Whirlwind Romance

by

M. S. Spencer

This is a work of fiction. Names, characters, places, and incidents are either the product of the author's imagination or are used fictitiously, and any resemblance to actual persons living or dead, business establishments, events, or locales, is entirely coincidental.

Whirlwind Romance

Cover Art by *Rae Monet, Inc. Design*

The Wild Rose Press, Inc.
PO Box 708
Adams Basin, NY 14410-0708
Visit us at www.thewildrosepress.com

Publishing History
Previously published by Secret Cravings, 2014
First Champagne Rose Edition, 2016
Print ISBN 978-1-5092-0898-2
Digital ISBN 978-1-5092-0899-9

Published in the United States of America

How could she admit she had to get out of there quickly or she wouldn't be able to go at all? His handsome face—the strong chin covered with stubble, the pearly teeth contrasting with his tan skin, not to mention the long, graceful fingers he held out to her—all conspired to lure her closer. Her heart led the way, propelling her to his side. She sat down. "What is it?"

"Lacey...um."

Her body tensed as desire fought to get out, and she fought just as hard to keep it in. *I have to go. I have to...go.* "What?"

His words came out in a rush. "Lacey, the other day—the first night—when you rescued me. When we...we..."

Don't say it. Don't say it. Christ.

"I...uh...want you to know I don't do that on a regular basis."

His air of shy ambivalence gave her courage. "I see. You don't have sex on a regular basis?"

"No, no, it's not that." He stopped, flustered. "Er, I mean...I don't sleep with women indiscriminately."

Should she let him off the hook? *Nah.* "But you do sleep with a lot of women?"

"No! Lacey, you're being difficult on purpose. I meant, that I didn't mean to...you know. It just happened. Forgive me?"

"I—"

Armand interrupted her. "Not that it wasn't enjoyable." He seemed distracted, running a finger down her arm. "Wonderful. Fantastic. Too short." He peered at her. "Lacey, you must know how beautiful you are. You have the most perfect cheekbones I've ever seen."

Dedication

To my sister-in-law Karen,
who introduced me to jelly-making

"They slipped briskly into an intimacy from which they never recovered."

~F. Scott Fitzgerald, *This Side of Paradise*

Chapter One

The cocoplum is native to South Florida and occurs naturally in cypress hammocks and wetland areas. Evergreen, it forms a dense, clumping bush. The fruit is a dark purple drupe one to two inches in diameter, and ripens May through August. The nut is also edible.

Cocoplum Jelly

200 cocoplums, peeled
2 cinnamon sticks
4 cups brown sugar
1 box (1.75 oz.) powdered pectin

Place plums and cinnamon sticks in water to cover. Bring to a boil and simmer for about 1 1/2 hours, or until liquid is dark purple. Remove from heat and strain, reserving the nuts. Add water if necessary to make two cups of liquid.

Shell the nuts and chop. In a jelly pan add the juice, nuts, and pectin and bring to a rolling boil. Pour sugar in all at once and bring back to a rolling boil. Boil exactly one minute.

Standard Procedure: Remove pot from heat, skim off any foam, and ladle into hot, sterilized jelly jars to within 1/4 inch of the top. Wipe rims and place the two-piece canning lids on the jars, but do not tighten completely. Turn the jars over and leave upside down for five minutes on a padded rack. Turn upright and tighten the lids completely. Makes about 4 half-pints.

Alternate method: Process filled, tightly closed jars in boiling water for 15 minutes. Cool on rack.

****

"There's one." Lacey picked up her machete and hacked through the tree ferns and wild coffee to reach a dense, dark green bush heavy with purple fruit. She had almost reached it when she stumbled over the root of a strangler fig and sank into the soggy soil. Black water sloshed up over the tops of her wellies, soaking her feet. She felt the mud squishing up between her toes…and something else. Something that tickled. She peered inside the boot. Two unblinking, liquid eyes stared up at her. A brown frog clung desperately to her ankle, its huge padded fingers glued to her skin. Yuck. Rummaging around in her knapsack, she pulled out a large pair of tweezers, plucked the creature off, and threw it as far as she could. It bounced off a gumbo limbo tree and scrabbled away into the hammock.

Wait—didn't the Florida wetlands guide say some frogs leave a noxious slime? Lacey pulled a stained and worn paperback from her back pocket and thumbed through it. "Here it is." She read aloud, " 'The Cuban treefrog is an invasive species that eats practically anything that moves, including other Cuban treefrogs. It secretes a toxic substance that can irritate human mucous membranes.' " She stuffed the book back in her jeans, drew out a wipe from her pack, and carefully cleaned the goo from her leg. Then she wrung out a washcloth and dried her dripping face. *Gawd, it's hot.* According to her neighbor Sheila, the temperature would hover in the nineties until at least mid-September. Another two months of hell to go.

A rumble sounded overhead. Massive charcoal-colored clouds scudded across the sky, blocking out the midday sun. *Better harvest this last cocoplum and head back to camp.* Using a garden fork attached to a long pole, she raked the grape-colored drupes into a plastic bag. As she picked the last plum, a heavy raindrop hit the top of her head. *Uh oh. Good thing I remembered the poncho.* She drew the hood up and began to slog back through the swamp.

By the time she reached her campsite, the rain had soaked through to her skin. The wind tore at her little pup tent, yanking the stakes out of the ground. She managed to grab one end and pull it down before it sailed off into the tall cypress. As darkness cloaked the hammock, Lacey huddled under the tent listening to the whoosh of nearly horizontal rain. The squall didn't worry her much—she'd been through worse since she'd moved to the Gulf Coast of Florida in February. Even though they were well into hurricane season, the weather bureau predicted a quiet year—at least the last time Lacey checked it did. As the sabal palms creaked and groaned overhead, a little voice whispered, "Exactly when was the last time you checked, anyway?"

No matter—Sarasota usually missed out on the big ones. Thanks to Sara de Soto. Her thoughts turned to the story of Hernando de Soto's beautiful daughter and the Seminole prince who loved her. Chichi-Okobee had come to parlay with the Spanish conquistador. When he saw Sara, he immediately fell in love with her and she with him. He asked de Soto for his daughter's hand but was refused. Brokenhearted, the prince left. Soon after, he fell ill. Sara pleaded with her father to be allowed to care for him. Over the months, she nursed him back to health. He recovered, only to have her succumb to the disease. Neither the Spanish monks nor the Seminole medicine men could save her, and she died.

De Soto, in honor of the bond between the two young people, gave Chichi-Okobee permission to bury Sara at sea with full Seminole honors. The next day the prince and his warriors poled the funeral boat out to the middle of Sarasota Bay with her coffin. They dropped it into the water, but then, to the Spaniards' horror, Chichi-Okobee and his men deliberately capsized the canoe and drowned. As the conquistadors stood frozen on the shore, black clouds rolled across the sky and the wind roared. At the spot where the Seminoles went down, a waterspout erupted. It whirled onshore and whipped around de Soto before heading out to sea.

The conquistador expected the prince's father to demand retribution, but instead the Seminole chief came bearing gifts. He said, "Our people believe that only true love can keep evil at bay. My son and your daughter will be together forever, and together they will protect us and our descendants from the great winds, the *ho-tah-lee-mas-tchay*."

As the rain slackened and the wind died down, Lacey reflected that the two lovers had kept their promise. Sarasota hadn't had a direct hit by a major hurricane since they started keeping records in the nineteenth century. Nestled in her blanket, she dozed.

When she awoke, wispy sunlight peeped through the canopy. Unfortunately, the rain had only concentrated the steamy, moisture-laden atmosphere. She threw back the canvas and shook off the raindrops, thankful her son Crispin had presented her with the waterproof tent before she left Virginia. "I know you,

Ma. You'll wander off into the swamp with nothing but a rake and a berry pail."

A wild sight greeted her, ebullient with life. Instead of the matted foliage and uprooted trees she expected, the hammock plants stretched and popped with new growth. Under the shade of the live oaks and Australian pines, a riot of palmetto, buttonbush, and red stopper flourished. In every crook of every bush, bromeliads and epiphytes inhaled the saturated air. A tiny orchid bravely opened its purple and white blossoms on the branch of a lignum vitae.

Lacey packed up her gear and made her way down to the estuary that led to the river. As she pushed the kayak into the water, an alligator sashayed off the bank and sank up to his nose, following her with soulless eyes. She paddled out into the center of the stream away from the spidery roots of the mangroves, giving an overhanging manchineel tree a wide berth. Sheila had told her of the dangers of the fruit Columbus called "little apples of death." Not only its fruit, but the leaves, bark, and even raindrops cascading off the tree could produce horrible welts that only wore off after hours of agony. *That's one fruit I ain't makin' no jelly out of.* Her lip curled at the joke.

The channel flowed out into the Manatee River. Only a few days earlier, sunlight had dappled the flat, clear water and not a single white puff had interrupted the solid blue sky. Today, sepia waves crashed on the shore, leaving dense yellow suds in their wake. Splitting the air like guided missiles, adamantine clouds raced across the heavens. *What the hell happened since I left Longboat Key?*

She shaded her eyes and gazed down the thin strip

of beach. The storm had vomited up all kinds of trash, from palm boots to fishing line to chunks of cement. Broken beach chairs, rainbow-striped umbrellas, even the occasional dinghy, were wadded into large bundles as though a giant trash compactor had swept through the area. The sun dipped behind a wall of light fog.

Might as well venture out. She had almost reached the bay when she ran into whitecaps. Water splashed over the bow, puddling in the cockpit. She steered into the wind, but the undertow kept pushing her athwart. Before she could turn around and head back to the lee of the river mouth, a wave spun her around and flipped the boat. She came up sputtering and barely managed to grab her pack and the bowline before everything drifted away. Stretching a toe down, she gratefully touched the sandy bottom. By dint of slow, wobbly steps, she dragged what was left of her investment to the bank.

Okay, now what? She checked the sky for signs of clearing. *There.* At the horizon, a tiny splotch of blue moved steadily toward her. A few minutes later the fog lifted. She pulled the clothes and blankets out of her back pack, stripped off her shorts and T-shirt, and hung them up on a fig tree. Then she lit her camp stove and sat down on a rock to consider her options.

Is there anyone who'll worry if I don't get home today? The simple answer to that was no. Lacey had been living in the house she'd inherited from her grandmother for six months, renovating, studying the local flora, and boning up on harvest times preparatory to setting up her jelly business. She hadn't had time to greet any of her neighbors other than to say "Hello" or to pat their invariably tiny dogs. Crispin called now and then, but his farm work kept him busy seven days a week. *He's not a child anymore—I have to cut him some slack.* The familiar cloud of depression floated nearer and dropped down an inch or two closer to her mind. Her son was all she had now. Her parents were gone, and her sister had recently decided to give up on ever finding a mate and moved to Morocco. "I hear it's a dissolute place," she'd said with a wink. "I should be able to keep busy. Commitment is overrated anyway."

Since Lacey's husband Damien had walked out when Crispin was only a year old, mother and child had depended on each other. Crispin had been her rock through all the lean years. *And now he's a grown man with his own life.* She stood. *All right, when everything's dry, I'm going home.*

Three hours later, she headed out again. It was still choppy, so she hugged the bank, careful to avoid the flotsam ebbing and flowing. Where the river narrowed near De Soto Point, she took a chance and braved the open water. Safely across, it took another three hours to cut through Perico Bayou, cross Palma Sola Bay at its mouth, and head down the Intracoastal toward Longboat Key.

The little point she called home hove into view just as the sun flashed its good night in a brilliant display of tangerine, scarlet, and carmine. The channel marker blinked encouragingly in the eerie darkness, but no light shone from any of the houses. Even more disheartening, only a few lit up the Sarasota skyline. She pulled the kayak up and overturned it on the lawn.

Peering through the deepening twilight, she checked up the street. The trees and houses seemed unscathed, but there were no signs of life in the neighborhood. *They must have evacuated the island.*

Yeah, yeah, okay, I shoulda listened to the forecast before I went camping. Still, people should be coming back by now—the bays and bayous on her way home were calm, and she'd seen no sign of major destruction. She unlocked her door and went inside.

Yup, no electricity. No Internet, no television, no cell service. She smiled. *How will I ever survive?* She could just hear her mother launch into her stump speech about the Depression and ungrateful children. She turned the tap. No water either. Thank God she had a commercial-sized water purifier for her jelly-making. She started the generator and filled a bucket with water from the bay. *At least the rain barrel's full.* She opened all the windows, but the air in the house still smelled musty, so she found her battery-powered fan and turned it on. *Now where did I put that emergency radio?* She poked around in several drawers, but hunger eventually won over her desire for news, and she decided to settle for a sandwich, a bottle of wine, and the stars.

The waves lapped quietly on her seawall, accompanied by the pitter-patter of tiny lizard feet in the palms. Over in the mangrove-choked channel that flanked the northern side of her property a family of raccoons squabbled over their dinner, their shrieks of outrage almost human. She sipped the wine and tried to appreciate the quiet, but it still bothered her. *It's unnatural.* She didn't mind being alone when camping, but here the tomb-like hush unnerved her. *It's not…it doesn't feel whole. Something's missing. What is it?* People. It needed the hum of human activity, the warm air produced by bodies moving, talking, eating. Was this how it felt to be the lone survivor of an apocalypse? She took another slug of wine.

The chattering of the raccoons grew more strident. Lacey got up and tramped over to the mangroves. "Scram!" Dead silence greeted her. She returned to her chair, satisfied. A minute later, the racket began again. "What the hell?"

She picked up her flashlight and marched to the canal. "Yo, beasties! Pipe down!" For answer she heard a splash and a groan. Shining the light into the swamp, it picked up something white, caught among the knee-like pneumatophores. She took a step closer and sank into black muck. Grabbing her ankle, she tugged until her foot came free with a loud *schluck*. She shook off the mud and backed up. *Forget it. It's probably just a piece of trash.* But just as she made it to dry ground, she heard another groan. *Okay, now* that's *definitely human.* She ran back to the house, pulled on some thigh-high rubber boots, and returned to the canal. Wading slowly toward the white object fluttering in the half-light, she made out a hand. She edged closer, batting at mangrove spider webs. "Hello?"

The whisper came low and raspy. "Help....me."

Lacey didn't hesitate. Taking hold of the hand with both of hers, she pulled the form upright. About as bedraggled a man as she'd ever seen—at least alive—slumped before her. He started to fall again, but she caught him and, wrapping her arms around his chest, managed to drag him to the bank where she dropped him. He lay still. She was about to shake him when he spoke. Through a voice thick with mucus and an unfamiliar accent, she made out, "Thank you."

"Well, you seem to be alive. Who are you?" He didn't answer. Lacey leaned toward him and caught a whiff of sulphur. "How long did you stew in swamp water, anyway? Well, never mind. Let's try and get at least some of these rags off you before I take you into the house."

She set the flashlight so it shone on the man and gingerly pulled his socks off. The jacket sleeves tore away from the shoulders when she tugged at them. She tossed them on the heap. As she was about to extricate him from the sodden trousers inspiration struck. Lugging the fellow over to the hose, she turned it on him. It washed the mud off a few of his toes before trickling down to nothing. "Damn, I forgot there isn't any water." *Thank God I didn't dump him in the rain barrel.*

Hands on hips, she took stock of the stranger. All she could make out in the dark was a thin body, the lower half covered in shredded jeans. Something obscured his face. She considered her options. *So how do I make him presentable enough for genteel company without any water or power?* Now that the storm was over, the utilities had to come back on line soon. Meanwhile, what to do with Popeye here? He stirred and groaned. She nudged him. "Are you awake?"

He nodded and grimaced. "My ankle."

"Look, I can't see you very well here. Can you walk if I help you?"

"I shall do my best."

"Okay, on three. One…two…urk. How much do you weigh anyhow?"

That prompted a chuckle. "Twelve stone stripped, if you must know."

"What's that in pounds? Never mind. Your clothes must weigh a ton all by themselves. How about if we amble on over to the bayside and you jump in? Works for a dog."

He obliged, and together the two of them hobbled to the boat ramp. He sat down and shunted on his bottom until he reached the water. There he stopped. "How deep is it here?" His voice cracked with terror.

Oh dear, I forgot he must have almost drowned. Probably not too gung ho about taking a dip right now. "Not to worry—it's only about five feet. I'll get in first and help you in, okay?"

She looked at the water and then up at the sky, now pitch black. Heavy rain clouds obscured the stars. *I sure as hell don't want my last pair of shorts to get wet with no way to dry them.* She shimmied off her shorts and pulled her T-shirt over her head and tossed them under the kayak. As if on cue, the moon broke through and bounced off the water, illuminating both the yard and Lacey's body, clad only in panties. She heard a gasp, and hastily sank under the water. *Poor guy, I shouldn't have subjected him to a nearly forty-year-old physique.* She held out her arms. "Sorry about exposing myself, but we've no electricity and I don't want my one clean shirt to get soaked. Now come on. I'll hold you."

He raised his eyes from her breasts and nodded. With the moonlight full upon him, she saw that he sported a rough, dark beard and shaggy hair. Homeless? Or grooming for a movie role? Standing about six feet tall, he was younger than she'd thought at first. His dark eyes glittered in the pale light.

"If you're ready…" He slid down the ramp into her waiting arms. She bent down and pulled the torn jeans off, then unbuttoned the remnants of his shirt. He clung to her, his body trembling. She tried to ignore the stench rising from him, but as she worked, somewhere down below her bellybutton parts of her kindled and something that wasn't bay water oozed out of her. It had been five years after all—five long, desolate years since she'd been with a man. She'd accepted the possibility that she might never have sex again. *Haven't thought about it in weeks.* Now the steady throbbing of a hard penis on her thigh unexpectedly liberated buried desire, and she butted against him.

He fell over in the water and came up spluttering. "What did you do that for?"

Good question. Hand to mouth, Lacey backed away. Her foot landed on a crab, which did not take kindly to the assault and chomped down hard on her instep. Yowling, she lunged forward, landing in the stranger's arms again. This time he took advantage and crushed her to him. One hand pulled down her panties. She didn't argue but spread her thighs so his cock could slide into her vagina. The water and mud made entering her all the easier, and they clung to each other, swaying back and forth. He must have found a purchase on the ramp for his thrusts grew stronger. Lacey reveled in the power of the man. She loved that he took control, that she could simply acquiesce and enjoy. The orgasm floated up from the depths and roared out of her mouth. "I'm coming! I'm coming!" He redoubled his pistoning, and as she began to shudder, he gave one last shove and sighed. She felt something warm mix with the cold bay water sloshing around her. The man didn't speak but, keeping his penis inside her, bent to kiss her lips.

Lacey let the water ripple around her, washing off the mud and the smell. After a minute, the man released her and ducked under the water. He came up shaking his head. A passing cloud veiled the moon and all she could make out were two brilliant eyes, streaks of starlight flashing in them. He whispered, "I'm so sorry."

The words smacked into her like her father's belt did that day he caught her smoking in the alley. *Oh. My. God. What have I done? How wanton could I be? And how stupid?* This guy could be a rapist, an escaped convict—or worse, married! Here she was, acting like some Hollywood harlot screwing in an airplane lavatory. Yeah, it felt wonderful. *But...oh, dear.* What to say? "Never mind?" How about, "I do this with all shipwrecked sailors?" "Do it to me one more time?" Instead, she slogged up the ramp and turned. "You coming?"

He limped after her. She picked up her clothes and together they crossed the yard. Lacey left him on the porch and went inside. In Crispin's room she found a pair of sweatpants and an old work shirt she thought might fit. Tossing them out to him, she lit the Coleman lantern and rummaged around the kitchen for something to eat. When the stranger appeared, she had crackers and peanut butter, along with the wine, set out. He inspected the table. "A meal fit for a king." His eyes twinkled as if from some private joke.

Shyness engulfed Lacey. *I just had mindless, abandoned sex with this man—how can I possibly look him in the eye?* Finally, she peeped at him from under her lashes. Thick, black hair curled becomingly over his ears. His fading smile gave a hint of bright white teeth in a tanned face. The nose between two iridescent black eyes could only be described as patrician. *Close to my age, I'd say—but much better preserved.*

She surveyed her own figure. If you ignored the

slight bulge of a thirty-nine-year-old belly, her breasts were still perky and her legs slim and shapely. Despite pressure from her sister to cut her long, red-gold hair into a more mature style, she still wore it in a ponytail most of the time. Add to that eyes that alternated between turquoise and dark teal, and she presented a fairly decent picture. At least so her ever-loving son Crispin maintained. *Preserved, ha.* If only she could do with her body what she did with huckleberries and sea grapes.

"Er…forgive me…is that wine?"

She removed herself from the daydream and squeaked, "Yes, yes it is. Would you like some?"

"Most definitely." He took the paper cup and gulped down its contents. She poured again. "Thank you, I needed that."

He wolfed down half a box of crackers and most of the peanut butter before holding out his cup again. "I hope this does not deplete your larder, er…Miss?"

"Lacey. Lacey Delahaye. And no, we have plenty of food." Lacey tittered, thinking of what her family sarcastically called her nuclear winter pantry. "I always store enough provisions to last half a year. You know—the basics, like canned tamales and pickles."

He didn't take it as a joke. "I hope it doesn't come to that. Delahaye, did you say? Are you perchance descended from the pirate Jacquotte Delahaye? She frequented these waters, as I recall."

Lacey sucked in a breath. No one—not even Crispin—knew her ancestry, not to mention her real name. Keeping her voice neutral, she asked, "Who did you say?"

"Jacquotte Delahaye, known as Back from the

Dead Red because of her red hair and the fact that she faked her own death, only to return with a vengeance." He reached out and pushed a damp tendril from her forehead. "Her portrait shows her with the same copper-colored tresses as yours. She prowled the Caribbean in the 1660s, possibly in partnership with the other great female pirate Anne Dieu-le-Veut. You've never heard of them?"

Oh my God. What do I say? "Um...maybe in a book. Somewhere."

He seemed disappointed. "Too bad. I believe she spent some time on my...in my country."

"Excuse me?"

He didn't answer but picked up the bottle and poured himself another cup of wine. After taking a long swallow, he remarked casually, "How did you fare in the hurricane?"

Lacey gratefully consented to the change of subject. "Hurricane? How bad was it?"

His eyebrows rose. "You weren't here?"

"No, I've been camping north of Tampa. Near Terra Ceia Bay."

"How far away is that?"

"About fifteen miles, as the kayak floats."

"Surely you must have encountered some rain and wind then?"

"Yes, but nothing out of the ordinary. Was it worse here?"

He raised his eyebrows. "I believe Category Two is considered serious?"

Lacey almost spit out her wine. "Really? Did it hit Tampa?"

"I don't know where it made landfall, but when

I…capsized, they were predicting it would strike Sarasota."

"Capsized?"

He nodded. "We must have caught the tail end of the storm. The waves were high, but I was quite close to shore when the…accident happened. I've been hid— hanging out in your mangroves for two days."

He's obviously got a secret. Good or bad, Lacey didn't have the energy right now to ferret out the truth. She finished her cracker. "I only just returned this evening and haven't had a chance to look around. No one seems to be in the neighborhood, so they must have evacuated. I have no water and no electricity. And no cell service."

He seemed perplexed. "But your refrigerator is working?"

"I have a generator. We'll be fine for a while. When I find my radio, we'll be able to learn more."

"Did you say radio?"

Was that panic in his voice? "Yes, I have an emergency radio here somewhere. The authorities are sure to broadcast when the power will be restored."

"I see." He made a pretense of yawning. "Might I trouble you for a cot or sleeping mat?"

Sleeping mat? Where does this guy come from? "You can sleep in my son's room. He has a real bed."

He stood, then listed to the right, clucking his tongue in pain. "I forgot all about my ankle."

Lacey jumped up and took his elbow. "We'd better put something cold on that." She led him to the former storeroom she'd fixed up for Crispin's visits. The man lay down while she bustled around wrapping ice cubes in a dish towel. When she saw the ankle—swollen to twice its size and bright blue, she gasped. "It's either broken or a very bad sprain."

"It bloody well hurts."

"How did it happen?"

He didn't look at her. "I'm not sure. Sometime after the boat foundered."

Lacey pressed the ice pack on his ankle and tied it tight with some string. "Okay, we'd better keep your foot iced all night. I'll come in and refresh the pack in a few hours."

His ebony eyes settled on her cerulean ones. "How can I thank you?"

She sent the lump back down her throat and fortified her voice. "Not now. Tomorrow. Tomorrow you will tell me your story."

He blinked. "Yes, tomorrow, then."

She left him and went to her own room. Question after question spouted, inhibiting sleep. *Why do I get this...this fibrillation when I'm near him? Why did I literally jump his bones before I'd even gotten a good look at his face? Is swamp slime some kind of pheromone? Am I still going to feel this way tomorrow or is this a function of—what?* As she lay awake puzzling, it occurred to her that he hadn't answered the most important question of all. *Who the hell is he?*

Chapter Two

Sea grapes are tall, multi-trunked trees with round leaves that grow along Florida's coast. The clusters of grapes ripen in the summer and should be picked when fully purple (if you can get there before the birds do).

Sea Grape Jelly

8 cups ripe sea grapes
4 cups water
5 cups white sugar
1 box powdered pectin
1/4 cup lime juice
1/2 teaspoon butter

Wash grapes. Place in large pot with the water and cook over medium heat until the skins are soft. Press the pulp through a sieve, then place it in a jelly strainer or two layers of cheesecloth and let drip. Add water to the clear juice to make five cups.

In a large pot, bring the juice, lime juice, pectin, and butter to a rolling boil, stirring constantly. Add the sugar and bring again to a boil, stirring constantly. Boil exactly one minute, then remove from heat and continue with the standard procedure given in Chapter One.

****

The grating croak of a hungry great blue heron woke Lacey the next morning. Gazing out the window to the east, she spent some time trying to come up with a description other than "rosy-fingered" for the spears and darts of coral light shooting from the horizon but gave up. Why fuss with the perfect phrase? She splashed cool water on her face to prepare her for the cold shower she knew awaited her, but when she tried to open the bathroom door, she found it locked. From inside a lyrical tenor belted out "La Donna e Mobile."

Blushing furiously—more at the choice of an aria that translates as "Woman is fickle" than at being locked out of her own bathroom—she crept back to her room. When the music stopped, she waited another five minutes, then zipped down and through the door, to be confronted by a wasteland. Two towels lay on the floor, water pooling from them. Toothpaste splotched the sink, and the bar of soap had somehow ended up behind the toilet. She opened her mouth to yell but realized the curse wouldn't mean much without a name attached to it. Pulling her robe together she marched down to Crispin's room and threw the door open. "Hey, you!"

The stranger, clad only in her son's boxer shorts—rather too snug for her peace of mind—stood in the center of the room. He had a comb in his hand and an indignant scowl on his face. "Do you mind?"

"Yes, I do." From the depths of her exasperation Lacey managed to take note of a strong, now clean-shaven chin, a barrel chest covered in soft black hair, and a swimmer's broad shoulders and narrow hips. "You left the bathroom in a mess."

His face registered utter bewilderment. "I'm sorry—I'm not sure what you mean."

I can't believe this bozo. Lacey snapped, "Where were you raised—in a barn? Or are you the pampered prince from some fairytale kingdom who never had to lift a finger for himself?"

He stared at her, open-mouthed. When it appeared that his expression had no intention of altering any time soon, she regrouped and managed in a reasonably steady voice, "In this house, we pick up after ourselves. Please go hang up the towels and clean off the sink. I'll make some breakfast."

By the time the man appeared in the kitchen, Lacey had made coffee and set out dried apricots, bread, and a crock of her own sea grape jelly. Freshly-squeezed grapefruit juice from the tree in her neighbor's yard stood in a pitcher on the table. She left him to take her shower. He had done a fair job of tidying the bathroom, but she had the impression the task was an unfamiliar one. *Maybe he* is *a frog prince.*

A few minutes later she joined him in the kitchen. He was licking jelly off his hands. "What is this condiment? It's intriguing."

"Sea grape jelly. Haven't you ever had it before?"

"No. It's delicious. Did you make it?"

"Thank you. Yes, I did. I had a shop up in Virginia for many years and made and sold jams, jellies, and preserves from local wild fruit. Now that I've moved to Florida, I plan to open a business here. It's amazing how many edible plants grow on the Gulf Coast."

"Ah. I've always admired people who make things. Especially things you can eat."

Lacey studied her guest. Definitely foreign, with his luminous ebony eyes and hair that shone like black ice. His long, aristocratic fingers were scraped from his ordeal, but she noted the nails were carefully manicured. He had an air about him that said "seriously indulged." "What do you do?"

"Me? I…uh…I'm in administration. Yes, that's it."

"And your name?"

He suddenly developed a tic in his left eye. Taking a long sip of coffee, he wiped his mouth with his napkin. Lacey waited him out. Finally he muttered, "Armand."

"Armand who?"

"Um…Armand…Straniero. Um." He kept his eyes on his plate.

Why do I sense that's a lie? "I see…and where are you from, Armand?"

The question seemed to startle him. "From?"

"Yes. You have a strange accent." Why did his lips turn up at that? "What country do you come from?"

"I…uh…it's a small country. Quite far away. You have probably never heard of it."

"Try me."

He raised his eyes to the ceiling, almost as though he were turning over choices in his head. "Er…Todoacabado. It's an island." He blinked.

"I see. And how did you end up in my mangroves?"

He rose. "It's a long story."

Lacey put out a hand and pulled him back down. "We've got plenty of time."

Armand pursed his lips. "I don't think it's wise to tell you, all right? Let's say I fell in with a rough crowd, and I'd rather not meet up with them again."

"Did they throw you overboard?"

"What? No, I…uh…I left when they were otherwise occupied."

"You mean, by the hurricane?"

"Yes, but that's all you really need to know." This

time she let him hobble back to his room.

She took her coffee and walked out to the jetty. The sun hit her eyes, and she shaded them, searching for any signs of activity in the bay. No boats, not even any birds. They must have flown inland to ride out the storm. She scanned the horizon, then decided to walk up her street. Hurricane shutters secured the windows of every bungalow. All the cars were gone. It reminded her eerily of the old rock song "Everyone's Gone to the Moon." She saw only minor damage, however. Two pygmy date palms had been blown down and some roof tiles lay on the ground. She called, "Halloo! Anyone around?" Silence. *It's not like I know many of the locals anyway.* She'd been so busy the last few months she'd only made the acquaintance of Sheila, her next door neighbor, who worked for a resort management agency on the island.

A horrible retching sound rent the air. Lacey thought it came from a conch house a couple of blocks away and headed toward it. A long, low building with cheery yellow walls and a pink door, it squatted under the Brazilian pepperwood like a giant spider. She heard another screech and looked up to the roof. A peacock strutted around on the tiles emitting what he evidently believed to be a stirring serenade to his mate. It worked. A peahen landed near him, and the pair joined in an ear-splitting duet. *They must have been blown down here from the Village.* She'd learned from Sheila that Longbeach Village, at the north end of the island, had been battling a Mongol horde of peacocks for decades.

A few more minutes' exploration only turned up a couple of raccoons happily finishing off some poor kid's stash of M&Ms. Armand waited for her in the living room, his ankle propped on an ottoman. "Where have you been?"

"Scoping out the area. Most everything seems to be in order, but I'm guessing the county evacuated the island to be on the safe side. People should start trickling back soon."

He sucked in his breath. "Oh dear."

Lacey tried to tamp down the effect those sable eyes had on her. She chose a chair some distance away. "Look—what did you say your name was?"

"Armand. Armand Straniero."

"Well, Armand, you've got to tell me what happened to you. Maybe I can help."

For a second it looked as though he might confess, but then he shook his head. "I don't want to put you in danger. You've been more than kind. I should be able to travel by tomorrow."

"Nonsense. Your ankle won't be healed enough to walk for days. Look, my car's almost out of gas, but I saw a bike in my neighbor's carport. I think I'll ride up the island and see what's going on. You stay here." She waved at the piles of books he'd pulled from her shelves. "And clean up again."

He looked chagrined. "Sorry."

Lacey filled a travel mug from the rain barrel and headed up the Gulf of Mexico Drive, all that remained of John Ringling's grandiose plans for Longboat key. By the time she reached Whitney Plaza, her mood had deteriorated, but even then she wasn't prepared for what she found round the bend. The drawbridge over Longboat Pass had been raised, and from the looks of it, simply left up. She turned around and rode home.

"Okay, I'd better find that radio. We need to know

what's happening in the bay area."

Armand avoided her eyes. "Yes, by all means."

Lacey paused. *He wouldn't dare.* She began in the obvious places—the pantry, the tool drawer, under her bed. Nothing. She searched the attic, the garage, even the car. No sign of the radio. Stomping into the den, she stood before Armand, hands on hips, steam rising from the top of her head. "All right, man, where have you hidden it?"

Armand raised his head from a book. "It?"

Boy, does he do innocent well. She checked the title of the volume—*Debrett's Peerage. That's the one Crispin memorized during his Royals phase.* "You know what I'm talking about. What have you done with the radio?"

He made a show of canvassing the room, then, when Lacey continued to fume, reluctantly drew the little portable radio from under the couch. She snatched it from him. "Look, I know you're in trouble and you claim to want to protect me, but I need to know what's going on in the outside world. The bridge to Anna Maria Island is out, and I don't fancy schlepping the seven miles to New Pass if I'm going to find that bridge out as well." She marched out to the garage and rummaged around for her supply of batteries. Coming up with five of the six she needed, she headed back to the house to ream Armand out. He met her at the door. "Is this what you're looking for?"

Without a word, she grabbed the battery from him and inserted it into the radio. Static. She took the box outside and started fiddling with the dials. Armand watched her from the doorway. She finally found a local station. They were discussing the upcoming mayoral race in Saint Petersburg. "Yup—Bud Carney's got a heckuva campaign team, but he's going to catch hell from the voters for his handling of the evacuations."

"Yeah, Hank, we're hearing a lot of noise about Chicken Little Bud and the wussification of Americans. Hell, we got two inches of rain and a few gusts, and he has every key and all of Pinellas County evacuated. At last count, the recovery estimate totaled a piddling ninety thousand dollars."

"Why don't we open up the phone lines, Chuck? I want to hear what our listeners have to say. Hildegard from Ellenton, you're on the Daily Cuppa with Chuck and Hank. Hello."

"Am I on? Hello?"

"Yes, Hildegard, you're on the air. Go ahead."

"Hello?"

"Could you turn down your radio, Hildy? We can't hear you."

"Hello?"

Hank muttered something under his breath. Chuck shushed him. "Maybe we'd better take another call. Who've we got, Clara? Francine? Francine from Longboat Key, you're on the air with Chuck and Hank. How did you weather Hidalgo out there?"

"Hi, Chuck." The woman let out a dramatic sigh. "It took two hours to get off the island, and I tell you we're beat!"

"Where are you, Francine?"

"What? Oh, we're here at the Sunrise Inn in Bradenton." Her voice faded. "Stop that, Pudgy. Mummy's on the phone! Get off me!" Lacey heard scratching noises and a dog whining.

"Francine? Are you still there?"

"What? Oh, yes, sorry." Her voice rose a decibel. "Norman! Come get Pudgy! I'm on the radio." More scratching and whining, followed by a high-pitched yelp. Lacey guessed Norman had removed the objectionable Pudgy, although not without repercussions.

"Francine? Are you with us? Chuck, maybe we should go to another caller."

No! She's from Longboat. I need to hear this.

"Wait, wait—I'm back. Like I said, we're holed up in the Sunrise Inn here for the duration. All of Longboat Key was evacuated. I hear the Longboat Pass drawbridge is stuck and one of the pylons on the New Pass bridge is cracked. There's no word on when we'll be allowed back."

"Gee, that's terrible. Power and water's back on here in Tampa. We haven't heard of any problems elsewhere. What about Anna Maria? Any word from there, Chuck?"

"Just a minute." Lacey listened to the sound of papers shuffling. "Says here Bradenton Beach still has some clearing to do, but Anna Maria and Holmes Beach are back to normal. Both Manatee and Cortez bridges came through Hidalgo fine. Francine, are you still on the phone?"

"Yes, but—"

"Well, you hang in there. I'm sure the authorities are working like crazy to get all you Longboaters back home."

Lacey muted the radio and stared out across the bay. "We're alone here."

Armand did not respond. She spun around. Gone.

She ran into a house that echoed with only her own footsteps. His room was empty, the bed made. He'd even returned the books to their shelves. Except for the *Debrett's. Now why did he take that?*

She wandered around the yard, feeling at loose ends. *It's really for the best.* After all, he admitted to being in a tight spot. Whether he was on the lam or being pursued, the longer he stayed with her the greater chance his enemies would find his hiding place. Still…that oh so brief lovemaking had wrought a change. She felt better about herself and the world. *Amazing what a little sex can do for your morale.* She began to tidy up the coffee table. Only when a teardrop landed on a copy of The Atlas of the Gulf of Mexico did she realize she was crying.

My God, woman, you've only known the man two days. This is ridiculous. But then she thought of his effervescent eyes, the way his lips curled when he made a joke, and that little bump on the top of his regal nose. The vaguely foreign accent that enriched his tenor. The strength of his arms as they held her that night in the water. *I can't believe I miss him. I must be the most pathetic creature on Longboat Key. Oh wait, I'm the* only *creature on Longboat Key.*

She picked up the radio and turned it on again. "Hank, what's the latest on that boat they found abandoned in Sarasota Bay after Hidalgo passed through? Were there any survivors?"

"Not that we've heard. The boat was registered to Colombia, so I gather the Coast Guard is checking with Bogota. They found a whole cache of automatic weapons in the hold."

"Gun runners?"

"Drug dealers more likely. Or maybe pirates." Both men laughed. "That's just what we need here in Tampa Bay, Hank—more buccaneers."

Could that be Armand's boat? Is he a pirate? But the conversation had shifted.

"—have they caught him yet?"

"Nope, and boy, does it make the TSA look bad. The fellow slipped between their fingers right there at the boarding gate."

"SRQ is a pretty small airport compared to Tampa International. He's gotta still be around somewhere."

"Not necessarily, Hank. Remember? We had Chief Miller of the Sarasota police on earlier, and he said they're sure he's left the city."

"But where would he go? A lot of roads are still closed."

"Yeah, and that accent is pretty distinctive. Someone's sure to recognize him."

Ding, dong, ding. "Well, that's it for us, folks. Come on by tomorrow for another Daily Cuppa with Hank and Chuck. Stay tuned for Macarena Momma's Bayou Cooking." *Ding dong ding*.

Lacey played with the dial. The radio only picked up AM, and most of the channels were either Spanish-language or evangelists. She finally found a local talk station. Glenn Beck was telling a funny story about a congressman who sneered at his opponent's poor academic record, only to have the congressman's mother tweet that he had flunked the bar three times. They went to a break, and Lacey waited for the news.

After a report on hurricane cleanup efforts, the announcer said, "The police and TSA have had no sightings of the man calling himself Loganathan. He entered the U.S. on a Malaysian passport and was scheduled for extradition but slipped away while the plane was boarding."

A female with a strong North Carolina accent asked, "What are the charges against him, Phil?"

"He's accused of trapping manatees for export to China, Megan. According to Professor Hua at the University of South Florida, there's an expanding market there for manatee bones."

"Manatee bones! What would the Chinese want them for?"

"Hua says the bones are ground into a paste and used as both an aphrodisiac and a treatment for shingles." The announcer paused, then, in a slightly tremulous voice, continued. "He...er...didn't mention what shingles and sex drive have in common." He broke off, and Lacey could hear giggling in the background.

"In other news..."

She turned the radio off. If only they'd described the man. All they said was he had an accent. And the name—she automatically picked up her laptop to Google it and realized she had no power. The battery had long since run down.

Frustrated, she closed the lid and sat back. Could this Loganathan be her Armand? Armand might be an alias—*of course it is, dummy.* Still, hunting manatees seemed a little out of character. What a horrible crime, even if their bones did relieve shingles. *Wait—they're also an aphrodisiac. Maybe he took some of his own medicine?* She smirked.

Her stomach rumbled, reminding her that she'd missed lunch. The sun had already begun its majestic descent toward the gulf. As it fell, it shot golden arrows back and forth across the sky, punching holes in the creamy clouds. A school of snook roiled the water, and far out a mullet jumped a foot in the air. She missed Oscar, the dolphin who used to hang around the point. *Hurricane probably blew him offshore.*

Back in the kitchen, she opened a new jar of peanut butter and made a sandwich, brooding while she worked. *Should I have gone after Armand? He could hardly get very far on that ankle. Maybe he stole the bike. He'd better not have—it's my only means of transportation.* Sandwich in hand, she wandered out the back door and checked Sheila's carport. The bike lay on its side where she'd left it. She scanned the street. Nothing. Wait. Up there, where the canal came to an end. A huddled shape. She loped toward it.

The cloth she'd used to wrap Armand's ankle lay in a heap by the side of the road. She picked it up and looked around. No sign of life from any of the houses. The twilight thickened. High up in a side yard she saw a pinprick of light. *Is he hiding in a tree?* She stepped between the houses. Little Tommy Forster's tree house, built of bits and pieces from abandoned fishing boats, hung slightly askew from the gnarled old mango. The light wavered and went out. *Must be a match.* She put down the sandwich and tiptoed toward it. Tommy had nailed wooden boards into the trunk for a rough ladder. She climbed quietly, hand over hand. As she reached the last board, a soft, but menacing voice purred, "Well, my sweet, you've found me."

Okay, here's where we find out if he's a bad guy. "Give me a hand up, will you?"

Other than a slight intake of breath, he complied

without a word. Lacey's head rose up over the floor to find a cubicle lit by a small pencil torch and cluttered with toy guns, candy bar wrappers, and crushed Dr Pepper cans. And Armand. Who took up most of the rest of the space. He still held her hand, but he had stopped pulling her. "Where did you plan to sit, on my lap?"

At least he's toned down the threat level. "Or you could come down. I don't think Tommy Forster allows uninvited guests in his palace."

His jaw dropped. "Palace?" After a brief interval, he said, "Oh. I see. I can't."

"Can't what?"

"Come down."

"Why not?"

"I...I...think I reinjured the ankle. I can't put any weight on it."

Lacey toyed with the idea of leaving him there for little Tommy, but his mother would have been appalled. "All right, just a minute." She climbed down and went back to her house, grabbed a coil of rope from the shed and sprinted back up the street. "Armand?"

"At your service."

"I'm bringing up a rope. I want you to tie it to something, then you can shimmy down without using your feet."

"Um, what about when I get to the ground?"

How much did he say he weighed? Twelve stone? Lacey calculated swiftly. *Must be over a hundred sixty pounds.* "I'll try to ease you down." She threw the coil into the darkness and backed down the tree.

A few minutes later the rope tumbled down and Armand emerged. "For the record, this was my worst sporting event in public school." He held on for dear life and inched down the rope.

Five minutes later he'd descended a foot. "Come on, Armand—hurry it up."

"I'm doing my best." By dint of a lot of swearing and some wild swinging, Armand made it into Lacey's waiting arms. He sat on the ground, legs splayed out in front, panting. "Now what?"

Lacey hadn't really thought that far. *If he's a fugitive, I can't trust him. And I have no way of contacting the police.* Maybe this wasn't such a great idea. "Er, I guess we'd better get you back home. Then you can tell me what this is all about." He didn't argue, but when he tried to stand, he fell over. She considered the situation. "What we need is some kind of transport. Like…like…what was that thing the Indians used?" Lacey cast about for the word.

"Travois?"

"That's it—aren't you clever. A sort of triangular thingy to carry a wounded man. Made of logs and deerskins." She stopped, not—as one might assume— due to the lack of readily available logs and skins, but to savor the picture in her mind. An injured warrior, lying spread-eagled before her—bare-chested, sexy, bravely enduring the pain. *Wow.*

Armand didn't seem to notice her heightened color and pointed at the carport across the street. "Could we use that little red wagon?"

She followed his gaze. *Story of my life—instead of Geronimo I get Ralphie.* "That'll do. Wait here."

"Yes, I think I shall." Armand kept a straight face. Lacey brought the little wagon to him, and he lay down in it, arms and legs hanging over the sides.

"You'll have to lift up your extremities if this is going to work."

And so, with Armand looking like an upside down turtle and Lacey with tears of laughter streaming down her face, they staggered along the road to her house. By the time they reached it, darkness had descended. She helped him inside and onto the couch. "I need a drink." She went to the kitchen, filled a highball glass with ice, and poured bourbon to the top.

When she came back, Armand eyed the glass. "Might I have one too? For medicinal purposes only of course."

"I have a limited supply of whiskey, you know. And you've hardly been a model guest so far."

"I know." He hung his head. "I'll make it up to you. I'll…I'll reveal all if you wish."

Oh shit. Where did I put that pistol? Maybe I only need a baseball bat—after all, he's handicapped. Right—handicapped. He can't be too dangerous. You'll be fine, Lacey. "All right." She got him a drink and sat down on the club chair opposite him. In the darkness, his eyes glittered like a panther's. She shivered a little. "Now spill."

Armand took a big gulp of bourbon and a deep breath. "I—"

An ear-splitting crash interrupted him, followed by men shouting. Armand's face went white and he whispered urgently, "Hide me."

Chapter Three

The beautyberry is a small, deciduous shrub found in Florida pine scrubs and moist woodlands. Fruiting in late summer through winter, the striking purple berries cluster around the stems at the leaf nodes.

Beautyberry Jelly

1 1/2 quarts berries, washed
2 quarts water
5 cups white sugar
1/2 cup lemon juice
1 box powdered pectin

Boil the berries in the water for twenty minutes and strain through cheesecloth or a jelly bag to make three cups of juice. In a large pot, bring the juice, lemon juice, and pectin to a rolling boil. Add the sugar and bring again to a boil, stirring constantly. Boil exactly one minute, stirring constantly, then remove from heat. Continue with standard procedure described in Chapter One.

****

"Quick, quick!" Lacey pushed Armand up the ladder, forcing herself not to think about how hard and firm his ass was. He scrambled up and sprawled on the attic floor. She followed, pulling the ladder up after her, and shut the trap door. They lay side by side, listening. After the initial hubbub, the noise had died down outside. Before they fled, Lacey had glimpsed a launch painted in camouflage colors, its running lights dimmed. It seemed to have run aground in the shallows. Three men in bandannas and filthy T-shirts huddled around it.

Lacey crawled over to the dormer window that faced south. The full moon gave just enough light for her to see. The men had dragged the launch up her boat ramp and now sat cross-legged in a circle on her lawn. The red tips of the cigars they smoked burned bright in the semi-darkness. She could hear them talking but couldn't make out the words. Armand wormed in next to her. "Who are they?" she whispered.

"Pirates."

Aha. "And you're with them?"

He snorted. "In a manner of speaking."

The men's voices rose in some sort of argument. Lacey cocked an ear. "Do you understand what they're saying?"

"Yes."

"What is it? It's certainly not Spanish."

"Actually, it's a creole—a mixture of several languages. Spanish is one of them."

"Really? What are the others?

"Dutch, Taino, English, among others."

She listened to the harsh, guttural voices of the men. "How do you know it?"

"I learned it as a child."

"Come on, Armand. You can do better than that."

"It's true! I grew up in the country those men come from."

He shifted his weight. She felt his hip bone touch hers. She considered edging away but only for a moment. "So what's the name of this country?"

"I told you…Todoacabado."

Did he just snicker? "Todoacabado, huh. Weird name." *That was definitely a snicker.* "Tell me about it."

"It's a very small island, so small that you won't find it on many maps. My family, along with ten other families, was stranded there when our ship broke up on its reef in the Year of Our Lord 1629. We've been there ever since."

"Sort of like Pitcairn Island?"

"Precisely. Only we weren't mutineers. We were simple pioneers heading to the Promised Land."

"Promised Land?"

"Yes." In a low, melodious voice he sang—

O'er all those wide extended plains shines one eternal day,

There God the son forever reigns, and scatters night away.

No chilling winds or poisonous breath can reach that healthful shore,

Sickness and sorrow, pain and death are felt and feared no more.

I am bound for the Promised Land,
I am bound for the Promised Land,
Oh who will come and go with me?
I am bound for the Promised Land.

Lacey, nearly mesmerized by his crooning, murmured, "But you didn't find what you were looking for."

"Oh, yes, we did, just not where we expected to. Par—I mean, Todoacabado, is a lovely island. It has all the usual tropical accessories—palm trees, azure waters, pink coral, beautiful long-haired virgins…"

She cuffed him. "So how did you come by the British accent?"

"I went to Oxford."

"Huh. That means people can leave this island of yours."

"Oh, most certainly."

"And what is the main industry?" She felt silly lying there in the dust, peppering him with questions, but it would while away the time while they waited for the men to leave.

"Smuggling. Although that's really more of a hobby."

"A hobby? What—"

"Shh." Armand listened intently. "They're pissed they've had to make this detour. Marko thinks they're wasting their time. Tubal says the merchandise should have been picked up already and that they're losing money. Belasco disagrees. What he sneeringly calls the 'human cargo' is worth much more than any manatees."

"Huh? What human cargo?"

Armand ignored her. "The leader—the one they call Belasco—has decided to head toward their rendezvous with…somebody. Didn't catch the name. He says they have to come back this way anyway, and they'll resume the search after they've got the manatees."

"The search…for you?"

His voice was grim. "For me."

The two watched as the crew shoved off and revved the motor.

They climbed down the ladder into a pitch-black house. Lacey thanked God she hadn't gotten around to lighting the lantern or starting up the generator before the pirates landed. They would have definitely tried to break in and search the place if they thought people were inside. She looked out toward the middle of the bay but could see nothing.

Armand lay down on the sofa and lifted his foot onto the coffee table. "They'll keep the running lights off until they reach the channel."

"Oh, I hadn't thought of that. How will we know when they're gone?"

"More importantly, how will we know when they come back? We've got to get out of here."

Lacey sat on the ottoman. "There's just one teensy problem with that. I've only got the one-man kayak and a bike. And you're not fit to walk anywhere. Besides, where would we go?" Armand was silent, and eventually Lacey's attention wandered. "I presume the launch is just for shore excursions. How big is the pirate ship? How fast is it?" *Do you even hear yourself, Lacey? Did you trip and fall into a Disney movie?*

"*Raven's End*? It's a long line trawler. A fishing boat like that has a regular cruising speed of six to ten knots, but Tubal bragged that he'd retrofitted the engine to make fifteen. I never found out if he succeeded, since they were weighed down by a load of contraband guns when they captured me. Belasco complained even then that they were making terrible time."

"I imagine the manatees are pretty heavy too."

"Oh, they haven't picked them up yet. I believe they were going to exchange the guns for the manatees somewhere north of here."

Lacey thought this over. "Guns need a dry place for storage, but manatees would need water to survive. Or will they be dead?"

"No—Belasco said his partner insists that they be delivered alive."

Lacey remembered the radio show. "Manatee bones are used to treat shingles and something else…let me see…" She pressed her lips together. "That's it, as a love potion."

"Really?" He leaned toward her and twisted a ringlet of her hair before letting it slip through his fingers. "Perhaps I should give myself up?"

Lacey hastily moved to the chair. "Wait…according to the news, the Coast Guard found a boat filled with guns. Would that be *Raven's End*? Maybe they abandoned it in the hurricane."

"If only that were true. It's an old smuggler's trick—they always have a backup boat…one they keep anchored somewhere out of sight. When they see a cutter they take off, leaving the substitute boat adrift to distract the law."

"But what about the guns?"

"My guess is they left a token pile of guns in the decoy's dry hold. Belasco didn't say anything about losing his cargo."

"So you think they're on their way to the rendezvous to exchange guns for manatees. Again, where will they store the animals?"

"In the live well. This is a deep draft boat—meaning almost half of its height is under water. Below the deck amidships, there's a large hold called a live well. It has air holes punched in the hull which allow water to circulate in and out."

"So…it's sort of like a great big aquarium in the bottom of the ship?"

"Yes. The well is usually used by fishermen to

keep their catch alive until they reach port."

"I see." Lacey thought this over. "Live manatees must be a lot heavier than fish. You'd need a pretty powerful winch to lift them out of the hold, wouldn't you?"

Armand shook his head. "In this case it's not necessary. Belasco installed a hatch door in the hull. They'll load the animals in from under the boat and transfer them the same way. The manatees will never be out of the water and never exposed to prying eyes. It's ingenious. "

Lacey didn't agree but had too many other questions to waste time arguing over the definition of ingenuity. "Do you know where they're supposed to deliver them?"

"I'm not sure. I only snatched bits and pieces of conversation while they held me captive on the ship."

Lacey had to know the truth. "Captive? You mean you weren't involved in the smuggling?"

He snapped, "No! How dare you suggest that?"

His tone—a mixture of outrage and arrogance, got her back up. "I can dare anything I like, mister. A man accused of smuggling manatees to Malaysia slipped through the hands of the police just before Hidalgo hit. It could have been you. You could be lying to me."

Armand sat still, but Lacey could hear his fingers tapping furiously on the table. Finally, he said, "It's probably okay to light a candle now. Put it on the floor though."

Lacey did as she was told, even though it gave him time to think up an alibi. *Let's see what he comes up with.* "Are you?"

"Lying? No. I don't know anything about any

Malaysian. I can tell you this. I was sailing my yacht, and when a squall came up—"

"The hurricane?"

"No, this was a couple of weeks ago and far away. My boat took on water and sank. The pirates came alongside to pick me up. When they recognized me, they decided I'd make good ransom material. They had to finish their transaction first though, so they tied me up and left me below deck for days."

Lacey decided to believe him. With his black eyes shining in the dancing light and his male scent enveloping her, she couldn't bring herself to dislike or fear him. Worse, she felt a terrific urge to kiss him. She clutched a throw pillow and searched desperately for another question. "Could they have been held up because their partner was in police custody?"

"Possibly."

Lacey put down the pillow. "I'm going to make some supper. Are you hungry?"

He perked up. "Am I! Say…" He winked at her. "…you don't have any more wine, do you? My…uh, ankle is throbbing. It might help."

"I'll see what I can find." She lit the Coleman stove, opened a can of Spaghettios and another can of green beans, and set two pots on to heat. Then, checking to make sure Armand didn't see her, she slipped into the garage and retrieved a bottle from a footlocker under the workbench. *Let's see…ah. I think a Beaujolais will do nicely with the Spaghettios.*

They ate at the kitchen table, the candlelight lending a romantic glow to the little room. By mutual consent, they didn't discuss their predicament. Lacey led off the conversation with a spirited defense of the

Washington Redskins, but, finding that Armand knew next to nothing about football, she let him take the floor. As the wine flowed, he discoursed on Ayn Rand's philosophy, whether the West Indies would beat India in cricket this year, and the relative superiority of Verdi versus Puccini operas.

The full moon shone through the window, illuminating Lacey's nodding head. Armand touched her cheek. "I think it's your bedtime."

Stung, she shot back, "I'm taking care of you, remember?"

He held up a hand. "Sorry! I'd forgotten." After a moment, he asked, his tone diffident, "Can you help me up?"

Lacey put an arm around his back and together they limped to Crispin's room. She took his pants and shirt off and folded them neatly. As she turned to leave, he touched her arm. "Stay a minute?"

How could she admit she had to get out of there quickly or she wouldn't be able to go at all? His handsome face—the strong chin covered with stubble, the pearly teeth contrasting with his tan skin, not to mention the long, graceful fingers he held out to her—all conspired to lure her closer. Her heart led the way, propelling her to his side. She sat down. "What is it?"

"Lacey…um."

Her body tensed as desire fought to get out, and she fought just as hard to keep it in. *I have to go. I have to…go.* "What?"

His words came out in a rush. "Lacey, the other day—the first night—when you rescued me. When we…we…"

Don't say it. Don't say it. Christ.

"I…uh…want you to know I don't do that on a regular basis."

His air of shy ambivalence gave her courage. "I see. You don't have sex on a regular basis?"

"No, no, it's not that." He stopped, flustered. "Er, I mean… I don't sleep with women indiscriminately."

Should she let him off the hook? *Nah.* "But you do sleep with a lot of women?"

"No! Lacey, you're being difficult on purpose. I meant, that I didn't mean to…you know. It just happened. Forgive me?"

"I—"

Armand interrupted her. "Not that it wasn't enjoyable." He seemed distracted, running a finger down her arm. "Wonderful. Fantastic. Too short." He peered at her. "Lacey, you must know how beautiful you are. You have the most perfect cheekbones I've ever seen."

"Cheekbones?" *What the hell is he talking about?*

"I'm an amateur photographer. Those cheekbones could belong to a supermodel. Perfectly sculpted. And your nose…" He tapped the tip. "A little pixie nose. It even turns up slightly. Your long, fine hair is the russet-gold of burnished copper pots I once saw piled high in a shop on Martinique. Your eyes…" He closed his. "Your eyes are the blue-green of a freshly mowed cricket field, of the emeralds that grow deep in the mountains, of the lagoon ncar my home on a blustery day." He touched her hand. "Then there's your body—as I remember it—a soft, comfortable, pillowy—"

"Hey!" Lacey shook her head to break the spell. "I think you've said enough. Get some sleep."

She tried to rise, but he slipped his arms around her

43

and drew her close. She wanted to struggle. She tried to struggle. It was no use. The long kiss filled her with a warmth that matched a fire on a cold night, a cup of cocoa, or a hot bath. When he lay back, the warmth turned to blazing passion. The power of it frightened her. *I've got to go.* She ran out of the room before he could stop her.

As she lay in her bed, panting with the effort to compose herself, she wondered at the explosion of libido in her. *How does he do that? Do I really care about him or am I just horny?* Thank God she'd had the strength to leave. This whole affair had become way too confusing. If only the bridges were fixed, and normal, everyday people reappeared. That would dissipate this aura of magic—this feeling that they were shipwrecked on Shakespeare's savage isle.

She found herself repeating what Armand had told her. *My hair—burnished copper. And my eyes…my eyes were like…what did he say? Emeralds.* Her heart began to pound. *No, Lacey, stop it! Quick—think of something else. What had he said about being abducted?* The pirates were after manatees. His boat sank, and they rescued him. And when they recognized him…wait—recognized him. *He calls himself Armand, but who is he really?*

****

Despite her distraction, Lacey fell quickly into a deep sleep. As the orange haze of a July morning stole through the window, she woke. Rolling over, she fetched up against an arm covered in soft black hair. She felt up it to a familiar chin. "Armand!"

He opened an eye sleepily. "Yes, dear?"

"What are you doing here?"

His sheepish face said it all. "I couldn't sleep. I thought maybe some company would help."

"And did it?"

He lifted his arm so she could snuggle under it. "Slept like a baby. You?"

She couldn't deny it—sometime in the night she had felt a wave of peace wash over her, calming her nerves. She didn't remember much after that.

But now his nearness bothered her. Her breasts tingled. Her vulva opened and shut, the organ grasping at air, longing for a thick penis to fill it. Casually, she shrugged Armand's hand a little closer to her breast, then arched to let his palm cover the sensitive nipple. It stiffened under the weight. Beside her Armand went quite still. She took a quick peek at his face. Impassive, stoic—until she checked his mouth. His lips stretched tight across his teeth, and his nostrils flared. Suddenly, he flicked the nipple and rubbed it between his thumb and forefinger. A nub of orgasm flared, and Lacey threw caution to the winds and moved Armand's hand lower. He slipped a finger inside, then two. As he rubbed her clitoris, she lost control, stuffing herself onto his moving fingers, panting and groaning with lust. As the climax raced through her, she rose up off the bed, carrying his arm with her.

When she fell to earth, he rolled her over onto his chest. Her vagina found his cock, now hard and smooth as glass, and slid down on it. Lacey held Armand's gaze while their hips began a slow dance, accelerating gradually to rocket speed. Her breasts swayed just out of reach of his mouth, and he shifted his eyes to watch them, all the while relentlessly grinding into her, frictioning the clinging tissue, scratching the itch.

Finally he gave a great sigh and fell back. Lacey lay across his chest, breathing only lightly.

An hour later, she woke to an empty bed. She heard the shower running, this time accompanied by "Celeste Aida." She lay quietly, drinking in the music. Armand's tenor was mellifluous and pure. She smiled to herself and stretched like a cat. *Life ain't bad.* From outside came the cree cree of an osprey, a lonely sound. It reminded her that her neighbors had still not returned to the island. A dismaying thought intruded. Would the pirates come back? If they'd already searched this area, wouldn't they move on up the island?

She rose and found her robe. As she padded down the hall, Armand emerged naked from the bathroom, shaking a wet head. He saw her and stopped, allowing her a breathtaking view of his glorious masculinity. "By the way, we're out of dry towels."

She threw him a washcloth, her blush not fading fast enough for him to miss. He grinned, caught the cloth, and limped off toward Crispin's room. By the time he made it to the kitchen, she had bacon sizzling in a pan and biscuits baking in a Dutch oven. He took the tray she handed him, his mouth open in surprise. "How did you come up with such a sumptuous feast?"

"I had precooked bacon in a box—very convenient. And flour and water mixed with a little baking powder and dry milk make a nice dough. We'll have my beautyberry jelly, I think."

She poured coffee, and they went outside and sat at the picnic table. Armand wolfed down the food, remarking on the distinctive fuchsia color of the jelly. "It's delicious, but what's it made of?"

"Beautyberries—*Callicarpa americana*. The

berries are a unique lilac color, so they're easy to find in the pine scrublands."

He took another bite. "You made this as well as the sea grape jelly?"

She nodded. "Yes. I'm still experimenting with jelly recipes. I've had to start from scratch learning all the local fruits here."

"It must be nothing like the vegetation in the mid-Atlantic region."

"Oh, you can still find mulberries, blackberries, raspberries—that sort of thing, but there are so many hundreds of edible warm-weather plants in Florida. The fun part is getting acquainted with all the different ecological niches here. Besides the hydric hammocks and salty coastal plains, you've got upland forests, pine flatlands, and scrubs in the interior. I can gather shore fruit like sea grape and roselle, plus hammock plants like the beautyberry and pigeon plum."

"What about the mangrove swamps?"

She chewed on a piece of bacon. "There's not much there except mangroves and buttonwood, although I've heard you can make pickles from glasswort—they're those little translucent green and red fingers."

"Doesn't sound very appetizing." He popped the last biscuit, slathered with jelly, into his mouth.

They finished breakfast, and Lacey helped Armand into the living room. She left him watching the bay with his foot propped up and returned to the kitchen to wash the dishes. When she came back he remarked casually, "We must prepare for Belasco's return."

Lacey sat heavily. "Mightn't they just go on, figuring they'd covered this area?" Her pitch rose on the last word, hope spilling out of it.

"Maybe, but we should still weigh our options for escape."

Lacey touched his ankle. "Until you can walk, our only choice is to hide."

"I guess you're right." He gave a little snort. "Hell, we can try little Tommy's tree house. They'd never find us there."

He looked so handsome and so helpless. Lacey was sorely tempted to lie down next to him. She'd forgotten how safe she felt with a man near, how cozy it could be. And domestic. It had been—she made a quick calculation in her head—twenty years since she'd lived with a man. *If you don't count Crispin.* Even when they were together, Damien hadn't been much of a husband. The marriage lasted two years—just long enough to give birth to a son and for Damien to plow through four jobs and a warehouse of cheap vodka.

Lacey smiled at Armand. He looked back at her with affection. She dropped to the seat and swung her legs up. His arm went round her shoulders, and they closed their eyes. Just as she began mulling over what to do with the ten pounds of cocoplums in the larder, he nudged her. "Sorry, kid. Nature calls."

The day passed quietly, and the next and the next. Like a latter-day Robinson Crusoe and his man Friday, the two castaways fell into a routine. Lacey would get up, set the water to boil, and make biscuits. Armand was allowed to choose the jelly. He pronounced the roselle his favorite, followed by beautyberry and pigeon plum. "Roselle, you called it? Excellent. Lemony and not too sweet. Reminds me of cranberry jelly. It's strange to think it's made of a flower."

"The calyx. The part that enfolds the flower."
"Whatever."

After that they would spend an hour or so exercising Armand's ankle. The swelling had gone down, but it was still bruised and purple. Lacey fashioned a crude cane from the root of a red mangrove, and Armand limped about getting in her way. At night she would put him to bed in Crispin's room and in the morning he'd be lying next to her. The arrangement was acceptable to both.

She had scouted out the island a bit more. There appeared to be some activity at the other end of the bridge over New Pass, but it was too far away for her to attract anyone's attention. When she came home and mentioned it, Armand dropped the book he'd been reading.

"Did they see you?" he asked anxiously.

"No. I thought maybe I'd make a flag or something. If I attach it to a pole—"

"No! I mean, don't do that. Who knows when Belasco will reappear?"

Lacey stopped. "I hadn't thought of that." She'd been so content she had almost forgotten about the men who kidnapped Armand. It brought up another point. "You know, it won't be long before they repair the bridges and the locals start coming back. We won't be able to hide then."

Armand said nothing. After a minute, Lacey continued. "On the other hand, we'll be protected with all those people around us. We can go to the police." She watched him carefully. Fear, apprehension, and something furtive passed over his features. *He's still hiding something.* "Look, you'd better come clean.

Admit it, you were actually working with those guys."

"Absolutely not. It's as I said. My boat capsized, and they pulled me out of the water. I told you the truth, Lacey. As much as I can."

"Wait." *He said they recognized him.* "Who are you? You said they were going to hold you for ransom. You must be rich or famous, or both."

He shook his head. "Neither, I'm afraid. But I am important."

"Huh?"

"Lacey, please." He rubbed his ankle, keeping his eyes on it. "All right, but I must swear you to secrecy. Will you?"

"Will I what?"

"Swear?"

Lacey was about to argue but thought better of it. "Sure."

He stared at her a minute. "All right, I told you my name is Armand Straniero. I…uh…I'm a minor dignitary, accused of embezzlement and banished from my country. They sent me off to…to Jamaica, but the ship was boarded off the Caymans. Belasco and the others took me and two others hostage. The others were…were…they killed them. But they kept me, hoping to use me as a human shield should they be pursued by the authorities."

"And when the storm came up, you gave them the slip?"

"Yes."

"But what about the ransom? You said they were holding you for ransom?"

"I did? Oh, well, yes. After a few days they decided they might demand money from my family in exchange for my freedom."

"But if you were banished, why would your family pay anything? You wouldn't be allowed back."

"I…uh."

Lacey went to the kitchen, poured herself a glass of water, and stood at the sink staring out the window. The late afternoon light wobbled uncertainly over the bay. She watched a flock of pelicans soar just above the waves in a perfect vee formation. When she came back, she sat on the ottoman. Armand hadn't moved, except to cross his ankles so the injured one rested on his good leg. "You'd think after all this time you could come up with a better story, Armand."

He didn't equivocate. "I know. My only excuse is I've been preoccupied with your beautiful eyes. Today they're a deep indigo blue, like the water beyond the coral reef in my country. It must be because of the clouds."

Lacey refused to be disarmed. "Can you at least tell me why you're giving me this cock-and-bull story?"

"To—"

"Protect me, I know. So, what is this great peril you're shielding me from?"

"If the pirates find me with you, they'll seize you as well. I told you what happened to the other two hostages."

"Assuming your story is a fabrication, there were no other hostages."

"But there are pirates. You've seen them."

"All right, so there's one itty-bitty fact swimming around in the morass of lies. Any others lurking in there?"

He picked the book up from the floor and

pretended to thumb through the pages. "Why won't you let it go, Lacey? I can't tell you the truth. There. I've said it. I will not drag you into my problems. You mean too much to me." His eyes blazed with frustration, and he panted, his breath coming in hot bursts.

Lacey stood stock still. "What did you say?"

He paused and his gaze wavered. "Lacey, I think I'm falling in love with you. I don't know how it happened. It shouldn't have happened. I'm involved in a real mess, and the last thing I need is to care about someone."

Images whirled through Lacey's brain—a mud-covered man stuck in a mangrove tree, an attic filled with dust and smelling of ginger, a warm chest against her naked back. His eyes shimmering with fun, his mouth full of biscuit and purple jelly. A penis pulsing in her vagina as they lay, sweat-covered and happy. "I…I do—"

She didn't finish her sentence. Banshee screams hurtled through the window from the bay outside. Men waving guns charged the house, broke down the door, and swooped down on the helpless couple.

Chapter Four

'Twas Friday morn when we set sail,
And we were not far from the land,
When our captain he spied a lovely mermaid,
With a comb and a glass in her hand.
~*~
Oh, the ocean waves do roll, they roll
And the stormy winds do blow.
But we poor sailors go skippin' to the top,
While the landlubbers lie down below, below, below,
While the landlubbers lie down below.
~*"The Mermaid," a traditional sailing song*
****

"Who's the broad?"

The pirate captain Belasco shook Lacey, apparently for the hell of it. He spoke to his companion in broken English. "Dunno. Was wit' da prince."

Lacey stopped shivering and stared at the man. *Did he say "prince"?*

"Why's she all wet?"

Belasco scowled. "She tried to break loose, and when Tubal grabbed her, she fell off da launch."

The man facing Lacey and Armand stood, legs planted wide to steady himself in the swaying cabin. "Fuck that, Belasco. You shoulda just left her there. Or whacked her." He surveyed his prisoners. "I suppose she may come in handy. At least now we have two chips to bargain with. You're sure no one saw you?"

"I know what I'm doin', Loganathan." Belasco's voice held a barely disguised threat.

Loganathan said mildly, "Of course you do. That's why I hired you. And don't call me Loganathan anymore. He's gone—lost at sea. It's Traficant now."

The pirate cackled. "Oh, yeah, I forgot."

Lacey jerked at the name, tightening the knots that bit into her wrists. Loganathan. The Malaysian manatee smuggler who got away. *At least that lets Armand off the hook for one crime.*

"So you didn't stop anywhere between Longboat Key and Honeymoon Island?"

Belasco shook his head. "I didn' leave da boat till we rendezvous'd wit' you. Marko and Tubal"—he indicated his two cohorts, one huge and one short and squat—"went inta Sain' Petersburg for supplies, but dat's it."

"And you didn't see anyone on Longboat when you went back for the prince and the dame?"

"Nah. Marko went ashore and cased da island afore we raided da house. We nabbed 'em and came back here, no problem."

Lacey examined the man who used to be Loganathan. Dressed like an amateur yachtsman, he wore neatly creased khakis, a Ralph Lauren polo in a painful lime green color, and brand new deck shoes. Measured against the husky pirate, he stood maybe five feet seven. Baby pink scalp glistened through the strands of graying hair. He had a bottle-fed tan and faded blue eyes. His nose had been broken in several places. When he spoke, his raspy voice indicated a lifetime of allergies. Lacey placed his accent as deep

South with a hint of Hackensack. *The talk show host called his accent exotic. Hackensack exotic?* Maybe to Floridians.

Traficant snapped his fingers. "We'll haul her along then, but if she's any trouble, dump her over the side."

Belasco gave Lacey a once over, lingering on her chest, and showed his teeth in a wolfish grin. "I's sure she won' be no trouble."

To his credit, the American shot a fist out and landed a right cross on the pirate's chin. Tubal and Marko lunged forward. Traficant whirled on them, the glint of a knife in his palm. They backed out the door. "Forget it, Belasco. I can't stand that kind of old world thuggery. Leave her alone. And tell your crew"—he stuck a thumb back in the direction of the wheezing thugs—"she's off limits."

The big man shrugged, although Lacey noticed a venomous flicker in his eye. "Can we get underway now?"

"Yeah, it's dark enough." Traficant nodded at the porthole. "Turn off the running lights, and we'll slip through New Pass. I want to be at least a hundred miles out by midnight. What's today, Monday? We've got to make Aruba before the weekend."

"What about the manatees?"

"We drop them off with Sandalio on Aruba. From there it's more than six hundred miles to Paraiso, but we should make better time without the cargo. You think Tubal's modifications can get us up to fifteen knots?"

Belasco swaggered. "He's a genius, dat Tubal. You know he's my cousin? Us Sendoas are all real smart."

Traficant was unimpressed. "We'll need that speed if we're to finish the business on Paraiso and get back to Aruba."

"Why do we haveta go back to Aruba?"

"To wait for confirmation of the delivery. Sandalio will take the manatees to Caracas. I've made arrangements to ship them from there to Malaysia."

"When do we get our money?"

"Not until the manatees arrive in Penang. The client won't pony up until he's made sure they're alive and healthy. They'll be slaughtered there and kept on ice for the trip to China." He spit into a brass spittoon, confirming Lacey's guess that the lump under his lip was chewing tobacco. She suppressed a gag.

The pirate brought a beefy fist down on the table. "You promised us da money when we picked up da merchandise. I ain't goin' nowheres till I get my tousand dollars."

Traficant raised a calming palm. "I can't give you what I don't have. The contract clearly states you get your money when the animals are delivered."

The staring contest went on for a second too long. Belasco dropped his eyes when he saw his adversary's hand edge toward the bulge in his pocket. "Well, just so's we get it."

The other man gave him a mean little smile. "Tell you what. I'll give you an advance in Aruba. And since we have two to ransom, I'll even split the take with you when we get to Paraiso. How's that?" He tried to slap the pirate's shoulder but could only reach the small of his back. "Agreed?"

Belasco appeared to ponder the pros and cons of Traficant's proposal. Lacey hoped he wouldn't pick up on the fact that the American's deal left him with only half the ransom money, money which technically belonged solely to the pirates. Not to mention the real possibility that, since the people forking it over didn't know her from Adam, she might not be ransomed at all. She blinked a tear away. In the chair next to her, Armand, his arms tied behind his back like hers, pressed her thigh with his reassuringly. "It'll be okay," he mouthed.

The pirate made up what little mind he had. "Okay. Sure. I'll be in da wheelhouse."

"Swell. Who's on guard duty?"

"Marko. Tubal's workin' on da engine." He left.

Traficant barked out the door. "Hey you, come here." Marko, a Sherman tank of a man, strutted in. Traficant thrust his chin out at Lacey. "There are some extra clothes in that compartment over there. Find something to fit our girlfriend." He looked Lacey up and down, his expression too similar to Belasco's for comfort. "She should get out of those wet clothes."

Marko untied Lacey and tossed a T-shirt and a short skirt at her. She waited a moment on the off chance that chivalry might triumph over voyeurism. No such luck. Finally, dogged by the leers of two men, she peeled off her soaked dress and pulled the dry clothes on over her wet underwear. *I'm not giving them the satisfaction of seeing me naked.* She avoided Armand's face.

Traficant ordered, "Tie her up again."

Marko did as he was told. His boss tapped the top of her head. "Okay. I'm going to get some shuteye." Lacey caught a glimpse of Marko taking up his position in the corridor before the door closed. She waited until she heard the key turn in the lock, then, twisting her head to glare at Armand, she hissed, "Prince?"

Armand, who looked about to explode, stopped short. "Oh. Er…you heard that? Um…yeah, I'm a prince—but it's not all that big a deal."

"Yes, I guess a king trumps it."

"Actually, in this case, my father is a grand duke. Not a king."

"Let me guess. He rules a grand duchy, then, right?"

"Yes."

"And you're his son."

"His second son. My older brother, Jakome, will inherit the dukedom. I'm the one they used to pack off to the priesthood."

Lacey reflected that, had they done so, it would have saved her a lot of trouble. "So that's why they kidnapped you."

"'Fraid so."

"Wait a minute." Lacey tried to remember Armand's fake story. "Didn't you say you came from a country called Todo…Todo…something?"

"Todoacabado. Spanish for 'all washed up.' I had to come up with something quickly." Armand's voice shook with mirth. "Rather clever of me, don't you think? Like picking 'Straniero' for a surname."

"Which means?"

"Foreigner—in Italian." His face smug, he said, "You never would have guessed."

Lacey ignored the jibe and shot her own condescending arrow. "So what's the real name of your washed up duchy?"

"Paraiso."

"Isn't that where Traficant said we're going after Aruba?"

"Uh huh. It's in the Saint Andrews archipelago off the coast of Nicaragua. We're a small but proud-hearted nation."

"Small?"

"The island's only twenty-one square kilometers."

"It would be in an atlas though, right?" Lacey gulped, her tone edged with anxiety.

"Only a very detailed one. You'd need a microscope to see it even on a map of the Caribbean."

"Oh dear, Crispin will never find it then."

Armand blinked. "Crispin?"

"My son. Presuming he'll come looking for me, that is."

"You have a son?"

Lacey studied Armand, detecting notes of jealousy, disappointment, and apprehension as they radiated across his face. She was tempted to let him stew a bit longer, but just then the boat's engines started up, reminding her that their time alone was limited. "Yes. Crispin is twenty-two. His father and I were divorced twenty years ago."

The muscles of his face smoothed out, but then he twitched, causing the chair to tip. He threw his weight to the other side, righting it. "Forgive me, but how would this son of yours know where to look for you?"

"I managed to scribble a short note during the attack."

"And what did you write?"

"Whatever I could piece together from the trifling bits of information you'd confided. When Belasco grabbed me, he knocked a glass over and the note landed in a puddle. I don't know if any of it will still be legible by the time Crispin finds it. If he finds it."

"Did Belasco see it?"

"I don't think so. I kicked it under the couch."

"Good girl. It will likely be a useless attempt, but you did your best." He beamed at her.

"Good girl? You make me sound like a well-trained puppy. I—"

"Shh. Someone's talking to Marko." They listened. Armand whispered, "I only made out a couple of words—'dinner' and 'rum.' "

"I like the sound of both."

"Somehow I doubt they'll ply us with liquor."

"Food at least would be nice."

A few minutes later the door opened to reveal Marko's elephantine silhouette. He set down a large tray and filled two coffee mugs from a pitcher. Sticking a straw in each he barked, "Punch."

Steam filled with spicy, buttery aromas rose from plates piled high with jerk chicken, fried plantains, and rice. Only the tight knots on her wrists kept Lacey from lunging forward and grabbing a juicy piece of meat from the plate. Marko slipped the knots off their hands, and left without another word.

The two fell on the food. Neither spoke until at last Armand sat back with a muted burp. "Not bad for prison chow. I could stay here awhile."

Lacey sipped her rum. "How long will it take to reach Aruba?"

"From Sarasota? It must be over a thousand miles. Didn't Traficant want to reach it by the weekend? That's five days." He looked around. "This trawler can probably make ten knots easy, but the cargo is slowing it down."

"And from there to your island?"

"Presuming they offload the manatees at Aruba, another couple of days. Paraiso is in the western Caribbean, miles from both the mainland and any other island group."

"Is that why it's not familiar? I'd never heard of it before."

"Yes, and we like it that way." Armand winked. "No tourists, no crime, no crowding. The only outside entity we interact with is the Campbell Metals Company LLC."

"Oh? What do they do?"

"They basically own the island. When a rare metal was discovered there, the company came in and bought all the subsurface mineral rights. The islanders receive a very generous royalty, which has kept the grand duchy in the style to which it's been accustomed for three hundred years—and without the necessity to…er…forage for ourselves."

"I see." Lacey popped the last plantain slice into her mouth. "So how did you become a grand duchy anyway?"

"Ah, this is what makes my home so special."

"Tell me."

Armand poured more rum. "I told you that a group of ten English families settled on the island in the seventeenth century. The soil was unsuitable for the crops we wanted to plant, but we found abundant fish and coconuts—enough to keep us alive. Scavenging from ships that foundered on our reef gave us building materials and rum, and the survivors—Dutch traders, Spaniards, African slaves—even pirates—augmented our little community."

"No Indians lived on the island?"

"No. The local Taino natives only maintained temporary fishing camps there—that is, until we'd developed a lucrative…shall we say, extra-legal shipping industry. Then they were happy to participate."

"Shipping? Oh, you mean smuggling."

"With a little piracy on the side." He grinned. "After a hundred years or so, the population had grown large and diverse enough that they needed some form of government. The Spaniards wanted a kingdom. The English and Dutch thought a republic would be better. The Africans didn't care so long as slavery was outlawed. Finally, they agreed on a constitutional government, but, in a nod to this one old salt who hailed from Luxembourg, compromised with a duchy rather than a monarchy. The grand duke holds considerable power, tempered slightly by a small legislative assembly."

"Sort of a cross between Saudi Arabia and England?"

"Yes, but with better food and flags."

"Flags?"

He gave her a mischievous pinch. "You'll see."

He refused to elaborate, so she gave up and moved on. "Okay, so what is your role as the second son?"

Armand's face darkened. "Minor. I wish I had more influence. We're going through a troubled time. My brother—"

A key turned in the lock, and Traficant entered. He surveyed the remains of their dinner. "I'll say one thing for Belasco—he employs an excellent chef. I'm glad I persuaded him to feed you as he does the crew. We don't want your father to find his son in poor health when he welcomes you back."

He waited a minute, but when neither prisoner responded, he went on. "Perhaps I should introduce myself. My name is Ulisses Traficant, and I'll be your cruise director for the next few days." He stepped toward Lacey and held her chin up with one finger. "Not bad. Who are you and how did you get mixed up with Prince Armand Eneco Cromwell de Montegue, second son of his Royal Highness Xavier, thirteenth Grand Duke of Paraiso?" He cocked an eyebrow at Armand. "You see, I've done my homework. At first I had no idea what Belasco was talking about when he said you were an aristocrat and worth a pretty penny. Now I know all about your little paradise. I also know about the dysprosium. So I repeat—" He swung on Lacey. "Who are you?"

Lacey shot a questioning look at Armand. He continued to stare at Traficant. *The most likely way to get me killed is to tell the truth. On the other hand, he'll find out soon enough if I'm lying.* "My name is Lacey Delahaye. I rescued this man after the hurricane. I know less about him than you do."

"Ah." He continued to gaze at Lacey speculatively. She fidgeted, uncomfortable under the scrutiny. At last he dropped his eyes and put his hand on the doorknob. "Do let Marko know if you require anything. I don't think it's necessary to keep you tied up, but you will be locked in the cabin." He slammed the door behind him.

Lacey let out a long, slow breath. Armand was the first to speak. "Well done. As long as Traficant—or Belasco—doesn't decide to make you walk the plank, they'll probably let you go when we get to Aruba. You're of no use to them."

"But I know their identities! I could finger them to the cops."

" 'Finger them?' Where were you raised, South Side Chicago?" He sniffed. "Not to worry—Belasco could care less about that. He's from Paraiso—pirates are a dime a dozen there, and he's a two-bit player. Hell, Henry Morgan, the renowned buccaneer, made us his base of operations, whence he sallied forth to prey on Spanish treasure ships!"

"He what?"

"He what what?"

" 'Sallied forth'?"

"Huh? Oh, pardon me. A legacy from my grammar school days. Pirate history formed a large segment of the curriculum."

"I see." *Not.*

Armand continued to muse. "As for Traficant, that's an obvious alias—it means 'smuggler' in Portuguese. This manatee operation must be his baby. Belasco and his crew aren't usually involved in such complex schemes. Whatever, he seems to be the pragmatic type. I don't think he considers you a threat."

No, not a threat. But…The female in Lacey had recognized a glimmer of interest in the American's eyes.

The afternoon wandered on. Through the porthole they watched the sun prepare for departure. Shyly, Lacey sought Armand's hand. He squeezed it and kissed her temple. "We'll be all right."

As the light paled into evening, Marko came in and pointed at Lacey. He said something. Armand translated. "You're wanted on deck."

"What for?" Fear clogged her throat.

Armand asked Marko and received a one-word reply. "Orders."

Losing all control, Lacey clung to Armand. "No! Armand, don't let them—"

Marko grabbed her arm and spat something out at Armand.

"Lacey, go. He says they're not going to throw you overboard. I won't tell you what he called you." He patted her hand awkwardly.

She went. They climbed the stairs up onto the deck. A half-moon gave just enough light to make out the figure of Ulisses Traficant in the stern. Marko pushed Lacey toward him and disappeared.

Traficant summoned her to the railing with a smile. He indicated a folding plastic table set with glasses and a bucket. "Welcome to *Raven's End*."

Lacey surveyed the empty deck. "Where are the others?"

"Below." He lit a lantern. The light filtering through the brass openwork lent an eerie glow to his face. "Pretty nice digs, huh?" She heard the pop of a champagne cork, then the clink of a glass. Traficant handed her a flute. "One of the perks of working with brigands—they'll strip a victim of everything, including a case of Bollinger. Salud."

Lacey saw no reason to refuse. Better to stay on his good side. And besides, Bollinger was her favorite champagne. She downed the liquid and held out her glass for more. He poured, and watched her drink. "You're probably wondering how a nice guy like me ended up with a bunch of loutish pirates."

M. S. Spencer

I'm guessing it's the money.

Traficant sipped from his glass. "I needed their trawler for my current endeavor, and they rudely insisted on coming along for the ride. Then, when I learned they hailed from Paraiso, well, my fertile mind recognized the potential for yet another source of income."

"What are you talking about?"

He refilled her glass. "I'd better back up a bit. About a year ago, I was in Bangkok setting up a rather intricate deal involving elephants and a Moroccan leather merchant, when I happened to run across the executive of a company named Campbell Metals. After a very generous round of drinks, he told me Campbell had a monopoly on half the world's supply of a rare earth element called dysprosium. He said they extracted it from a deep vein of bastnasite on a Caribbean island named Paraiso. I thought nothing of it at the time—my business usually involves more animate things…" His lips curled in an unsuccessful attempt at humor. "But when I learned Belasco et al. derived from said Paraiso, an idea began to percolate."

Despite herself, Lacey was intrigued. "What is dysprosium used for?"

"Oh, things like nuclear reactor control rods, lasers, magnets. It's hard to find in commercial quantities, so it's extremely valuable. The deposit that runs under the island is substantial enough to be worth millions. And Campbell owns all the rights."

"I don't…see."

"You don't? Ah, you must understand I'm a man of much imagination but not given to long-term planning. I'd been tossing around ways to get a cut of the dysprosium revenue when Belasco rescued a man on his way to our rendezvous. Right in the middle of my operation! You can imagine how annoyed I was."

"Er."

"Until, that is, Belasco told me that this particular castaway would make great ransom material, being a prince of Paraiso. Paraiso, says I. Dysprosium, says I. Perhaps this chance encounter could serve to enrich one poor struggling businessman such as I. So I forgave Belasco and signed on for Paraiso to seek my fortune."

She watched as he poured the last of the champagne into her glass. The wind picked up, and the boat suddenly rolled under her. She lost her footing and slammed into Traficant. He caught her, but instead of letting her go, he tightened his grip. His cock pulsed against her thigh. His voice thick, he muttered, "You know, you're a very sexy woman."

Careful, Lacey. "I…I think I'd better sit down. It must be the champagne."

He reluctantly let her go, but as he did his hand cupped her pubic mound. She stumbled and grabbed the rail. "There's more of that to come," he whispered in her ear. "Don't worry, you'll enjoy it."

A cloud passed over the moon, and she felt a raindrop. "Oh dear, it looks like rain. I should get back to the cabin." She headed toward the ladder, stepping a little unsteadily. He caught her arm. "I'll help you."

She so badly wanted to shake him off but knew she couldn't afford to provoke him. As they walked, his hand snaked down to her ass and started to rub it. She walked a little faster. A line coiled on the deck caught her toe, and she pitched forward. As she raised herself to her knees, Traficant bent over her and hiked her skirt up to her waist. She heard the sound of a zipper opening. Breathing heavily, his fingers locked onto her breasts through the thin cotton and pinched the nipples. "Woman, I want you," he panted. A hard rod nudged at her. "I saw the way you looked at me in the cabin. You want it too. Come on, come on, let me fuck you."

"No!"

He stopped. "What did you say?"

"No…please. Not with…not with all these people around. When we get to Aruba." She hoped she'd managed to sound flirtatious, that he wouldn't hear the hysteria in her voice.

"Shit, woman, what do I care about other people? They can watch if they want to."

"But—"

A shout from the bow drowned out her protest. "Hey, Traficant. Where are you? Sandalio's on the radio. He's landed at Aruba." Tubal stepped over a capstan. "Is that you? Come on!"

Traficant pulled himself upright and zipped his trousers. Through the side of his mouth he spit out, "We'll take this up later," and headed to the wheelhouse.

When she was sure he'd gone, Lacey crawled down to the cabin door. Marko opened it, and she fell into Armand's arms. "What happened?"

She couldn't tell him. She felt so humiliated. *I should have been nasty to him—bitten him or something. Anything would be better than what he just did to me.* "Rain…rain's coming."

Armand stared into her eyes a minute, before growling, his deep voice filled with rage, "I'm going to kill him."

"No, Armand—they'll kill you first. We'll figure something out."

His fists clenched, he nodded. "Maybe we'll have a chance at Aruba. Or Paraiso. Either way, I'm going to kill him."

"Fine, fine." Lacey just wanted to wash the filth off. She went into the tiny bathroom.

Later they lay in the narrow bunk holding each other. She hoped Armand wouldn't want to make love. She wanted the memory of the evening to wash away before she could touch him. He seemed to understand, and they fell into a fitful sleep.

She woke to a dark day. Rain pounded the deck above, and black clouds covered the sky. A slice of red shot from the horizon. Armand recited absently, "Red sky at night, sailors' delight. Red sky in the morning, sailors take warning. We're in for a blow, I think."

Sure enough, it poured all day and the next. The seas grew rough, and they listened to shouts and commands from the sailors as they lashed things down and tried to keep a steady helm. Lacey thanked the weather god, since it meant she could stay in the cabin and not face Ulisses. They whiled the days away playing word games and telling jokes. Lacey only knew one or two from childhood, but Armand was a master storyteller and kept her in stitches.

The evening of the third day the gale moved north and the seas calmed. A balmy breeze swept the dankness out of the cabin. Thursday night Lacey went to bed feeling almost as peaceful as she had the day she came home from her camping trip. Before the whirlwind.

At dawn a shout woke her. She shook Armand.

"What is he yelling?"

Armand cocked an ear. "Land ho."

Chapter Five

Fifteen men on a dead man's chest
Yo ho ho and a bottle of rum
Drink and the devil had done for the rest
Yo ho ho and a bottle of rum.
~*~

The mate was fixed by the bosun's pike
The bosun brained with a marlinspike
And cookie's throat was marked belike
It had been gripped by fingers ten;
~*~

And there they lay, all good dead men
Like break o'day in a boozing ken
Yo ho ho and a bottle of rum.
~Traditional sea chanty

****

The trawler maneuvered through a gap in the coral reef and chugged toward the beach. A stone groin jutted out into the water, and Tubal tossed a stern line toward it, catching it on an iron spike. They came alongside a floating dock. Marko threw another rope and tied the boat off. From her post at the scuttle, Laccy saw a man come out from behind a divi divi tree and wave at them.

Belasco jumped onto the dock and trumpeted in English. "Sandalio, my old friend! All is well?"

Sandalio opened a mouth empty of all but one tooth. "It goes, it goes. Welcome to Bachelor's Beach."

Belasco guffawed. "Bachelor's Beach? We've just come from Honeymoon Island, and we go on to Paradise after this. Are we lucky bastards or what?"

The other man pounded his chest. "That we are. I understand you have some pets for me?"

Traficant shouted from the deck above. "He sure does. How soon can you take them off our hands?"

Sandalio checked the sky. "Not till nightfall. Too many sailboats and fishermen about. Drop the anchor and come ashore. I have made camp. We can eat and talk awhile."

"Where's your boat?"

"*Wolf's Bane*? Hidden in a small bay around the point." He indicated a rowboat on the beach. "I'll go back to it this evening and rendezvous with you at midnight."

"This part of the island is uninhabited, right? How far are we from Oranjestad?"

Sandalio pointed northwest. "About twenty kilometers. It's on the western coast. People rarely visit these parts. The tourist beaches are all on the leeward side."

"Good, it's perfect for our transaction then." A minute later Traficant stuck his head in Lacey and Armand's cabin. "I have to go ashore to discuss some matters with my associates. I'm leaving the door unlocked, but Tubal will be guarding the boat. If you try anything, he has orders to shoot you. Any questions?"

They both shook their heads. He jumped into a dinghy that bobbed beside the dock and motored with Belasco and Marko toward the waiting Sandalio. As she watched them recede, endless options for escape raced through Lacey's mind. "Okay, they're gone. So how do we get out of here? I could swim—"

"Where? You heard them—there's no one within miles to help us." Armand slapped his knee. "Damn! I assumed we'd come ashore nearer civilization. I'd forgotten about Bachelor's Beach. It makes sense they would land here."

"There must be weapons stashed in the boat. We could find them and—"

"What? Stage a shootout?"

Lacey flounced onto the cot. "Well, what do you suggest? I suppose you'd rather sit around like a housebroken sheep." She glared at Armand. "Could we at least break open the hold and free the manatees?"

Armand chuckled, then paused. "You know, that's not a bad idea. They'd have to go after them—those animals are their cash cow."

"Ha, ha."

"What? Oh, yeah. I get it—sea cows, cash cow. Funny." He waited for her to subside. "Anyway, they only left Tubal to guard us. We would be two against one."

"That's right!" They mulled the idea over in silence for a minute, Lacey dreaming of riding a manatee into Sarasota Bay to the cheers of Floridians thronged along the shoreline.

Armand broke into her happy reverie. "So, any idea how we release the animals?"

"You said they were in the—what did you call it? The wet hold?"

"The live well."

"Right. And that Belasco installed a hatch in the hull—right?"

"Right."

"So all we have to do is find the lever that opens those hatch doors. It's got to be on the deck or in the hold somewhere…"

"Or outside the hull."

"Let's hope not." Lacey wondered how long she could hold her breath under water.

Armand drummed his fingers on the table. "Okay, here's the plan. We wait until midnight—"

"But that's when they're going to transfer them."

"Oh, yeah. How about…*hmm*."

"*Hmm*." Lacey rose. "I'm hungry."

"That's because they forgot to bring us breakfast."

For answer, Lacey's stomach grumbled. "I'm going to find the galley and see if there's anything to eat."

"Good idea. Bring me back something. Oh, and you might reconnoiter while you're on deck—maybe there's a secret hatch topside that leads to the hold."

"Yes, master." Hands on hips, she looked him up and down. "How is the ankle, by the way?"

Armand opened his mouth and closed it. "Better. Not quite healed."

"You'll tell me when you're no longer totally helpless, right?"

"Of course. I *am* a man, Lacey. You don't think I like having you wait on me hand and foot?"

"Isn't that the definition of a man? Or at any rate, a prince?"

Armand kissed her forehead. "Get along with you."

When Lacey came out on the deck, Tubal was scanning the open sea and paid her no attention. She poked around as casually as she dared. Toward the

74

stern, she found a hatch door and opened it. She couldn't see anything, but she heard splashing and the snuffles and bleats of several large beasts. She closed the door carefully and went in search of the cook.

Using a mix of English and hand gestures, she persuaded him to make her some breakfast. As he cooked, he griped about the *piratas* and extra mouths to feed. As soon as he handed her the tray, he began boxing up food and bottles. She returned to the cabin to find Armand gazing out the porthole. "Looks like they're planning to hang out on the island awhile. Tubal is rowing the cook over."

"You're right. Ooh, if they all stay on the island until midnight, we'll have plenty of time to let the manatees out."

"Okay, let's keep an eye on the activities over there." He picked up a plate. "What's this? An omelet? Cookie must be sweet on you."

As the afternoon wore on, the men stayed onshore. The prisoners could just make out a tent among the pines. When twilight descended, someone lit a couple of lanterns. Lacey ventured out onto the deck. She could hear shouts and now and then the crash of a bottle breaking. There was no sign of Tubal, and Sandalio's rowboat had disappeared.

She hurtled down the steps to the cabin. "Armand? Sandalio's gone. It looks like the rest of them are inside the tent, and from the sound of it, rum is heavily involved. We should make our move."

"Let's go." Armand limped toward her. Together they went up the stairs, then, crouching low, Lacey dashed to the hatch. Armand tried to follow her but stopped. "I'll have to crawl."

By the time he reached the opening, Lacey was already inside. She called up softly. "I'm standing on some kind of landing. I can hear the manatees, but it's too dark to see anything."

Armand whispered, "There's probably a lever that opens the hull door. See if you can find it."

Lacey felt around blindly until one hand touched a long wooden stick. "Found it."

"Okay, now push it forward."

"It's stuck."

"Put your weight into it."

Lacey panted, "It's starting to shift!" At the halfway point, it suddenly stuck again, but Lacey's momentum propelled her headfirst into the well. She came up in a pocket of air about a foot below the landing and grabbed hold of the coping. *Should I call? Did he hear me fall in?* A shadow passed behind her, then another. Something soft and pulpy gave her a push. She turned to find herself face to face with a bewhiskered, canine face. The manatee made a whuffing sound and butted her again. "I'm sorry I'm in your territory. Instead of ramming me, maybe you could give me a lift up."

From above her Armand trilled, "I don't think they understand you, Lacey. Did you fall in?"

She snapped, "What do you think?" A strange sound floated down. *He had better not be laughing.*

Armand called, a slight quaver in his voice, "Are the hold doors open?"

"Only partway. The lever stuck."

"Good. So the manatees are still inside?"

A fluke slammed into her back. "Ouch! Yes."

"Stay put. I'm going to climb down."

Lacey waited, trying to keep out of the way of the increasingly irritated bull. She heard groans from Armand and creaks from the ladder. All of a sudden the noise stopped.

"Armand?" Silence greeted her cry. "Armand?" She tried to keep the panic out of her voice. *Where is he?* She had to get to the lever. If it came unstuck and opened all the way, she'd be sucked down and out with the manatees. The sides of the well were slippery with fish guts, and she edged slowly, hand over hand, along the coping, hoping to find a ladder up onto the ledge. She touched a knotted rope. *If I can get a good grip and climb up...* She had wrapped the rope around her hands and shimmied up one knot when a light shone full in her face. Temporarily blinded, she fell back in the water. An arm shot out and caught her under the shoulder, hauling her up. She teetered on the ledge, holding onto the arm for dear life.

"You care to explain why you chose this evening to swim with the manatees?"

Traficant. "What have you done with Armand?"

Ulisses held her tight as his flashlight swept the water. "The little prince? He's fine, just getting his forty winks. Come on." He rammed the lever closed and pushed her up the ladder.

When they reached the top, she found Armand sprawled on the deck, out cold. Otherwise, the boat was empty. She took a quick look toward shore but could see no lights. "What's going on?"

"Shouldn't that be my question?"

Wet, cold, and worried, Lacey lost her temper. "Isn't it obvious? We planned to release the manatees. Why else would I be down there?"

Her attitude seemed to have a cooling effect. "No need to take that tone with me, Lacey," Traficant said mildly. "After all, freeing the manatees hardly constitutes a gracious gesture toward a man who saved you from pirates…not to mention drowning."

"All right. What are you going to do with us then?"

"Just what I planned to do. Once Sandalio takes the manatees off my hands, I'm taking you both to Paraiso for the ransom."

"Where are Belasco and the others?"

He spat—not a pleasant sound. "I have decided not to share the proceeds with them."

"They won't take that very well."

"I don't think they're in a position to argue."

Lacey sat heavily on a barrel. "You killed them."

Without answering, he dragged her up on her feet. "Come on, you should change out of those wet clothes. Again. It's a good thing Belasco's wife left a cache of female attire on board." He ran a hand down her chest, lingering on one breast. "Unfortunately, I lack the time to enjoy the view. Sandalio will be here in five minutes. Beat it."

As she cleaned up and changed into shorts and a T-shirt, she heard a boat come alongside. Grappling irons were tossed over the gunwales and the two trawlers bumped, knocking Lacey off her feet. She grabbed the window frame, pulled herself up, and looked out. With much splashing and squealing of chains, the manatees were transferred to the other boat. The two men said almost nothing, and a few minutes later, Sandalio and his cargo steamed off.

Lacey sat in the cabin, ruminating. Should she go up on deck and revive Armand? Would that just encourage Ulisses to assault her again? Did he really kill all three pirates? Or worse, the cook? And if so, why? Could he handle this cruiser alone? At first blush, he'd seemed at least semi-civilized. But now…Apparently, he'd stop at nothing to gain his ends. *Although those ends are pretty open-ended.* He jumped onto the ransom wagon without so much as a "Hey, can I play?" Which meant that he wouldn't harm Armand—at least until they reached Paraiso. *But what about now? What if Armand needs my help right now?* She held her fingers over her ears to stop the questions. When she'd collected her wits into a rational pile, she listened, hoping to locate Traficant by his footsteps. The engine started up, and the boat began to move.

I can't just wait here. I'm a sitting duck. She got up, brushed her hair, and cast about for a weapon with which to defend herself should the need arise. She chose a wooden yardstick over the miniature embroidery scissors. *Better to keep some distance between us.* Climbing up on deck, she spied Traficant in the wheelhouse, silhouetted against the moonlight. Armand still lay sprawled by the hatch. She shook him and whispered, "Armand! Wake up!"

He caught her arm. "I am awake, dear. Just resting. I saw no reason to draw our captor's attention. I gather you were unable to accomplish your mission." He peered at her. "He didn't hurt you, did he?"

"No, but I don't know how long that will last. Armand, I think he killed the pirates."

He sat up. "Come on, let's get below."

She helped him along the gangway and down to the cabin. When he'd caught his breath, he said, "Well, if Traficant's the only one on the ship, he'll have his hands full."

"How long did you say it would take to get to Paraiso?"

Armand squeezed his eyes shut. "If I remember my nautical charts correctly, it's about seven hundred miles from Aruba to Paraiso. Traficant will be able to increase his speed now that the boat's lighter. If Tubal's engine modifications worked, I'd guess a couple of days."

"That's not very long." She looked about the cabin, wondering if anything could be fashioned into a better weapon than the flimsy stick in her hands.

"I've already looked—the best I could come up with are those." He gestured at the rusty pair of scissors Lacey had already rejected. "I doubt if there's anything we can do till we get to our territorial waters. With any luck a local fisherman will recognize me and sound the alarm."

"I don't know…I don't think we should wait. Why can't I jump him?"

"Because he's stronger than you. And remember, he may not consider you worth saving."

Lacey put her chin in her hand. "Okay, you trip him and then I whack him on the head with a spanner?"

"Do you even know what a spanner is?" Armand rolled his eyes.

"As long as I use a heavy object, what difference does it make?"

"Look, my head's killing me. And my ankle isn't too boffo either. I'm going to get some sleep. We'll consider our options in a few hours."

Lacey let him lie down and turned to the table, where their plates from breakfast remained. "I hope

Traficant didn't kill the cook."

"It's considered unlucky to do more than complain about the food when at sea."

"Unfortunately, the cook was on shore." She mused, picking at the crumbs left on her plate. "I don't suppose there's any food left in the galley."

The only response was a snore. Lacey went back to observing the dark sea. Just as she decided to join Armand, she saw a light on the horizon. It came nearer. A ship! "Armand! A ship's approaching!"

He didn't stir.

"What if they hail us? Maybe I can send a signal."

Just then, Ulisses blew the ship's horn. An answering blast came from the other boat. As it pulled alongside, Lacey saw with a sinking heart that Sandalio stood amidships. The two men shouted across the waves, but she couldn't make out what they said. From the scowl on his face, Sandalio seemed to be upset about something. Traficant simply shrugged and revved his engine. Sandalio shook his fist at the retreating boat.

A voice spoke behind her. "Do you suppose he's angry about the mess o' dead bodies he just had to contend with?"

Lacey took Armand's hand. "I don't know—he doesn't seem the squeamish type. Maybe Ulisses double-crossed him too."

"If we're lucky, Sandalio will turn on him, and our troubles will be over."

"That would be nice, but Sandalio has the manatees. He's under a deadline to deliver them. I doubt he'll waste time following us."

As if in answer to Lacey's comment, *Wolf's Bane* came about and headed back east.

Raven's End picked up speed, and they bumped through the whitecaps. Lacey lay down, but the rocking made it impossible to sleep. Armand leaned out the porthole. "He must be going over twelve knots. At this rate, we'll get to Paraiso early Tuesday."

"And then what?"

He turned. "I have no idea. My family will be…er, unprepared for my return. I fear Traficant may be caught off guard by their reaction to his demands."

"Unprepared? Why? Do they…do they think you were lost at sea?"

Armand's tone was dry. "They probably hope I was. Let's just say my homecoming will not be met with loud hosannas."

"What on earth do you mean? Wait—your story of banishment. Is it true?"

"No, not exactly. Look, it's really complicated. And the less you know the better—plausible deniability, that sort of thing."

"The less I know? Armand, I'm totally in the dark here. How can I help you if you only drop little hints and clues? It's not like I'm not already up to my eyeballs in this affair. Or that I'm not already at risk. Why won't you fill me in?"

"Because—"

The door swung open. Traficant strode in, twisted Armand's arm behind him, and manhandled him out of the room.

"Where are you taking him?"

Traficant spoke over his shoulder. "To make a phone call."

****

An hour later the door opened again, and Armand

stumbled through. Traficant slammed it after him and turned the key in the lock.

"What happened? Who did he want you to call?"

"Just a minute." Armand pulled a bottle out from under the cot and poured himself a whiskey. He hobbled over to her and sat.

"Where the hell did you find that?"

"I forgot to tell you…when you were on one of your forays to the galley I discovered a full bar tucked away by the loo. We sure lucked out in the prison cell amenities department. Cheers." He held up another plastic cup and poured Lacey a generous dose.

After downing it, she commanded, "Speak! Who?"

"Who did he want me to call? My father."

"And did you?"

"No."

Lacey took the bottle from him and poured another tot. Where to start? "All right, it's time to tell me everything, my lad."

Armand polished off his drink. "Not right now, if you don't mind. I'm going to get some sleep. We'll have all day tomorrow to talk."

Leaving her gaping at him, he threw himself on the bed and immediately fell asleep.

Lacey finally managed to drift off as the dawn seeped over the horizon. When she awoke, hot sun poured into the cabin. Armand handed her a glass of orange juice. "Compliments of our captain." Behind him the table was set with a loaf of bread, jam, and butter.

She sat up and drank the juice, then ran a hand through her tangled locks. "I need a comb."

He produced one from a pocket. As she dragged

the tines through her hair, tearing out the knots, she fixed Armand with a determined look. "I believe the schedule calls for a full report today."

"A promise is a promise. At any rate, we should have some extra time. The boat's slowed down— something must have gotten Traficant's wind up. He seems to be idling, waiting for a signal or something. If we stay at sea for another day, I'll have time to enlighten you on the situation in Paraiso."

Foreboding clutched the tiny hairs at the back of Lacey's neck and yanked. What if Armand were a criminal? Or a traitor? "Just…um…tell me as much as I need to know."

"Okay." He tore a piece of bread off and slathered it with jam. "Not as good as yours, but it'll do in a pinch."

"You were saying?"

"As I explained, I'm the second son of the Grand Duke Xavier. By law, my older brother Jakome inherits the throne."

Lacey dipped a finger in the jam and licked it off. "How much older is he?"

"Less than a year. We left for university at the same time, but he returned and spent some fifteen years on Paraiso before going back to the States for graduate school. I only came home a few months ago."

"How come?"

"After Oxford I did some traveling—"

"The customary Victorian Grand Tour for young gentlemen?" Lacey drawled in her best BBC accent.

"Something like that. I spent a year helping a village in Botswana build an aqueduct, then had a grant to teach carpentry in Peru. Later on, I worked with the king of Morocco to establish a school for the arts. Similar projects have kept me away from Paraiso for the last twenty years, with only short vacations there every year or so. I finally settled down last January."

Wanna take that appendage out of your mouth, Lacey? "Oh."

Armand appeared not to notice her discomfiture. "Coffee?" He filled her mug. "Jakome attended Princeton University rather than Oxford. About four years ago he decided to go back for a master's degree in political science." He shook his head. "In retrospect, Father was so wrong to let him do that."

Lacey bristled. "Why do you say that? Princeton's one of the best schools in the world. My father, all my uncles, and both my grandfathers went there."

"It may have been great at one time, but now it's overrun by left-wing dinosaurs." At her shocked look, he shrugged. "I guess the ivory tower is the only place left that nurtures the faith that someday, somewhere, socialism will actually improve an economy. My brother returned to Paraiso with all kinds of unhelpful ideas."

"Like what?"

He tore off another chunk of bread. "Where do I begin? He tripled taxes on the off-shore accounts we're known for hosting and doubled the individual income tax so he can fund cradle-to-grave government welfare. He ordered price controls on staples to punish what he calls 'those greedy farmers,' and required businesses with at least three employees to replace their equipment with new 'green' machines."

"I thought you said he's only the heir apparent. Does he have the authority to make all these changes?"

"Not technically, but he's always been Father's favorite and…well, Father's not as young and sharp as he used to be."

"You said Paraiso had a legislature. Don't they have to agree to any changes?"

"Jakome claims he has the executive power to 'tweak' the law, as he refers to it. So far, the assembly has gone along with him. And he's got this smooth-talking adviser who's convinced Father that Jakome's reforms will make life fairer for everyone. All it's done is drive fifty mom-and-pop stores out of business, prompt international companies to pull their assets out of our banking system, and create shortages of everything from tea to sugar. If we didn't have the regular royalties from Campbell coming in, we'd be bankrupt."

"What can you do? Where can you go for help?"

Armand refilled her glass. "That's just it. We've been virtually isolated for two hundred years. We voted not to join the United Nations, and the Caribbean Tourist Organization isn't interested in us because we have very few tourist facilities. Worst case scenario, we'll have to abandon the island."

"But that's awful! Surely your brother doesn't want that to happen? How has he reacted to the problems?"

"He doesn't believe they *are* problems. He declares that 'the few must give more for the good of the masses,' or some such nonsense. The fact that we have a population of six thousand—hardly even one mass, let alone multiple masses—seems to have escaped him. It's as though he's been brainwashed by some kind of cult."

"Oh dear."

Armand went to the window and stood looking out,

lost in thought. "Have you ever heard of cognitive dissonance?"

"No, what is it?"

"It's a term in psychology that describes a condition in which a person believes so strongly in something that he's unable to distinguish fact from fiction. Like the wacko who proclaims the world will end tomorrow. When it doesn't, what does he do? Stop believing? No sir. He picks himself up, dusts himself off, and announces that the end of the world will be a week from now. He's so consumed by the idea that he can't conceive of being wrong. Reality has no effect."

"I remember hearing about a guy—what was his name?—who predicted the end of the world in 2012. Are you saying Jakome's like him?"

"Ronald Weinland? Yes. When I came home and found Jakome systematically uprooting our laws and substituting his personal edicts, I tried to reason with him. It quickly became obvious that reason had long since left the building. So I did some research—hoping to understand the basis for Jakome's intransigence. It led me to messianic cults and cognitive dissonance and ultimately to Weinland. He first predicted the end of the world in 2008, and when that didn't materialize, he claimed he really meant May 27, 2012. May 27 came and went without so much as a peep, but that didn't faze Weinland. He announced that the apocalypse had in fact occurred—we just didn't know it. Apparently it takes a while to kick in, so we could expect the end to be sometime in 2020."

"I guess I should check my TV guide, huh?" Lacey tittered.

Armand threw her a disapproving look. "It's not so

funny when it happens to you. Thousands of our people are hurting, and I can't get Jakome to accept that his policies are at fault."

"Is that why you left?"

Armand stopped, his mug halfway to his lips. "No. Well, in a way. Edrigu—"

"Edrigu? Who is he?"

"He's the man I called instead of my father. He's First Secretary Edrigu Boudewijn Cacicana Proctor. His family accompanied my ancestors to Paraiso in the seventeenth century. The Proctors have served as liege to the Montegues since the establishment of the grand duchy."

"Wait, stop there. What did you say his name is?"

Armand recited patiently. "Edrigu Boudewijn Cacicana Proctor."

Lacey goggled at him. The familiar New England last name sounded so outlandish in conjunction with the exotic ones. "I recognize 'Proctor,' but what do the others mean and why does he have so many?"

Her question seemed to flummox Armand. "Everyone on Paraiso has at least two forenames and two surnames. I never thought about it much." He pursed his lips. "Let's see. Edrigu is Paraisan for 'council commander.' Cacicana was the native chief who greeted the pilgrims upon their arrival. Each name refers to an ancestor."

"So yours—"

"Armand Eneco Cromwell de Montegue. Eneco means 'hot' or 'furious' in Paraisan and Cromwell…well, Cromwell—"

"I get it," Lacey jumped in hastily. "You were saying about Edrigu?"

"Yes. When I returned to Paraiso this past winter, he came to me. He was concerned about the effects of Jakome's changes. He told me Jakome had bribed or threatened all the members of the legislature to rubber stamp his decrees. I agreed that we had to take action before the damage was irreparable, but Father wouldn't listen to us—he's walled up in that chamber of his in the castle writing his memoirs."

Lacey could hear the dejection in his voice. "He cut you off?"

"Yes. He got tired of my constant warnings and banned me from his office."

"What about...Edrigu? "

"My father trusts him as an old retainer but refuses to hear any criticism of Jakome. Edrigu reluctantly came to the conclusion that only a coup d'état could end the madness."

"I don't understand—if you deposed your father, Jakome would have all the power, wouldn't he?"

"No! No, I didn't mean that. He...uh...Edrigu wants to...to..."

"To what? Banish Jakome? Imprison him?"

Armand hung his head. "Yes. Arrest him for treason. He believes it's the only way. I disagree. Jakome is the rightful heir to the throne. Besides"—he twisted his lips into a wry expression—"it could set a precedent, and then where would I be?"

"You'd also have to contend with the grand duke. From what you've said, he wouldn't take kindly to the impeachment of his best beloved."

"True, but even if we succeeded in placating Father, it would still be wrong."

Lacey sipped her juice, not sure whether to voice

her disagreement. *Not yet.* "So what happened?"

"We went back and forth for weeks. Meanwhile, Jakome kept introducing new 'reforms'—restricting water use, censoring the newspapers. He's now requiring doctors to submit their treatment plans to a government committee for approval. All in the name of 'fairness.' When lines began to form for food and rum, Edrigu redoubled his pleas for me to do something. I had to make a decision."

He broke off. Tearing the crust from the loaf, he chewed slowly. "I told Edrigu I needed some time to clear my head and took my little sloop the *Celeste* out alone. I sailed to Cozumel, then down to the Caymans. On my way to Jamaica, a waterspout capsized the boat. That's when Belasco and the others rescued me."

"They recognized the prince, saw a chance for ransom money, and took you prisoner."

"Yes. They weren't aware of how much the state of affairs back home had deteriorated or they might have left me stranded."

"And this was how long ago?"

"I left Paraiso more than a month ago. The pirates held me for two weeks before I got away."

"That's a long time. If the people were discontented, they may have already taken matters into their own hands."

"Maybe. Maybe they have."

"You don't know?" Lacey stood up. "I thought you spoke to Edrigu?"

"He couldn't talk freely—apparently my brother's advisor was in his office when the call came through. I still don't know what kind of reception I'll receive."

"I guess we'll find out soon enough." Lacey stifled

a yawn. "I didn't get much sleep last night. I think I'll take a nap."

Armand took her mug and placed it on the table. "Good idea. I'll keep watch."

Lacey gazed at him. His handsome profile showed lines of worry she hadn't noticed before. Something pressed on her heart. *He's so alone. I want to help him so badly.* She reached a hand out, but let it fall. *I can't be…no. Now is not the time to indulge in feelings—not with tomorrow hanging over our heads.* What would Ulisses do with them? How did he plan to handle his ransom demands? The lump of affection dissolved, and dread straddled her chest. *We could both be dead by morning, or at least separated.* Her heart told her the latter would be worse. She closed her eyes, hoping to push the thought away. Soft lips touched her forehead.

"Sleep, my dear. All will be well."

She slept.

Chapter Six

"Aloft there, aloft!" our jolly bosun cries,
Blow high, blow low, and so sailed we;
"Look ahead, look astern, look aweather and alee,
Look along down the coast of the High Barbaree."
~*~
There's nought upon the stern, there's nought upon
the lee,
Blow high, blow low, and so sailed we;
But there's a lofty ship to windward, and she's
sailing fast and free,
Sailing down the coast of the High Barbaree.
~*~
"Oh, hail her, hail her," our gallant captain cried,
Blow high, blow low, and so sailed we;
"Are you a man-o'-war or a privateer," said he,
"Cruising down the coast of the High Barbaree?"
~*~
"Oh, I am not a man-o'-war nor privateer," said
he,
Blow high, blow low, and so sailed we;
"But I'm a salt-sea pirate a-looking for my fee,
Cruising down the coast of the High Barbaree."
~Traditional sea chanty
****

A change in the rhythm of the ship's engine woke her. "Are we slowing down?"

"Yes." Armand turned from the porthole. "We're within sight of our capital city, Port Huntington."

"Huntington. Not much of a name for a Caribbean city."

"The first settlers—my ancestors—were cousins of Oliver Cromwell. They named the city after his birthplace."

Lacey took his place at the window. Whitecaps blew foam in frothy drifts as waves crashed over a hidden reef. She could see calm water through a narrow gap in the breakers. A shrimper chugged slowly past them into the channel. "Is Paraiso a coral atoll?"

"Volcanic originally, but over the millennia a coral reef built up around it—one of the most beautiful in the world." He sighed. "It is truly paradise here. I have missed it."

Lacey stretched. "I wish we could see it from the deck."

"Me too, but Traficant told me he plans to keep us locked in until he makes contact."

She peered out. In the near distance rose a high, mountainous island. They approached a town nestled under the watchful gaze of a ridge of hills. From the waterfront, a wide pier jutted out into the lagoon, its buildings painted in colors straight from Gauguin's palette. Two castles, turreted and fortress-like, perched on cliffs at either end of the island. Flags flew from each tower. "I can't make out the flags. What are they?"

"On the left—to the south—is the grand ducal palace. The flags are those of our family—the Montegues—and the grand duchy. The first is a shield of white with three red diamonds below our emblem, the gryphon. The flag of the Grand Duchy of Paraiso is a simple cross together with a yoke and galleon on a field of purple."

"Strange combination. What do they represent?"

"The cross symbolizes our original Puritan quest for religious freedom. The galleon depicts our ship, the Swan. The purple stands for sovereignty, justice, and majesty. The yoke..." Armand paused. Lacey turned to find him squirming in his chair.

"The yoke?" prompted Lacey. "As in, for oxen? Farming?"

"N...no. I told you that the land here isn't suitable for the type of crops we were used to, so we turned to the only means of support available—scavenging shipwrecks. From there it was a natural transition to the slave trade."

Lacey's jaw dropped. "That doesn't sound very religious!"

"Nobody said we were consistent. You'll find Paraiso an odd mix of beliefs and customs."

"I do not approve."

A twinkle in his eye, Armand kissed her. "Do you approve of buried treasure?"

"You mean that rare earth stuff?"

"The dysprosium? No, I mean doubloons, Spanish silver, Colombian emeralds, golden goblets. Pirate treasure."

Lacey leaned forward eagerly. "Buried, you say?"

"Yes. The infamous corsair Henry Morgan had his base here for more than a decade, and rumor persists that he hid much of his hoard somewhere in the mountains or in one of the inaccessible coves up and down the coast."

"No one's found it yet?"

He shook his head. "We're all praying a native Paraisan will come across it before Campbell Metals does."

Lacey looked out again. "What's the other castle, the one on the northern point?"

"It's the ancestral estate of the Proctors. The first secretary has always come from their ranks. Edrigu is the current officeholder."

"The first secretary is like what, a vizier?"

"Yes. And treasurer, chief steward, commander of the army—"

Lacey stifled a giggle. "An army of one?"

Armand looked down his nose at her. "For your information, our muskets still work, and both Stefan and Luis are well trained in hand-to-hand combat."

"Should it ever be needed."

He turned grave. "I hope to God it never will be."

It reminded Lacey of their predicament. "Where is Ulisses, do you suppose?"

Almost as if he'd been listening, the door sprang open, and Traficant entered, carrying a coil of rope. "I have an appointment with a man named Damiano." He put Lacey on the cot and tied her hands to the bedposts. Dragging a chair to the other side of the room, he lashed Armand to it. "Now stay put. I won't be long." He left.

They heard the splash of the anchor. A little later, the sound of oars dipping into the water told them their captor had taken the dinghy. Spread-eagled on the bed, her arms stretched painfully, a familiar panic smothered Lacey's senses. She had never been able to stand having her arms pinioned. She laid her head back and tried to relax, but her breathing quickened and hysteria washed over her. She concentrated on the gentle rolling and pitching of the boat.

"Here, let me." Warm breath misted the back of her head.

She tried to jerk upright, but the ropes pulled her back down. Her eyes wild, she opened her mouth to scream, but a rough hand went over it. "Shhh, quiet, Lacey! You'll wake the dead."

"Armand! You're…you're free! I thought…I thought…"

"Now if you will kindly wiggle your fingers."

Lacey did so and soon felt a loosening of the bonds around her wrists. "How did you manage it?"

Armand held up his hands, free of rope. "Unlike American prep schools, Eton teaches useful skills such as fencing and lock-picking."

"I bet you're a big hit at parties."

"As a matter of fact…" He picked up her hand and kissed the tips of her fingers.

Lacey took a deep breath, and peace flooded back into her body. "So, your degree is in Houdiniomics?"

"Among other things."

She rubbed her wrists. "What do we do now?"

"We get off this boat."

"You mean, swim?"

"If we have to." He stood up and paced the cabin.

She stopped him, hand to his chest. "You can walk!"

"What?" He looked down as though discovering his feet for the first time. "Oh, yes. The ankle is nearly healed."

"But you were limping heavily only last night when Ulisses took you."

"That was for his benefit. If he thinks I'm still lame, he won't worry about our getting away."

"I see." She went to the door and tried the handle. "Locked."

Armand held up what looked like a needle. "Standard school supplies." He fiddled with the lock until the door sprang open.

"Why didn't you use that before?"

"And go where?"

"Good point." Lacey stuck her head around the corner and checked the gangway. "All clear."

"All right." Armand picked up the yardstick and the scissors. "Let's get out of here. Traficant may not be gone long—especially when he discovers his ransom demand falls on deaf ears."

Up on deck the island loomed over them, much closer and larger than it had seemed below. Armand checked a storage bin in the bow. "There's an inflatable life raft in here. See if you can find a pump."

Lacey moved along the deck, looking into the bins that lined the port side. Something moved near the hatch to the live well. "Armand!" she whispered urgently.

He followed her pointing finger. "What did you see?"

"Someone's there. I think Ulisses left a guard on the boat."

"Don't be silly—we know he's alone."

"Then who is it?"

Armand strode toward the hatch and lifted it. He caught a small brown hand before it slipped down into the water and hauled a boy up. He looked about fourteen years old, with black hair, a deeply tanned body clad only in wet shorts, and striking blue eyes. Armand barked in English, "What's your name?"

The boy drew himself up, a proud lift to his chin. "Inigo Carolus Azarola Mather, at your service."

"Well, Mister Fiery Fox, what are you doing here?"

The boy pursed his lips. "I reserve the right to investigate any strange vessel that drops anchor on our shore without proper authorization."

"Ah." Armand nodded gravely. "Do you know who I am?"

The child looked him up and down. "You are His Royal Highness, Prince Armand Eneco Cromwell de Montegue, a little the worse for wear."

Armand threw back his head and roared. "Oh, my. Yes. Yes, I am. Tell me, are your parents in my father's service?"

The boy frowned. "No, Your Highness. My father is sergeant-at-arms to His Excellency First Secretary Edrigu Boudewijn Cacicana Proctor."

"You're Koldo's boy? Good." Armand wasted no time. "Where is your boat?"

Inigo indicated a painter tied to a cleat on the gunwale. They bent over the side. A rough dugout canoe bobbed in the water. "I made it myself. Cut down the ceiba tree, shaved off the bark, aged it, and burned out the core." He beamed.

"Can it hold three people?"

The beam faded. "I don't know, sir." He brightened. "However, it will easily carry the both of you. I can swim alongside."

Armand contemplated the boy, then patted his shoulder. "Good man. Let's do it."

Inigo went first and steadied the boat while Armand climbed into it. Lacey clutched the side of the trawler as she crept down, almost losing her nerve when a wave washed over the canoe. Armand caught her around the waist and lifted her into the bow. He picked up the paddle and headed toward the northern point, Inigo kicking alongside.

The boy guided them to a break in the reef, and by dint of hard paddling they made it into the calm waters of a small lagoon. Lacey trailed her hand in the warm sea and on a sudden whim slipped over the side.

"Lacey!"

"Oh, Armand, it feels so delicious." She wiggled out of her T-shirt and tossed it in the canoe, then started toward the shore. Underneath her, brilliantly colored fish flashed and dipped among the corals. Something shimmered in the sands. "Treasure, Armand! I see treasure!"

His eyes sparkled with humor. "I told you—pirate gold is everywhere." They reached the beach, and Lacey flopped down on the sand. Inigo took one look, blushed fiercely, and turned away. Armand threw her shirt to her. "Now look, you've frightened the lad."

Unrepentant, Lacey dragged the shirt over her wet skin.

Inigo pulled the canoe up and tied it to a coconut palm. Eyes glued to the sky, he spoke to Armand. "Did you need anything else, Your Highness?"

Lacey realized the boy had to this point asked no questions. He seemed incurious about how they came to be on Traficant's boat, why they wanted to leave it, or even where Armand had been all this time. *Maybe it's just that a fourteen-year-old boy has other interests.* Or maybe questions were not encouraged in this grand duchy.

Armand said, "Yes, I do. Tell your father I am here and have him come to me. Quietly."

The boy saluted, then clambered over the sharp rocks and disappeared from sight in a grove of saw palmetto. A few minutes later, he came into view racing across an open field. Lacey watched him climb the hill. "How long will it take Inigo to reach the castle?"

"Maybe half an hour. Depends on which path he takes. After that he'll have to find his father."

"Can he be trusted to keep mum?"

"I'm sure he can. He seems a bright boy."

Lacey sat down on a log. The sun shone brightly, and a soft breeze dried her hair. She dug her bare toes into the powdery white sand. "What did you call him? Fiery fox?"

Armand skipped a pebble across the water. Lacey silently counted. Six. *Not bad.*

"His Para names—Inigo and Azarola mean fiery and fox. I was teasing him."

"But his other names—his surname—"

"Mather. Yes. Remember I told you the original settlers were religious separatists. They had set out across the Atlantic as part of a large flotilla. About five hundred miles out to sea, a storm came up. Our ship was cut off from the fleet and blown way off course. The others went on to Massachusetts, while we made our way south—don't ask me how we missed every island in the Lesser Antilles—and settled here. Over the years we intermarried with the local Indians, former slaves, and shipwrecked sailors. Everyone here has a name from two or more of the various ethnic groups represented—Taino, Dutch, English, Portuguese, Spanish, and an amalgam we call Para."

"Like you."

He skipped another pebble. "It's worse for me. As a Montegue, I'm saddled with names from every country and every ancestor to which we have any connection. If I gave you my full name, we'd be here until next week."

"Ah."

"Speaking of, is Lacey your only name? It sounds like a nickname."

"It is."

"A nickname. And?"

"My Christian name is on a need-to-know basis only."

"That bad, huh?"

She threw a handful of sand at him.

"Do you have a middle name you can divulge?"

"That's even worse."

He sighed. "All right, is there another game we can play while we wait?"

They looked at each other and then around the area. Lacey remarked, "Do people come here often?"

Armand shook his head. "I've never even been to this cove. That's probably why Inigo uses it—I imagine it's his private duchy."

"*Hmm.*"

"*Hmm* indeed. Come here."

Lacey's T-shirt joined her shorts on the sand and was followed soon thereafter by Armand's clothes.

A while later she laid her head on Armand's chest and breathed in his scent—a mix of brine and pheromones. "I wish we could stay here forever," she whispered.

"Better dress," he whispered back. "We won't be alone for long."

The din of someone crashing through the underbrush broke the spell. Armand stood up quickly, leaving Lacey to scramble up on her own. A large man, barrel-chested and clad in a uniform bristling with medals, skidded to a halt in front of the couple. "Your Highness," came out on puffs of air.

Armand bent his head. "Koldo."

"Inigo…my son…"

"Yes. He's a good boy, Koldo. He will be a man like his father—trustworthy, honest, brave."

Lacey guessed this was some kind of code, for the older man nodded. "I am at your command. Where do you want to go?"

"To the first secretary. Not a word to anyone, you understand? Did you come alone?"

"Yes. My son understood that your presence is to be kept secret."

"Take us then. Edrigu's in Castle Aresti?"

"At present. Prince Jakome has summoned him this evening. The word is the prince intends to announce more regulations, this time on the fishermen." Koldo did not look happy. "The situation worsens by the day."

Armand slammed a fist into his palm. "The sooner Edrigu and I take counsel, the better then."

Koldo bowed to Lacey. "Ma'am?"

Armand started. "My apologies. Lacey, may I present Koldo Maarten Rackham Mather, Sergeant-at-Arms to First Secretary Edrigu Boudewijn Cacicana Proctor. Koldo, this is Ms. Lacey Delahaye. She rescued me from the pirate Belasco."

"Belasco! We thought we'd run him off for good."
He inspected Armand with a critical eye. "It appears
you have a story to tell."

"I do, and the sooner I tell it to Edrigu the better."

Koldo saluted and led the way out of the clearing.
They climbed the mountain, the older man chopping
through vines and ferns with a huge saber. At last they
came out on a path wide enough for two to walk
abreast. "Keep close behind me," ordered Koldo.

Around a bend, he struck off into some thick
bushes. Just as Lacey opened her mouth to ask if they
could rest a bit, they came to a small wooden door set
in an ancient stone wall. Intertwined jasmine and
passionflower climbed up and over it. Koldo produced
a skeleton key.

The door opened with a creak. The old man went
first, followed by Lacey and then Armand. They
climbed a narrow spiral of stairs, the dark breached
every few feet by small slits in the wall. Lacey kept her
head down, knowing if she looked up or at the walls her
claustrophobia would kick in and she'd be reduced to a
gibbering idiot. At last they came to a wider portal that
opened on the flat roof of a tower. She rushed to the
parapet, drawing in lungful after lungful of fresh, free
air. When the terror had subsided, she unclenched her
eyes. Spread out before her was the classic layout of a
medieval castle. She stood on the southeast tower.
Towers also buttressed the northeast, northwest, and
southwest corners. In the northern wall crouched the
castle keep, a solid masonry inner fortress. Below her,
green courtyards made up the baileys, areas that in
Europe had been used to quarter livestock, forges, and
workshops. Here instead she spied a tennis court, a

horseshoe pit, and a swing set.

Outside the castle walls, the mountain sloped down to a wide band of white beach. The sea spread out in concentric circles, the color progressing from light aqua to ultramarine. Above her, the sun in a cloudless sky watched over paradise, spreading contentment.

Armand came to her and touched her shoulder. "You'll be all right here if you want to stay while I go and talk to Edrigu."

"I'd rather come with you."

He seemed to weigh the pros and cons of this, and finally said, "All right." He turned to Koldo. "Take us to him."

Five minutes later, the little band arrived at the castle keep. Armand crossed a large hall and knocked on a metal-studded wooden door. A deep voice called, "Enter."

Lacey walked into an incongruously homey, comfortable room. A blue velvet sofa with lace doilies on the arms held up one wall. Two straight chairs gathered around a chessboard. In one corner, she spied a card table with a half-finished jigsaw puzzle on it. An old man with flowing white hair, his heavily lined skin darkened with age and sun, rose slowly from an overstuffed armchair. "Your Highness." He bowed his head.

Armand met him in two steps, and they embraced. The man continued to stand until Armand ordered him to sit. Koldo bent down and whispered in Edrigu's ear. He regarded Lacey with solemn cordiality. "Welcome, Ms. Delahaye. I understand the thanks of a grateful nation for rescuing our prince are in order."

The blush shot up her face and blew red spirals out

the top of Lacey's head. She already knew there was no place to hide in the big room, so she stood there, blinking rapidly, until Armand took pity on her. "Ms. Delahaye is...overcome by your kindness but is much too modest to take credit for my liberation." Out of the corner of her eye, she noted his mouth twitching and swore under her breath. Revenge would be swift and hopefully chafing.

Edrigu either chose to ignore the silent interchange or missed it entirely. He harrumphed. "Armand, tell me what happened to you. We've had no word since you left in the *Celeste*."

A servant knocked and came in with a tray. Armand poured a glass of iced tea for Lacey and one for himself. "It started when the *Celeste* sank off the Caymans."

As the afternoon sun slanted at a greater and greater angle, Armand told his story. Edrigu's aristocratic face suffused with indignation and worry. "This disgraceful treatment of you shall not go unpunished. I have not heard anything of this Ulisses Traficant. Presumably, Jakome will throw him out on his ear, but who knows? If they pay the ransom for you, they will not tell me."

"Has Jakome excluded you from his deliberations?"

"Not entirely, but this advisor of his, this Damiano, has his ear—and his brain, I fear. He will not listen to my counsel. Your father has withdrawn completely. Jakome only summons me when he has new laws he wants me to execute. He grows more arrogant by the day."

"And the people?"

"He seduces them with free handouts—things like medications and subsidized rent. Do you know he ordered Maxim's—the little electronics store—to give a telephone to any customer who claimed he couldn't afford one? When the policy forced Max out of business, Jakome pulled money from the roads fund and gave it to him. He did the same for the fishermen who lost their livelihoods when he announced that their engine fuel was polluting the waters and cut the fleet by half. With all that help flowing from the palace, people have been lulled into thinking his policies aren't costing the economy. If anyone asks where the money is coming from to pay for all his largesse, he shrugs and starts to talk about how we should be building more roads."

"A little difficult to do if the roads fund is depleted to save Maxim's."

"Indeed."

Lacey put in, "I don't understand. Where is he getting the money then?"

Edrigu put his head in his hands. "I don't know. It may be running out though. He's started to make noises about nationalizing the dysprosium operation."

Armand gaped at him. "You're kidding."

Lacey started to ask but then remembered what Ulisses had told her about the dysprosium. *A rare earth element he said. Very valuable. And Paraiso has a large supply of it. Didn't he say some company owns all the rights to it? Campbell, that's it.*

Edrigu, his eyes worried, said, "I wish I were kidding. Jakome claims they've been hiding revenues overseas and that the royalty payments are unfairly low. He is demanding Campbell Metals double them."

"Have they responded?"

"Not yet." Edrigu stood and began to pace. "We have had a very good relationship with them—it has kept us going for the last sixty-five years. Many of our citizens are employed by Campbell. If they pull out, we're doomed. I tell you, Armand, we must stop Jakome."

"We've been through this before. Unless we can get Father on our side, Jakome can declare us traitors if we do anything to hinder his activities. We have to find a way to block him without it being too obvious."

Koldo entered. "Sir, it's time to leave. Prince Jakome is expecting you."

The first secretary turned to Armand. "I've had a suite prepared for you, and food brought in. It would be best if you remain in the castle. Perhaps I can learn more about this man Traficant at the meeting." He left, and a servant led Lacey and Armand through a maze of corridors to the northwest tower. They entered a spacious living room. Two bedrooms and a small kitchenette opened off the main area. Pictures of early sailing ships adorned the walls.

A balcony lay beyond sliding glass doors, beckoning Lacey into the twilight. No lights pierced the forested slope below her. She called to Armand. "Doesn't anyone live on this part of the island?"

"Not many. The capital city is midway down the east coast, as are most of the villages. Much of the northern region is included in the UNESCO Seaflower Biosphere. We don't have to worry about being observed."

Lacey watched the sun dip down below the horizon as the sea darkened from teal to navy, before going back inside. Another servant entered with a large tray piled high with food. Armand indicated a small table, and he set the tray down on it. "Thank you, Richard."

Lacey sat down. "I'm starving!" She tasted everything—from the jerk chicken to the goat stew to the omelet-like codfish and ackee. She marveled at the variety of the fruits. "What's this one? The one that looks like a pine cone?"

"It's an atemoya."

She took a tentative bite, then a much larger one. "Yummy. It tastes like candy."

"It's been described as a cross between wintergreen, vanilla, and pineapple."

"Very close, yes. But not overly sweet." She pointed to a bright yellow oval fruit. "And this one?"

"We call it eggfruit here, for obvious reasons." He handed her a slice.

"Mmm. It's creamy—like ice cream or custard." She chewed thoughtfully. "I don't think it's suitable for jelly though."

Armand laughed. "Not everything is suitable for jelly making, my dear."

She was too hungry to argue. "More, please."

He watched her, his eyes alight with pleasure. "Yes, Paraiso is truly a paradise, isn't it? We even make our own rum." He sighed. "Too bad it may all cease to exist."

Lacey had never dealt with a royal before and wasn't sure whether bouncy optimism or sober agreement was in order. She opted for supportive encouragement. "If anyone can fix it, Armand, you can. I have faith in you." She donated a brave smile to the cause.

He patted her hand. "It's about time I confessed something to you, Lacey. Not to put too fine a point on it, I am the…er…black sheep of the family—the ne'er-do-well as it were. My father has little patience with me now because I gave him so much trouble in my youth. We almost went to war with Saint Andrews over a prank I pulled when I was sixteen. It made me none too popular with the citizens."

"What did you do?"

"Let me back up a little." He picked up a handful of red berries that resembled tiny pincushions. At her look of inquiry, he said, "Surinam cherries." Between bites, he explained. "Our archipelago consists of three main islands—Paraiso, Santa Isabella, and Saint Andrews. Spanish conquistadors conquered Saint Andrews in 1502, long before the English contingent fetched up on Paraiso. As with most Spanish expeditions, a complement of Dominican priests tagged along to convert the natives. When the explorers moved on, they left Fra Diavolo and Fra Bartholomé behind, along with Bibles, rosaries, and a ten-foot-tall wooden statue of Jesus. The locals were most hospitable and listened politely to the two friars while they waited for the cauldron to boil."

Lacey giggled. "Oh dear."

"Precisely. Anyway, in honor of a memorable meal, the villagers erected the statue on their highest peak. In later years Dutch, Spanish, and English settled the island, and Christianity took hold. The statue remained on the mountain for five hundred years—a landmark and symbol of Saint Andrews. That is, until a juvenile delinquent by the name of Armand stole it."

"Ah. And the people of Saint Andrews were not

amused."

"Nor was the Grand Duke Xavier of Paraiso. Said Armand had to return and reinstall Jesus, and only by promising to pack me off to Eton did Paraiso avoid hefty reparations. Suffice it to say, my departure went unheralded."

Lacey kissed him. "At least you cleaned up good."

Armand grimaced. "Unfortunately, due to my adolescent high jinks, the population does not hold me in high regard, which has hindered our ability to thwart Jakome's plans. Edrigu trusts me, but he's about the only one."

The door opened, and the same servant ushered in the first secretary. "I see you two have settled in. I hope the accommodations are to your satisfaction?" He bowed to Lacey. "Sylvia, the housekeeper, made sure there were…er…feminine items for your convenience."

"Thank you," returned Lacey gravely.

"Yes, Edrigu, thank you. You chose our rooms well. Now, what happened with Jakome?"

Richard took the tray away, and Edrigu sat down next to the desk. "He wants to board all the island children in one school away from their parents, where they will be taught using a curriculum Damiano has devised. I saw the summary. Armand, it rewrites our history to exclude all references to our Christian roots. It mentions neither the dysprosium nor our native industries, and attributes our prosperity solely to the grand duke's generosity."

"What? Does he think anyone will buy that?"

"Who knows?"

Lacey was confused. "Why wouldn't they believe that?"

Edrigu scowled. "If you think the duke is independently wealthy, he is not. The family receives a small stipend to cover ceremonial expenses, but like everyone else on Paraiso, the Montegues have always worked. Xavier's grandfather fished, and his father ran a pawn shop."

"A pawn shop?" *It's a wonder their pilgrim ancestors haven't risen from their graves to smite the apostates.* "What is Xavier's profession?"

"He's an accountant."

An accountant? Really? With some effort, Lacey kept mum.

Armand put in, "So, in answer to your question, our island's prosperity is due entirely to the people's industry and the royalties from Campbell. Every public project Jakome comes up with must be paid for with taxpayer money. And since there are only a few thousand people on this island, the income tax can't possibly cover all he proposes to do."

"That's why he's doubled the sales tax and increased the processing fees for international companies to bank here."

Armand went to the window. His back to them, he asked, "Did Jakome ask you for your opinion?"

"He no longer does that. Armand, he's like a crazed beast—crazed for power. He doesn't care what damage it will cause. He doesn't care that he's destroying our culture, our way of life, our freedoms."

Armand spun around and strode to the door. "I must talk to him."

"Wait!"

He turned his head. "What is it?"

"I haven't told you the other news. Damiano came

in with your abductor, Ulisses Traficant. He did not mention any ransom demand, so I presume Damiano had summarily refused, but he did announce that you are here."

"Here? That I'm on the island? Or did he say I am here in your castle?"

Edrigu looked thoughtful. "I believe he only said 'here.' "

Armand steepled his fingers. "That might mean Traficant doesn't know we've escaped yet. He may be expecting to go back to the boat and bring us in, hoping for a reward, if not the ransom. That gives us some time."

"Don't forget Jakome will be looking for you too. And when he finds you, he intends to arrest you."

"For what?"

"I don't think he knows yet—they'll likely trump up some charge. You're still not very popular here, Armand. I doubt it would cause much stir."

"Well, I can hardly stay here indefinitely. And if Jakome finds me here, he'll arrest you as well. Ideas?"

In response, the old retainer suppressed a yawn. "Jakome is holding a banquet tonight, honoring Saint Andrews' finance minister, so he can do nothing until tomorrow. I think a good night's sleep is in order. We will talk after breakfast."

When he had left, Lacey wandered about the suite, checking out the books and ornaments. An antique map of the Caribbean showed the three islands of the archipelago, nestled in the elbow of the Central American isthmus. Paraiso was labeled "The Promised Land" and a three-masted, square-rigged sailing ship was anchored offshore. It reminded her of the picture of the Mayflower she'd seen in school. Behind a door, she discovered a well-appointed bathroom with a large square tub. Over her shoulder she called, "I'm going to take a bath."

She turned on the taps and poured a few drops of rose water from a small flagon into the tub. Slipping off her shorts and shirt, she sank blissfully into the water. Armand came to the door. "You look happy."

"At this point it's the little things."

"Yes. I have a feeling tomorrow will not bring good news. I wish you weren't here, Lacey."

"Well, thanks a lot." She batted her eyelashes at him.

"You know what I mean. This is a very precarious situation." He sat on the edge of the bath. "I never should have let you help me."

"You didn't have much choice, Armand. Besides, I couldn't leave you in the mangrove swamp. It's not done in my family."

He shook his head. "And then I seduced you in the first five minutes of our acquaintance. I am a wicked man."

Lacey thought back to that night—to the smells of sulphur, mud, and sex. She'd felt guilty then, believing it was her fault, that she'd thrown herself at him. Not the other way around. She looked up into Armand's face. Black stubble covered his chin. His unruly hair, a little long now, matched his glistening black eyes. *Might as well let him wallow in his ignorance.* She reached an arm around his neck and drew him toward her. Just as their lips touched, his eyes went wide, and he fell on top of her.

Bathwater spilled out, leaving Lacey half exposed

and shivering. "Ack! What are you doing?"

He struggled out of the tub, his clothes dripping. "It's your fault. You pulled at me, and I slipped."

"Well, I never. You leaned in and lost your balance." She turned the tap on again. As the bath refilled, an idea crossed her mind. Her eyes danced. "Now you're wet, you might as well get in. You could use a wash."

He cast her a look from under the thick eyebrows. "Might as well."

She moved over and he squeezed in beside her, then rolled her over on top of him. She felt gloriously sensual and rubbed her body over his, massaging the hard parts. He found the soap and lathering up his hand, inserted two fingers inside her. The scent of rosewater filled the room. She slowly rotated her hips while his fingers kept up their pressure, then pulled away, allowing them to slip out. Locking her eyes on his, Lacey lowered herself onto his cock. The soap lubricated her opening, and he slid in to the hilt. She began to rock, slowly, then faster, as he kept his hands on the tub's sides to steady himself. She concentrated on the thick penis scraping the sides of her vagina, nicking the tip of her clitoris, nudging her orgasm into flower.

"Oh God, Lacey, don't stop." He closed his eyes, and she redoubled her efforts until she came to the tipping point. Shuddering, she collapsed on top of him. They lay in each other's arms, water sloshing and bubbling around them.

Someone knocked on the outer door. They held their breath. A female voice called from the living room, "Your Highness? It's Maitea. Cook told me you

114

had returned. I've brought champagne." The two in the other room heard the clunk of a tray being set down, then the voice came again. "You must be bathing. Shall I come in and dry you off?"

As Lacey gurgled, Armand—his embarrassment palpable—bellowed, "No! I mean, no, that won't be necessary, Maitea. If you don't mind, I'm very tired. I shall see you tomorrow. Thank you, Maitea. Good night, Maitea."

There was a heavy silence, then the outer door slammed. Lacey jumped out of the water and drew a terry bathrobe around her naked body. "Maitea?"

"Er."

"I gather you have more than one confession to make."

"Er."

"Armand, are you married?"

"No, of course not. Maitea is my second cousin. We grew up together. She's seen me naked before—it's no big deal."

"And did you always share champagne?"

Armand pulled the drain plug and stood up. As he toweled off under Lacey's open glare, his face went from white to crimson. "Look, you have to find out some time. Paraisan custom dictates that my father's father's sister's daughter's daughter and I must wed. We would have been engaged by now, but I haven't been here long enough to arrange for the betrothal ceremony. So I'm not. Engaged. To Maitea. And besides"—he hurried on to drown Lacey out—"I'm not in love with her. I'm in love with someone else."

"What? Who?"

"A beautiful woman. You'd like her."

The sinking feeling that had started when he spoke of love now threatened to drag her body down to the floor. She wrapped her arms around her stomach to stop the rocking. She managed a weak, "Really?"

"Yes." He moved toward her and touched the tip of Lacey's nose, his expression soft. "She has long, russet hair and ocean-blue eyes. She makes delicious jelly. And she graciously shelters gentlemen who drop from trees."

Lacey didn't wait for him to kiss her. When they broke apart, he panted, "And with any luck and the mercy of the gods, she loves me too."

Chapter Seven

Then up spoke the cabin boy of our gallant ship,
And a brave young lad was he.
"Oh, I have me a girl in Plymouth by the sea,
And tonight she'll a'weep for me."
~*~
Oh, the ocean waves do roll, they roll
And the stormy winds do blow.
But we poor sailors go skippin' to the top,
While the landlubbers lie down below, below, below,
While the landlubbers lie down below.
~*"The Mermaid," a traditional sailing song*
****

Edrigu knocked just as they finished breakfast. Armand ushered him in. "Any news?"

"Not yet. Evidently the American Traficant stayed for the banquet. He returned to his boat this morning, so he will soon discover your absence. We'll see how he reacts."

"No one knows we're in Castle Aresti?"

"Only the servants. And Maitea." He peered at Armand. "She has been staying with me while her house on Saint Andrews is painted and overheard the servants talking about you. I believe she meant to come to your room last night." He seemed to be waiting for an answer.

Finally, Armand said, "She dropped by, but I

117

was…was indisposed. Edrigu, will she keep silent about me?"

"I'm not sure. Armand, you must talk to her." He glanced at Lacey. "You owe her that much."

Lacey shifted in her seat. Armand said, "I will. I'm sure she'll understand that we don't have to abide by ancient traditions anymore."

Edrigu, his face somber, said, "She may, but your father may not. He has so little power left, he clings to the old ways."

Armand put his fork down. "Well, there are more important things on our plate right now. My marriage is a low priority. First we must find a way to defuse Jakome's ambitions. Have you heard from Campbell?"

"We have a meeting with Gerald Pandanus this afternoon."

"The CEO? Good. Report to me when you return."

"Of course. What is your plan?"

"I don't know. I must gain admittance to Father before Jakome does anything rash."

The old man clucked his tongue. "I fear it's too late for that, Armand."

"I can't help that, Edrigu. You said Jakome wants to arrest me. How can I get into Castle Zeruko without being detained?"

"*Hmm.*" Edrigu tapped his chin. "Perhaps a very public homecoming? Jakome could hardly take you into custody in front of the whole citizenry. After all, he has no grounds. You did nothing other than disagree over policy."

Armand brightened. "A splashy arrival? Brilliant! I make a grand entrance to Port Huntington—the prodigal son returns home. Flag waving and fireworks—then I retire with Jakome to Zeruko for consultations. He can hardly turn his own brother away."

"And Traficant can hardly demand a reward for delivering you if you're already here." Edrigu rose. "Perhaps we should continue in my office."

Armand nodded and the two men left, Armand promising to return for lunch. Lacey let him go. She didn't mind a little down time anyway. Her mind in a whirl, she wanted a chance to savor the long hours spent talking, snuggling, and making love the night before. Armand imbued her with happiness, like that moment when the sun breaks out from behind a cloud and illuminates the world, or when a mother sees her baby's face for the first time. Joy flooded her and, when it filled her to the brim, shot out in all directions. She couldn't stay still. *I'll just take a walk on the walls— maybe that will take the edge off.*

As the balmy breeze fluffed her hair, she gazed out over the northern reaches. She knew from the map that over four hundred miles lay between her and the Cayman Islands directly north. Paraiso and its sister islands were virtually alone in the big bend formed by Nicaragua, Costa Rica, and Panama. *No wonder it's remained a backwater, beneath the world's notice.* It might be uninhabited now if it weren't for the assorted human detritus who washed up on its shores—the slaves, the traders, the seekers after religious freedom, the pirates. *Come to think of it, Todoacabado—washed up—isn't such a bad name for the place after all.*

She continued to walk past the southwest tower to the southern battlements. The sun, rising toward its peak, beat down on her. She leaned on her elbows and gazed along the mountain ridge. In one spot, the underbrush shook as though something large were slashing through it. A wild animal? Maybe goats? Or Inigo? She missed the child. *I never properly thanked him for his help.* She traced the path of the intruder, who seemed to be skipping from tree to tree as though hiding from sight. *Has to be a person—a goat wouldn't hide.* She waited. There. The top of a head came into view, yellow hair bobbing just above the tall sunflowers. *It can't be Inigo then.* The figure hit an open clearing and sprinted across it, but not before Lacey recognized him. "Crispin!" *How the hell did he get here?*

She watched as her son approached the castle. Another figure stepped out from under a trellis heavy with trailing glorybower and went to greet him. A female, dressed in a long, flowing, white shift. The scarf wound around her head covered her hair, and, since she faced Crispin, Lacey couldn't make out her features. She took the young man's hand and led him to the secret door Lacey and Armand had gone through the day before.

I'd better get back to my room. She walked quickly around the walls and downstairs to the empty suite. Five minutes went by. Lacey strummed her fingers on the desk. *What if he doesn't come here?* She resolved to wait ten more minutes, then make her way downstairs. Nine minutes later, she heard a tap on the door, and Crispin came in. He was alone. Lacey threw her arms around him.

"Hello, Mother."

His shy grin put everything right. After the preliminary hugs and kisses and routine questions,

Lacey sat on the couch holding her son's hand. "Crispin, how on earth did you find me?"

"It wasn't easy." His brown eyes glowed. "When I heard that hurricane warnings had been issued for Sarasota and Tampa Bay, I tried to get in touch with you. Longboat Key Fire and Rescue didn't answer the phone, so I called Sarasota police. They told me Longboat had been evacuated and that the bridges were out. I checked the hotels and shelters within a twenty-mile radius, and no one had any record of a Lacey Delahaye, so I decided to come down."

My boy really turned out remarkably well, didn't he? "How did you get on the island?"

"By the time I arrived, they'd repaired the Anna Maria bridge, and almost everyone had returned to their homes. They were still working on New Pass bridge, so I rented a car at the airport and drove up to Cortez, crossed the bridge and down Longboat to Buccaneer Drive."

"And found the house abandoned. You must have been so worried."

"Especially when I saw the mess. I couldn't tell if the hurricane were responsible or if someone had attacked you. Then I found the note."

"Note?"

"Yes. It had fallen under the sofa—"

Lacey put a hand to her mouth. "Oh my gosh, I'd forgotten all about it! While Tubal and Marko concentrated on Armand, I managed to jot down a few words. Then Belasco grabbed me and I dropped it."

"Tubal? Marko? Belasco?"

Lost in the memory of that awful night, Lacey julienned her words. "Belasco. Marko. Tubal. Pirates."

"Huh?"

Get a grip, Lacey. "Sorry, hon. They're smugglers who held Armand captive. He managed to escape, but they tracked him down to my house and took both of us prisoner."

"Whoa, hold on, you're only confusing me more." Crispin got up and went to the desk. Sitting on the edge, he held a hand up. "Start at the beginning please."

"Okay." Lacey described her adventures since the day she returned to find Longboat Key evacuated and Armand in the mangroves, leaving out the more lurid elements for obvious reasons.

"Who'da thunk it? In the note, I could only make out 'pirates,' 'shipwreck,' and 'Armand.' The rest was smudged."

Pride swelled. "And that was enough for my extraordinary son to figure it all out."

"Yeah, yeah." Crispin rolled his eyes. "Actually, the Internet helped a lot. I Googled the name Armand for news items and found something in the Jamaica Observer about a Prince Armand who was presumed lost at sea while sailing alone in his sloop. Natives on Little Cayman Island found the wreckage of the *Celeste*, but no sign of its master. The article noted that Armand was the son of the grand duke of an island called Paraiso in the western Caribbean. Other articles mentioned a resurgence of piracy based in Paraiso. I couldn't find anything else that included all three words from your note, so I took a chance and booked a flight. I figured it didn't matter whether you'd gone willingly or unwillingly—you wouldn't have left Florida without telling me. So I took a plane to Saint Andrews, and then hopped a ferry to Paraiso."

Lacey opened the door to a servant, who placed a large basket of fruit on the table and silently withdrew. "All well and good, but how on earth did you find me here in the castle? No one is supposed to know we're hiding here."

"Ah, that required another stroke of luck—although this place seems small enough that no secret could last very long." He plucked a banana from the basket and peeled it. "Do you mind? I'm starving."

This statement did not come as a surprise to his mother.

He swallowed a large bite and resumed. "I had no idea what to look for or who to ask, so I registered at the only hotel in Port Huntington and wandered around the market square. Funny—the place is a modern version of the Garden of Eden, but most of the people I passed seemed rather despondent. Any idea why?"

Lacey picked up a bright yellow carambola and cut a piece from the middle, popping the star-shaped slice in her mouth. "It's a long story. Let's finish yours first."

"Okay. I stopped at a cafe for a cup of…coffee." His eyes sidled away from her, leading Lacey to guess he'd accepted a jigger of rum as well. *Hey, he's twenty-two—not much point in scolding him.*

"I met a woman there." He blushed, a rosy glow tinting the pale skin he'd inherited from Lacey. "A very pretty woman. When I told her I was looking for my mother, she said she knew of you and that you were hiding here in Castle Aresti."

Oh no. If it's common knowledge, we're in deep trouble. "Where had she heard this?"

"She said she's staying at the castle. Her name is Maitea. She's…uh…quite lovely, Mother."

"Oh dear."

"It's not like that," he said hastily. "For one thing, she's way too old for me—I'd guess maybe twenty-four. And remember, I've got Nancy."

Oh, yeah. Nancy. Not one of Crispin's more attractive conquests. Lacey found her bossy and disrespectful in a sly sort of way. "Nancy. Right."

"Nancy said it was okay for me to come down here. She sent her respects." He seemed anxious for Lacey's approval.

"Oh, I'm not worried about you and Nancy." *At least not until you stop appreciating other women.* "I meant it's worrisome that Maitea knows not only that Armand is here but that I am as well. That could make things more complicated."

Crispin gave her a speculative look. "Why is it complicated?"

Lacey assumed Crispin wouldn't be too thrilled to hear about his mother's implication in a love triangle with Armand and Maitea, so she merely remarked, "The fewer people who know about us the better. For Armand's sake."

"All right, it can wait." Crispin had apparently decided to let her off the hook, temporarily at least. "At any rate, Maitea was kind enough to give me directions and let me into the castle. More important, she's arranged for a boat to carry us back to Saint Andrews. We can book a flight home from there."

"Home!"

Crispin stared at her. "You don't sound too happy about it."

"Oh, er, yes, I am. Very." She looked around vaguely. "I guess I'd better pack."

Her son gave her a quizzical look. "You have things to pack? Normally when a person's kidnapped, you leave with just the clothes on your back. Did the pirates let you take your makeup kit with you?"

"Don't be snide, Crispin. I...I do have a few things to gather. You run along down to the kitchen and see if they can rustle up some food."

"I really don't think—"

Someone knocked. Crispin stepped into the bedroom while Lacey went to the door. Inigo stood there. He saluted. "I'm here to save you again, Missus Delahaye."

Save me? Jeez. Saviors are coming out of the woodwork like...like cockroaches? No, that's not right. "Thank you, Inigo."

He marched in. "You can come out now, Mr. Delahaye." Crispin emerged. "I am Inigo Carolus Azarola Mather, and I have come to lead you to the boat. Lady Maitea's orders."

Lacey saw herself losing control of the situation and made a last attempt to reclaim seniority. "Great. Good. Now you two go get some food. I'll be ready to leave when you return."

She hustled them out. Once they were gone, she went into the bedroom and flopped on the bed. Staring at the ceiling, she reviewed her reaction to her imminent deliverance. Crispin had been surprised at her lack of enthusiasm. *Well, why wouldn't he be? Unless I'm suffering from that Stockholm syndrome where I fall in love with my captors, I should be leaping at the chance to get away.* Could it be frustration at unfinished business? *Maybe. How can I go without knowing whether Armand is able to stop Jakome's runaway train—or whether the grand duke will listen to reason?* What would Traficant do? Would he wander off looking for other deals or stay here making Armand's life miserable?

Frustration—yeah, that's it. *No, it isn't. I don't want to leave Armand. There, I said it.* She wondered whether Paraisan law allowed a commoner to marry a prince. The memory of a lilting soprano calling to Armand from the living room and the popping of a champagne cork reared its ugly head. Maitea. If Edrigu were right, and Xavier insisted, Armand would have to marry Maitea. *So I have no chance with him anyway.*

A hawk landed on the windowsill, shook its feathers, and cocked its head at her. *Interesting— Maitea running into Crispin like that. Fortuitous?* He'd told Maitea about Lacey, and she'd instantly guessed it was the mysterious woman staying in Aresti Castle. She must have seen her chance to be rid of her rival. Lacey's eyes narrowed. Crispin said Maitea was lovely. Was she also a jealous fiend? Or—here the pressure on Lacey's heart forced her knees into her stomach—could she be in love with Armand? She sat up. Her arms encircled her calves, and she rocked. *Armand said they grew up together—that she had seen him naked.* The image of his powerful torso, his slim waist, his extremely manly parts, rose before her. The painful truth slammed into her already aching heart. How could Maitea *not* be in love with him?

Be that as it may, if the girl had used Crispin to help her fulfill her romantic dreams, she had every right to do so. She could have gone further—she could have turned Lacey in to the police. *Bringing Crispin to me was a generous and possibly hazardous act on her part.*

126

She sighed.

Footsteps stopped at her door. "Lacey?"

"Yes, Armand. I'm coming out." Wiping a tear away, she got up and went into the living room.

Edrigu spoke. "We have news."

"Oh?" *So do I, unfortunately.*

"The CEO of Campbell Metals, Gerald Pandanus, has delivered an ultimatum to Jakome. Either he desist from threatening to seize their assets, or they will close down the mining operations entirely. He says the company has already transferred its bank accounts to Colombia."

Edrigu spoke. "If he follows through, it will put half of our population out of work, and we'll lose the royalties we depend upon."

Lacey tried to refocus on this new crisis. "Can't the government simply run the operation? Then Jakome could rake in all the profits for himself?"

"That, we fear, is his plan."

Armand strode to the window, whipped around, and strode back. "It won't work, though. Campbell imported all the engineers and many of the supervisors. They'll leave if the plant closes. Plus Campbell's equipment is patented—"

"Which means they can haul us to court if we confiscate it. It would be impossible to run the mine without the technicians, and who knows how much infrastructure they'll remove?"

The two men remained standing in the middle of the room facing each other, oblivious to the woman sitting on the couch. Armand said slowly, "That might work in our favor. Jakome is hardly going to shut down our main source of revenue, is he?"

Edrigu blew out his cheeks. "He will, if Damiano tells him to. That man is evil."

Lacey interrupted. "Who is this Damiano?"

Armand broke his gaze from Edrigu and turned to her. "When Jakome came home from Princeton, Damiano accompanied him. He claims to be a lecturer in political science there, although he isn't listed in the university directory. He may be simply a charlatan, but he's an exceedingly artful talker. Jakome hangs on his every word. He has the prince wrapped around his little finger."

"How can you stop him?"

Edrigu pursed his lips. "That's where Armand and I differ. I think we must use force. The prince feels differently."

Armand took the floor. "If I can just get Jakome alone—talk to him brother to brother. We were close once. We must find a way to keep Damiano away from him long enough for me to reach him. I'm sure I'll be able to open his eyes to the misery he's causing with his policies." He gave the first secretary a sidelong glance. "Edrigu has agreed to try my plan before we do anything more incendiary."

The old man hesitated, then nodded. "We may have an opportunity at the Settlement Day festivities that begin tomorrow. Armand plans to make a grand entrance into the capital. Jakome will be forced to greet him formally."

Armand took Lacey's hand and gazed earnestly into her eyes. "Lacey, I'm going to have to escort Maitea. It will be expected, and will show the people that I am back for good and serious about solving our problems."

Edrigu added, "Maitea's presence will also make it harder for Jakome to show disrespect to his brother."

Armand continued his silent entreaty. Lacey took a minute to gather her strength, then in a strangled whisper, muttered, "That makes sense."

"You can stay here, and I'll be back as soon as I can."

Lacey made a decision. "No, Armand. I won't be here."

"But—"

At that moment Crispin and Inigo appeared in the doorway. Crispin gazed from Armand to Edrigu to Lacey. "Mother? Are you ready?"

Armand turned astonished eyes on the young man. " 'Mother?' " He spoke over his shoulder. "This is your son?"

Lacey moved to stand next to Crispin. "Yes."

"And may I inquire how he came to be in Paraiso?" Armand's face alternated between bafflement and anger.

"Remember the note I left in the house when the pirates attacked? Crispin found it and followed the clues to Paraiso. Maitea guided him to the castle and has arranged for a boat to take us to Saint Andrews. I'm going home, Armand."

Armand continued to stare at Crispin. "Maitea?"

His furious tone frightened Lacey. "She wanted to help, Armand. She met Crispin in the market, and he asked about me. She thinks she's doing a good deed. She doesn't…know."

Edrigu interrupted, his face bland. "This is good news. Ms. Delahaye will be safe and sound in her own country, and we can hold the engagement ceremony right away. It will be one more indication that you are assuming your rightful role in the duchy."

Armand said nothing but raised a hand, his intention clear. All except Lacey filed out, Edrigu tossing a look full of meaning at Lacey.

The two of them stood a few feet and miles apart. Finally, Armand whispered, "Lacey, I can't lose you."

So this is how it feels to die inside. Lacey took a deep breath and let it out slowly. "Edrigu is right. You must marry Maitea and do what's expected of you. If you want to save Paraiso, you have no choice."

"Lacey, I…"

She could clearly see the battle raging in his ebony eyes. Flashes of swordplay, lofty words warring with desperately passionate ones, duty and honor brought to bear. She couldn't stand to watch it, couldn't stand the pain. *I have to go.*

"I have to go home, Armand. I want to go home." She bit her lip so hard blood welled up.

He blinked, spun on his heel, and strode out the door. Two words left his mouth and floated back. "Then go."

Lacey collapsed on the sofa. If only the tears would come—they would lighten the unbearable weight on her chest. Finally, she rose and went to the door. Crispin stood out in the hall. He took a step toward her. "Are you all right, Mother?"

"Yes, Crispin. I…I'll be all right."

He touched her hand, his eyes concerned, then led her down the winding stairs. Inigo waited for them at the bottom. They took the path back to the tiny beach where they had first landed. Lacey stopped and closed her eyes, reliving their lovemaking on the sand, memorizing it for the long, lonely nights she knew lay ahead. She held her lips tightly closed and stepped into the dinghy with Crispin. Inigo pushed it out into the water and jumped into his canoe.

A small fishing boat lay anchored just beyond the reef. Inigo waved at a man standing in the stern. When they reached the aptly named *Breaker Heart*, he tied the dinghy to the vessel, threw a rope ladder over the side, and Lacey and Crispin climbed aboard. Lacey leaned over the gunwale and shook Inigo's hand, then impulsively kissed his cheek. "Be a good boy. I'll always remember you."

Inigo's brown skin reddened. He pushed away from the boat and sat in his canoe watching them as they came about and headed out to sea. The man introduced himself. "Captain Barca at your service. I'm to take you to the marina next to the airport. From Saint Andrews, you can catch a plane to anywhere in the world." He rapped his chest proudly.

Lacey stared straight ahead. She didn't have the courage to look back. When they were beyond the lagoon and in open sea, she asked Crispin, "Did you see anyone up at the castle? Anyone waving...goodbye?"

Crispin's face held a mine of sympathy. "No, Mother. I saw no one there."

Chapter Eight

The kei or caffir apple is a drought-hardy and salt-tolerant shrub, used in cooking and as a thorny hedge. Because of its high acidity and pectin content, the plum-sized, bright yellow fruit makes excellent jelly. Harvest August to September.

Kei Apple Jelly

2 lbs. kei apples
2 lbs. sugar
1/2 cup water

Cut fruit in large chunks and place in a pan with water to cover. Bring slowly to a boil, stirring occasionally. Reduce heat to medium and simmer ten to fifteen minutes. Strain pulp. If necessary, add water to make about four cups of juice and return juice to pan. Simmer about ten minutes, skimming any foam off. Stir in sugar and cook until dissolved, about ten minutes. To check whether it has jelled sufficiently, dip a teaspoon into the jam and let it cool. If it sets, bring the juice back to a rolling boil. Continue with standard procedure described in Chapter One.

****

"Watch those thorns, Crispin!"

"What did you—ouch!" Crispin sucked his thumb.

"I told you to wear gloves, dear." Lacey reached into the center of the dark green shrub and plucked several small, bright yellow fruits from the branches, dropping them into the basket slung around her neck. "That's why Harry uses it as a barrier hedge. Keeps raccoons and foragers away from the kei apples."

"That is, all the foragers except my intrepid mother." Crispin took one from the basket and popped it into his mouth. Instantly his mouth puckered, and he spit it out. "Pah! It sucked all the moisture out of my mouth. Why are we picking them if they're inedible?"

"Because they make wonderful jelly. Duh."

"More jelly? At last count, you had ten varieties of jelly or jam in the pantry and the garage is full. When are you going to start selling them?"

"Soon." Lacey didn't want to tell her son that she wasn't ready to face people yet. For the last six weeks, she'd immersed herself in the study of the native plants that grew in the coastal areas and hammocks of north-central Florida. She'd spend hours perfecting jam recipes for parsley haw, passion fruit, Barbados cherry, and Simpson's stopper, but whenever a neighbor asked her over for dinner, she would turn down the invitation. Crispin must have sensed her misery, for he left his job in Illinois and found work at the local community college teaching sustainable agriculture. Together, they explored the many beautiful state preserves of Florida, gathering fruits and berries for her recipes. Lacey refrained from asking about the situation with Nancy, and Crispin didn't volunteer much except that they were "taking a break." The news prompted a slight uptick in her mood.

"It's past time to transition into the business end of this endeavor, you know. The season's almost here."

"Okay, okay!" She plucked another apple from the bush. "I'll have to find some commercial space first."

"That's why I brought home that real estate guide." He pulled out a water bottle and took a long swig. "Gawd, September's just as hot as August was. When does it cool off around here?"

Lacey wiped the back of her neck. "Not until October or November. Then we'll have a couple of glorious months before winter arrives."

"Winter! I thought everybody came south to Florida for the warmth. It doesn't get cold, does it?"

"Oh, it can get down to the fifties—even the thirties at night. That's why I told you to bring a jacket."

Crispin laughed. "To a snowbird that's warm, Ma." He squinted at the sky. "It'll be dark soon. Come on, we'd better get back."

They walked along the hedge until they came to a dirt road where they had left their bicycles. As they rode out to Gulf of Mexico Drive and took the bike path south, Crispin whistled a few bars of a sprightly melody.

"What's that tune, Crispin?"

"What? Oh, it's the Paraiso national anthem. Inigo taught it to me. Catchy, isn't it?"

Lacey didn't respond, mainly because the need to cry overwhelmed her vocal chords. She breathed deeply, willing the pain away. Her grief had to subside someday—she would eventually forget Armand, forget the eyes and the face, forget the hard body that could bring her to such heights of passion, forget the sonorous baritone that spoke such wondrous words of love. *But do I want to?*

They reached the house just as twilight dropped into the bay. The usual lineup of cormorants sat on the long cement seawall. Out in the mud flats a reddish egret flapped his wings and jumped about in a dazzling display of avian grace. For a grand finale, he stabbed the water, snagging a fish. As he held it up, his shock and triumph obvious even to a human, a herring gull swooped in and ripped the fish from his bill.

Crispin gave a disapproving snort. "Damned gulls."

"The circle of life, my dear, the circle of life." Lacey warbled.

"Yeah, well, with any luck, what goes around comes around."

As if in answer to his plea, a massive phalanx of crows exploded from a live oak and launched an attack on the gull, forcing him to drop his prize into the water. Crispin gave a delighted chuckle.

"Happy now?" Lacey headed into the kitchen.

After dinner, Crispin came into the study. "I'm supposed to meet some friends for a drink in St. Armand's. Will you be okay?"

"Sure, honey." Crispin no longer asked her if she'd like to come. When he first arrived, he'd try to get her out of the house, but whenever he suggested the theater or a happy hour, she would cheerfully decline. After a while, he found his own friends and began spending less and less time with his mother. He still kept a watchful eye on her, and she was grateful for his attention.

"I'll see you later then."

Lacey went back to her book on the fruiting trees of Tampa Bay. When her face hit the page a second time, she decided to accept the inevitable and go to bed. As she slipped under the covers, she prayed her usual little prayer. "Please, God, watch over Armand and protect his people." The ritual concluded, she turned out the light.

A crash and a curse woke her. "Crispin? Is that you?"

"Mother, would you please stop leaving buckets everywhere? The alarm system I installed is working fine. You don't need a second line of defense."

"Sorry." She lay back on the pillows. Her son knocked and came in. "Are you decent?"

She switched on the lamp and sat up. "Why?"

He stepped aside to reveal a young woman dressed in a brilliant red sheath. Lacey guessed her to be in her early twenties. With her softly rounded figure and rosebud mouth, she stood in vivid contrast to Crispin's thin frame and blond thatch. Her sable hair fell to her waist, and her eyes sparkled as brilliantly black as Armand's. In fact, she could have passed for his sister. Lacey put a hand to her mouth to stop the cry. Longing filled her. *Oh God, I miss him.*

Crispin was speaking. "May I introduce Maitea Pulawi Abasolo Abbot of Paraiso, Prince Armand's second cousin." He smiled. "I hope I got that right. Maitea? This is my mother, Lacey Delahaye."

The girl stepped forward and gave a little curtsy. Lacey nodded as regally as she could, considering she lay in a rumpled bed wearing a torn flannel nightgown. "Crispin, would you mind taking Maitea to the living room while I make myself presentable?"

"Huh?"

Maitea pushed the young man gently toward the door. "I'm so sorry to inconvenience you, Ms. Delahaye. Crispin said it would be quite all right to come to your bedroom." A coquettish smile crossed her delicate features. "Like most men, he has no clue about women's sensitivities."

They left, and Lacey threw on a shirt and jeans, combed her hair, and trotted out of her room. Crispin had poured Maitea a glass of wine, and they sat on the couch, scrupulously leaving several inches of space between them. He jumped up. "Would you like something, Mother?"

Lacey, glancing at the girl's perfect legs and flawless complexion, straightened her spine and pulled her stomach in. "Bourbon, please. A stiff one."

Crispin went off to the kitchen, and Lacey sat down in her favorite high-backed wing chair. Maitea perched on the edge of her seat, holding the wine glass with two fingers. As the silence lengthened, she began to fidget. "It's so nice to meet you at last, Ms. Delahaye."

"That's right—we missed each other at the castle, didn't we?" Lacey cringed at the memory of a wet, sudsy interlude interrupted by a disembodied voice offering to towel Armand off.

"Yes, it is a pity. However, I've heard so much about you."

Lacey gulped. "From whom?"

"Why, from Edrigu—you know he's actually my great uncle—and of course Inigo. Inigo talks about you constantly. He says you are a very brave lady. I think he has a little crush on you." Maitea's eyes crinkled. She obviously found the notion amusing.

Lacey resisted the urge to ask if anyone else had mentioned her. She thought she knew the answer anyway. Crispin returned and handed her a glass. "I was at Tommy Bahama's when Maitea called me from her hotel. She's at the Ranola, so I picked her up and brought her out to meet you."

"Oh?" Lacey turned startled eyes on her guest. "You're staying in Sarasota? What brings you here alone?"

The young woman spoke demurely. "Customarily, I would not leave Paraiso without a chaperone, but Uncle Edrigu gave his consent, provided Crispin escorts me while I'm here. I…I come to beg a favor."

Crispin interrupted. "Maitea wrote me last week. She—"

Maitea put a tiny hand on his forearm. "I think I had better tell her."

"Oh, all right." He blushed and avoided her eyes. "I'll just go and get myself a drink." He loped toward the kitchen.

"Ms. Delahaye—"

"Please, call me Lacey." *We should be on a first-name basis if you're going to marry the man I love.*

"All right. I very much need your help. Crispin was sure you would know what to do."

"Yes?" *Out with it, child.* The suspense rippled up and down her spine. She took a swallow of bourbon to calm her nerves. *Is it about Armand? Is he hurt? In prison? In love with someone else?* Lost in her frantic speculation, she almost missed Maitea's next words.

"Prince Armand insists on marrying me, and I have no idea how to prevent him."

"Prevent him?" A seedling of hope twined its way through the confusion. "I don't understand. Why would you want to stop him? Doesn't Paraisan custom demand it?"

"Yes." Maitea took a delicate sip of wine and put the glass down. "But our generation considers it more of a guideline. We're not Puritans after all." She seemed to think this required clarification. "Well, not anymore. Nowadays, it's accepted that both parties must agree to the match. And I don't want to marry Armand. I want to marry Gorka."

"Gorka?"

Maitea's furrowed brow relaxed. "Gorka Jaso. He owns fifty acres down near Ekaitz on the west coast. It's been in his family for three generations. He's very rich."

Despite the mercenary tinge to Maitea's description, the seedling blossomed from hope into likelihood, choking out every other emotion. *She doesn't want to marry him!* Lacey took another swig of bourbon and waited for her heart to defibrillate. Unfortunately, the pause left room for an alarming idea to insinuate itself. "You want to marry Gorka, but Armand still wants to marry you?"

"Yes, but I don't believe he really wants to force me into a loveless marriage. It would make me so unhappy." She folded her hands in her lap, her expression of prim complacency a tribute to her youth and self-absorption.

Lacey—herself wallowing in a sinkhole of self-doubt—found it refreshing. "Then why is he insisting?"

"Oh, I'm sure it's only to prove his bona fides to the people." Crispin appeared, mug in hand. Maitea made room for him on the couch. "Perhaps I should fill you in on what has happened on my island since you left. Grand Duke Xavier is very ill—the physicians don't expect him to live much longer. Meanwhile,

Prince Jakome has been consolidating power in his own hands. Armand and Edrigu lead a faction that wants to repeal his enactments. As for the people, now that the consequences of Jakome's edicts are beginning to cause real harm, they are gradually aligning themselves with Armand."

Crispin spoke up. "Prince Armand thinks that if they hold a big official wedding, it will confirm his status as an alternative to Jakome and strengthen his position. Edrigu agrees."

"So you see, if we don't change their minds, I'll have to go through with the wedding and Gorka will lose me."

"Is Xavier aware of any of this?"

Maitea shook her head. "It's said he drifts in and out of consciousness now. If he dies before this conflict is settled, well…"

"Jakome takes the throne."

"Yes."

"Does Armand intend to depose him?"

At this question, Maitea's eyes shifted. "N…no. But Uncle Edrigu thinks it's our only choice. And so do most of Armand's advisors—including me. Armand continues to resist. Jakome and his—what was Richelieu called? The French king's eminence something?"

"You mean *éminence grise*." Crispin patted her hand indulgently. "Actually, the *éminence grise* referred to a man named Père Joseph, and he was not the king's, but Richelieu's secret advisor." He wagged his chin. "European History 105."

"Thank you, Crispin. You do know so much." Maitea sparkled at him.

Lacey's barely stifled guffaw went unremarked.

Maitea tore her eyes from Crispin and resumed. "Prince Jakome has an advisor, an *éminence grise*"— she blushed—"named Damiano. He is said to be the one pushing Jakome to more and more radical acts. However, with opposition to his policies on the rise, the two are losing some legislative battles. In his frustration, Jakome is beginning to act irrationally."

Lacey knocked back her drink. "The question is obvious. Why are you here? What on earth do you think I can do about any of this?"

Maitea held her hands out, palms up. "Ms. Delahaye—Lacey—I know you love my cousin. I can see it in your eyes when you say his name. That is how Armand feels about you. He has been a changed man since you left—cold and driven. Even if he married me and took the crown from Jakome, he would never be a good ruler. He needs his true love by his side. He needs his grace, his mercy, his judgment back. He needs his sanity. For the good of Paraiso, will you come back with me?"

When you put it like that..."I'll think it over. Right now, we all need a good night's sleep. Where did you say you were staying?"

"At the Hotel Ranola."

Lacey knew the posh establishment off Main Street in downtown Sarasota. A very nice address. *I bet* her *father wasn't an accountant.* "Crispin, would you drive her back to her hotel, please?" She took Maitea's hand. "It took courage to come here. I'll give you my answer in the morning."

Not that it was ever in question. *Armand needs me.* Lacey hummed a tune as she wrote down the confirmation number for her reservation. Crispin entered and read the screen over her shoulder. "Ha. And Maitea was worried you would take a lot of persuading."

Lacey swiveled in her chair. "Crispin, you have been so patient with me. I couldn't talk about my feelings—not just because it hurt too much, but because I didn't think you'd approve."

"Approve? Mother, that's ridiculous. You've been alone for so long—you deserve some happiness. Of course, a prince is a little beneath you."

She threw a cushion at him.

He caught it. "You made a reservation for me too, didn't you?"

"You? Not on your life. You have your job, Crispin. You can't go traipsing about the world after your mother."

"But you could find yourself in a real jam!" He stopped short. "Er…I mean, pickle."

"Whatever. Look, if it's safe enough for Maitea, it's safe enough for me. I presume Traficant is long gone."

"I have no idea—Maitea didn't mention him. I'm more concerned that civil war is about to break out."

"If I recall correctly, the Paraisan army consisted of two men trained in stick fighting."

"If the situation is as dire as Maitea describes, they may be overwhelmed. The relative strength of the two sides is unclear."

Lacey thought about the Caribbean island she'd left six weeks ago, presuming she'd never return. How shocking it would be if that lush, exotic, rainbow-colored paradise were the scene of mayhem and violence. "Tell you what, I'll call you if I need backup."

"All right. Maitea leaves tomorrow, but she will meet you in Saint Andrews and bring you back to Paraiso herself."

"Perfect."

Crispin hesitated, then clinked her glass. "To a successful reunion."

The words hung in the air, filled with the helium of doubt. *What have I done?*

****

As she looked out the airplane window, Lacey reflected that the view of Paraiso from above was much more pleasant than from below decks on a boat. Undulating circles of progressively darker blue fanned out from the island, its hills covered in green forest. She could make out Port Huntington on the east coast and the two tiny castles bookending the northern and southern tips. The L4T Turbolet banked and headed south to Saint Andrews.

Maitea met her on the tarmac and led her to a waiting taxi. "I have a small villa a few miles from here. If you'd like to freshen up before we head to Paraiso, I'd be glad to take you there first."

The sight of the young woman with her dark tresses, her pink cheeks, and her luminous eyes made Lacey feel like something the cow dragged in. "That would be nice."

The car took them to a vine-covered, white stucco house set among luxuriant gardens. Curved-bill bananaquits played in the areca palms, and a fountain tinkled softly. Maitea helped Lacey out. "Welcome to Euskara."

Lacey trailed her hand in the fountain, sending the

143

orange and white butterfly koi skittering away. "It's beautiful. Is it your family's house?"

"Yes. Or rather, it was, but it's mine alone now. I have no close kin left. My parents and brother were lost at sea when I was fifteen, and I inherited a fortune. My great uncle Edrigu took me in—he's been like a father to me."

Lacey remembered something. "And Gorka?"

A spasm of woe crossed her lovely features. "Gorka is not a member of the First Families. He is descended from Spanish immigrants and African slaves. If my parents were alive, I would never be allowed to marry him—even if I weren't by custom betrothed to Armand."

"I thought you said Paraiso had moved beyond that kind of intolerance!"

Maitea opened the carved mahogany door. "Oh, it's not his parentage—it's his profession."

"You told me he's a farmer. What's wrong with that?"

"Here on Paraiso, we have a rich tradition of smuggling and piracy. Sedentary occupations are frowned upon."

"Sedentary?" Lacey pondered this before understanding dawned. "I think you mean agrarian. Farming can hardly be described as sedentary. Now, if you felt that way about, say, lawyers, I'd see your point. You have an odd little country, my dear."

Maitea sniffed. "Odd, perhaps, but we love it." She led the way into the front hall. Its blue and yellow Spanish tile floor, dark furniture, and white walls lent the room a very Mediterranean flavor. Maitea indicated a graceful staircase, the oaken banisters carved in the shape of climbing monkeys. It reminded Lacey of the 1920s-era Boca Raton Cloisters hotel, where miniature primates run amok on walls, lamps, and finials. "Upstairs on the right is the guest room. I trust you'll find all you need. The boat will be waiting for us at the pier when you're ready."

At the top of the stairs, Lacey passed a large-bosomed woman of about sixty. She bowed to Lacey but didn't say a word and walked down the hall. When Maitea came to fetch her, Lacey asked, "Who was that older woman?"

Maitea, her expression marked with disdain and a touch of acrimony, said, "That is Mary Fede Aconi Bacon, a distant cousin of my mother's. She lives with me here."

Her tone made it clear that further questioning would not be appreciated. An hour later, they chugged out of the harbor and headed north. "How far is Paraiso from Saint Andrews?"

"About seventy kilometers—more than forty miles. It'll take us an hour."

When they hit the open sea, they were surrounded by a spectacular turquoise sky shot through with baby pink clouds. Dolphins raced along beside them. Lacey's heart raced with them. Maitea shouted over the engine. "You'll stay with me at Uncle Edrigu's castle."

"Is Armand at the duke's castle?"

"Oh, no—he'd be too vulnerable at Zeruko. He has a house down on the beach on the west side."

"Maitea, does he know I'm coming?"

The girl didn't answer. Thirty minutes later, they pulled up at a pier, and the captain tied the boat to a pylon. Maitea gave him some money, and they climbed onto the landing. A servant waited on the shore in a little cart drawn by a pony. Lacey shook her head, her eyes bright with humor. "A transport fit for a princess!"

Maitea gave her an astonished look. "Excuse me?"

"Never mind."

When they reached the castle, they were ushered into Edrigu's study. He greeted Lacey warmly. "Maitea has filled you in on recent events?"

She nodded.

"We must bring Armand to his senses. He refuses to force Jakome to abdicate."

"Why is he against it?"

"He says it would deal a deathblow to our way of life. Paraiso has not seen an interruption in the line of succession in all its four-hundred-year history."

Maitea interjected gently, "Except those twenty years when Henry Morgan and his buccaneers controlled the island."

Edrigu waved a dismissive hand. "The grand duke remained on his throne during that time—a figurehead to be sure—but Captain Morgan respected our traditions. Not like Prince Jakome." His face darkened. "Armand says Jakome is the first-born and therefore heir to the grand duchy. He won't consider removing him in any manner other than as the Constitution allows, which takes time. Too much time." He slapped the desk in frustration. "With Xavier on his death bed, Jakome could become grand duke any day now. That would be disastrous for Paraiso. We must dislodge him before Xavier dies. We need your help, Lacey."

Lacey's eyes swiveled to Maitea. This wasn't what Maitea had asked her to do. The girl's face closed down. *Did she tell her uncle why she wanted me here?*

Not sure what to divulge, Lacey murmured, "What do you want of me?"

Edrigu patted her hand. "Didn't Maitea explain? Armand hasn't been himself since you left. He's like a demon, working twelve to fourteen hours a day. He's everywhere—checking on the mine, the docks, the fields. Jakome believes he's wasting his time, that this hands-on approach only diminishes his stature. Instead, Armand's support among the people strengthens by the day. We hoped that would steady him, but there's still a simmering bitterness in him that could ignite into violence at any moment. He needs you, Lacey. He loves you."

"Again, what do you want me to do?"

"Do? Nothing. Once Armand sees you, the rest will take care of itself."

Lacey's heart sank. "But…but what about Maitea?"

Edrigu shot a swift glance at the girl. "Maitea is a good girl and understands where her duty lies. She will marry the prince." Giving his niece a wan smile, he said, "It is common practice for the grand duke to take a mistress. She accepts that."

So Maitea hadn't confessed about Gorka to her uncle. *Wait a minute…Mistress? Does he mean me?* Lacey pressed her lips together to avoid lashing out at the old man. He couldn't possibly understand how insulting she found his assumption. Maitea claimed Paraisan culture had moved into the modern time, but their proposal smacked more of Henry the Eighth's era. *Isn't that what the original Puritans rebelled against?* Longing filled her—oh, to be back with her jellies and jams and her house on the bay! She tried to picture

147

Armand and couldn't. Panic clouded her thoughts. *I've got to get out of here.*

The door opened, and a uniformed footman stepped in. "Dinner is served, your Excellency."

"Thank you, James." Before Lacey could bolt, the first secretary took her arm and escorted her down to a cavernous dining room. Maitea trailed behind.

Watching her footing on the worn flagstone floor, Lacey did not look up until she reached the table. When she did, she caught the gale force winds of an enraged Armand full on. "What the hell are you doing here?" His voice, throbbing with malevolence, sliced through her ribs and ripped into her heart.

Edrigu stepped between them. "We asked her to come."

Armand turned to Maitea and opened his mouth, but before he could say anything she cried, "I brought her here. And don't make that face at me, Armand. You haven't been yourself since she left."

"You are not in a position to order me around, Maitea." He swung on Edrigu. "Nor are you. I may not be grand duke, but I outrank you both. I will not be treated like a child."

Edrigu put a hand on Armand's shoulder, forcing him into a chair. "You can have your official wedding if you like, but it would only create a temporary diversion in the battle with Jakome. We must move aggressively."

Maitea took the floor. "We decided that you had to be confronted with your true feelings—"

"An intervention, if you will." Edrigu didn't seem to notice the absurdity of his remark.

"—before you will recognize how obsessed you've

become with this marriage. You're not being reasonable, Armand. Marrying me won't make you happy."

Edrigu waved a dismissive hand at Maitea. "That's not the point. Armand, you've let your emotions drive you since Ms. Delahaye left. This frenzy of activity does little to bring the throne closer to you. Now have a drink and calm down."

Armand searched the faces of his relatives and finally put his head in his hands and groaned. "You're killing me."

Lacey had hung back, searching madly for an avenue of escape. Now she halted at the anguish in his voice. Blind rage routed her shame, and she stepped forward. "Let me speak." The three before her, Armand huddled in the middle, paused mid-bicker. "Edrigu, Maitea, I understand what you're trying to do, but I will not be a pawn in your game." She turned to the girl. "As I see it, you, Maitea, want me here so you can weasel out of your duty. And you, Edrigu"—she pointed a trembling finger at the old man—"you want to force Armand to strike at his own family. I won't be a party to any of this." She pivoted and charged toward the door. As she flung it open, she cried, "I can't believe you talked me into this. Armand, I apologize. I'll be leaving in the morning." She swept out of the room.

Fury impelled her all the way to her suite, but once there, as she looked at the empty bed where she and Armand once lay, grief overwhelmed her. *I've lost him all over again. This is too cruel.* How could they use her like that? How could she have been so blind? She knew the answer. *I wanted to see him so much I didn't care.* She went out to the terrace. Below her, an osprey glided along the wind currents, its distinctive cry echoing in the valley, reminding her of home. The tears gushed, and she laid her head on the stone wall. Wrung out by the stress of both passion and travel, she slumped on the bench and closed her eyes. The sun dipped under the mountain, leaving a chill twilight behind.

Finally, she went inside. The covers had been turned back and her suitcase unpacked. A tray of food lay on the table. She tore a chunk of bread off and chewed it but had no appetite for more. *I could use a belt.* A small bar in the corner proved to be well stocked. Bourbon in hand, she drew a bath, hoping the warm water would soothe her, but her jumbled thoughts clanged and pinged in her head. *What if they don't let me go?* It hadn't occurred to her until now that, with the stakes so high, she may not have a choice. She rose and, pulling a towel around her, padded to the door. Sure enough, it was locked from the outside.

This is like something out of a tawdry romance novel. The damsel locked in the tower. She thought she'd better look around for a possible weapon. Or a ladder. Instead, she found herself yawning. She checked her watch. Eight o'clock. It had been eighteen hours since she boarded the plane in Sarasota. *I'll just take a quick nap. When I'm fresher, I'll be able to think more clearly.* She slipped on her nightgown and plumped a pillow.

****

A light tapping woke her. She lifted her head as the mantel clock chimed once. One a.m. "Who is it?"

"It's me. Armand. Can I come in?"

150

No! "What do you want?"

"We have to talk."

"Do I have a choice?"

"Of course."

"I mean, you've locked me in. I'm hardly in a position to refuse."

The doorknob rattled. "Damn it, you're right—those two blockheads must have ordered it. Hang on." She listened to some scratching and bumping, and the door yielded. Armand stumbled in. He held up a small pin with a grin. "I believe I'll double my donation to Eton this year."

"*Hmmph.* Look, I need some sleep. I'm getting out of your hair tomorrow morning, so you don't need to threaten me. I apologize for being such a fool."

He took a step toward her, and she drew her knees up to her chin. "May I sit down?"

"Be my guest."

He gazed at her a minute. "It's...it's good to see you."

She was too busy clenching her jaw to say anything.

He tried again. "I missed you."

"Huh."

"I...uh...look, Lacey, you have no right to take that attitude. After all, you were the one who left me." He stood and paced.

"I—"

He swung on her, his face pinched, his voice brittle. "Why did you do that? Why did you go?"

"I had to, Armand. I was in the way. You had a family crisis—a national crisis—on your hands. My presence just made things worse."

"No...no. That's not true. I wanted...needed you. Lacey—" He bent toward her, his beseeching eyes filled with shade upon shade of black and mahogany and gold.

They reminded her of Maitea's eyes. "Really?" She tossed her head. "I see you wasted no time getting engaged."

He lifted his chin. "What else could I do? I'd lost the only woman I've ever loved. All I have left is my honor. And honor dictates that the second son of the grand duke marry his second cousin."

Lacey remembered that awful night in the castle, with Edrigu and Crispin and Inigo, and...Armand—the night when all her options were so cruelly eliminated, leaving her with the one, the inevitable choice. "You didn't lose me, Armand. You let me go."

His stricken face shot shards of pain out, piercing her heart. Defenses crumbling, she held out her arms. He fell into them.

A long kiss, followed by a rambling conversation in which the words "love" and "forever," figured prominently, went on for a few minutes. Armand's hands roamed over Lacey like a blind man memorizing her body, finally reaching the hem of her nightgown. He lifted it up and over her head, pausing to kiss each nipple. She unbuttoned his shirt, planting kisses on his chest. He wiggled out of his jeans and returned to her.

She pressed closer, squashing her breasts against him, wrapping her thighs around his hips. They held still, savoring the moment, savoring the knowledge of what was to come. He inched down her stomach, pausing to lick her belly button. "Hurry, hurry," she panted. Instead, he lingered on her inner thighs, trailing his lips down the bare flesh. She writhed on the bed, aching for her climax, begging him to unleash the passion building in her.

At last, he came to her toes. He peered up at her, and she caught a mischievous gleam in his eye. Lacey, who a minute before had been consumed by impatience, wanting her orgasm, wanting to come with him immediately if not sooner, settled down to watch. He took each toe gently between his lips and kissed the tips, then ran a finger along her instep. One hand cupped her heel while the other gently stroked the back of her calf. The kneading calmed her. *This must be the way a cat feels when she's petted—all warm and cozy and loved.* Her restlessness muzzled, she lay quietly, rejoicing in his caresses.

Armand whispered, "Lacey, I've waited for this moment for six weeks. Every night I'd fall asleep thinking of you, and every dawn I dreamed you were lying here next to me. I'd wake happy, until the real world crashed in. And here you are, as beautiful and desirable as you were the moment I first set eyes on you."

"Come to me, Armand."

The world stood by as two lovers met and enfolded. A roll of thunder and crash of lightning from beyond the window echoed the thrumming of flesh on flesh. She couldn't breathe, couldn't think. His scent filled her nostrils, and she let go.

Fingers intertwined, lips touching, they rested. The storm faded into the night.

As dawn peeked in through the open window, a knowing smile on her cream-colored face, Lacey pulled Armand close and reminded him again of what he'd missed. Almost sated, they slept again.

A knock woke them. A servant entered and without a word left a breakfast tray. Lacey stretched. "Dibs on the mango." Armand rolled away and pulled the pillow over his head. A gentle snore came from his vicinity. Lacey shrugged and sat down to eat.

An hour later Armand still slept. Lacey wondered if he was making up for weeks of insomnia. She dressed and went in search of Maitea. The girl took one look at her and smirked. "Things are progressing, I see. Are you still angry with us?"

The events of the evening before tore through the veils of contentment. "Yes, I am. You put me in a terribly awkward position. I still don't know how to resolve this."

In the tone of one mature beyond her years, Maitea replied, "Give it time, give it time." A servant rushed past them toward Edrigu's study. She held out a hand to block him. "What is it, Yuli?"

"It's Prince Jakome. He's had both the Chief Justice of the Ducal Court and Bishop Bunyan arrested."

They followed him to Edrigu's room. The old man stood at his desk. Maitea cried, "Is it true?"

Edrigu nodded. "Yuli, take this note to Prince Armand. Quickly!" The boy ran out before Lacey could stop him.

Maitea continued to stare at Edrigu. "But why would he do such a thing?"

The first secretary picked up a piece of paper. Lacey could see the coat of arms of the Montegues embossed at the top. "He claims the bishop planned to conduct an illegitimate marriage ceremony—yours and

Prince Armand's—and that the judge had unlawfully sanctioned it."

"But…but it's tradition!"

Lacey wondered if she were the only one in the room to see the irony in Maitea's protest.

Edrigu spoke slowly. "It appears that Jakome—or perhaps Damiano—senses the danger of letting the wedding proceed. He probably thinks by imprisoning the only officials authorized to perform ducal weddings, he can stop it."

Maitea pursed her lips. "He may be able to delay it, but he can't hold back the burgeoning preference of the people for Armand. I think he fears he's losing the upper hand and intends to resort to strong-arm tactics."

Edrigu shook his head. "That would be most unwise."

Lacey spoke up. "Arresting a bishop sounds pretty unwise to me. What else could he do? Surely he wouldn't dare go after Armand?"

Edrigu shook his head. "No, not Armand, but Maitea…"

"Maitea? No! You know Jakome, Edrigu. Is he capable of such an act?"

Before he could reply, a horn blared outside. The sound of a heavy instrument hitting the great iron door echoed through the castle. A voice cried, "Open up in the name of the prince!" Several young men swarmed into the study. They grabbed Maitea and marched back out—all without a word. As they left, one tacked a sign on the door. Two others took up positions on either side of the high gate leading to the castle keep.

Edrigu and Lacey followed them down the steps. The first secretary tore the paper off the door and read.

By order of His Highness the Grand Duke Xavier, Chief Justice Cornelius du Plessy Mozes Winthrop and Bishop Increase Jeremias Estebe Bunyan have been arrested for conspiring to commit illegal acts against the Crown. The grand duke finds the Lady Maitea Pulawi Abasolo Abbot to be an accomplice in the conspiracy and commands that she be brought to trial for treason. As punishment for harboring said traitoress, First Secretary Edrigu Boudewijn Cacicana Proctor has been placed under house arrest.

It was signed with a wax seal.

Chapter Nine

The sun came up on the Spanish sea
Our homeland far behind us
Being hunted by the King's Navy
It's sure he'd never find us
Pull away, me lads o' the Cardiff Rose
And hoist the Jolly Roger.
~*~

We brought her into the leeward wind
And made for the Caribbean
For thoughts of what it might have been
Destroys a human bein'.
~*~

But thoughts about the Spaniards' gold
And learnin' to desire it
Can make a man so brash and bold
He'll soon become a pirate
Pull away, me lads o' the Cardiff Rose
And hoist the Jolly Roger.

~Traditional pirate song

****

The two young men who guarded the gate wore Jakome's livery—the ducal cross and yoke but on a background of orange. They also wore the sneering expression of the schoolyard bully.

Edrigu marched back to his study, Lacey in his wake. He picked up a telephone and began to dial.

She put a hand on his arm. "Who are you calling?"

"Armand, of course."

"Um. He's…um…here. In my room."

The old man put down the receiver. "I don't understand. He stormed out of here last night soon after you left, vowing all kinds of retribution. Why would he…oh." He blushed, a very sweet look for one so distinguished. "I see. Well, you had better go tell him what happened."

Lacey climbed the stairs to her room. The bed was empty, and she could hear Armand singing in the shower. "La Donna e Mobile" again. Her mood softened, but then she remembered her errand. She went to the bathroom. "Armand."

In response, a hand slithered out from behind the curtain and grabbed her, pulling her in. She spluttered when the stream of water hit her face and tried to push him away. He held her tight with one hand and stripped off her wet skirt and panties with the other, then hitched her up on his hips. "Armand, no!"

He cut off the protest with a kiss and eased his soapy penis inside her. She had no choice but to ride him and braced herself against the wall. Before long, they slipped into a cadence, her movements clicking in sync with Armand's like the gears of a clock. The tempo increased, the cogwheels revolved faster and faster, and *wham!* They exploded in simultaneous orgasm. She bucked against him, lust stifling all rational thought. Armand gave a great thrust and a sigh. "Oh, God, Lacey!" His hands ran down her sides and around to her ass, and he spanked her lightly.

Her legs trembling, Lacey slid off him. They stood close together, letting the warm water wash them off.

At length, Armand kissed her and stepped out of the tub. He passed a towel in to her. "Is there any breakfast left?"

"I don't know. Armand, there's something I have to tell you." She pulled her soaked blouse off and wrapped the towel around her middle. When he'd thrown his clothes on and had a sip of cold coffee, she said quietly, "Maitea's been arrested."

He froze, a piece of mango halfway to his mouth. "What?"

"Jakome's men. They came a few minutes ago and took her away. Armand, he's charging her with treason."

He said nothing but strode out to the hall. She knew he'd go to Edrigu, so she dressed and followed him. She walked in to hear the first secretary saying, "—and I am under house arrest."

Armand tore Jakome's proclamation into pieces and tossed them on the floor. "He knows imprisoning you would be going too far. As for Winthrop and Bunyan—where are they?"

"In Castle Zeruka's dungeon. Things are coming to a head, Armand."

"Yes. Maitea's arrest is the last straw. I'm going to the palace."

"Wait! We need a plan. Right now Jakome holds all the cards."

"I can't just sit here." Armand slammed his fist into the wall. His eyes widened, and he shook his hand. "Ouch."

Lacey coughed. "Perhaps I could go into Port Huntington. I could nose around, see what I can find out. Jakome doesn't know anything about me, does he?"

Armand stopped rubbing his fingers. "I never thought of that. No, he doesn't know about you."

Edrigu spoke slowly. "Jakome assumes Armand is in love with Maitea. He expects his brother to come charging over when he hears about her arrest and challenge him to a duel or some such thing. At which point Jakome will take Armand into custody. That, of course, would be our undoing."

Reluctantly, Armand nodded. "I guess it wouldn't hurt to bide our time for a bit. Lacey may be able to get a sense of how the people are reacting to this new outrage."

"With any luck, it will awaken them to the situation, and you will be able to challenge Jakome with the citizens at your back." Edrigu turned to Lacey. "Inigo will guide you. You'll be less conspicuous with him by your side. Koldo must stay here to protect the prince. See what you can find out and come back."

"I'll be back by this evening."

****

As they came over the ridge, Port Huntington spread out before them. "It's not very big, is it?"

Inigo looked at Lacey as though she were daft. "It's our capital city. It has many monuments. Look up there—see the grand duke's castle?" He pointed at a huge stone monstrosity sitting like a great blob on the hill to the south. Assorted gables and goiters had been added here and there, and a lumpy tower squatted in the middle. Flags flew from turrets that looked more like chess pieces than real architectural features. Lacey peered at them. "Are those *semaphore* flags?"

"Yes." Inigo didn't seem to find this strange. "We

love flags here in Paraiso. All kinds of flags. We have ten national flags—one for every occasion."

"Really." *So that's what Armand meant by "better flags" than in England.* "Sounds like an innocuous enough custom."

The boy proceeded to elaborate with enthusiasm. "We fly the Pilgrim banner on Settlement Day, and on Buccaneer Day we fly Captain Morgan's original battle flag—the one that flew over his ship Satisfaction."

"Buccaneer Day?"

"That's when we celebrate Henry Morgan, the most famous of all the privateers. He made Paraiso his base. He said our island was the key to control of the Caribbean." He flushed with pride. "We were notorious throughout the Spanish Main."

Yes, indeed, an odd little island.

They took a path down to the central square. Market booths had been set up around the perimeter, vendors selling everything from fish to tennis socks. Behind the kiosks, Lacey made out two- and three-story houses painted in cheerful chartreuse, hyacinth, and saffron hues. People holding glasses filled with pink liquid hung over balconies and shouted at the pedestrians below. Others swayed and sang to a steel drum band. Lacey recognized the old sea chanty "Hoist the Jolly Roger." "Is today some sort of holiday?"

"Holiday? No. It's always like this. We are a fun-loving people."

"But weren't the first settlers Puritans?"

"Indeed, yes, but, as my father says, centuries of living by piracy tends to temper one's morals. Plus we have Dutch, Spanish, Indian, and even African blood in our veins."

Lacey listened to the pandemonium. "It certainly makes for a vibrant food and music scene." *That reminds me, I'd better pick up a brochure if I'm to be a tourist.* She stopped at a booth and bought a glass of passion fruit juice. As she sipped it, they wandered around eavesdropping on passing conversations. Most were in English, but some were in the language she now recognized as the Paraisan creole—a blend of English, Spanish, Dutch, and a couple of other unfamiliar tongues.

Inigo translated where necessary. "The people are philosophical. They do not like all these changes but see no way to alter the situation."

"Has anyone mentioned Armand?"

"Oh, no. Prince Jakome has spies everywhere. No one would risk an overt show of support."

"But in private?"

He made a face. "We do not approve of Prince Jakome's activities, but Damiano—his advisor—is truly detested."

"Who is this Damiano? He's an American, right?"

"Yes. He taught at the university where Prince Jakome studied. He accompanied the prince when he returned. Most people believe he's responsible for all the new regulations and restrictions."

A commotion at one end of the square distracted them. A man in the uniform of the Montegues pushed through the crowd. "Oyez, oyez!"

Punching Inigo in the side, Lacey whispered, "Did he really just say that?"

The boy ignored her. The herald shouted, "His Highness Prince Jakome will make an announcement from the north balcony in ten minutes."

Someone in the back of the crowd spoke loudly. "Another one?" A few people snickered. The man glared at the group. "All citizens are requested to gather on Cromwell Boulevard to hear the proclamation."

The crowd broke up into small groups and meandered down an alley. Lacey and Inigo went with them. The alley opened onto a wide avenue that led to the duke's castle a mile away. A balcony projected from the second floor. Inigo led Lacey through the throng to a spot just below it.

After a few minutes, another herald appeared and announced His Highness Prince Jakome Zigor Cromwell de Montegue. He stepped aside to reveal a man about Armand's age, but shorter. Sparse black hair covered his round head, and the heavy brocade cape he wore seemed to weigh him down. He moved slowly to the rail.

"Friends and fellow citizens, good day to you." He raised his arms up as if expecting exuberant cheers. The response from the crowd—a kind of low hum—did not convey warmth. "Today I have sad news. We have uncovered a plot—yes, a plot—to undermine the wonderful changes we've instituted in the last few months. I'm sure you all join me in my great relief that the perpetrators were detained before they could execute their plan. His Highness the Grand Duke Xavier has commanded that they be tried for treason."

A man in the crowd shouted, "Who are they?"

"They are Cornelius du Plessy Mozes Winthrop, Chief Justice of the Ducal Court, Bishop Increase Jeremias Estebe Bunyan, and the Lady Maitea Pulawi Abasolo Abbot."

"And what are they accused of?"

The interruption appeared to rattle Jakome. He turned away from the balcony and was seen whispering to a man standing in the shadows. When he turned back to his audience, his voice shook slightly. "They conspired to arrange a marriage between my brother Prince Armand and Lady Abbot."

Another man yelled, "But what's wrong with that? It's Paraisan custom!"

A third voice chanted loudly, "It's written that the second son shall marry his second cousin."

The herald stepped forward. "Silence! There will be no discussion. His Highness is merely making an announcement. Any further interruption will not be tolerated."

Jakome waited for him to move aside and continued. "I intend…rather, Grand Duke Xavier intends, to bring Paraiso into the modern world. Truly progressive cultures are no longer mired in outmoded customs such as marriage…I mean marriage between relatives. The grand duke has determined that arranged marriages like that of Prince Armand and Lady Abbot are no longer valid." He warmed to his subject, oblivious to the strident buzz rising from the milling people below. "He has also determined that the primitive dependence on religion is nothing more than a tool to subjugate the people. His Highness the Duke recognizes that religion enslaves humans, that it is an…an…"

A hand appeared on Jakome's shoulder, and the man he had earlier consulted leaned forward and said something in his ear.

Jakome nodded and raised his voice. "An opiate of the masses. That is why Grand Duke Xavier proclaimed last week that religious ceremonies would henceforth be prohibited. Thus, the three conspirators attempted to subvert not one, but two of our enlightened reforms."

The buzzing stopped, and the crowd grew ominously silent. Jakome hesitated, then plunged on. "Of course, we still require that justice be served, and so His Highness has appointed Damiano Wynn as interim chief justice to the high court and bestowed upon him the title of Sir."

The man behind him stepped into the sunlight. At the same time a third man appeared at Jakome's other side. Lacey's eyes widened when she recognized him. *Traficant.* Looking sleek and self-satisfied. She stared at him a minute before her eyes swiveled to the man Damiano. "Oh, my God."

Inigo tugged her sleeve. "What is it, Miss Lacey?"

She pointed. "Is that the man they call Damiano? Jakome's evil advisor?"

"Yes."

Without another word, she twirled and began fighting her way through the spectators. "We have to get out of here. We must find Armand. Quickly."

Inigo caught up with her as she started up the path over the mountain. "What is it? Why are you so frightened?"

Lacey couldn't bring herself to voice the words. "When we get back," was all she could manage.

They made the rest of the journey in silence. Since the island ran less than five miles tip to tip it didn't take long. Armand must have seen them arrive for he was waiting in the great hall.

Inigo raced to Armand and stood before him, teetering on his toes in his agitation. "It's true! It's true!

Prince Jakome has arrested Bishop Bunyan and Chief Justice Winthrop. He says they conspired to repeal all his regulations, including the ban on religious ceremonies. Jakome claims the grand duke ordered all this, but we know better." Inigo seemed to have added three inches and ten years.

Edrigu entered with Koldo. "So he is trying to prevent the marriage. He must think it would be costly to him."

Koldo shook his head. "Or he wants to distract the people from the standoff with Campbell over the dysprosium mine."

"Both threaten him, Koldo. Whatever his purpose, we must preserve the possibility of the marriage, if only to keep him off balance." He bowed to Armand. "Even if you and Maitea don't intend to go through with it."

Armand kept his eyes on Lacey. "We can hardly discuss a wedding when the judge and presiding bishop are out of commission."

Koldo mused, "It was clever of him to arrest Winthrop as well. He would have tossed out the charges against Bunyan and Maitea."

"Wait! Wait! I have more news!" Inigo appeared to have forgotten that he was talking to the first secretary and a prince of the ducal house. "Guess who he's named to replace Chief Justice Winthrop?"

His father frowned. "Inigo, your manners!"

Armand interrupted. "It's all right, Koldo. Your son has earned his stripes. Inigo, what did you find out?"

The boy's eyes shifted from one man to the other, clearly weighing the prospect of later punishment against his current spot in the limelight. "I…uh…"

"Inigo! Don't play games. Who did Jakome name as chief justice?"

He blurted out, "Sir Damiano!"

"Damiano?" Armand and Edrigu looked at each other. "Does he really think he can get away with that? He's not even a citizen!"

The boy sidled over to a large dish of candy that lay on the desk. "I don't think the people liked it. There were murmurs."

Lacey, who had been wandering around the room absorbed in her thoughts, finally muttered, "And Jakome has acquired another advisor—or bodyguard. Ulisses Traficant."

She halted before Armand. He took her hand. "Traficant! Did he see you?"

"I…I'm not sure. I don't think so."

"Let's hope not." Armand wiped his forehead. "This is getting out of hand. Edrigu? Do you think we have the people on our side?"

The old man shook his head. "I have no way to gauge, but my scouts tell me they're definitely moving in our direction. Inigo, what were these murmurs from the crowd like?"

The boy spit out the jellybean he'd just popped into his mouth and stammered, "A few actually questioned Prince Jakome when he claimed the prince's marriage would be illegitimate, and many showed their displeasure at the arrests. But no one actually denounced him. I think they're still afraid to challenge his authority."

Koldo saluted Armand. "With all due respect, Your Highness, I don't think you should remain here in the castle."

"I agree." Edrigu nodded.

Armand picked up a knapsack. "I'm way ahead of you. I have a secret hideaway in the Sister Cays where I used to camp as a boy. I'll go back to my house and grab some things, then head out there."

"It would be wiser to flee entirely. To Saint Andrews, or farther."

The prince shook his head. "Not on your life. That would be surrendering my people to Jakome. No, I must stay here and try to mobilize support."

Lacey found her voice. "I'll go with you."

Armand kissed her. "No, my dear. It's too rugged. Besides, the farther you stay from me the better."

Edrigu said, "Perhaps she should continue her role as tourist. You know, hide in plain view as it were."

"The more conspicuous, the less suspicious, eh?"

"Something like that."

"What about Traficant? What if he sees me?" She didn't mention her other concern. *I want to tell Armand about it first—before anyone else finds out.*

Koldo shrugged. "He'll hardly be wandering the city. And what can he do to you? Out you as the woman he held for ransom along with Armand? There's no evidence that he told Jakome about you before this, and if he identified you now, it could only jeopardize his new position as the prince's bodyguard."

"Good point. So we're agreed. Lacey will stay on but as a simple visitor to the island." Armand kept his voice casual, but Lacey sensed he was on edge—needing her here but out of harm's way.

Edrigu regarded his prince gravely. "Yes, for now. She can stay at the hotel in town. As long as she remains under the radar, no one will suspect her of being involved with the so-called conspirators."

"Hotel?"

"The Hotel Azure. It's in the market square." Edrigu signaled to a servant. "You can stay there until we can make arrangements for you to fly to Saint Andrews."

Lacey's hand went to her throat. "You're sending me away?"

Ignoring the others, Armand took her in his arms. "Not yet, but I may have to if conditions become more unstable." He gave her a lingering kiss. "Now that I've got you back, I won't let you go unless I absolutely have to." He pushed her toward the stairs. "Go pack. The donkey cart will take you around the island so it looks as though you're arriving from the airport."

She went. *I have to find a way to tell him.*

****

The hotel proved to be a graceful pink building almost hidden behind a sprawling bougainvillea on the edge of the square. Behind it rose the gray stone walls of Castle Zeruko, the grand duke's palace. She pushed the revolving door and entered the lobby. As Edrigu had advised, she registered under her own name. There didn't seem to be any other guests. A short, dark-haired man of indeterminate age bustled out from the office. "Welcome to the Hotel Azure. I'm Mr. Pusey, your concierge." He checked the book. "How long will we have the privilege of your company, Ms. Delahaye?"

"A few nights I think. I'm…I'm on an extended sabbatical. Visiting Caribbean islands." The cover sounded as artificial as it had when Armand came up with it. *I mean, what serious university would pay its faculty to compare beaches and sample rum punches?*

Armand had winked and suggested, "Princeton?"

She made a show of surveying the lobby. "Paraiso is certainly a beguiling place. It feels very friendly."

"We think so." Mr. Pusey rang the bell on his desk. A bellhop skipped over. "Apal, please take Ms. Delahaye's luggage to 4B." He turned back to Lacey. "And how did you hear of us, if I may ask?"

"I…I was on a cruise and some of the passengers mentioned it. I hadn't planned to visit, but you have such a…unique history and government. I thought, why not?"

"So true." The concierge wagged his head in agreement. "You know we are a grand duchy—the smallest in the world. And our climate is perfect. The windward breeze is warm and constant, and the water temperature averages eighty degrees Fahrenheit year-round. If you're interested in snorkeling, our coral reef is the third largest in the world."

"Sounds fascinating." She checked her watch. "Oh, my. Is it four o'clock already? I didn't have time for lunch in…in Saint Andrews. Do you have room service?"

"I'm afraid we only serve breakfast in the garden."

"Thanks."

She strolled around the city as the evening came on, then had a bath and ordered dinner. Her balcony overlooked the harbor. Fishing boats were returning, the crews shouting at the stevedores on shore to help. Far out at sea, beyond the reef, she saw what looked like a freighter. *Is that how they transport the dysprosium?*

A few hours later she turned in, wondering if Armand had made it to his island. *I should have told him.* They hadn't had any time alone, and by the time she finished packing Armand had left Castle Aresti. *If only I knew what to do about it.* She fell asleep.

Something moved in the darkness. Armand? She sat up and turned on the light. Stifling the scream, she pulled the covers up to her chin.

"Hello, Lacey."

The flat but amiable tone reassured her.

"Hello, Damien."

Chapter Ten

> *Oh, better far to live and die*
> *Under the brave black flag I fly,*
> *Than play a sanctimonious part,*
> *With a pirate head and a pirate heart.*
> *Away to the cheating world go you,*
> *Where pirates all are well-to-do;*
> *But I'll be true to the song I sing,*
> *And live and die a Pirate King.*
> *~W. S. Gilbert, Pirates of Penzance*
> ****

"So you did recognize me. I wasn't sure you would after so many years." He touched her cheek. "Just as beautiful as I remember. How is Crispin?"

She was too tired to throw him out. *Besides, I want to hear how he ended up the* éminence grise *to a Caribbean prince.* "He's well. He turned into a fine young man." *No thanks to you.*

Damien hung his head. "That's good to hear. I am so sorry, Lacey. I just wasn't cut out for marriage." He raised his eyes. Up close she could see he had aged much too gracefully for a man of his dissolute character. *Still remarkably handsome.* Crispin had inherited Damien's sandy hair and chestnut brown eyes, but credit for his strong chin went to Lacey. Now that she wasn't blinded by infatuation, she could see the evasive look in Damien's eyes and the thin, bloodless lips that never quite smiled—or at least not with genuine feeling. "I did provide the child support though."

For the first year. Then nada. Lacey had long since left her rancor behind. It wasn't worth going over past sins again. "Yes."

He sat at the foot of the bed. "Forgive me for coming by so late. I have to avoid my fans." His mouth twisted. "You may have guessed I hold a relatively high position here."

"Really?" *Remember your cover—first visit, tourist, etc.* "I don't know anything about this island. Friends recommended it. I'd only just arrived today and noticed the crowd going to the castle. What do you do?"

"We'll get to that." He leaned toward her and gently pulled the blanket down to her stomach. Running his eyes over her body, he lingered on the twin mounds of her breasts. She kept still, her body tense, hoping his old sexual obsession with her had flagged. "So, you still have a jelly business?"

She edged away from him. "Yes. I've moved, though. I'm in Florida now—Tampa Bay area. I'm just getting started. You know, building inventory, learning about the local fruit, that sort of thing."

"It must be very lucrative."

"Not really."

He pounced. "You could afford a trip to the Caribbean."

"I—" *Does the bastard think he's laying a trap? Or does he expect a cut?* "I...uh, sold the Virginia house when I inherited the one on Longboat Key from Grammy Delahaye and set some of the money aside to travel. I've always wanted to travel, but I couldn't while Crispin was young." *Zing.*

"Oh." The dart didn't appear to penetrate. His finger touched her chin and trailed down her neck to one breast. He flicked the nipple. She flinched, and his hand shot up. His face tightened.

Quick, distract him. "You haven't told me what you're doing here."

He got up without answering and rummaged around on the bureau. "You don't have anything to drink, do you?"

She indicated the minibar. He opened it and took out a couple of little bottles. Pouring them into a water glass, he held it up. "Put it on my tab, okay?"

She reflected glumly that it wouldn't be the first time he'd done that. "Well?"

He took a swig and sat down on the bed. "That's better. Okay. You remember I got that teaching assistant job at Roanoke College, right? Well, when I finished my degree I landed a post at Princeton. Just research—not much money, but I built up my reputation and a couple of years ago they gave me a visiting assistant professorship in political science. Jakome took my precept, and we got to know each other."

He sounded so normal, so rational. Did he have a clue what havoc he was wreaking on little Paraiso?

"Anyway, he asked me to come back with him and…well…look at the place. Is this paradise or what? Who in their right mind could leave?"

"It seems very…charming. I noticed a bit of unrest among the people in the square though. Do you know what's bothering them?"

He jerked back as though she'd slapped him. "Unrest? Here? Not at all. It must be your vivid imagination at work again. It always was a bit over the top. Jakome is very enlightened, and the population has welcomed his ideas. He's instituting some much needed reform. Did you know they've had the same system of government for three hundred years?" He shook his head in amazement. "There are a lot of inequities. Entrenched power. Too much money in too few hands. You know, like the States. Why, one company—an American one, natch—is draining us of our natural resources and paying us a bare pittance as our share. It's…it's insulting."

"Us?"

He sipped his vodka.

Playing for time?

Finally he mumbled, "I know it sounds bizarre, but I tell you, Lacey, this place has become like a second home to me. Jakome has asked me to stay and help him out in his efforts. You heard him today. He's appointed me chief justice. Of course, it's only temporary," he added hastily. "I don't intend to spend the rest of my life here, but there's so much to work to do. We both want to make some real, progressive change. By the time we're finished, it will be a new Paraiso."

Lacey kept her voice mild with some effort. "That sounds…nice. The American company. Are you talking about Campbell Metals? I read about it in a brochure I picked up at the airport. It said they provide a very generous stipend to every citizen in exchange for the mining rights. It said the average Paraisan income is higher than in the States. That isn't true?"

His brows drew together in a vexed frown.

"Technically, yes, but that's my point. Everyone's doing okay, but a few people—and the Campbell folks—are making out like bandits." His voice took on a nasal whine. "It's not fair."

Lacey could see that debating a world view like Damien's was like arguing with a child. It reminded her of the old joke going the rounds of mothers when Crispin was small. Her friend Joanna called it "the toddler's code of ethics." How did it go? *Oh, yeah.*

If it's yours, it's mine.
If I like it, it's mine.
If I think it's mine, it's mine.
If I saw it first, it's mine.
If I had it, then put it down, it's still mine.
If you had it and put it down, it's mine.
If it's broken, it's yours.

A quick peek at his fretful face and she settled for an oblique approach. "You say Jakome is making reforms. What about the grand duke? The brochure says he's the ruler. I believe his name is Xavier. Is he Jakome's father?"

Damien got up and pulled two more small bottles from the refrigerator. "Yes, but he's bedridden. And an old fool at that. Luckily he goes along with whatever Jakome wants."

"I see." Lacey gently pushed his hand away from her knee. "At the risk of repeating myself, Damien, why are you here?"

"Me? I thought we could catch up. It's been a long time. When I saw you in the crowd, I couldn't believe it. I had to come by."

"How did you know where to find me?"

He chuckled. "There's only one hotel in town. I

assumed you'd be here."

Good. So he doesn't know I've been here before. That means Traficant either didn't see me or didn't tell him. "By the way, who was that other man on the podium today?"

Damien broke off his hungry gaze. "Other man? Oh, you mean Traficant. He showed up in my office a few weeks ago claiming to be holding Prince Armand hostage and demanding ransom. I tossed him out on his ear."

"Did you tell Prince Jakome?"

"I didn't think it necessary to bother him. Wish I had though. When Traficant realized Armand had slipped through his fingers, he didn't slink off like the rat I think he is. Oh, no. He waltzed back to Port Huntington and claimed the pirates had kidnapped *him*."

Why didn't Ulisses mention me? Not sure how to find out without giving herself away, she kept quiet. Damien continued to grouse. "Now Jakome's taken a shine to the little weasel and made him his bodyguard." He curled his lip. "Can't stand him myself. Something sneaky about him."

Takes one to know one. "And who is Prince Armand?"

"Armand? Sniveling little brother of Jakome. Talk about sneaky. He's been going around behind my back trying to undermine support for our reforms. He's had little luck, although he's influenced a few weak souls with his negative rants and hostile attitude. That's probably what you sensed today. The prick. If I had my way…"

"What? What would you do to him?" She held her

breath, praying her repugnance didn't show.

"Me?" Damien seemed to realize he'd gone too far. "I can't do anything to him. I'm just the advisor. The grand duke is the ultimate arbiter, although he's given Jakome as his heir a great deal of latitude."

Lacey persisted. She had to know what Damien was capable of. "Still, if you had your way, what would you do about Armand? I mean, has he broken any laws?"

But Damien had evidently decided to clam up. He bent closer, his breath warm on her cheek, and wheedled, "Forget politics. It's really good to see you again, Lacey. You don't look a day over twenty-one." He pawed at her, grabbing a handful of the negligee.

Lacey wiggled out of his grasp, stood up, and went to the table. Pouring water into a glass, she gulped it down. "Thanks, Damien. Listen, I'm really tired."

His eyes narrowed. "I see. Of course." She tensed, hoping the old Damien wouldn't appear, the one who could never keep his hands off her, the man who, when in his cups, hadn't balked at forcing her to have sex. Finally he stood. "How about if I send someone to pick you up tomorrow—I'll give you a personal tour of the castle. I'm sure Jakome would love to meet you."

She relaxed. "Ah, gee. I'd like that. But, but…I've arranged for a boat excursion with a friend I met on the ship. He's counting on me. So sorry."

"He?"

Hmm. Is it better to make him jealous or to reassure him? She checked his face. The cheekbones had hardened, and his chin wobbled under the wispy little attempt at facial hair. *Reassure.* She said airily, "He's an older gentleman—must be in his eighties. I met him in the buffet line. A bit rotund for my taste, but he's all alone and likes the company. How about the day after tomorrow?" *That will give me some time to figure out the best approach.*

"Yeah, okay." He rose. "I'll have someone from the castle keep an eye on you though. Believe me, you'll appreciate my protection. This island isn't as benign as it appears." Before she could feint, he caught her shoulders and kissed her full on the mouth. "See you later." He walked out, leaving the door open.

Lacey waited until she heard the elevator clang shut, then closed and locked the door. Upon reflection, she pushed a chair under the doorknob. Then she went into the bathroom and scrubbed her face. Five minutes later, she was asleep.

****

The sultry rays of the morning sun heated the little room, and shouts and cries sounded from the square below. She jumped out of bed and went to the balcony. The harbor was bustling, fishing boats chugging out, pleasure yachts putting up sail. Farm carts, piled high with fruits and vegetables, rattled down the cobblestone alleys. Lacey thought of Maitea and her Gorka. Would she be ever be free to marry him? For that matter, would she ever be free?

Back in the room, she tripped on an empty vodka bottle, deflating her good mood. What to do about Damien? *I wish I'd had a chance to tell Armand about him.* Too bad she had to stay here and play tourist and couldn't ask advice from anyone. *Might as well do some sightseeing then. And listening.*

After a light breakfast in the hotel garden, she set out to explore. She would later describe Port

Huntington as a town laid out by a man chasing a greased pig. One street split around an ancient kapok tree, another came to an abrupt end at a blank wall. A few crossed each other two and three times. Except for Cromwell Boulevard, the broad avenue that led to the castle, most turned into dirt after a block or two. But the houses were all painted in vibrant colors, their window boxes overflowing with lantana and geraniums, and the people who passed her never failed to greet her. *This is a lovely place.* She could see how Armand wouldn't want it ruined.

She stopped for a cup of coffee at a cafe on the edge of the market. Watching with delight the boisterous exchanges between customers and vendors, she thought back to Damien and his "progressive reforms." *Why do these do-gooders have to stick their noses into other people's affairs? Why do they always think they know better?* Both Jakome and Damien were academics. Like Lacey's grandfather and uncles— professors all—they lived in a theoretical world, a world where you could argue as the devil's advocate and win without anyone suffering any lasting ill effects. Men like Damien had no clue how the real world worked. *If people don't act the way he wants them to, he says they're stupid and should be forced to do what he thinks is in their best interest.*

She remembered one professor of hers who claimed that every social institution—even down to the family and sexual reproduction—was an artificial creation and therefore kept humans from reaching their full potential—whatever that was. The obliteration of all those false constructs—family, property, faith— would lead to nirvana, he opined. That particular professor had been divorced three times and then expelled for lying on his resume. Lacey last saw him pushing a shopping cart and babbling to himself. *So much for nirvana.*

By the time she'd finished her coffee, she had made up her mind. Mr. Pusey was happy to put a call through to the castle. She remembered in time to call him Damiano.

"Well, hi, Lacey. What can I do for you?" He sounded pleased.

"Turns out my old gentleman gets seasick on small boats. He's gone back to Saint Andrews. If you're not busy, I'd like to take you up on your offer."

Damiano put his hand over the receiver. She heard a voice raised peevishly. He came back on. "The prince and I have some business to attend to this afternoon. How about if I send a car for you around five?"

"Wonderful. See you then."

Now what? She wished Inigo would turn up—at least she could send a message back to Edrigu. *I'll just have to play it alone.* She wandered down to the waterfront and spent the afternoon haggling for souvenirs.

At five, a chauffeur in the purple ducal livery presented himself at the hotel and handed her into a Bentley. The trip took five minutes, partly because the driver refused to stop for traffic or anything else, including donkeys, and partly because the hotel stood only a mile from the castle. Damien met her at the door. "Welcome."

"Thank you."

"Shall we?" He took her arm and proceeded to lead her on an exhausting trek through myriad chilly rooms and galleries overflowing with portraits of grim ancestors in starched white collars and black hats.

At one particularly ghastly picture of an early Cromwell, she remarked, "It's funny how the settlers here went from strict Puritans to jolly Caribbean rum swizzlers."

Damien shrugged. "Change with the times—that's what I always say."

She saw a winding stair at the end of a long hall. "Where does that go?"

"That leads to the private apartments of the grand duke. We won't disturb him." He checked his watch. "Oops, cocktail time. Jakome is anxious to meet you."

"What, I don't get to see the dungeons?" She said it as playfully as she knew how.

He looked at her, bemused. "Why would you want to?"

"Oh, you know, chains and iron maidens—tools of torture—very romantic." *Too perky? Not perky enough?*

He stiffened. "My dear Lacey, I have never appreciated your taste for the melodramatic. For your information, our cells are clean and equipped with the latest amenities. Except, of course, for communication devices." He didn't crack a smile.

My God, he's serious.

They came to a double wooden door adorned with rusty iron plates. The dark varnish had peeled off in long strips, leaving the impression of prison bars. "Ah, here we are."

A large room opened before Lacey. Heavy burgundy drapes covered the stone walls. Pinpricks of leftover sun filtered through tiny apertures. Wall sconces provided a bit more light, while candles set here and there failed to pierce the rest of the gloom. Lacey wondered if the darkness were a salute to medieval ambience or just mean-spirited penny-pinching. *Those light bulbs can't be more than twenty-five watts.* A man rose from a heavy wooden chair and came forward. "You must be Ms. Delahaye. Damiano has spoken highly of you. Welcome to Paraiso."

In person, Jakome seemed even shorter than he'd looked on the balcony—or was it more shrunken? Thin shoulders protruded through the orange T-shirt emblazoned with the Princeton tiger. He'd covered his balding head with a baseball cap. Baggy shorts and worn flip-flops completed the ensemble. Lacey did not feel compelled to curtsy as she had with Edrigu. This man held no awe for her. He had no stature, no regal presence that she could feel. She thought of Armand and the power and authority that emanated from him even as a forlorn castaway. *One is a king. The other's a wannabe, an intruder, a supplanter.* "How do you do?"

Jakome indicated a brass-studded leather armchair and sat down again. Damien pulled a velvet rope, revealing a well-stocked bar behind hidden doors. He turned to Lacey. "As I recall, you like vodka gimlets. Straight up?"

She nodded.

Damien handed her her drink in a large martini glass and filled a snifter with brandy for himself. Jakome held up his glass of pilsner. She noted it had the Princeton logo on it. "Chinchin!"

Lacey sipped her gimlet and watched the prince, wondering if he'd ever really moved on from his college days. He dressed like a student, swilled his beer like a student, and talked like a twenty-something radical. When he spoke, every phrase on his lips reminded her of some screed from the latest Hollywood celebrity cause.

He had gone on for a solid ten minutes before Damien interrupted. "Jakome, you had something you wanted to ask Lacey."

"What? Oh, yes. I understand you make jellies and jams. You use nothing but organically-grown fruits I presume?"

Sigh. "Yes, sir. I gather wild fruits found locally. I don't use farm-raised produce of any kind."

His nod of approval lapsed into a palsied quiver. He took another slug of beer. "That's good. I'm thinking of establishing a communal farm here—settle all the independent growers on the island in one central location so we can turn more acreage into productive farmland. You may help me."

Lacey gasped. "You mean take the farmers' land away from them?"

Jakome stared at her. "No, no of course not. They would still be able to work it, but the whole operation could be run more efficiently from here. Isn't that right, Damiano?"

Lacey rotated her horrified face to Damien, who stood in the center of the room, his face alight with religious fervor. "Absolutely. This island is a patchwork of small tracts—there's so much waste. The new department of agriculture that Jakome is going to establish will transform the system—centrally run, it will be leaner and cheaper. Plus, we can control what crops we cultivate. For example, instead of the current bunch of acre-sized plots of fruits and vegetables, we'll consolidate them into one big sugarcane plantation. The new department of trade will handle all imports and exports. That way we can redistribute the income more fairly."

Jakome broke in excitedly. "And if we took over the dysprosium mine, we'd have complete control of the economy. We can make it a veritable utopia!"

"Now, now, one step at a time, Jakome…"

Lacey forgotten, the two men talked over each other, visions shining in their eyes like sugarplums of a new and glorious state in which everyone received what they needed from a benevolent government. *That is, what Jakome and Damien think they need.* She put down her drink and began to back slowly out of the room.

Just as she reached the door, Damien stopped and lunged for her arm. "Oh, my dear, I apologize. When we start expanding on all the wonderful things we can do for the people of Paraiso, we tend to forget all in the pursuit of it. Do have another drink, and we'll talk of the weather."

Lacey wanted to protest but knew it was important to keep the atmosphere friendly and calm. *These two are totally off their rockers.* She accepted a second gimlet but didn't drink it.

An hour later, Damien escorted her to the front hall. "You're sure you won't stay here? The hotel isn't as…comfortable."

The last thing on God's green earth Lacey wanted was to be stuck in this loony bin of a castle, even if it gave her a perfect spot from which to observe the two inmates. "I don't want to impose, and besides, all my things are at the hotel, Damien."

"It's no trouble. I can send Dries with the Bentley to pick up your luggage, and you can get settled here."

"No! I mean, I'm a little tired. It's been an…an interesting evening. I'd like to chew on all your fascinating ideas." *And spit them out.*

"All right." He opened the great double doors. The full moon floated high above, bisected by the northwest tower. Thousands and thousands of stars blazed a paean to it. A soft breeze caressed her cheek. She wondered how long this paradise would last if Damien and Jakome had their way. Damien touched her elbow. "I'll see you tomorrow?"

"I…uh…"

Before she could stop him, Damien pulled her into his arms and kissed her. He must have felt the shiver of disgust that went up her spine for he hugged a little tighter. "You cold?"

She stepped back. "No, no, I'm fine. Goodnight, Damien."

He watched her take the steps down to the waiting limousine. As she climbed in, she looked up at the castle. Only one faint light shone from the hall. The rest was dark. She started to tap the glass to alert the chauffeur but paused when she saw an oleander bush twitching unnaturally. It parted, revealing Inigo. His lips were set in a furious frown, and his eyes shot daggers at her. She stared back at him, mouthing the question. "What is it?"

Inigo pointed above him, where Damien still stood. *Oh my God, he saw the kiss. He thinks…he thinks…* The car pulled away, carrying Lacey back to the hotel. *Will Inigo tell Armand? How do I explain? What, oh what, do I do now?*

Chapter Eleven

Then up speaks the mate of our gallant ship,
And a well-spoken man was he,
"Oh, I have me a wife in Salem town,
But tonight she a widow will be."
~*~

Oh, the ocean waves do roll, they roll
And the stormy winds do blow.
But we poor sailors go skipping to the top,
While the landlubbers lie down below, below, below,
Oh, the landlubbers lie down below.
~*"The Mermaid," a traditional sailing song*
****

The hotel concierge greeted Lacey with barely disguised terror. "All is well, mademoiselle? You are satisfied with your accommodations? You made no complaint at the castle?" He prodded the elevator button with an anxious finger. "I have taken the liberty of sending up a bottle of champagne and some of Paraiso's local shrimp fresh from the lagoon."

"Thank you, Mr. Pusey. It's most kind. Yes, my room is lovely."

Lacey got in the lift, but the little man held the door open. "You're sure there's nothing else I can do for you? Anything? Anything at all?"

Oh dear. "I told Jak—I mean, Prince Jakome that your hotel was magnificent." She almost added,

"Although perhaps you could stock beer in the minifridge," but thought better of it. *That would probably reduce him to tears.*

In her room, she found the bedclothes turned down, a lamp lit, and champagne snuggled in a nest of ice. She opened the bottle and filled a glass. As she raised it to her lips, Damien's scent filled her nostrils. She set the flute down, went to the bathroom, and turned on the spigot. While the bath filled, she tore her clothes off. Only after thoroughly soaping her body and brushing her teeth did she feel clean enough to deserve the wine.

She sat for a while gazing out the window. Below her, the marketplace was quiet. A single fisherman worked on his nets by the light of a kerosene lamp. He whistled a sea chanty she recognized. *Papa used to sing me to sleep with that one.* What was it called? "Blow the Man Down." She began to sing along—

Come all ye young fellows that follows the sea
To me, way hey, blow the man down
Now please pay attention and listen to me
Give me some time to blow the man down
I'm a deep water sailor just come from Hong Kong
You give me some whiskey, I'll sing you a song
To me, way hey, blow the man down.

She wondered what tomorrow would bring. Damien still had feelings for her—that was obvious. *It could work in my favor. If I can string him along, he might reveal more of his plans.* Although they hardly seemed reticent about wanting to remake Paraiso into another Cuba. How could Armand combat their mindset? How could he prove to the people that he—not Jakome—had the island's best interests at heart?

She finished off the champagne and crawled under

the covers. Inigo's outraged face made an unwelcome appearance. *I've got to explain to them, but if I contact Edrigu I'll blow my cover.* She drifted off to sleep.

The dream was short and dramatic. Unblinking feline eyes—black, but with flecks of greenish light—watched her from the jungle. A snarl curled the cat's lips, leaving the fangs exposed. She felt rather than saw it crouch. As it sprang she sat bolt upright. "No!"

Armand, his eyes glittering in the candlelight, sat at the end of the bed. His mouth was set in a thin line. "You're awake."

Lacey fell back against the pillow. "I am *now*. How did you get in here?"

"The same way your boyfriend did—bribed the ineffable Mr. Pusey. At this rate, he may suspect you're doing one-night stands." He didn't laugh.

"My boyfriend—what are you talking about?"

"The infamous *éminence grise*—Damiano. Or is he not the only one?"

"Armand, you're being ridiculous."

Lacey tried to get up, but Armand held the blanket down, pinning her. His face inches from hers, he ground out, "Am I?"

"Let me go!" She pushed him off, swung her legs out, and fell off the bed. He made no move to help her. She stood up. The nightgown had bunched up as it always did around her waist, and she quickly pulled it down, but not before she saw an odd mixture of frustration, hurt, and lust blow across Armand's features. "I can explain."

"Do."

Lacey wished she'd left a little of the champagne. Alcohol would steel her nerves. "Damiano is...is my ex-husband."

Armand's jaw dropped, which gave Lacey some slight satisfaction. "Your husband?"

"Ex. Father to Crispin. Real stinker."

Armand did not seem pacified. "And yet you kissed him."

"I didn't kiss him. He kissed me." She attempted to sit next to him, but he stood and moved to a chair. "I swear I didn't know until yesterday that he was even here. When I saw him on the balcony with Jakome, I tried to lose myself in the crowd, but he recognized me. He insisted I go to the castle and meet Jakome. Armand, they're crazy—both of them."

"Don't I know it." His face softened slightly. "Did he tell you how he came to be my brother's advisor?"

"They met at Princeton. Damien's a lecturer there, although I'll bet it's short-term."

"Damien?"

"Damiano. Damien's his real name. Damien Wynn."

"Ah, that explains why I couldn't find him in the faculty directory."

"I have no idea why he's using this silly alias. Armand"—she put a hand on his arm and this time he let it stay there—"Damien—Damiano—is a true fanatic. You should have heard him go on and on about radically transforming Paraiso, redistributing land and wealth, and centralizing control in the grand duke's hands. It's bizarre and terrifying."

He nodded. "You've seen Paraiso—imposing his expansive plans on this tiny island smacks of demented folly. Hell, it would be funny if they weren't in charge, wouldn't it? Now you see what Edrigu and I have been fighting."

Lacey took a sip of water. "I don't think Jakome is wicked, but he's totally mesmerized by Damien and his rhetoric. For that matter, I don't think Damien is evil—"

Armand shook off her hand. "Lacey—"

"—but he's not a nice man. I hate him. I do." A little lame, but it had the advantage of being the truth.

He wasn't mollified. "Why did you kiss him then?"

"For the last time, I didn't kiss him."

Armand's face showed no sign of believing her. "Well, evidently he wants you back. I can't have that."

"Oh, really?"

Her sarcasm fell on deaf ears. "Really." He gazed out the window, distracted. "I'm beginning to think Edrigu is right—I should kill him."

"What!"

"It may be the only way." Armand began to pace. "We'll lay a trap. You—you go back to Florida." He nodded to himself and continued to pace, muttering under his breath.

Oh great, just what I need, another nut job. "How about if I stay here for a bit, continue to play along with them? I can still be your inside man—even more so now that I have their ear. I could beg for mercy for Maitea."

"Absolutely not."

She paid no attention to him. "Inigo can be our go-between. We'll set up a system to get messages to you. When I hear he's considering a new regulation or reorganization, I'll pass it along and you can leak it to the news media and the public. You might be able to build enough opposition to stymie his plans." She paused for breath but not long enough to let him get a word in. "For some reason, Traficant didn't blab about me, so right now, they have no clue that I know any of you. It's perfect. I'd be in no danger."

Armand stopped. "You're right," he huffed, "but only because your boyfriend will protect you. He may even think you'll be safest in his bed." His eyebrows waggled like a spider on a hot plate.

Sensing an opening, Lacey pressed on. "I can handle Damien. Don't worry—I'll keep him at arm's length with one finger."

"Now there's a mixed metaphor."

"Nonetheless." Lacey let her lower lip tremble only slightly and batted moist eyes at him.

The tic in Armand's cheek subsided, and his mouth relaxed. "I don't know. The thought of that monster's hot breath on you makes my blood boil." He gazed at her speculatively. "I don't deny it would help to have an ally inside the enemy camp." When Lacey threw her arms around his neck, he grimaced. "But I want Inigo watching you at all times. Maybe he can recruit a friend so you're observed round the clock."

She kissed him. His arms went slowly around her. He touched his forehead to her lips. "I can't ever say no to you, can I?"

Lacey began to unbutton his shirt. "I hope not." She unbuckled his belt.

"You realize you're making love to a wanted man?"

She slipped a hand under the waistband of his shorts. "I sure do. Want you."

"I didn't mean that. I meant—"

"Shhh. I know."

The cool, gossamer-light material of her silk gown did nothing to diminish the heat rising from her skin, so she drew it slowly over her head. Armand took it from her and tossed it on the floor. Lacey knelt before him and drew out his penis. As she stroked, it grew stiff and long, pulsing in her hand. She kissed the tiny hole where a drop of fluid hung, then in one swift movement took the entire cock in her mouth. Armand gasped and steadied himself on the bed. Lacey's tongue swirled around the pole, licking in a spiral motion until she reached the tip again, then sucked hard on the head.

He ran his fingers through her hair, scrunching it as he raised his hips to get closer to her lips. When he began to moan, she let go and crawled up his body. He reached up and grabbed her ass, bringing the bursting flesh closer. She held still, anticipating the first touch of his tongue. *There.* But instead of taking her into his mouth, he started tickling the sensitive labia, nipping and lapping. She tried to sit on his mouth, but he held her just out of reach and proceeded to drive her into a frenzy of desire. "Please, baby! I want it now!"

In response, Armand pushed her on her side, then flipped her on her stomach. He lifted her hips so her ass just grazed his face, then spread her knees. She felt wide open and vulnerable to whatever he planned to do. And ready to submit to whatever he planned. Time slowed, then sped up as he began manipulating parts of her body in new and hitherto unprecedented sensations. "Oh my God, Armand!"

"Shhh—quiet!" he commanded. She stuck a fist in her mouth to stop the joyous yelp of ecstasy, and they crested together.

The moon grazed the horizon when Armand rose.

"I'd better go. Remember, you're not the only one who wants me."

Lacey went to the door and listened for signs of life in the hallway. "It seems quiet. Be careful. And send Inigo to me as soon as you can."

"I will. See if you can find where they're keeping Maitea."

"She's in the dungeon along with the bishop and the judge."

"Talk about archaic."

"Oh no. Damien says the cells are state-of-the-art."

Armand stared at her. "Excuse me?"

"I mean…er…"

"That does it. You're getting out of here."

"No, wait! I may be able to persuade Damien to show them to me. I can…what's that expression? Case the joint? If we find the prisoners, maybe we can spring them."

Her lover rolled his eyes. "You're as bad as Edrigu. I will not fight lawlessness with lawlessness."

"Well, at least I can visit them—make sure they're all right. If they're not—"

"If they've been mistreated"—Armand's face went rigid—"I will rethink my position." He checked the hall again. "I must take my leave." He kissed her cheeks, her palms, and her lips, and sprinted down the stairs.

Lacey went to the window, but Armand must have used a secret entrance for she saw no one in the street. As she turned back toward the room, a movement caught her eye. She looked down. A shadow detached itself from the bushes by the hotel door. As it passed under the streetlight, she glimpsed a familiar face.

Traficant.

****

The Bentley pawed at the curb when Lacey returned from breakfast. Damien sat in the back seat. "Come on, I'm taking you on a tour of the island."

The refusal formed on her lips, but she stopped in time. *Stick to the plan. You can fend him off easily.* She checked the impassive face of the chauffeur. *Besides, the driver will put a damper on any advances from Damien.* "Give me a moment to get my things."

The maid had already made up the room when she reached it. She headed toward the bathroom but a hand snaked out from under the bed and grabbed her ankle. "What the hell?" She fell back on the mattress.

"Ouch!" Inigo's head emerged. "Did you hab to land so heabily?"

"Inigo! How did you get in?"

The boy crawled out and stood up, massaging his nose. "I worked here one summer as a busboy. I know this hotel like the back of my hand. Also, Molly the scullery maid likes me."

"I see. So Arm—Prince Armand explained?"

"I am to watch over you and protect you with my life from all who would do you injury. Especially if it's Sir Damiano."

And you will too, won't you? "More important, you're to ferry messages back to the first secretary and Prince Armand when I have information."

"Yes, yes. Walter will do that. He will come to the kitchen door of the hotel when you give the signal and follow your instructions. Me, I shall protect you."

"Do I know Walter?"

Inigo gave a low whistle. A boy of about ten slunk out of the bathroom and stood staring at the floor.

"Walter! Stand up straight! Shoulders back! Now look your new mistress in the eye, and tell her your name."

The child straightened manfully and whispered, "Walter Umea Potter Knaap. Ma'am."

Lacey resisted the urge to dub him Sir Walter and said formally, "I am delighted to meet you and welcome you into my service." The boy remained standing, ramrod straight, knees locked, until she relented. "At ease, Walter." He let out a puff of air and sagged. Lacey turned to Inigo. "You mentioned a signal. What is it?"

For the first time, Inigo seemed rattled but soon rallied. "I…uh…can you whistle?"

"You mean, can I put my lips together and blow?"

"Pardon me?"

I guess he's too young for Bogart and Bacall. "Yes, I can."

Inigo braced himself, elbows out, and let out six descending notes. He squinted at her. "Can you do that?"

Lacey reproduced the melody. "How'd I do?"

Inigo pursed his lips as though contemplating upping the ante, then seemed to reconsider. "Okay, when you have need of Walter, whistle that tune. He'll come to the kitchen door."

"All right." The two boys faced her like soldiers ready for inspection. Lacey wondered what else she was supposed to do. Finally, she said, "I have to get ready. Mister—Sir—Damiano is waiting for me downstairs."

"Oh."

"Oh." After a minute, Inigo got the message and, pulling Walter behind him, left. Lacey picked up her purse and went to meet Damien.

"What took you so long?"

Lacey didn't think the question required an answer. "Where are you taking me?"

"I'm going to give you the seaside tour of the island." Damien settled back. "Dries, take us to the boat."

The car started up and drove down a narrow cobblestone street to a small landing. Damien handed Lacey into a dinghy and a sailor rowed them out to a large cabin cruiser. As they crossed the gangplank to the main deck, she admired the polished mahogany rails and bright brass trim. "Is this the ducal yacht?"

"Oh no—that's much grander. Jakome gave me this little number as a welcome gift. I named it Satisfaction, after the pirate Henry Morgan's flagship. Not bad for an assistant professor, eh?" Damien stroked the side lovingly. "Come on below for a minute."

They stepped down to a saloon that took up the entire stern. A man in a crisp white uniform wiped the gleaming bar. The captain entered. "Orders, sir?"

"We'll be sailing around the island, Stiles. Slowly." He touched Lacey's elbow. "Mimosa?"

Lacey didn't like the prurient spark in Damien's eye. "It's a little early for me, thanks. Can we go up on deck now?"

"What? Oh, sure." He picked up two glasses. Over his shoulder he called, "Seaman, bring up a pitcher of mimosas."

The boat pulled out of its slip, reversed, then headed east into the sun. As it neared the white caps that indicated the coral reef, it turned north, hugging the shoreline. Green squares bordered by low hedges marched up the hillside. "How much of Paraiso is farmed, Damien?"

He glanced at the verdant fields. "Not enough. See how broken up the fields are? If we cut down those hedges we could produce twice the sugarcane."

Lacey suspected the farmers would not react well to losing the plots of land their ancestors had worked so hard to cultivate. Off to starboard a fisherman pulled his nets in, his brown body covered in tattoos and not much else. He started to wave, but when he saw the name *Satisfaction* painted on the stern, he dropped his hand and went back to his nets. Lacey wondered just how unpopular Damien—or Jakome—was. "Damien? Why did you name the boat after a pirate ship?"

"Why indeed?" Damien waved at the blue lagoon. "Captain Henry Morgan was the most notorious buccaneer in the Caribbean in the late seventeenth century. He sacked and burned cities from Maracaibo to Panama over the course of eleven years. It's reported he used Paraiso as his base after 1665."

"That's right. I read about him in the brochure. The concierge claims he buried much of his loot here."

"At least that's part of island lore." He chuckled. "I did my share of digging for treasure when I first arrived. It didn't take long to figure out that taxes are a lot easier to collect and guarantee a more reliable revenue stream for our projects. Of course, if we received a bigger chunk of the profits from the dysprosium, the sky would be the limit."

It's as good a time as any to probe. "What about the company—Campbell, isn't it? How do they feel about being nationalized?"

Damien drew back. "Nationalized? Who said

anything about that? We're simply demanding our fair share of the money. Campbell's been sucking us dry all these years and leaving us with little more than subway fare. It's not fair. Not to mention the wholesale environmental destruction they've caused on the island. Look, I'll show you. We're coming up on the mine."

Nestled in a hollow valley just below the ridge that formed the island's backbone, Lacey saw a structure rather like an oil rig only much smaller. Surrounding the tower were lush gardens, in the midst of which she could just make out a long, low building painted green. "I don't see any destruction, Damien. I don't even see any smoke. How do they mine the dys...dys..."

"Dysprosium. They actually mine a mineral called bastnasite, which contains the dysprosium, then extract the element from the ore. The deposit is very thin but long. They siphon it out through a tube under a great deal of pressure."

"Sort of like a straw?"

"Yes. They claim the pressure has no effect, but we've recorded earthquakes since they began operations."

"Earthquakes! Have they done much damage?"

Damien reluctantly shook his head. "Not yet, but who knows when a big one will strike?"

Back on Longboat Key, Lacey had spent many nights researching Paraiso. It helped ease the longing. "I read an article in National Geographic that said this whole area is on a fault line and therefore subject to quakes. What makes you think Campbell's operation is causing them?"

In response, her companion hurled his glass on the deck, smashing it. Through gritted teeth Damien spat out, "I know about that article. Bunch of hooey. National Geographic sent some Mickey Mouse cub reporter. Spent his time at Winston's bar listening to the bozos from the National University of Colombia. Those guys don't know their ass from their elbow." A steward appeared and mopped up the mess, silently handing Damien a new flute. He poured more champagne into his glass. "I have an ecologist from Brown who's made a valid case that Campbell's drilling is responsible. I say that trumps some punk geologist."

Lacey thought it best not to argue. "So, you intend to shut the mine down?"

This turned out to be a mistake. Damien's eyes bulged, and his face went blotchy. "Stop badgering me, woman. What's wrong with you? I don't need to justify myself to some female who's just passing through. If we take over the mine, we'll do it right—not like those greedy bastard capitalists. So shut the fuck up." He threw his glass overboard and stalked down the deck.

Five minutes later, he returned, shamefaced. "Lacey, I'm sorry I blew up. Don't know what came over me. I guess seeing you again has started my male juices flowing—you always said I had too much testosterone for my own good. Forgive me?"

Considering she was stuck on a boat two miles from shore, Lacey felt it prudent to let it go. "No, no, I'm to blame. I shouldn't have asked so many questions."

That seemed to satisfy him, and he sent the steward down for more mimosas. They rounded the northern tip of the island as Damien finished off the second pitcher. He threw an unsteady arm around Lacey's shoulders and pointed. "There's Edrigu's castle. Poor sap. We had to put him under house arrest—although I don't think the old fart has much fight in him anymore. Jakome disagrees. And Jakome's in charge, isn't he?" He hiccupped.

Lacey tried to move away, but Damien's arm tightened around her. He pulled her closer, his lips nuzzling her neck. "Lacey. You know what you do to me…" He bent his head and began to nibble on the mound of her breast. Lacey tensed, trying not to recoil. With his temper, any show of repulsion would set him off. The staff had disappeared. She doubted they would help her anyhow.

His other hand had snaked down to her ass and begun to pinch it when she heard a ping. Damien ignored her jump and ripped the buttons off her bodice, pulling down the bra to expose her nipples. She tried to slip sideways, but he pressed her against the railing, his hard-on pulsing way too close to her groin. "Lacey, you're going to let me do this. No point in trying to get out of it like you always used to." His guttural whisper sent chills down her spine. When they'd been married Damien had had an insatiable desire for her, which only seemed to intensify the more she withdrew. She remembered one awful night when she had demurred, citing a headache. He'd thrown a fit, forcing her to service him in the backyard where the neighbors could hear her slurping and gurgling. She submitted that time, but she never let him touch her again.

The sun beat down on them as Damien ripped her underwear off and grabbed a fistful of pulsing red flesh. She heard another ping.

"What was that?"

"Wha—?"

"That sound. Like something ricocheting." In quick succession they heard two more pings.

Damien dropped to the deck, pulling Lacey with him. "Those are gunshots. What the hell's going on?" He rolled away from her. Lacey took advantage of his absence to tie the torn ends of her dress together and retrieve her underwear. Nothing happened for a few minutes. Damien sat up. All was quiet. He groused, "Must be hunters. The west side is pretty empty, and some of the villagers come over to shoot rabbits and squirrel. Goddamn rubes sure have lousy aim." He stood up. Crack! Lacey saw a black object lodged in the bulkhead a foot from Damien's head. He sprinted down the gangway yelling for the captain.

She peeped between the railings at the shore. The land appeared uninhabited—forests of Caribbean pine marched up the ridge. Here and there she saw puffs of smoke—from outdoor fires? Or chimneys? She looked west. Three islets floated a mile or so away, mangroves creating a lacework ring around them. *Wasn't Armand's hiding place on one of those? Could he have seen them on the boat? Could he have seen Damien mauling her? And shot at us? He could have killed me! Honest to God, Armand, this jealousy has got to stop.* Nevertheless, it seemed wiser to continue sitting on the deck. Damien did not reappear. *The bullets did some good at least.*

The boat turned around, picked up speed, and skimmed the waves, heading north. Damien must have ordered the captain to make for home as fast as possible. He didn't show his face again, and after a while Lacey went down to the saloon. The steward silently poured her a double rum neat, his eyes averted.

She weighed the idea of asking him if the crew would have come to her aid, but it seemed irrelevant at this point. Half an hour later, they berthed at the castle pier.

Damien said not a word as he helped her out of the cruiser and into the waiting limousine. He dropped her off at the hotel. "I have to follow up on whoever's out there shooting at people. I'll see you later."

"Er, yes. Thanks for the tour. I do have plans to see that old gentleman from the cruise this afternoon. Tomorrow would be better." She hoped she sounded upbeat.

"Yeah, okay."

She trudged down the hall to her room. The door stood slightly ajar. *Please God, don't let it be Armand—I couldn't deal with any more raging male hormones today.*

She pushed the door open. A man stood in the center of the room, holding a hat in one hand and a briefcase in the other. "Ms. Delahaye?"

"Y…yes."

"I'm Jonathan Dooley. I represent Campbell Metals LLC. Could I have a word with you?"

Chapter Twelve

Passion fruit is a woody vine with unusual, yet beautiful flowers. It thrives in humid tropical lowlands. Ripening in the fall, the round fruit about the size of a plum is either golden or dark purple.

Passion Fruit Jelly

5 lbs. passion fruit

2 oz. water

Halve the fruits and scoop out centers. In a blender, quick pulse for a couple of seconds. Strain the juice. Repeat procedure 2-3 times, thinning with water if necessary, until juice is clear.

2 cups juice

1 3/4 cups water

7 1/2 cups sugar

6 oz. (2 packets) liquid pectin

Combine juice, water, and sugar in a large pot. Bring to a full, rolling boil over high heat, stirring constantly. Add pectin. Remove from the heat and continue with standard procedure described in Chapter One.

****

Remembering just a minute too late that letting your mouth hang open is unladylike, Lacey gestured at a chair. "Could you give me a minute?"

"Certainly."

Lacey ran into the bathroom and retrieved a light

shift from a hook. She dragged her torn dress over her head, threw on the new one, and returned to the bedroom. Sitting down on the bed, she asked brightly, "What can I do for you...Mr. Dooley, is it?"

Dooley remained standing but laid his briefcase on the desk and opened it. "As I said, I represent Campbell Metals, which holds the subsurface mineral rights for dysprosium on Paraiso."

"All of Paraiso?"

"You mean all eight square miles of it?" He made a little chirping sound, almost as though she'd told a good joke. "I think so. Just a minute." He checked a document, then began to scrabble through the paper, reading what appeared to be rows of figures. He looked up, his face ashen. "I stand corrected. We control six square miles. A tiny portion seems to have remained in Montegue hands all these years. Interesting." He stared at his files, lost in thought.

Lacey studied him. If asked, she would have described him as a cross between Polonius and Millard Fillmore—in other words, stodgy, a bit dull, and better with numbers than people. His rather worn suit had been pressed with care—she guessed by an equally stodgy wife—and he wore his mousy hair cut short. Faded blue eyes and a weak chin rounded out the impression of a life based on tedium. Still, he exuded a kindly aura. "I'm sorry, but again, why are you here?"

He emerged from his preoccupation. "Forgive me. Let me just make a note about those two acres, and I'll be right with you." He jotted some words down, folded the paper and slipped it into his briefcase. "As I said, my name is Jonathan Dooley, and I'm here at the behest of our CEO, Gerald Pandanus. If I may provide a little background?"

Lacey nodded.

"When Campbell Metals discovered a commercially viable source of dysprosium on this island in 1952, we signed a contract with the reigning grand duke, which provides for the right to extract and sell the metal in exchange for an annual distribution to every adult citizen of Paraiso of eighteen percent of the profits. Up to now this has proved a satisfactory arrangement for all."

"Yes?"

"Recent developments have threatened our very positive relationship."

How long is this going to take? "Yes?"

"Before I go any further, we have been informed that you are acquainted with Prince Armand, second son of the Grand Duke Xavier. Mr. Pandanus would like you to confirm that."

Lacey thought swiftly. She was supposed to be incognito. The fewer people that knew of her business the better. On the other hand, if Jakome planned to appropriate their mine, Campbell would hardly be on good terms with him. She decided to hedge. "I've heard of him. I'm on vacation visiting Paraiso. There's been talk in the town about a Prince Armand, but I understand he's not in the capital at present."

Dooley's eyes glazed over in what he obviously thought was an inscrutable stare. "We have reason to believe he is currently in hiding, possibly to avoid arrest. On Prince Jakome's orders, the chief justice, together with the bishop of the island, is already in custody, and First Secretary Proctor is confined to his castle."

Proctor? Oh, yes, Edrigu. I'll never keep all these names straight. "And what does this have to do with me?"

"Ms. Delahaye, we know you have some means of communication with Prince Armand. We need his help. Our source tells us Prince Jakome intends to take over our facilities. This would not, to put it mildly, be a welcome move as far as we are concerned."

"Yes, yes. I understand." *Get on with it, man.*

He held up a hand as though he read her thoughts but had no intention of complying with them. "It would also be devastating to this economy. Campbell and Paraiso have had a long and mutually advantageous connection. While not a large company, we have the resources to fight a takeover attempt. However, that would involve closing down the mine and transferring assets out of the country. Unless we stop Jakome, the industry that employs two hundred people and provides a source of income to all seven thousand inhabitants will dry up. Now, will you help us contact Prince Armand?"

Finally. Lacey took a deep breath. "Yes."

"Excellent." Dooley shuffled the contents of his briefcase and pulled out a purple folder. "We'd like you to deliver this to him. It contains documentary evidence of Prince Jakome's game plan. He is conspiring to use tactics that are illegal both under Paraisan and international law to gain control of our company. Armand can use it to show the people of Paraiso just what Jakome is capable of."

"Where did you get this information?"

Dooley's face went blank. "That's better left confidential, Ms. Delahaye. Suffice it to say, it's from a source with access to confidential communications."

"I see." Lacey took the file from him. "What about Edrigu—I mean, the first secretary? And the bishop and judge? What about Maitea? Can you do anything to free them?"

"Maitea?"

"She is Jakome's second cousin, by tradition promised to Armand. Jakome arrested her as well."

He shook his head. "Unfortunately, no. Our contract with the government does not give us the right to interfere in internal Paraisan affairs. But"—he pointed at the folder—"if we can stop this takeover scheme, the rest of Jakome's plans might disintegrate as well." He closed the briefcase and picked up his hat. "Thank you, Ms. Delahaye. I'll be in touch."

He left, stumbling only once on the threshold. Lacey checked her watch—six o'clock. She'd better wait until dark to signal Walter. Meanwhile, where to hide the file? She finally slipped it into the hotel's guide to services and settled down to wait.

When the moon rose—a tiny sliver of light—she went to the window and whistled Inigo's tune. A slight form came around the corner of the building and lounged by the back door. She surveyed the area. *Now what? How am I supposed to reach him?* It occurred to Lacey that they hadn't really thought this through. Surely someone would consider a guest hovering around the rear of the hotel a trifle suspicious. Still, she had no choice. She took the elevator to the hotel lobby and ambled casually out the front door. The bellhop stood there.

He tipped his hat. "Evening, Miss. Can I get you a taxi?"

"No! I mean, no thanks, Apal. I just thought I'd take a walk around."

He seemed dubious. "It's not a very good idea for you to wander around alone in the dark, Miss. I'll get you a cab." And before she could protest he waved a car down and turned to her. "Now, where would you like to go? There's a lovely restaurant down by the pier." Without waiting for an answer, he gave the driver directions.

With a sigh, Lacey accepted. When they reached the restaurant, she paid and waited for the cab to leave, then sprinted back toward the hotel. Not till she rounded the corner did she remember the file. The one she'd left in her hotel room. Walter looked up. "I thought you needed me, miss. You whistled."

She panted, "I was delayed. I have something for Inigo to take to Prince Armand. It's upstairs. Can you wait here while I get it?"

The boy bobbed his head. "My mother will have supper ready soon. She'll be wondering where I am."

"How far is Inigo?"

"Not far. I will take it to him, then go home."

Perhaps relying on a ten-year-old boy to execute clandestine operations had its limits. *What if Walter gets in trouble and his mother grounds him?* "I'll be right back." She found her way through the empty kitchen and up the back stairs, retrieved the folder, and brought it back to Walter. She saw him off and trudged back upstairs.

An hour later, hunger drew her downstairs. As she walked into the lobby, she suddenly recalled that she had supposedly gone out at seven. What to do? She tapped the doorman on the shoulder. "Hi, I think I left

209

my hat at the restaurant. Could you call me a taxi?"

"No need for you to trouble, ma'am. I can send Apal for it."

Ack. "I…um…said I'd meet someone there. For a nightcap."

That seemed to satisfy him, and Lacey managed to devour a seviche of bass, red onion, and yellow chilis, washed down with a glass of dry Peruvian rosé, before heading back. She hoped Walter had left a message or some sign that he'd completed his task. Instead, she found Inigo waiting for her.

"Do you have the file?"

"Yes, but I cannot take it to Armand."

"Why not?"

"Because Damiano has the rats—I mean his retainers—out looking for whoever fired shots at you. They are swarming over the west side of the island."

"That's where Armand's secret place is?"

"Near there. Yes."

"Will they find it?"

"Only if I lead them to it. We'll have to wait until tomorrow."

Lacey put a hand on Inigo's shoulder. "You're a brave young man, Inigo. Do you think Armand fired those shots?" He wouldn't look at her. "Inigo, were you with him this afternoon?"

He nodded.

"Did you—he—see anything? Out on the water I mean?"

"We…saw Damiano's boat. We saw Damiano and…and…"

"And me." *Oh my God, he saw Damien ripping my clothes off!* "Inigo, I want you to know that nothing happened. I can take care of myself. Damien—I mean Damiano—is someone I've known a long time. Armand must trust me. He took a great chance by reacting this way. Now we all have to lie low until Damiano calms down."

"Yes, ma'am."

"You'll go to Armand tomorrow?"

"Yes."

"Good. Now get some sleep. I expect a report when you return."

Inigo slipped out the window, crawled down a gnarly sea grape tree to the ground, and disappeared into the darkness.

The telephone rang.

"I understand you're visiting our fair isle."

She dropped the receiver. *Traficant.*

****

Lacey made her way through the market crowds. The morning sun was hot, and she pulled off the light jacket she'd shrugged on before leaving the hotel. Following Ulisses' directions, she found a small cafe in a side street and passed through the main bar to a back room, murky with smoke. He sat alone at an empty rum barrel that served as a table, a fat, hand-rolled cigarette between his fingers. At his elbow lay a jigger of brown liquid.

"I'm here. What do you want?"

He peered at her over his superfluous sunglasses. "You look well, Lacey."

"What do you want?"

"Now, is that any way to treat an old friend? Especially one that has...so far...neglected to inform my boss that you have...er...visited Paraiso before?"

At this point Lacey's store of patience was exhausted. She spoke sharply. "You didn't tell anyone because it would be admitting a woman slipped out of your grasp. It must have been pretty humiliating to go back to your boat and find me gone. Hard on the old male ego, huh? Not to mention your reputation. What did you tell Jakome?"

He rose an inch out of his chair, his eyes closed to slits. "Be careful, Lacey. You're speaking to a man with influence." He sat back and took a long drag on the cigarette, stubbing it out on the barrel. "To be clear, I did not mention your existence because I doubted they'd be willing to pay much, if anything, for a total stranger. Besides, I had…other plans for you." He leered, his lips drawn back to show long, sharp canines. "As luck would have it, that SOB Damiano refused to let me make my ransom demand directly to Prince Jakome, so I didn't also have to explain how I'd come to lose your boyfriend." He raised his eyes to the ceiling. "However, with Armand on the loose, my situation became rather tenuous. Who knew when he might show up and finger me?"

"Why didn't you just leave Paraiso?"

"And go where? No, finding myself temporarily between gigs, I figured I could work my magic here as well as anywhere. As you may recall, I can be quite resourceful—even flexible—if faced with fluctuating conditions. When I found you and Armand gone, I merely went in a different direction. In fact, your escape saved me from the dreary task of…er…discarding you. Jakome knew nothing of my original intentions, thanks to Damiano, so I offered my services as bodyguard to His Highness Prince Jakome, heir to the ducal throne." He snapped his fingers. "It's been a pretty cushy—and lucrative—job so far."

He probably has no reason to "out" me then—it would alert Jakome to his missteps with the abduction, maybe jeopardize his new career. "Glad to hear it. So— I do hope I'm not boring you, but I repeat, what do you want?"

"Ah." He leaned forward. The smell of tobacco and fish clung to him, reminding her unpleasantly of their last encounter. "I need your help."

"Me?"

"Yes. Jakome and Damiano don't know who you are. They think you're simply a tourist. I happen to know that a man named Dooley visited you last night and gave you something."

Shit. "I don't know what you're talking about."

"Don't play dumb. Dooley works for Campbell Metals. They're concerned that Jakome is contemplating seizing the mine—which he's going to do, by the way. They want Armand to lead a revolt against Jakome before that happens. The file Dooley gave you contains some damning information about Jakome's activities. I want it."

"Why?"

"Because, dear lady, if Armand makes it public, Jakome and Damiano will know who provided it to Campbell. And all my neat little negotiations will go up in smoke."

"Negotiations?"

He tossed off the drink and stood. "Don't worry your gorgeous head about it. But—" He snapped his fingers. "FYI, I might be able to actually save the mine for the humble peasants of Paraiso, a result which would be iffy at best if that idiot Armand is allowed to screw things up." He tossed a coin on the barrel. "I didn't find it in your room so I know you've stashed it somewhere. Go get it and bring it to me. I'll wait for you in the hotel lobby."

"What if I don't have it?"

"You don't…what did you do with it?"

"It's gone. Armand has it."

"Damn. You were too quick for me. All right, I'll give you until tomorrow morning to retrieve the file. Armand can't have done much with it yet."

"Or what? You have nothing to threaten me with."

"Really?" His face twisted, looking more than ever like a hyena salivating over its kill. "Did I mention I know where your boyfriend's bolt-hole is?"

Gulp. Wait…"Then why not just go get the file yourself?"

Traficant spat. "Because that prick Damiano is having me followed. The last thing we want is to have him find Armand."

"Damiano?" Lacey realized she had an ace in the hole. *He doesn't know my relationship to Damien. Maybe I can play them off each other.* She said slowly, pretending to reluctantly give in, "If I were to do this— which I'm not saying I will or even that I can—how would I get it to you?"

"Don't worry, I'll find you." And with that, Traficant melted into the shadows. Lacey was alone.

She was unprepared for the bright sunshine when she emerged from the cafe and shielded her eyes, waiting until they adjusted to the light. After a minute, she walked down the alley into the market square. When she stopped to buy a drink at a juice stand, an old lady barred her way. She held up a basket of dark purple fruit. "Passion fruit for a passionate lady?" The mass of wrinkles that made up her face funneled into a pinched mouth, reminding Lacey of an elderly fox.

"No, thank you."

The woman followed her. "Two for one? Half-price special today!"

"No. Thank you, no."

"They make a lovely jelly. Very special. Fit for a prince."

Lacey halted and stared at her. The woman's face could not have been blander. She tried to lose the crone in the crowd, but when she'd made her way through the carts and kiosks to the hotel entrance, there she was. She held out the basket. "At least buy one for your sweetheart Inigo?"

"My what?" *Is she trying to tell me something?* Feeling in her pocket, Lacey produced a silver coin. "Here, take this. Is that enough?"

The woman accepted it, but instead of giving Lacey her purchase, she grabbed her hand and pulled her around the corner. She whispered urgently, "Miss Lacey, listen to me. Damiano knows about Inigo. The boy cannot help you anymore."

"Damiano! Oh my God, did he find the file?"

"No, Inigo passed it on." She patted her voluminous skirts and cackled. "There's something to be said for old age—young constables are reluctant to search a smelly, toothless old lady." She pinched Lacey's arm. "Much more fun to let their lecherous hands roam over beautiful, nubile young women."

Lacey eyed her. "Who are you?"

"I am Inigo's bam-bam, his grandmother, Arrosa. I

will be your…your—is the word 'liaison'?"

Lacey made a little whiffling sound, her mind in total flux. *This whole affair is becoming way too convoluted.* "You mean you have the file?"

The old lady held a finger to her lips. "Shhh. The object will reach its destination tonight."

I need time to think. "I…I have to go back to the hotel. Come to me later." She raised her voice. "Bring a basket of fruit to my room this afternoon, and I will pay you handsomely."

Inigo's grandmother bobbed and curtsied, giving cover for Lacey to reach the hotel. Mr. Pusey waited for her. "You have a message."

She took it upstairs to read. The note was handwritten on heavy orange stock.

Lacey, I regret that I have to break our date for tonight. I will be in conference with Jakome. We must decide how to deal with the outbreak of criminal activity in the western areas of the island. Yours, D.

Setting aside the fact that they had made no such date, Lacey wondered whether the "crime" referred to Armand's potshots or to Inigo. *Damien doesn't mention the boy, though, or an arrest.* How had Arrosa put it? That Damiano "knew about" Inigo. Hopefully, that only meant he knew Inigo worked for Jakome's brother, and not that he was acting as a messenger between Lacey and Armand.

She went to the window. The square bustled but in a rather subdued way. From below came the sound of someone whistling a familiar tune. *What is that? Oh, yes, the Paraisan national anthem.* It reminded her of Crispin. *I'm so glad he's not here. I've got enough to worry about.* She returned to the table and reread the note. *Damien must be referring to the shots fired on the boat. Suddenly it's an "outbreak of criminal activity."* Simply an excuse to crack down on citizens? Or a reflection of Damien's persecution complex? No matter what the motive, if Jakome ordered a sweep of the western shore, they might discover Armand's hideout.

*I can't hang around here twiddling my thumbs. I'm going with Arrosa. Armand needs me—if they find him, all alone...*Her heart lurched. Besides, Armand wasn't the only one who stood to lose. She had to keep Damien from learning about her connection to Traficant...and vice versa. Here in Port Huntington, their paths would undoubtedly cross sometime, so lingering in town could be perilous.

The remains of her breakfast still lay on the table. She swiped a finger through the crock of purple jelly. *Delicious.* She read the label and chuckled. *Whaddya know—passion fruit.* Without warning, a wave of homesickness washed over her. How she longed to be out in the woods gathering pigeon plums and mulberries, or watching the magnificent frigate birds soaring over Sarasota Bay, or listening to the screak of mangrove trees in the wind! Mangroves. Where this whole thing began. A tear spilled out. Do I wish I'd never met Armand? Images of brilliant black eyes, flecks of gold crackling in them, of a dollop of ebony hair falling across a tanned brow, of the light of love on a cherished face, rose before her. *Do I wish I'd never met Armand? No.*

She went through to the bathroom and turned on the tap. *On the other hand, why couldn't he have been a vacuum salesman or something?*

Chapter Thirteen

Then up spake the cook of our gallant ship,
And a red hot cookie was he
"Oh I care much more for my kettles and my pots,
Than I do for the bottom of the sea."
~*~
Oh, the ocean waves do roll, they roll
And the stormy winds they blow.
But we poor sailors go skipping to the top,
While the landlubbers lie down below, below, below,
And the landlubbers lie down below.
~*"The Mermaid," a traditional sailing song*
****

Arrosa seemed to have the same knack for appearing and disappearing as her grandson, for Lacey heard no sound and suddenly the old lady stood before her. This time she carried a basket of coral-colored roses. A rich, spicy scent filled the room. "I go tonight to Armand—do you have a message?"

Lacey plucked a rose from the basket and sniffed. "I'm going with you."

Arrosa did not protest as Inigo surely would have, but merely said, "I thought you would want to." She pulled a package from under her skirts. Lacey wondered just how much she could store between the layers. "Here."

Lacey opened it to find a neatly folded pile of dirty

clothes, looking as though they'd last been worn by a
truant child scrambling through Spanish bayonet. She
shook the skirt out, sending bits of mud and pebbles
flying. "This is certainly…er…becoming."

"You do not have the advantage of age to protect
you, my dear." Arrosa crooked her finger at Lacey.
"These will help. Now dress. I shall wait for you."

Lacey put on the rags. Arrosa had included a
shapeless felt hat, which she pulled down over her ears.
After a moment's thought, she took some makeup and
spread it thickly over her face. When she came out of
the bathroom, the old lady tittered. "A woman only an
infatuated prince could love. Come."

She led the way down the corridor and the
servants' stairs to the back door.

The sun sank behind the mountains with the
panache only a star 865,000 miles wide could have.
Ribbons of salmon and sapphire streamed across the
sky, dotted with puffs of white cloud. Five minutes
later, twilight fell. The two women set off up the alley
behind the hotel.

The path petered out halfway up the mountain. A
wasteland of prickly pear cactus, mother-in-law's
tongue, and spiky yucca faced them. Lacey dropped
onto a large stone, panting. Arrosa, unwinded, stood,
hands on hips. "You are not a country girl, I see."

"Oh, yeah?" *I'm not letting an old lady beat me up
the hill.* She dragged herself up and strode ahead of
Arrosa through the undergrowth. It was dark by the
time they reached the summit. Lacey scrambled up a
large outcrop to see most of the island spread out before
her, lit by the crescent moon. Two or three yellow
circles indicated villages among the dark green,

forested slopes. Behind them Port Huntington sparkled, an Emerald City in the wilds of Oz. Steel drum music drifted up to them. Lacey looked left, where Xavier's castle loomed. Only two lights split the darkness—one on the ground floor and one high up in a tower. She pointed. "Who's up there?"

Arrosa followed her finger. "That is the grand duke's chamber. They say he hasn't left it in months. There are villagers who believe his son is poisoning him so he can take over the throne."

"What do you believe?"

"That Xavier is an old and feeble man. That he has lost his power and his will to live. He is no good to us." She pointed to the other light. "We need youth and strength to combat the evil that lies down there. We need Prince Armand." She picked up her skirts. "Hurry."

They crossed the ridge and began to descend the western slope. Here and there Lacey made out the lights of farmhouses. After about two miles, they took a break. Arrosa handed her companion a flask and a small bag. Lacey gulped down a mouthful of water and opened the bag. It held a few mottled red and green oval fruits and a sandwich of tomatoes and grilled fish redolent of lime and salt. She tore into the sandwich, then picked up one of the fruits. "I've never seen this before—what is it?"

"Jujube." Arrosa sniffed one and took a nibble. "My favorite."

"I thought jujubes were candy. Who knew?" Lacey bit into it. The white flesh tasted like a very tart, crisp apple. She swallowed. "So, can you make jelly out of it?"

The old lady spat out a large seed. "Of course! You can make jam or jelly out of most of our fruits. This jujube is sometimes called a coolie plum. We also have June Plums, hog plums, cocoplums, Spanish plums, cherry plums—"

"Anything besides plums?"

"Oh yes. Atemoya, jackfruit, breadfruit, papaya, granadilla, starfruit…"

Thinking she was through, Lacey opened her mouth to speak, but the old lady was apparently only catching her breath. "And apples—we have custard apples and cashew apples, Jamaica apples, Chinese apples, mountain apples, Mammy apples—"

"Okay, okay, I get it—there are a gazillion kinds of fruit on Paraiso." *If I ever settle here, my work will definitely be cut out for me.*

When they finished the meal, Arrosa led the way down, but about half a mile from the coast, she made a sharp right. They cut through prickly hawthorn hedges and trudged across goat-infested fields for what seemed like forever. Lacey drew her thin shawl around her shoulders to ward off the chilly air. At last, Arrosa turned back toward the sea. They fought their way through a thicket of saw palmetto, tearing the remains of Lacey's skirt to ribbons.

Just before they emerged on the shore, Arrosa halted. She pulled a candle from her pocket, lit it and held it up for a second, then shielded it, then held it up for two more seconds before blowing it out.

Lacey heard one twig snap, and a man stood before them wearing nothing but a pair of ragged shorts. She recognized the fisherman who had turned his back on Damien's boat. Arrosa looked him up and down.

"Emilio?"

He nodded, then wheeled around and loped toward a dugout canoe that lay tied to a fallen coconut palm. The two women got in, and Emilio poled them out into the lagoon. When he reached the reef, he paddled alongside it until they came to a break in the solid wall of coral. Ahead Lacey could just make out a bridge rising a few feet above the water. The canoe went under it and turned to starboard and the open sea. Fifteen minutes later, they entered a tiny cove and landed on a beach. The man pulled them up, tied the canoe to a rock, and disappeared.

"Lacey?"

The whisper carried surprise, trepidation, joy, and puzzlement in equal amounts.

"Armand?"

For a long minute, Arrosa sat on the rock watching reunited love play out. She seemed to enjoy it almost as much as the two reconnecting did, but finally she barked, "Your Highness, it's time to move."

Armand extricated himself from Lacey's arms with many a kiss and a fondle. He took her hand and led the little group back up into the woods. Clumps of paurotis palms interspersed with red-flowered firebush and wild guava impeded their progress. Lacey unhooked her skirt from a root and asked, "Where are we, anyway?"

"Anna Cay. It's one of the three atolls, the Sister Cays, you saw off the northwestern shore."

"And the bridge we poled under. What does that lead to?"

"Ah, that's called Lovers' Bridge. It connects Paraiso with Santa Isabella, the third island of our archipelago. A beautiful spot, but a little too exposed."

He shook his head regretfully. "No one would think to look for me here on Anna Cay, since it's been used by the other islands as a garbage dump for decades."

Lacey sniffed. "Thank God. I thought the smell came from me."

At last they reached a clearing. In the center stood a structure covered with moss and branches. From a distance it would look like a shell mound or hammock, but a darker square indicated an opening. Armand ducked his head and entered, beckoning Lacey to follow. Inside he threw his arms out, fingers touching each wall. "Welcome to my humble abode."

What she saw was a far cry from both the Gothic, moldering splendor of the ducal palace and the cozy comfort of Edrigu's Castle Aresti. In one corner a dirty plate and a plastic tumbler indicated the remains of a meal, and in another crouched an unmade cot. Clothes, books, and tools lay scattered on the floor. "Humble indeed. What a mess!"

Armand frowned. "I wasn't expecting company, at least not of the female persuasion."

Arrosa came in, took one look, and started tidying up. Lacey caught muttered words—"men," "males," "pigs"—coupled with various pejorative terms. Armand and Lacey took the opportunity to neck. Finally, the old woman stopped. "You know about Inigo?"

Armand gave Lacey's chin a chuck. "No, what about him?"

"Damiano caught him on his way back from here. He's been combing the western hills looking for the man who shot at him."

Armand's lips curved up. "That was me."

Lacey glared at him. "What on earth possessed

you? If Damien hadn't been so terrified, he might have realized where the shots were coming from."

He flushed. "I'm not that stupid. He couldn't have placed them. I was out on the water fishing when I saw the boat. I saw him, Lacey. I saw him assault you, try to…try to…I guess I lost my head."

"I could have taken care of him myself, Armand. You put yourself at unnecessary risk."

They drew together. Arrosa coughed. "Right now we're worried about Inigo."

"Was the boy close enough to Anna Cay for Damiano to include the island in his search?"

"No, thank God, but he knows Inigo is loyal to you. He doesn't trust our family, including Koldo. He didn't arrest Inigo, but he set a man on his tail. I will have to fill in for now." She pulled the purple folder out from under her skirt.

He took it. "What's this?"

Lacey explained about Dooley and Campbell Metals. After some hesitation, she told Armand about her meeting with Traficant as well. "Traficant knew about the file. He wants me to bring it to him tomorrow."

"He does? Why?"

"I'm not sure, but he claims he's working on some deal that will save the mine."

"Santa Claus he's not. I'm not letting him have the documents until we know what he's up to."

"But he's expecting them! He's quite powerful now, Armand—not as powerful as Damien, but he can make a lot of trouble."

"Has he told Damien you were his hostage?"

"No, not yet. I'm not sure why." She picked up a

coconut. Armand had painted a face on it in charcoal. It reminded her of someone.

"Maybe he has other plans for you." Armand's fists clenched.

Where have I heard that before? "No—I...uh...don't think he's interested in me that way." *Let's hope Armand believes that—I can't have him wandering around popping off at every man who ogles me.* "More likely he thinks I could be a bargaining chip if things go wrong. At any rate, Damien still believes I'm merely a tourist who happened onto the island." She hefted the coconut.

Armand gently pried it from her hand. "Let's just put Wilson down, shall we? We don't want to crack his skull."

"Wilson?"

He winked. "A man needs company on a lonely desert island."

Lacey considered pursuing the topic, but only for a second. "Another thing. Traficant doesn't know about my relationship to Damien."

"Really? That's good. I think. There must be some way we can work their ignorance to our advantage. Meanwhile"—he slipped the papers out of the file—"I'll simply substitute some fake papers for the real ones. You can give the file to Traficant. If he asks, you have no idea what's in it."

"I don't know how well that'll work—he's not the trusting type."

"At least it will buy you time. I want to take a look at these. Then I'll get in touch with Dooley."

"You'll need me for that."

He touched her hair. "I wish you hadn't been

drawn into this struggle. Who knows how it will end? No, my love, I have Arrosa, and Koldo, and others. I won't need you. You must get away from the island. If Jakome discovers you're involved…I don't think he'll care what nationality you are."

A nasty little troll climbed down Lacey's throat and wrapped his warty fingers around her heart. *If Armand doesn't prevail…* She refused to consider any possible outcome except a positive one, even if it meant they couldn't be together. Armand had a duty to his country. If what saved Paraiso didn't turn out so hot for her, that was just too bad.

Arrosa tapped her shoulder. "It's time to leave."

Armand waved the old woman out and turned to Lacey. "Lacey, promise me you'll go back to Florida."

"I—"

"Please."

"I promise." He didn't need to know the unspoken rest of the sentence—*when this is over.*

"Good." He led the way outside. "I don't know when I'll see you again. If I succeed in convincing my brother of the error of his ways and we cleanse Paraiso of these vermin, I will come for you."

"Whether you succeed or not, Armand, you won't be able to."

He raised his eyebrows. "Able to what? Come for you? What are you talking about?"

"Armand, no matter what happens you're going to have your hands full. You're never going to change Jakome's mind. He's a fanatic—I know, I heard him. What did you call it? Cognitive dissonance? He'll never admit he's wrong even if his ideas devastate the island. The only viable solution is to attempt to depose him. In which case you'll either be in prison or on the throne."

His face hardened. "I beg to differ. Jakome is my brother. I know deep down he has a good heart. If only I can get him alone, I can convince him to repeal all these ridiculous regulations. He'll make a good grand duke." He touched the tips of his fingers to her lips. "Once Paraiso is back to normal, I'll be free." He kissed her lightly, but she saw no optimism in his eyes.

Arrosa clapped her hands. "Now, Lacey. We must get back to the city before dawn."

Lacey took one last, lingering look at Armand, and left.

Emilio waited by the canoe and took them across the lagoon. They reached the hotel just as the sky lightened in the east. Arrosa took her leave and Lacey slipped up to her room. She tore off the filthy garments, took a quick shower, and fell into bed. God being merciful, she was asleep before she had time to grieve.

****

"Do you have it?"

Lacey woke with a start. Traficant sat at the end of the bed. *People come and go so quickly here. And I'm getting awful sick of it.* "What?"

"The file. Do you have the file?"

"Y…yes. I do. Do you mind? I'd like to get dressed."

"In these?" He picked up the pile of filthy skirts she'd forgotten to throw out. "What on earth have you been doing? Wading through a mudslide?"

"Um…er…I took a walk last night along the waterfront. I…um…fell in." She took the rags from him and stuffed them in the wastebasket. "Pretty disgusting, aren't they? I'll have to shop for something new this morning."

He contemplated her, a speculative gleam in his eyes. "I don't have time to pick apart your sorry little alibi right now, but rest assured, I'll check it out. Give me the file."

Lacey pulled the purple folder out of her desk drawer. He began to open it. She held her breath. *What do I do if he sees we've tricked him?* They hadn't really considered the possibility that Traficant would open the file in front of Lacey. She opened her mouth.

Knock, knock. "Ms. Delahaye? Sir Damiano has arrived. He awaits you in the car."

Traficant grabbed her and snarled, "Damiano? What does he want with you?"

She shook him off. "He's taking me sightseeing. Not that it's any of your business."

"I'm sure the prince's comrade has better things to do than cart a female tourist around all day. How did you meet him? On a guided tour of the castle?"

"If you must know, he's an old acquaintance of mine. He saw me in the square the other day and offered to show me the island."

He gave her a hard stare. "I don't know what your game is, Lacey, but I'll deal with you later." He left, nearly knocking Mr. Pusey down as he stalked down the stairs.

A few minutes later Lacey ventured to the lobby. The Bentley stood out front. Damien leaned against the car reading a newspaper. She went out. "I wasn't aware we had a date, Damien."

"We don't—at least not right now. Jakome wants to see you. I think he's taken a fancy to you. Are you ready?"

I've had it with men bossing me around. "No, I'm not. Damien, I'm hungry and I didn't get much sleep last night. Why don't you come back this afternoon?"

He dropped the newspaper. "What?"

"I said, come back this afternoon."

"Uh, Lacey, that's not how we do things here. Did I mention Jakome is a prince and heir to the dukedom?"

Lacey stamped her foot. "Well, I'm not a Paraisan citizen. I'm a visitor, and I expect to be accommodated. Otherwise, I'll write a nasty review on TripAdvisor."

He raised his eyebrows and took his cell phone out. "Jakome? The lady is indisposed and requests the honor of waiting on you later today…Six o'clock? Dinner? I'm sure she'll be most flattered." He flipped the phone closed. "There. Happy?"

"Thank you." Lacey didn't want to give him a chance to invite her to eat, so she turned on her heel and marched back into the hotel. When she was sure he'd gone, she walked down to the square and found a restaurant.

After a nice brunch and a long nap, she was ready for the encounter with Prince Jakome.

Damien picked her up. He seemed in a sour mood so she kept quiet, grateful not to have to make small talk. She studied his profile, the one she'd fallen in love with so long ago. It reminded her of the ancient coins in the museum where she worked that summer. Her favorite was the silver Macedonian penny depicting the head of Alexander the Great. He had a long, regal neck, a strong Roman nose, and gentle curls framing a timorous face. Not at all the face of a conqueror, she had thought. But while in Alexander's case looks were deceiving, in Damien's they weren't. She'd soon discovered how weak and vacillating he was. He'd jump from one career to another, not always by design. If he came home with the same job he had when he left, she counted it a good day. A year into their marriage she became pregnant and hoped Damien would settle down, but there were complications and the doctor ordered her to bed for the last six weeks. This infuriated her husband, who was used to her waiting on him hand and foot. It didn't help that she now had an ironclad excuse not to sleep with him.

After Crispin was born, things went from bad to worse. Damien took to disappearing for days at a time. Lacey's mother helped out while Lacey tried to shore up her small jelly business. She remembered so well the summer day she brought the baby home from a doctor's appointment to see Damien sprawled on the couch, dead drunk, the television blaring. Under a pile of pizza crusts and half-eaten chicken nuggets, she found a pink slip of paper informing Damien Wynn of the termination of his employment.

She'd packed up Crispin and her cookbooks and fled to her mother. A week later, she returned to find he'd cleaned out both the house and their bank account. That was—*how old is Crispin?*—twenty-one years ago. She glanced at the man beside her. The years had been kind to him, which Lacey considered totally unfair. He still looked like Alexander the Great. *Only now he thinks* he *is Alexander.*

Damien growled, "Before we get to the castle, I have one question. What were you doing with Traficant this morning?"

"Traficant?" *Should I pretend not to understand? A look at Damien's face gave her the answer. Play dumb.*

"You mean Jakome's bodyguard?"

"I saw him leave the hotel."

"So?"

"So, don't get mixed up with that guy. I don't trust him. He's got something up his sleeve."

"Why don't you sack him?"

Damien grunted. "It's not that easy. For some reason, Jakome likes him. He keeps showering gifts and perks on him. I think he keeps him around just to annoy me."

"That seems awfully petty."

"I can't think of any other reason. Traficant's clearly not a believer. He's constantly putting our ideas down—argues they're impractical. Says he has a better way." He scratched the back of his neck, leaving a glistening red welt. "Obsolete capitalist notions like profit sharing or making Paraiso a tax haven. I tell you, Lacey, people like that should be lynched. The worst part is Jakome sometimes listens to him as though the son of a bitch's points are valid! It's enough to make a man puke." He lapsed into angry silence.

Damien sent the car away and marched into the castle four steps ahead of Lacey. Jakome sat in his usual chair in the dusty reception room. He rose when Lacey entered. She noted that this time he'd opted for the preppy look—a clean, white, button-down shirt and pressed khakis, finished off by loafers without socks. "Lacey, you look lovely this evening. I'm so glad you could make it." He raised a cocktail shaker and poured a clear liquid into a glass. "Martini?"

She took the glass and sat down in the chair a footman brought forward. Damien started to fill his glass, but Jakome said, "Damiano, Whitaker left some papers for you in your office. He needs them signed right away."

Damien opened his mouth, but Jakome said quickly, "Lacey, while Damiano is busy, why don't we take our drinks and go up to the battlements? We can see the sunset from the tower." He took her elbow and guided her out into the great hall, leaving a dumbfounded Damien behind.

The prince led her up a wide stairway to a landing. A small metal door slid open revealing an elevator that took them up to the castle walls. For a while they wandered the allure in silence, Lacey admiring the views of the sea and the city just north of them. When she looked down, however, she saw crumbling stone walls, a moss-covered keep, and a dry moat choked with brambles. On the verge of comparing Castle Zeruko to Edrigu's well-kept palace, she shut her mouth abruptly. *I'm not supposed to have been there.* "I…um…didn't expect to find a European-style castle on a Caribbean island."

"The Spaniards built the twin castles to protect the archipelago from pirates."

"The Spaniards?"

"Yes. Paraiso has had its share of conquerors and immigrants. When my English Puritan ancestors arrived in the early sixteen hundreds, they found only natives and Dutch traders. The Spanish took Saint Andrews and held Paraiso briefly. You've heard that Henry Morgan kept his fleet here for a while? That attracted sailors from all over the world, including freed African slaves—and women." Lacey could detect no hint of double meaning or amorous intent in his last word. *Thank God at least one man in this duchy doesn't want to ravish me.*

They rounded a corner and caught the full brunt of the sunset. Lacey gasped.

"Best view in the duchy, isn't it?" Jakome sipped his drink. "I brought you here for a reason, Lacey."

Uh oh, maybe I was wrong.

"I sense there's some history between you and Damiano. What is it?"

Lacey saw no reason to lie. "He is my ex-husband."

"Ah." He tapped a finger on the parapet. "And you've come to try to win him back?"

"Good heavens, no. Why would you think that?"

"I've seen the way he looks at you. He's still in love with you."

Lacey stifled a startled gasp. "I doubt that. We were only married for a couple of years over twenty years ago. We parted under less than civil circumstances."

"You're not pretending you didn't know he was here? That you just happened to book a vacation on Paraiso?"

"Small world, isn't it?" She said it lightly, but she could see the disbelief in his eyes. *Funny, when I tell the truth I get in more trouble than when I don't.*

Jakome put his hands on the battlement and gazed down at the desolation below. "Well, he's been distracted ever since you arrived. I can't get him to focus on our work. It's frustrating." He picked up his glass. "I don't have any patience for dalliance, so if you do have feelings for him, act on them and quickly. Understood?" He finished the drink.

Boy, oh, boy, how I'd love to act on my feelings—

but I don't think you'd appreciate it. "Believe me, Your Highness, I don't have any designs on Dam…Damiano. I'm sure once I leave, he'll be back to his old self."

Jakome didn't seem to be listening anymore. He mumbled something. She caught the name "Ulisses."

Now's my chance to find out what Traficant's been up to. "Who's that? Who are you talking about?"

"What? Oh, my new bodyguard, Ulisses Traficant. I'm well satisfied with his service so far."

"He was the third man on the balcony with you the other day?"

"You saw my speech?" He seemed gratified. "Yes. Ulisses showed up at the palace a couple of months ago. I think he spoke with Damiano. Whatever passed between them, he left in a hurry. When I saw him later that day in the boulevard, I had him brought to me. He told me he'd been caught by a band of pirates from this island and escaped after killing their leader. Belasco and his gang have been a scourge of the seaways around the western Caribbean for some time. I gave Ulisses a hero's welcome at the banquet that evening. He's been with me ever since."

My theory stands. He lies and gets the keys to the city. I tell the truth and…well, I don't. "So you made him your bodyguard?"

"He's much more than that. I trust him almost as much as I trust Damiano." A cunning look stole into his eyes. "It's very useful, having two faithful lieutenants at one's beck and call. Especially when they don't like each other."

"I think that's called triangulation," remarked Lacey absently. She was mesmerized by a volt of soaring vultures as they zeroed in on something lying on the ground. They circled lower and lower, ignoring the two people on the battlements, finally settling in a circle around the object. Lacey leaned over the rampart to get a better look. A cold, hard object nudged her in the small of her back, and she almost lost her balance.

Lacey whirled to find Jakome standing inches behind her. He gazed at her innocently. "You should be more careful. You almost fell." He pointed at the vultures. "And it's a long way down."

Hand at her throat, she could only goggle at him.

Jakome, perfectly composed, remarked, "Triangulation, I believe you said? Yes, it's an old political ploy. Works very well. As long as a fourth party doesn't insert herself into the delicate machinations."

Lacey abandoned any deference to his title. "Look, Jakome, I don't want anything to do with your 'machinations.' I'm here as a sightseer. That's all. I'll be leaving very soon."

Jakome took her glass and poured the contents out. One of the vultures below squawked and ruffled its feathers. "Yes, you will. Now, I believe my other guests are waiting. Shall we join them?"

He led her down a series of narrow, winding staircases and empty hallways to the keep. A butler met them. "Dinner is served, Your Highness."

They entered a large, high-ceilinged chamber. A carved mahogany table set for eleven ran the length of the room. Silver and crystal glimmered in the light from several candelabra. Lacey shivered as a chilly gust swept through the room, extinguishing most of the candles. The butler and a footman rushed forward with cigarette lighters to beat back the darkness but apparently didn't think to close the open windows. Jakome huffed petulantly and plopped in the master's chair with a noticeable thump. Damien sat down to his left, while Ulisses hovered behind him. The butler seated Lacey at Jakome's right. The eight other guests, none of whom looked very comfortable, followed suit.

On Lacey's other side, a paunchy man in a beautifully tailored suit he had managed to rumple and stain furtively slipped a syringe into his pocket. His pale gray eyes were clear, so she guessed the shot had contained insulin. Across from her and next to Damien sat an older woman in heavy makeup and a dinner dress that had seen better years. The woman nodded at Lacey as one gray curl escaped from under the pitch-black wig. *She looks familiar…and so does that necklace.* Nestled among the wrinkles on the lady's broad bosom lay an enormous heart-shaped sapphire on a thick gold chain. Teardrop pearls hung at intervals in a very baroque style. *Quite seventeenth century…wait, that's right—I saw it on the Spanish queen in the portrait upstairs.* Pirate booty perhaps?

The man on her right whispered, "Lady Bacon. The poor relative. Comes to every formal dinner and sneaks the rolls into her purse. Wears that stupid fake bauble everywhere, pretending Henry Morgan gave it to her ancestor for unspecified favors." He popped an olive in his mouth. "Gerald Pandanus, at your service." He did not offer her his hand but continued to whisper. "With her cousin in prison, I'm surprised Jakome's invited her."

"You mean Lady Maitea?" Lacey looked at Lady Bacon with renewed interest. *That's right—that's the woman I saw at Maitea's villa on Saint Andrews. I begin to see why the girl doesn't like her.*

"Yes, Jakome just had Lady Abbot arrested for conspiring to overthrow the grand duke. Ridiculous."

"Really?" A waiter slid plates of soup before them. The man fell to with enthusiasm, frustrating Lacey's hunger for more gossip.

Jakome kept the wine flowing, which helped wash down the vegan dishes. No butter for the rather spongy rolls. A wilted kale salad. Very wilted. The entree consisted of overcooked lentils and grilled tofu masquerading as a chicken breast. Lacey assumed the fruit and cheese platter would only contain fruit and was not disappointed. The prince called for more wine. Pandanus held up his glass. So did Lady Bacon, whose pale cheeks took on a pink flush as the evening wore on. Damien ate nothing. Traficant continued to stand behind Jakome's chair, his eyes roaming the room. Lacey half expected him to taste the food for the prince. As she pushed a lump of tasteless stuff from one side of her plate to the other, she thought, maybe that's where he draws the line.

Jakome's speech began to slur. He called out to Lacey, indicating her companion. "I see you've met Gerald Pandanus, CEO of Campbell Metals. Gerald, Miss Lacey is a visitor to our lovely land. I do hope you'll camouflage that monstrosity of a mine, so she doesn't go home with the impression that we're a smoke-spewing industrial polluter." He drained the last of his wine and held a silver chalice carved with the Montegue coat of arms out to the butler, who, a bit reluctantly, refilled it. When Pandanus did not respond, Jakome sniggered. "Just kidding, of course. Campbell Metals is a good corporate neighbor. Isn't that right,

Gerald?"

The CEO raised his glass. "To our continued partnership."

Jakome ignored him and turned to talk to Damien. Lacey gave Pandanus' elbow a nudge. "I met your assistant Dooley the other day."

He stopped, the bite of tofu pudding halfway to his mouth, and murmured, "That's not for public consumption, Ms. Delahaye." He finished chewing. "More wine?"

At the end of the meal, Jakome raised his goblet. "To a new Paraiso!" Glasses clinked, but no one seconded the toast.

The butler stepped forward. "Coffee and port will be served in the library."

Lady Bacon dropped a banana into her purse and took her leave. The other guests filtered out soon after. Traficant had vanished. Only Lacey, Pandanus, Damien, and Jakome remained. Lacey accepted a cup of coffee. She took one sip and realized why the other guests had declined. "Er, Your Highness, this is such an…an unusual taste. What is it?"

Jakome checked, his port halfway to his lips. "It's not coffee?"

Damien leaned forward, eyes bright. "No, it's made of something much healthier—dandelion roots. I had them imported from a little store in San Francisco. Excellent, isn't it? And gluten free!"

Lacey put the cup down and checked her watch. Only eight o'clock. *Time sure flies when you're hungry and nervous.* She rose. "Thank you for a lovely evening, Your Highness. I regret I must take my leave."

"So soon?" Jakome stifled a burp.

"Yes. I...I have an early flight tomorrow." *I might as well go—everyone else wants me out of here.*

The prince hid the spiteful smile behind his glass. "Ah, that's too bad. But then, you do have a life to return to, I presume. I hope you enjoyed your stay."

Damien, his eyes wide, sprang up. When Jakome glared at him, he settled back and remarked in a casual voice, "You didn't mention you were leaving so soon, Ms. Delahaye. It's a shame—we won't be able to finish the tour those hooligans so rudely interrupted."

Before Lacey could reply, Pandanus took her arm. "Allow me to escort you out, Ms. Delahaye."

She went willingly, hoping for a chance to talk about the file. He whispered, "I trust the package was delivered?"

"Yes."

"Good. I sense there's little time to lose."

As he shrugged on a raincoat, Traficant appeared. "Gerald."

"Ulisses."

Traficant took his arm and they moved off, speaking in low voices. Lacey, left to her own devices, decided to walk. Conspiracy permeated these mildewed castle walls, and she longed for some fresh night air.

Chapter Fourteen

The roselle, a member of the hibiscus family, is a medium-sized bush that flowers in the fall. The edible portion is the bright red calyx surrounding the flower. Harvest the calyces about ten days after the flowers have dropped, when they can be snapped off easily. Being very high in pectin, it makes a wonderful citrusy jelly.

Roselle Jelly

4 lbs. calyces

4-5 cups water

Wash calyces and remove the green seed pods. This will produce about ten cups of fruit.

Add calyces to water and cook over medium heat until reduced to a pulp, about twenty minutes. Strain through a jelly bag or two layers of cheesecloth. Boil juice fifteen minutes.

2 cups juice

2 cups sugar

Optional: juice of 1 lemon

Optional: 1 box powdered pectin

Add sugar and lemon juice to the roselle juice. Bring to a rolling boil and add pectin. Cook, stirring constantly, until it comes to a boil. Boil one minute, stirring constantly. (If not using pectin, cook mixture until it gels when dropped on a cold spoon.) Remove from heat. Continue with standard procedure described in Chapter One.

****

Lacey made her way back to the city, stopping for a beer and a Paraisan beef patty—"Extra meat, please." Hunger sated, she strolled around the port. A television blared from the interior of a bar. She drew near to listen. "Prince Jakome has the entire police force combing the capital for her. Both Stefan and Luis have been mustered up. The prince is said to be livid."

Lacey took a seat at the bar and signaled the bartender.

"Hello, young lady. Welcome to Winston's. Winston Cobus Willems Alsop at your service." The bartender pretended to leer.

"Nice to meet you, Winston Cobus Willems Alsop."

"Would you like something to drink?"

Lacey checked the blackboard. "You have real coffee, right? Not something made from a weed?"

The man winked at her. "We use Jamaican Blue Mountain beans for our coffee, but I can get you weed if you like."

"Oh, no! I didn't mean…er…What's going on?"

He swiveled around to look at the television. "It's Lady Maitea. She's escaped."

Lacey dropped her purse. "What?"

"She was freed sometime this evening, while the prince was at dinner. Apparently someone very small—"

A short, dark man with a heavy beard interjected, "We heard it was a monkey."

Another man yelled, "You always think it's a monkey, Ignacio. A monkey's not going to rescue a human. Doesn't make sense. They hate us. That wild troupe of green vervets over by Artizar? Can't hunt there at all anymore. They screech and throw their shit at you if you set foot in their territory."

"They only throw their shit at you, Ander." Raucous jeers filled the air.

"I tell you, it's biological. They know we're smarter than them, and it drives 'em nuts."

"Ah, you're a jackass, Ignacio."

The group fell to arguing about monkeys and the extent of their hostility to humans and Lacey slipped out. She was not surprised to find Arrosa in her hotel room. "I heard about Maitea."

"Yes, Inigo got her out of the castle. They're on their way to Anna Cay now."

An unexpected wave of jealousy flooded Lacey. "She and Armand will be alone on that island then."

The old woman shook a crooked finger at her. "There's no time for that now. Inigo was very stupid to do this. Maitea would have been better off in Jakome's dungeon than she will be with Armand."

Reality unhooked a heavy pendulum and let it slam into Lacey's sternum. "And Armand—this could lead Jakome directly to him."

"You see?"

Lacey slumped on the bed. "What can we do?"

"I for one will deal with Inigo. Maitea and Armand must fend for themselves. You—you should get out of Paraiso."

"I...I know." The pendulum swung back and cracked a rib. She couldn't breathe. *If I leave Paraiso, I'll never see Armand again.* Her mind raced. *Forget Jakome. Forget Arrosa and Edrigu. Forget Armand.* A reason—she needed a reason to stay. *Aha.* "I'm the only one who can handle Damiano. If I can coax him into…"

"Into what? Convincing Jakome to pardon Maitea? Welcoming Armand back into the fold?" Arrosa fretted, scrunching her skirts. Motes of dust and fabric cascaded to the floor. "The business is impossible. And you'll be sucked in deeper the longer you stay here." She threw her knobby hands in the air. "If only Grand Duke Xavier weren't bed-ridden. If only he would take charge."

Lacey shot up. "That's it! That's one thing I think I can arrange. I'll get Damien to take me to meet Xavier."

Arrosa lowered her arms. "Damien? Who is he?"

"He and Damiano are one and the same. He is my ex-husband."

The old woman's mouth opened and shut. "Your ex-husband? Does Armand know this?"

How many times do I have to explain all this? Lacey snapped impatiently, "Yes, yes." She couldn't miss the hurt in Arrosa's eyes, and taking a deep breath, forced herself to calm down. "Damien still loves me. I may have some influence with him."

Arrosa pursed her lips. "So you talk Damiano into introducing you to the grand duke. Then what? Armand tried and failed to persuade him of Jakome's wicked intentions."

"I won't need to persuade him. I'm sure Damien won't let me be alone with Xavier. All I have to do is mention Jakome's plans and ask Damien to elaborate on them. If I can get him really worked up, Xavier will see for himself how extreme Jakome's ideas are. Damien gets this frenzied look in his eye when he talks about a benevolent dictatorship and other nonsense. If Xavier were to hear him talk, he'd know all was not right in the duchy."

"What if he approves?"

"Approves?" Lacey gaped at the old woman. "How could anyone with any sense approve? These ideas have been tried and tried, and every time they've failed miserably. Surely the grand duke knows that."

"Not everyone agrees with you. There are always some who claim a system like Jakome's simply hasn't been executed properly or tried under optimum circumstances. I've seen this ideology rise and fall many times in my life. I no longer expect people to behave rationally. The duke loves his sons. He is on his deathbed. Mark my words" —she snapped her fingers— "he wouldn't repudiate his first-born even if it brought a swarm of locusts down on us."

"I still think it's worth a try."

"What about the reports that he's been poisoned?"

Lacey poured herself a glass of water. "I'll be able to tell when I see him, but I don't believe it. Jakome and Damien may be fanatics, but they're not murderers."

"We'll see." Arrosa went to the door. "Let me know if you succeed. I'm off to find the brat who got us into this mess."

****

For two days the streets teemed with uniformed policemen scouring every alley and interrogating every shop owner for information on Maitea. Lacey rightly guessed that Jakome and Damien would be too busy hunting the fugitive to care whether she actually left Paraiso or not, so she stayed at the hotel, keeping a low profile. She only broke cover to send a message to Damien.

By the evening of the third day, her cabin fever drove her back to Winston's bar. The bartender approached her. "Hello, miss. Welcome back."

"Hello, Winston. May I have a rum punch, please?" He went back to the bar, and Lacey found a table in a dark corner and sat, listening avidly to the general conversation.

"It's not hard to commandeer a boat and head to Saint Andrews. She's probably halfway to Florida by now."

Most heads in the bar nodded in agreement. Lacey thanked her lucky stars the patrons spoke mainly in English interlarded with only a few Paraisan phrases here and there.

The bearded man Lacey recognized as Ignacio turned to his companion. "You haven't heard from the Lady Maitea, have you, Gorko?"

Sniggers rippled through the crowd. A young man in overalls, his straw-like red hair roughened into a tangled nest, shook his head and spit out angrily, "Shut up, Ignacio."

Ignacio would not be deterred. "I heard she's in love with you, poor silly girl. And you thought you had a chance to marry up, didn't you?"

Gorko shook his fist at the man. "I told you to shut up. That's water under the Lovers' Bridge. Maitea's a traitor. Lord Jakome wouldn't have arrested her unless she were conspiring with Prince Armand to...to..."

"To what? The government hasn't leveled any concrete charges against her. What exactly is she accused of?"

"Ignacio's right." The speaker, a stout fellow in a red-stained apron, waved his mug, slopping beer on the unfortunate Gorko. "Jakome's wasting precious resources looking for her. How much of a danger can she be to him? She's his second cousin for crying out loud."

A wizened old man spoke up. "His second cousin, yes. Don't forget she is also second cousin to Prince Armand. Tradition has it she must marry Armand, and if that were to happen it would mean trouble for Jakome."

"Trouble for Prince Jakome?" Gorko seemed to have recovered his bravado. "Ha! His upstart little brother doesn't scare him. Besides, Jakome's the first born. He has the right to the throne—"

"You mean, after our gracious duke passes on."

Murmurs of "God save Xavier" wafted through the bar.

A new voice bellowed, "Jakome may be the first-born son of His Highness, the Grand Duke Xavier, but Prince Armand knows the soul of the people. He has their hearts. Only he can save us."

All eyes turned to the door where Koldo stood, his head nearly scraping the ceiling. Gorko swaggered toward him. "Save us from what, Koldo? What are you talking about?"

"You haven't heard? Gorko—and you, Ignacio—your precious Prince Jakome is going to take your farms away from you. He wants to force you to plant sugarcane, so he can collect the export revenue. And you, Ander, he plans to set prices for your meat. He's convinced all you merchants are gouging the poor."

"What, me?" The stout fellow spilled the rest of his

beer in Gorko's lap. "I'm barely making ends meet now. If he forces me to lower my prices, I'll go out of business."

Ignacio wailed, "I don't want to grow sugarcane. My hilly plot isn't suitable. Why can't I grow what I've always grown?"

Others chimed in, their voices rising. Just as the hubbub reached its peak, a loud report silenced the mob mid-howl. Traficant stood in the middle of the room, his revolver pointed skyward. A chip of paint fell from the smoking hole in the roof. He gestured with the gun at Koldo. "This man is telling lies. Your most magnanimous Prince Jakome has no such plans. Now go about your business. Scram!"

The bar emptied except for Koldo, Lacey, and Traficant. As Gorko tried to slink out, Traficant grabbed him by the scruff of his neck. "If I hear you've been harboring your girlfriend, Gorko, there will be hell to pay."

The farmer turned beet red. "I know nothing of Lady Maitea." He shook off Traficant's hand. "But if she came to me for help, I would turn her in to the police as I'm supposed to, not to some…some gringo."

So, he'd turn his own lover in and has the cheek to insult Traficant? Pitiful. Maitea had perhaps not chosen well.

Traficant merely grunted and shut the door after him. He turned to Koldo. "You, why shouldn't I have you arrested for slander?"

"It's not slander if it's true. And besides, we have a constitution here in Paraiso. Just like your American one, it gives me the right of free speech. On this, Gorko is correct." Koldo curled his lip. "You have no legal standing to arrest me." The big man towered over Traficant. His medals clinked, and his shiny black shoes tapped on the floor, as though at any minute he would launch himself at his adversary.

Lacey watched the old lion and the challenger. Finally, in a show of insouciance that fooled no one, Ulisses returned the gun to its holster. "Words are free, yes. Action engenders reaction. Be careful, old man." He sauntered out the door.

Koldo stood ramrod straight in the vacant room. "Miss Lacey, " he said without looking at her, "You must leave Paraiso, and quickly. The state of affairs is increasingly unpredictable here. Something is in the air."

All of a sudden, everyone wants to get rid of me. "Thank you for your concern, Koldo, but I have one more card to play."

Koldo didn't ask what she meant. Like son, like father, the Mathers seem to know when to pry and when not to. "I shall at least escort you back to your hotel."

Lacey consented. They walked back along the waterfront, quiet and peaceful now. Voices raised in song came from the upper stories, and the moon kept time, popping in and out from behind the clouds. The flags hanging from every rooftop fluttered in the soft autumn wind. In the lobby, Mr. Pusey approached her.

"You have a message, Ms. Delahaye." He handed her an envelope. She read it and climbed to her room. Arrosa sat on the bed.

"You arranged it?"

Lacey waved the note. "I'll see the duke tomorrow. Do you have any advice?"

"How can I give advice when I don't know what you expect to accomplish? Xavier slips in and out of consciousness. You might not be able to communicate with him at all."

"It may be our only hope, Arrosa."

The old woman clucked her tongue. "Then we are indeed in trouble." She went to the door. "Be careful, my dear. Armand will have my head if any harm comes to you."

As she left, Lacey closed the curtains. It would be a long day tomorrow, no matter what happened.

****

A horn beeped outside. She walked out to the Bentley and got in.

"I'm glad you decided to stay a little longer, Lacey." Damien tried to put a hand on her knee, but she crossed her legs just in time.

"I'm flying out tomorrow, Damien. It's been very…interesting, but I've done enough sightseeing. I have to get back to my business."

"And you want to meet Grand Duke Xavier."

"Yes. I know he's ill, and I won't stay long, but it would be so exciting to meet real nobility." She let loose a girlish giggle.

"Jakome's a noble."

"I know, but…a grand duke. How cool is that?"

Damien gave her an odd look. "I've never known you to be the groupie type."

Too much? Better dial it back. "You're right, but Crispin's always been fascinated with royalty. If I can tell him I met a grand duke…maybe take a snapshot of us—"

"Whoa, let's not take liberties. He may be an old

buffoon, but he is still the ruler of Paraiso. For now."

They rode in silence a few minutes. Lacey casually remarked, "Those rumors that Xavier's being poisoned are just rumors, right?"

Damien didn't respond for a minute. "Of course. Typical lies spread by the opposition. He's just an old man, Lacey. You'll see."

They reached the castle and climbed the stairs of the keep. A final set of stone steps led to a tower room. Damien knocked.

A woman's voice called, "Come in."

Lacey entered a large circular room, bright with fluorescent light. Two small windows faced south, away from the city and toward the open sea. Sleekly modern Swedish furniture filled most of the space, in striking contrast to the extraordinary Victorian walnut burl bed in the corner. Fluted bedposts supported a half-tester embellished with an ornate arched and pierced crest. Lacey thought she could make out the gryphon and three diamonds of the Montegues. Palm trees and galleons in relief adorned the headboard. An old man lay in the bed while a nurse took his pulse. Beside her stood a hospital cart filled with medicine bottles and beeping machines.

"Is he awake?" Damien asked the nurse.

"Yes. He's been expecting you." She piled some pillows behind Xavier and helped him sit up, then left.

Lacey approached the bed. Although pale and tired-looking, the grand duke had Armand's bright black eyes brimming with the same charm. He took Lacey's hand. "Hello, my dear." He looked over her shoulder at Damien. "Leave us."

Damien reddened and his lips thinned with

annoyance, but he obeyed. "As you wish, Your Highness."

Lacey watched him go with a sinking heart. Would her whole plan to alert the grand duke to the impending catastrophe fall apart? When she turned back, Xavier took hold of her other hand. "Now we can talk."

"Talk?" *Maybe he isn't as out of touch as everyone thinks.*

"Yes. I don't have much time. My strength is ebbing by the minute." He took a rattling breath. "I know you are not simply a tourist. Koldo informed me of Armand's abduction and of your connection to him. I have just learned that Edrigu is under house arrest, and that my son is in hiding. What I want to hear from you is why."

Lacey regarded him with concern. "You don't know what Prince Jakome's been up to?"

He shook his head. "He's told me of his ideas for reform in the duchy. I'm sure they are very progressive and wonderful, but I hear that the citizens are unhappy about them. Can you elucidate?"

"I'll try." Lacey told Xavier about Damien's and Jakome's policies, and of the rising backlash to them. "His latest threat is to nationalize the Campbell mine. Mr. Pandanus is taking it seriously enough that he's preparing to remove all his assets from Paraiso."

Xavier coughed and pointed at a cup near his bed. "Hand me the apple juice." Laccy gave it to him. He sucked noisily through the straw. "Appropriate the mine, eh? Jakome takes after his mother. She never could stand it that Campbell kept the major portion of their profits, even though they discovered the dysprosium and developed both the operation and the export distribution network. This rare earth element is very valuable on the global market, you know, and our share of the profits has provided our people with a very good income, but Amaia wanted more. I fear she filled her son's head with her greedy thoughts."

"Is she still alive?"

"Amaia? Oh no. She died when the boys were still teenagers. She raised both Jakome and Armand as her own."

"Wait—they weren't her own children?"

"Jakome is, but Armand…Armand's mother died in childbirth." He closed his eyes, remembering. "I loved Katerin with all my heart. God took her from me way too early."

Lacey tried to take this in. "So Armand and Jakome have different mothers?"

"Yes."

"I don't understand. If Jakome's the elder son, and his mother died when the boys were in their teens, how could…how could…" She raised her hands in helpless confusion. Did they allow bigamy in Paraiso?

Xavier took another sip and fell back on the pillows. One of the machines beeped loudly. The nurse came in and gave Xavier a pill. "Don't overdo it," she scolded.

"Go away, Dominica." When she'd gone, he beckoned Lacey to come close. He whispered, "It's time I told someone. Sit."

Lacey sat.

"Jakome is not my first-born son."

"What?" Lacey jumped up.

Xavier waved her back down. "Armand is ten months older."

"Armand! Then he's…he's…"

"Let me finish." He wiped a drop of spittle off his chin. "Armand's mother came from a farming family. As such, my father, the Grand Duke Bittor, refused to approve the match."

Lacey thought of Gorko and Maitea. *Customs die hard here.*

Xavier continued. "Madly in love, I would not comply with his wishes. Katerin and I were secretly married. When Father discovered our union, he banished us to Saint Andrews. A year later, she gave birth to Armand. He was healthy, but there were…were complications." His eyes glazed with ancient tears. After a minute, he resumed. "Soon after her death, I married Amaia, my father's original choice. She became pregnant with Jakome almost immediately, and he was born nine months later."

"Where was Armand?"

"My father wanted to put him up for adoption in Colombia, but Amaia persuaded him to relent, on the condition that Armand be proclaimed as her son. Her second son."

"But…but…how could she get away with that?"

"Remember, Katerin and I had been exiled to Saint Andrews. My father refused to let me come back to Paraiso, only giving in when she died and I agreed to marry Amaia. No one here knew of the baby or of my first marriage. We merely switched the boys' identities after a few months and no one ever knew. Amaia exacted a high price, but at least I could keep my son."

Lacey studied his face, lined by years of both sorrow and responsibility. "Armand doesn't know he's really the eldest?"

"No. That was part of the deal." He lay back on the pillows, his face ashen. "Now that both my father and Amaia are gone, I'm the only one who knows the truth."

"And me."

"Yes." He reached for her hand. "Miss Delahaye, I must make things right before I die."

Lacey heard again Arrosa's words of the evening before. "Xavier wouldn't repudiate his first-born even if he brought a swarm of locusts down on us." *How prophetic.* "What can I do?"

"You must bring Armand back so he can claim his rightful place."

She sputtered, "But he's in hiding! If he comes out in the open, Prince Jakome will imprison him."

He let her hand go and lay back, obviously exhausted. "I'm depending on you. You must find a way. Paraiso needs Armand."

Lacey stared at the old man, overwhelmed by the magnitude of his request. Exasperation slashed through the miasma of fear and her voice rose. "Why me? It's not fair. I'm not even a citizen. Why does it all have to depend on me? What if I just…just leave?" She stopped, panting.

Xavier said nothing, and Lacey slowly settled down. She knew the answers to her questions anyway. *I have no choice.* "Even if I tell Armand, how can I make him believe me? And how can he prove his birthright?"

He pointed at a small wooden chest, carved with pineapples and monkeys. "Bring it to me." When she did, he pulled a tiny key from under his mattress and opened it. He handed her an envelope. "In it is Armand's birth certificate, together with a confession signed by both me and Amaia, detailing the story I just told you."

She took it reluctantly and put it inside the notebook in her purse. "I will do my best."

"Of course you will." He smiled—the very same smile Armand used to ensnare her heart. "You love him."

Damien waited for her at the bottom of the stairs. "So now you've met an aristocrat. Just an old man, sick and senile, eh?"

Lacey had no intention of telling Damien what had transpired in the tower room. She pressed her purse to her side. *If he and Jakome believe Xavier is close to death, they'll leave him alone.* "He's very weak. The nurse said he won't last much longer."

"Let's hope she's right. As soon as he's gone and Jakome's proclaimed grand duke, we can get on with our work."

"How callous you are, Damien!"

"One man's life is hardly important, Lacey. Jakome and I—we intend to revolutionize the world. This is our stepping-stone. When countries see what we can do to bring social justice and equality here, they'll be clamoring to do the same thing."

Lacy reflected that in all those years he spent in school, Damien must have skipped history class entirely. Otherwise, he would have learned that his "experiment" had already been tried in big countries and small, in poor countries and rich, with identical results—a dispirited populace and crushing debt. *Everyone's equal, sure—equally poor.*

Damien led her down the steps to the waiting car. "Listen, why don't we get a bite to eat? I know a lovely place on the other side of the city—it's perched up on the ridge with a view to die for. How about it?"

Lacey's stomach chose that moment to gurgle. *Why not? There's no way I can take the papers to Armand until nightfall.* "Okay."

The place did indeed have a spectacular view. On the advice of the waiter, Damien ordered a Cipreses Vineyard 2011 sauvignon blanc. "First prize at the last Wines of Chile competition, you say? At that price, it had better be worth it," he grumbled.

Another waiter brought an iced tray, from which they chose trout and snapper, the fish so fresh the fins were still twitching.

"I swear that one looked at me, Damien."

"Was it a come-hither look?"

"More like a 'Take him! Not me!' look."

They sat at a table on the terrace and let the cool, sweetly scented breeze refresh them as they ate. The waiter cleared away the fish and brought out a bowl of fruit in a thick, syrupy glaze. "On the house."

Lacey sniffed. "What is it?"

"A compote of local fruits."

"I recognize the mango, but what are the other ones?"

He pointed. "Jackfruit, Barbados cherry, hog plum. In syrup made from roselle jelly. Lots of rum."

"Roselle? I make that at home."

Damien stuck a finger in the bowl and tasted. "*Mmm.* Tastes like lemon. What's roselle anyway?"

"It's in the hibiscus family. Sometimes called the Florida cranberry. I think they make Red Zinger tea out of it." She spooned some of the compote onto her plate.

The waiter watched her take a bite. "You like it?"

"Wonderful. Please ask the chef for the recipe." The man went off smiling, and Lacey pulled the bowl close and ate it all. As she scraped the last spoonful up, she caught Damien watching her. "Oh, gee. Did you want some?"

He took her hand and kissed the palm. "Your pleasure is sustenance enough."

Lacey was too full to stomp on his worn-out old line. The sun fell behind them, caressing their shoulders with a pink, fuzzy shawl of warmth as the temperature dropped. Lacey felt the stress trickle out. "It is nice here."

Damien moved his chair closer. "Do you think you could come for good?"

A shiver went up her spine. "Well, I don't know…"

He leaned across the table. "Lacey, I know I made a mess of things twenty years ago, and you were right to leave me, but I've changed." He lifted her chin and looked deeply into her eyes. "God, I've missed those eyes. Maybe that's why I love the Caribbean—it reminds me of you."

If it weren't for the wine she'd drunk—not to mention the abyss on the other side of the railing—Lacey would have stood up and walked out. As it was, she gently removed his clutching fingers from her thigh. "Damien, I don't think—"

"Wait, hear me out. Lacey, I never stopped loving you. I was a total wreck for the first year after you'd gone—drinking and vaulting from job to job."

Lacey opened her mouth to observe that he'd been doing that *before* he left her when he raised his voice, drowning her out. "Gradually I sobered up, though. I finished the doctorate, and the rest I've already told you." He broke off and poured himself more wine. Lacey held out her glass, but he waved it aside impatiently. "It's been marvelous working with Jakome—you don't know what it's like to be with a kindred spirit."

Lacey decided to let that one pass. She picked up the bottle and poured the rest of the wine into her glass. Oblivious, Damien continued his soliloquy. "There was always something missing, however. When I saw you in the crowd that day I knew what I missed. You."

Before she could stop him, he went down on one knee, held out a small velvet box, and opened it. The emerald shone bright in the mid-afternoon sun, its pillow of diamonds refracting the greens and blues of the stone. "The grand duke brought it back from Colombia—that's where the best emeralds come from. It belonged to Jakome's mother. Jakome gave it to me. I give it to you."

"Damien, I—"

The waiter came out in a rush. "Sir, Madam. Something terrible!" He burst into tears and ran back into the restaurant. Damien stood up and followed him. He quickly returned, his face taut. "Xavier is dead."

Chapter Fifteen

Then up spake the captain of our gallant ship
And a brave old skipper was he.
This lovely mermaid has warned me of our doom
We will sink to the bottom of the sea.
~*~
Oh the ocean waves do roll, they roll,
And the stormy winds do blow.
And we poor sailors go skippin' to the top,
While the landlubbers lie down below, below, below,
Oh, the landlubbers lie down below.
~*"The Mermaid," a traditional sailing song*
****

"Oh, my God—it must have happened right after I left him!" cried Lacey.

"We'd better go."

Damien paid the check, and they waited outside while the chauffeur brought the car around. When they reached the market square, they found it overflowing with people shouting and waving flags. Scattered among the semaphore, holiday, and pirate flags, Lacey noticed the Monteguc colors as well as the familiar yoke and cross of the grand duchy. As the Bentley nudged its way through the crowd, some split off to pound on the car, their faces distorted with fear and grief. Damien rolled the window down.

A man screamed in his face, "The grand duke is

dead! The grand duke is dead!"

Damien rolled the window up and barked a command at the chauffeur. "To the castle. Quick!"

Lacey saw her chance to shake him slipping away. "Damien, let me out. I want to go to my hotel. You have responsibilities. Jakome needs you."

She tried to open her door, but Damien clutched her arm. "No, Lacey, you've got to come with me. We're in for a rocky ride for a few days. I'll be at Jakome's side of course, but it's a sure bet Traficant will try to horn in. I don't trust him, Lacey. I need your help." Without warning, he pulled her to him and kissed her. "You can stay here with me, and we'll make a new world together." His eyes burned and a trickle of sweat coursed down his temple.

Terror gripped her. Not of him, but of the prospect of living without Armand. *Keep your head, Lacey.* She gulped. "I won't leave Paraiso yet, Damien, but you have things to do. Go." Before he could stop her, she jumped out, waving the chauffeur on. She watched the car roll steadily up Cromwell Boulevard toward the castle, then went into the hotel.

The concierge and all the staff were huddled in the lobby. The maids were weeping and wringing their hands. When he saw her, Mr. Pusey extracted himself from their clinging arms and came over. "Oh, Ms. Delahaye, terrible news! Our grand duke, our father, Xavier, has passed away."

"Yes, I just heard about it. I was with His Highness today. It is a great shock."

"You were? He was such a wonderful leader, so good to us. Ladies, did you hear? Ms. Delahaye was with the grand duke only moments before the end."

Oops. "No, no, Mr. Pusey. I went to see him this morning. He seemed weak, but very much alive."

The cook began to howl. "And now he's gone from us, in the twinkling of an eye." Lacey refrained from pointing out that Xavier was, after all, eighty-one. He'd been around for more than a twinkling.

"I'm going to my room." She went straight up and to her window. Opening the sash, she whistled the signal and waited. Minutes passed. Nothing. She whistled again. After a while, she lay down on the bed, only to leap up again. She still had the envelope in her purse. Where to hide it? She looked around. The room had been cleaned while she was gone, as it always was. *I can't leave it here.* She finally took it from her purse, folded it into a square, and slipped it into the book pocket of a library book she'd forgotten to return. Book and letter went back in her purse.

She returned to the window, but no one appeared from the shadows. *What should I do? Maybe Arrosa can't get near the hotel—I'd better go see what's going on.*

Immersed in mourning, people swayed and sang tuneless dirges in the square while passing around jugs of rum. One bear of a man strode to the center of the square and shook his fist at them. "You're all fools! We haven't been abandoned! We have a leader. Long live Jakome, the new grand duke!" Only one other echoed his words. Lacey wasn't surprised to see it was Gorko. A tomato came out of nowhere and smashed at the man's feet. He lunged toward a knot of boys. Lacey watched them swarm around him, grunts and curses rising from the melee. At length, the man shot out, blood pouring from his nose, and streaked up the street.

Gorko ran after him.

Lacey skirted the square and reached the bar. Winston threw his arms around her and moaned, "Our father's gone. What will we do?"

"I don't know, Winston." Lacey ordered tea and sat just out of reach of the chaos. She had seen no policemen and no sign of any government personnel. Were they still out searching for Maitea? Or for Armand? Or simply occupied with the assuredly complex arrangements for a ducal funeral? Once Jakome's supporters left, the noise level dropped, and after a while she made her way back to the hotel. Still no sign of Arrosa. No one stood at the concierge's desk. Even Apal, the bell hop, had disappeared. *Probably out marking Xavier's passing with all the rest.*

She took the elevator up. Rummaging around in her purse for her room key, her elbow hit the door. It swung open. Lacey took a step and tripped over something. "What the?" Looking down, she saw the Gideon Bible from her night table, lying open on the floor as if it had been hurled down. She raised her eyes to a room in total disarray. Drawers were pulled out, her clothes lay in heaps on the floor, even her toiletry bag had been emptied onto the table. She checked her jewelry case. The few gold chains and her diamond studs were still there. Not a robbery then. Could they have been looking for the purple file? Or... No. The intruder could only have been after one thing—the birth certificate. Thank God she'd taken it with her. She felt for the book in her purse. *Might as well keep it there.*

She straightened the sheets and sat down on the bed to think. Who would know about the papers? And who would want them? It had to be Jakome. Had he always known, or did Xavier tell him on his deathbed? Either way, he'd find the birth certificate gone from the monkey box. He knew Lacey had visited Xavier in the morning and probably put two and two together. *But it's broad daylight. How could he walk out of the castle and waltz in here without someone noticing?* Especially in the midst of all the uproar? He must have sent someone, but that would mean he'd have to take that person into his confidence. Someone whose career was inextricably linked to Jakome's. Damien? Or Traficant? Would Damien have had time to get down here, ransack the room, and leave while she was out? Possibly, but how would he know she wouldn't be here? For that matter, how would Jakome know? Answer—he probably didn't care. Whoever it was, she'd better avoid them both. Damien's love would likely take a back seat to political survival. *And where the hell is Arrosa?*

She saw no sign of the old woman for the next two days. The castle was a hive of activity—merchants, bakers, and green grocers trundling in and out day and night as preparations got underway for the state funeral. Excitement filled the air, tempered with sorrow. Paraisan custom dictated a full week of mourning, which consisted of heavy drinking, singing, and of course, flag-waving. Lacey found herself at loose ends. Affairs of state, including setting the stage for Jakome's ascension, kept Damien busy. The latter operation had to be very low key, he told Lacey in a quick phone call. "We don't want the celebration to overshadow the lamentation, you know? Not good politics."

Not very nice either. As twilight fell, she sat on her balcony, musing. *Should I leave Paraiso?* She didn't

263

want to be subject to any searches, nor to give Damien another opportunity to propose, so a speedy departure made sense. On the other hand, she had to get the birth certificate to Armand somehow, and Arrosa was nowhere to be found. *There's nothing for it but to take it myself. Then I'll go home.* She rose and set about packing her things.

At nightfall, she took the back stairs. She hoped to run into Arrosa, but the alley was deserted. Behind her in the square people still sang, although the voices wavered a bit more now, and the lyrics had turned maudlin. She left her suitcase in the garden shed and hitched her small backpack over her shoulder. No one stopped her as she walked up the alley to the country road that led over the hills. She hiked through a band of Australian pine and bracken fern, the sounds of the city fading behind her. Higher up she came to the field of prickly pear cactus she and Arrosa had crossed. Stumbling over rocks and slicing her palms on the vicious spines, she reached the top of the ridge and stopped to look back. To her left, Castle Zeruko was for once fully illuminated. She said a little prayer for the duke's soul. *If only Armand had been able to get through to him before he died, we wouldn't be in this mess.* She began the descent to the western side as the moon rose. At almost three-quarters, it shed enough light to help her find the way to the shore.

It took precious minutes to reach the beach where they'd met Emilio. Finally, the woods gave way to a small clearing. All seemed quiet. Someone had pulled a rowboat up on the sand, but she didn't see the canoe. She whispered, "Emilio? Hello?" No answer. She stepped out into the open and began to walk toward the boat, but halfway across the sand a floodlight switched on. A hoarse voice bawled, "Stop!"

She halted. A figure stepped into the light. "Well, Lacey, fancy meeting you here." Traficant smiled his signature mean little smile.

"What do you want, Ulisses?"

"Same thing you want. Prince Armand."

Lacey shielded her eyes. "Can you turn that thing off?"

"Sure." While he looked for the switch, Lacey quickly dropped her backpack and tossed it into the woods. Traficant turned the light to low and shone it on her again. "Better?"

"Not really. Let me see your face."

"For God's sake, Lacey." He set the flashlight down so his face was half lit. "It's not like you don't know who I am."

"Likewise."

"Yeah, but I need to know where you are."

"Nonsense. Where would I go?" Lacey moved toward him and away from her pack. She sat on a log facing Traficant.

He settled on a boulder across from her. "Now that we're both comfy, where's Armand?"

Lacey tried to spy out the edges of the clearing without turning her head. Nothing moved. "Are you alone?"

Ulisses raised his eyebrows. "Why? Do you think you can take me?"

"No. I'm just surprised a man like you would venture out into the wilderness by himself. You usually have backup."

"Oh, I've got my men close by. Not to worry."

She didn't believe him. Something didn't add up. *What does he want?* If he were out searching for Armand on Jakome's behalf, he'd have a whole platoon of people crashing through the woods. "You got your file. Isn't that what you wanted?"

"You know very well that the file didn't contain the documents I expected—but it did have fingerprints on it. Armand's fingerprints. And someone spilled a tiny amount of juice on the cover—chironja juice—a citrus fruit that only grows on the west side of the island." He chuckled. "You could say I followed a juice trail here. Then I only had to wait—I knew you'd be along. Can't stay away from your man for long."

"You couldn't be more wrong. I'm merely taking a last walk around the island before I leave tomorrow. And besides, you told me you already knew where Armand is hiding."

"I lied. But no matter—I have a pretty good idea where it is now. There's a bridge just up there that leads to Santa Isabella. It's a tiny island—the perfect spot for a rendezvous. I hear the bridge is even called the Lovers' Bridge. How apt." He sneered. "I'm betting that's where I'll find the little prince."

You'd lose that bet, but I'm hardly going to disabuse you. "So you don't need me to show you? Good, I'll just be toddling along then."

Lacey took a step toward the woods, but Ulisses caught her arm. "I don't think so. You might still be useful—perhaps in persuading Armand to give me the Campbell papers. I wonder what he'd say if he saw me do this?"

Traficant grabbed Lacey's other arm and pinned them behind her. She felt him tie her wrists together. He spun her around with a wicked grin. "Say, we never did get that roll in the hay, did we?"

Lacey gasped and pulled away from him. "Wait! I'll take you to him." She took a step but tripped over a root, landing heavily on her chest.

He leaned over her, his breath searing her neck. "I know you will, but not quite yet. You want it. I know you do."

What I want is to give you a hard kick in a very sensitive spot. She waited, ready to deliver the blow, but instead of turning her over, he seemed to be getting heavier. In fact, he felt like a dead weight on her back. "Hey!"

No answer. Lacey twisted to see what he was doing, and Traficant fell off her and rolled onto his back. She checked his face—leftover shock had drained all the color from it. He was out cold. She looked around, terrified of what she'd see. An animal? Another man who wanted his way with her? In the dim light she made out a small shape. A boy. He faced away from her. "Inigo?"

He mumbled, "Yes, ma'am. Are you all right, ma'am?"

Poor boy—what a sight I must be. "I'm all right. If you could untie my hands, I'll make myself more presentable."

Inigo backed toward her, stuck a hand behind his back, and pulled the rope free before fleeing to the other side of the clearing. Lacey straightened her clothes, then whispered, "You can come over now."

Together they checked the unconscious man. "What did you hit him with?"

He held up an oar.

"Oh, my. I hope you didn't kill him."

"I don't think so. I stunned him though." Now that his initial discomfiture had passed, he strutted around the body proudly. "I saved you, didn't I?"

"You surely did. You're my hero, Inigo."

"My father taught me to protect the weaker sex. He says you are delicate flowers, to be nurtured and cherished."

"Hold that thought, at least until you get married."

Traficant groaned.

"Shall I hit him again?"

"Perhaps just a little one, while we decide what to do." Inigo obliged, and Traficant stopped groaning. "Now, where is Armand?"

"On the island, ma'am. With Maitea."

Maitea. Young Maitea. *Why do I have to be "ma'am"?* "Please call me Miss Lacey, Inigo." She retrieved her backpack. "You must take me to Armand. I have something extremely important to give him."

Inigo kicked Traficant. "What about him?"

"First things first." As they untied the boat they heard shouting. Lights flashed in the woods. Traficant stirred. Lacey made a swift decision. "Get in the boat, quick!" She dropped the backpack next to Inigo and pushed the boat into the water. "Go! Go!"

"But…"

"I'll take care of this. You, take the long way to…you know where. I'm counting on you, Inigo." She gave one last shove, and the boat flew out into the lagoon and the darkness. Men began pouring into the clearing. She moved as far away from the shore as she could and stood under the palms. While two of the men helped Traficant up, the other two held her arms.

Traficant sat on the log rubbing his head. "What hit me anyway?"

Shoot, I hadn't thought of that. Scanning the clearing, Lacey saw a coconut lying on the sand. *Thank you, thank you!* She shook the guards off and picked it up. "This must've fallen on you."

He took it. "I guess so. Well"—he winked at Lacey—"you missed another good time. Yorge! Take her into custody." As she passed him, he whispered, "If you want to keep Armand alive, do as I say."

Puzzled, she whispered back, "What's going on?"

"Just look guilty." He raised his voice. "That'll teach tourists to snoop around Prince Jakome's private yacht. We've been scouring the area for you. Good job, men." He chortled at Lacey's face. "I told you I had men with me."

The one time he doesn't lie.

They took Lacey up to a dirt track where two Land Rovers idled and bundled her into the front seat of one. She cast her eyes back to the water. The half moon shone down on an empty lagoon. *Godspeed, Inigo.*

By the time they arrived in town, most of the celebrants had gone home. A light shone from Winston's bar. Traficant braked at the hotel. "Get out."

Surprised, Lacey looked at the man next to her. "Aren't you going to book me?"

"Nah." He pushed her out of the car and spoke loudly so the men could hear. "We don't want an international incident, so I'm letting you off with a warning. Just stay away from private property— especially grand ducal property."

Lacey saw no reason to argue and walked briskly into the hotel. The lobby was empty. *Good thing I didn't actually check out.* She retrieved her suitcase from the shed and, after a long bath, walked to the bar for a nightcap.

"Good evening, Miss Delahaye. You're out late."

"I know, Winston. I…couldn't sleep. Any news?"

The bartender pushed a glass across the counter. "This will help—it's hot buttered rum." He wiped the bar. "You want the news, eh? The funeral is set for next week. I hear construction of the dais is already underway for Prince Jakome's coronation." He seemed glum. When he didn't volunteer any more information, Lacey paid for the drink and headed home through the echoing market square.

Her head had just hit the pillow when all hell broke loose outside. She went out on the tiny balcony. People were milling around and shouting angrily. A few policemen stood on the corners but made no move to quiet the mob. She listened.

"He can't do this!"

"What about my job? My son's job?"

"He's not the grand duke yet. He has no right!"

She threw on a robe and ran down the stairs to find Mr. Pusey running his fingers through his sparse hair and talking frantically into the house phone. "I don't know, but the people are furious. I think he's gone too far this time."

Lacey shook his elbow. "What has he done? Who is he?"

He set the receiver down. "Oh, Ms. Delahaye—we were afraid you'd left without checking out. I'm going to have to charge you for the damages from the other night. Hotel policy prohibits wild parties, at least without permission."

She left that discussion for another time. "What's happened?"

"Prince Jakome has announced the nationalization of the dysprosium mine, effective immediately. Mr. Pandanus and Campbell's executive staff packed their stuff and flew out of Paraiso this evening accompanied by all the engineers. We are lost!"

It's too late for Armand to use the file against Jakome now. Would he have time to prove his birth? "Where is Sir Damiano? Do you know?"

"Jakome made the announcement by himself. Molly—she's the kitchen maid—she heard that Sir Damiano rushed to him directly after, and they are now closeted together. Let's pray he talks the prince out of this rash act!"

Lacey had her doubts but put a soothing hand on the concierge. "We can only hope so. I'm going back to bed."

Lacey had one foot in the elevator when a car pulled up in front with a squeal of brakes. A familiar voice called her. "Lacey, come. Now. I have to get you out."

She twirled. "You!"

"There's no time to argue. Get your suitcase—quickly. I'll take care of the bill."

She did as she was told. When she came out to the street, he stood on the sidewalk.

"Get in the car. I have you on a flight to Saint Andrews in half an hour."

When she got in, her rescuer leaned in the window. "Jakome has gone mad. I can't defend you here. I love you, Lacey. I always did. I'll come for you when I can."

"But Damien—"

He shook his head and stepped back. The car shot forward, heading toward the airport.

Chapter Sixteen

Sumacs are large shrubs that produce a tart, lemon-flavored berry in the fall. In Florida, shining sumac flourishes in dry, sandy soil. The malic acid on their skin gives them their flavor, so harvest the dark red berries on a dry day.

Sumac Jelly

2 cups berries

2 quarts water

Stem but do not wash berries. Soak in hot (not boiling) water for thirty minutes, stirring occasionally. Strain through several layers of cheesecloth to remove the hairs.

3 cups juice

4 1/2 cups sugar

1 box powdered pectin

Bring juice and sugar to a full rolling boil, stirring occasionally, until sugar is dissolved. Add pectin and, stirring constantly, bring to a rolling boil. Boil one minute. Remove from heat. Continue with standard procedure described in Chapter One.

❉❉❉❉

"Thank you, yes, it is a lovely color, isn't it? It's made from the berries of the shining sumac. Did you have a taste?"

The shopper, a local Lacey recognized from her walks on Gulf of Mexico Drive, licked the tiny tasting spoon. "Ooh, delicious. It's both tart and sweet."

"I'm so glad you like it, Kathy. You're in good company—it's one of my customers' favorites."

Kathy took another taste. "You know, it might go well with a meat dish. Grilled chicken maybe."

Lacey's eyes lit up. "What a clever idea! Perhaps I should have a suggestion box on the counter."

The customer pulled out her wallet. "I'll take two jars."

"Certainly. That'll be ten dollars with tax." Lacey popped the jars of jelly into a paper bag and handed them to her.

"Thank you." Kathy waved at a display of purple-hued jellies tied with colorful ribbons. "So, how does your business do in the off-season?"

"Remarkably well. Once people find me, they become regulars. I was lucky to lease this storefront right on the key."

"Us year-rounders are all delighted you're here. We needed something in the mall besides the massage parlor and Mickey's bike shop."

Lacey grinned. "It must have been empty for some time. The landlord was so happy to have someone interested in the property he cut the rent in half for me." She pointed at the stocked shelves. "I've been able to expand from jellies and preserves to teas."

"Teas! My sister loves tea. What kinds do you make?"

Lacey picked up a sheet of paper. "So far I have sassafras, sumac, pennyroyal, and sweet goldenrod. I'll be experimenting with various hollies and clovers in the summer."

"And all made from native plants you forage on

your camping trips. Impressive."

Lacey's cell phone buzzed. The woman flicked a hand and walked out of the shop.

"Mom? I'm at the airport. When are you closing up?"

"Oh, Crispin, I thought you weren't coming in until tomorrow! You'll have to take the bus, I'm afraid. I still have customers."

"Aw, Ma—the bus takes two hours. I don't mind waiting here for you. I can get a beer."

Sigh. "Okay, I'll be there as soon as I can. I'll call you when I'm near the airport." She hung up and dealt with the next four customers before flipping the sign to "Closed."

She surveyed the shop. Bright and cheery, it was painted a typical Floridian aqua and coral that matched the evening sky. A small semicircle of chartreuse right under the window represented the green flash—the brilliant streak of emerald light that shoots from the horizon as the sun sinks beneath it. She'd only seen it once, in Paraiso. Looking at it now, she felt the old hollowness come over her.

It had been a month—an achingly long month, since she'd seen Armand. She'd written a note to Edrigu explaining her sudden departure, but he hadn't replied. Nor had there been any word from either Armand or Damien, although she read news reports of riots and upheaval. Most of the global concern centered on what would happen to the dysprosium. Several international companies had voiced interest in managing the operation for the Paraisan government, but so far, Campbell Metals had resisted handing over its assets. The mine remained shut.

275

Political news from the island was a little harder to come by, so Lacey still didn't know whether Jakome had succeeded to the throne, whether he'd been deposed, or even whether Armand was alive and free. *Did Inigo deliver the birth certificate? Did Armand try to come after me? Why hasn't Edrigu answered my letter?* The lack of information galled her, but whenever she made noises about flying to Paraiso, Crispin put his foot down. He's been awfully bossy lately. *Must be the new girlfriend.* Lacey wasn't sure she liked her—her kittenish act came across as a bit too artificial. She'd have thought Crispin would prefer a more independent type. Like Maitea.

Gloom descended again as she sank back into the endless speculation that marked her nights. *Are they married? Are they happy? Is he slowly forgetting me? He probably didn't even try to come after me—well, he probably doesn't have time. He must have so many obligations—he's snowed under with work. Unless he's in prison. Or banished.* Out of all the scenarios she constructed, not one ended with her rushing into Armand's arms while a Rachmaninoff sonata played and the waves crashed romantically on the rocks.

"But I'd only go for a day or two. I'd even stay on Saint Andrews…"

"No, Mother. It's just not decent for an old lady like you to be gallivanting around the Caribbean and getting mixed up with pirates and grand dukes. I have no intention of rescuing you again." Then he'd hang up before she could pull rank on him.

Lacey picked up her purse and locked the shop door. Driving down Gulf of Mexico Drive behind a cavalcade of slow-moving Lincolns and Buicks, she tried to retrieve her good mood. If she could only forget Armand. *It's not that easy.* She missed the adventure—well, maybe not the kidnapping, but oh! The escape! And then slipping over the mountains to deliver a secret package to her lover, a prince in hiding. Definitely better than a book. All well and good, but more than the thrill, she missed the warmth of his fingers on her skin and the streak of gold in his dark eyes when he looked at her. Whenever she thought of him, she felt a tug, as though a wire connected their hearts across the miles. Even now, the memory pinched, compressing her ribs, making it hard to breathe. A tear dripped down, easing the pressure.

She wiped her eyes and blew her nose. As she pulled into the arrivals lane at Sarasota-Bradenton Airport, she dialed Crispin's number.

He answered on the first ring. "I'm coming out now."

She drove slowly along until she saw her son come through the sliding doors, a duffel bag slung across his shoulders. He turned back for a moment to talk to someone behind him. As Lacey cruised toward him, Crispin stepped aside and the man waved at her. *Oh. My. God. Damien.*

The only thing that kept her from stomping on the accelerator and roaring off was Crispin's startled face. With a sigh, she braked and pulled to the curb. What the hell was he doing here? Heart pounding, she waited.

"Hey, Mom. For a minute there, I didn't think you were going to stop." Crispin popped the trunk and dumped his bag inside. "While I was waiting in the bar, I met an old friend of yours, or so he says. He's heading out to Lido Key, and I thought we could give him a ride." He took Damien's carry-on. "Uh, what'd you say your name was again?"

Damien raised his eyebrows at Lacey. "Danny. Danny Wynn. I knew your mother before you were born, Crispin. You do her proud."

"Thanks, sir." Crispin opened the door. "Well, Mom?"

Before she could stop him, Damien slid into the front seat. "Great. I'm staying at the Holiday Inn. I really appreciate this." He pretended to size her up. "You look fabulous, Lacey. It's been, what, twenty years?"

"I don't remember."

Crispin wedged himself into the rear seat next to Damien's case, and Laccy headed south on the Tamiami Trail. They rode in near silence, only punctuated now and then when Lacey's internal seething erupted in a low snarl. They reached the hotel, and Damien hopped out. "I'd like to pay you back for your favor—and maybe get reacquainted. Can I take you to dinner tonight?"

Crispin put a hand on Lacey's shoulder. "That would be great. Mom, I forgot to tell you. I'm seeing Pat and Mike tonight. We're going to that new Peruvian brewery downtown, so you won't have to entertain me."

Her son appeared immune to the daggers Lacey shot at him. She thought quickly. "I wouldn't mind, except that I'm almost out of gas. Sorry!"

Damien straightened. "That's all right. I'm having a car delivered to the hotel. Your son and I were having such a pleasant time chatting that I sent it on ahead of me. Pick you up at seven?"

He didn't wait for an answer. For one brief moment, Lacey prayed that he didn't have her address, but Crispin happily explained he'd already given it to Danny. "He reminds me of someone. Have I ever met him?"

Heart sinking, she mumbled, "Only when you were a baby. I can't think how you'd recognize him." *Is he going to tell Crispin he's his father? What'll I do if he does?*

Her son prattled on cheerfully during the drive home. "I saw a review of your store on Yelp! Five stars! You're really on a roll."

"Thanks." Lacey tried to refocus. "How long can you stay, hon?"

"Only a week or so. We've still got some harvesting to do, and the winter rye has to go in."

"It'll be a cold winter in Wisconsin. I wish the community college had renewed your course here."

"Yup, but then I wouldn't have met Violet. She's a far cry from Nancy, isn't she?" Luckily, he didn't seem to expect an answer. "So where do you know Danny from?"

"Er...um...he was a friend of your father's."

"Oh." Crispin hadn't asked about his father in years. At the age of nine his questions had grown more insistent, and she'd come up with the lie that Damien worked as a security contractor for the Pentagon and had disappeared in Afghanistan when Crispin was a year old. The whopper seemed quite clever at the time, since it explained not only why they didn't have a military pension, but also why they didn't have a funeral. *If Damien breaks his promise and tells Crispin who he is, at least I can claim he's been alive all this time.*

She pulled into the garage. "I'd better go get ready for dinner."

"Yeah, sure. I'll unpack."

Promptly at seven the doorbell buzzed. Damien stood there in a dapper seersucker suit and bow tie. "Ready?"

He led the way to a sleek white Cadillac. "How about Marina Jack's?"

She nodded and touched the soft, white leather seat. "I'm guessing the recent unpleasantness in Paraiso hasn't crippled your finances."

"A perk of the company. I work for Campbell now—as their environmental consultant. They've been most attentive to my concerns about the mining operations."

Really? Is he that naive? "I see. So…there's been little news here about the events on the island. I presume you'll fill me in."

"Happy to. Ah, here we are." He led her into the restaurant and spoke briefly to the maitre d', who took them to a secluded alcove overlooking the Sarasota marina. "Two vodka gimlets, straight up, very cold."

"I thought you didn't like gimlets."

"I want to share everything with you." He leaned toward her and tried to take her hand. She quickly picked up a napkin. Undeterred, he locked his eyes on hers. "Lacey, I can't get you out of my mind. Awake, I think of you constantly. Asleep, I dream of your sea blue eyes, your silky hair the color of a wheat field in autumn." He touched a strand. "Still wearing it long I see. And in the very best dreams, I can almost feel the soft bits that are currently covered with fabric."

In spite of herself, she blushed. "Please, Damien, don't." A busboy placed a graceful, long-stemmed glass before her. She sipped. "So, tell me. Have they crowned Jakome yet?"

"Would that they had." He clinked her glass with his. "Remember the night I sent you away? Jakome took it upon himself to announce the appropriation of Campbell's mine without my permission—"

"Your permission?"

"Yes." He drew back, affronted. "Why does that shock you? He and I had a deal that I would set the pace of reforms. Jakome is such a child—he wanted to implement everything at once. I explained that the people weren't ready for such sweeping change, that we had to introduce them to the new order gradually. Plus, we had to tread delicately or risk losing the asset entirely. Which is, of course, what happened. Pandanus withdrew all his engineers and equipment and shut down the mine. Worse, he offered to pay for transportation and housing for any workers who wanted to come work at their new site. They'd discovered a vein of bastnasite—the mineral that contains dysprosium—in Brazil. So, not only did we lose the management and engineering staff, but the miners as well."

" 'We?' I thought you said you worked for Campbell. Did you move to Brazil?"

"Didn't have to. You're looking at a very persuasive man, Lacey. I'm in negotiations with Pandanus about reopening the mine in exchange for letting them have a slightly larger percentage of the profits and a stake in our new export trade in sugarcane."

"Wait…Sugarcane?"

Damien sniffed. "We told you about this, Lacey. Don't you listen? The arable land will be put to much better use as a single plantation. We expect a fairly sizable increase in revenue once we get the project going. The farmers are significantly happier in the commune. Or so they say in the government surveys."

Lacey stifled the curt retort. *I won't get any information out of him if I provoke him. Besides, we're veering off course.* "I see. And Pandanus is willing to reopen the mine on those conditions?"

"He's still wavering, but I think ultimately he'll agree." He finished his drink.

"Wait a minute. Did you say you'd give them a greater share of the profits? I thought you wanted them to increase your royalties?"

"That'll happen in time. I have to get the mine up and running again." He signaled the maitre d' for another drink. "Once Campbell's reinvested their capital on Paraiso, we'll have them in a bind. It will be cheaper to agree to our demands than to keep opening and closing the mine."

And here I thought he'd become more reasonable. Add cynical maneuvering to ideological mania. Lacey wanted to ask about Armand, but decided to take another tack. "You haven't explained why Jakome hasn't been installed yet."

The waiter brought another glass. "We're just waiting for this thing with Prince Armand to be resolved. Pandanus won't sign until Jakome is officially on the throne. Not sure what the holdup is, but it shouldn't be much longer."

"How does Jakome feel about your deal with

Campbell?"

"Ah, yes. Well, I had a little trouble with the prince at first." He shot a cautious glance at Lacey. "The revelation about his birth mellowed him a bit."

Lacey nearly choked on the gimlet. "His birth?"

"I guess that tidbit didn't make it onto MSNBC. I'd better start at the beginning. Let's order first."

The waiter materialized, panting only slightly. "Hello, there! I'm Rupert, and I am thrilled to be able to serve you today!"

Damien stared at him a minute before opening the huge leather-bound menu, obscuring his face. From its depths he said, a slight tremor in his voice, "I'll have the bouillabaisse…Rupert."

"Wonderful choice! It's Chef's specialty! He'll be so gratified!" Rupert pirouetted to face Lacey. "And for the beautiful lady?"

She scanned the menu. "What's the fish of the day?"

The waiter clutched his order book to his concave chest. "Oh, ma'am, I can't tell you how delighted I am you asked. We have a rare treat today—fresh blackfin tuna! Vincent—he's our house fisherman—brought it in this morning. I saw him myself." He closed his eyes, as though the image of a tanned, shirtless youth offloading baskets of fish, sweat running over his rippling muscles, was almost too much to bear. He sighed. "Yes, Chef can make you a lovely filet, cooked just the way you like, served with a delightful mustard and watercress sauce—on the side, of course! Then Chef has devised the most audacious little compote of brown rice and edamame tossed with sriracha sauce and ponzu."

He looked so eager and excited that she gave in.

"I'll have that, please—broiled, with extra lemon."

Damien ordered a bottle of Meursault Les Perrières 2003 and sat back.

Lacey couldn't keep her curiosity under wraps any longer. "Well?"

"Okay, okay, don't rush me. The night Jakome announced the expropriation of the mine, the city exploded in riots. I'm glad I got you out of there when I did. Stefan and Luis actually had to shoot their muskets once or twice to restore order."

"They didn't…"

"No, they shot them in the air. They only have blanks anyway. That reminds me—we should probably establish a real militia of some kind—or at least a palace guard." Damien lapsed into thought.

"Riots?" prompted Lacey.

"Oh, right. Jakome's idea of settling things down was to trot out the bishop, the chief judge, and the first secretary, and announce they would be tried as traitors. That helped soften the mood. Not." He snorted. "He had some idea that he would preside over a mass public trial, and the people would cheer him on as their new Thor, wielding his hammer of justice. Unfortunately, the constitution requires appointment of a real judge even for cases of high treason. Only two Paraisan judges had the necessary qualifications, and Jakome named the one he believed he had in his pocket. Imagine his distress when old Mather insisted on acting judiciously. He designated court defenders who quickly ripped the government's case to shreds. Even so, Jakome would have overruled him if it weren't for Armand."

Rupert arrived with their wine, which he displayed

before Damien with an eloquent twist of his wrist. Wine accepted and opened, he beckoned to his retinue—three busboys bearing plates of food, bread, butter, and a bucket—and flung his arms out like a master sergeant as they deployed the meal.

Damien made a fuss of tasting the wine and serving Lacey himself. She waited until he'd taken his first bite, then casually remarked, "Prince Armand? What did he do? I thought he was in hiding."

"He was. He came out of it. With Maitea. And a very significant piece of paper."

The birth certificate. "Yes?"

"He appeared in the court room with a birth certificate that gave the date of Armand's birth as ten months earlier than Jakome's. Jakome must have known about it since he didn't seem surprised, but that didn't stop him from immediately denouncing it as a forgery. Then, when the judge ruled that the prisoners be released on bond and that the court stand in recess until they could determine the certificate's authenticity, he flew into a rage."

"What...what happened to Prince Armand and Maitea?"

"Maitea went with Edrigu—he's the first secretary by the way, a kind of prime minister, only with no powers. Apparently, he's also her uncle. Armand left the court under guard."

Fear clogged her voice, making the question nearly unintelligible. "Is he...is he in prison?"

"No, of course not. He's a Montegue. He's at the palace with his brother."

Lacey studied Damien. Could he be trusted? Which was stronger—loyalty to Jakome or to his ideology? *As long as he gets his "new world order," I'm betting he'd throw his prize pig under the bus.* She came to a decision. "It is real."

Damien stopped with his fork halfway to his mouth. "What is?"

"The birth certificate. It's real. Grand Duke Xavier gave it to me."

"Gave it to you? How? When? Oh…wait." He took a swallow of wine. "When I took you to see him. The day he died. He told you Armand was the elder son? Did he explain how he managed to swing that with only one wife? A wife who I presume would know who she gave birth to and when?"

Lacey related Xavier's tale.

Damien whistled. "Is Paraiso a freaky country or what? This will definitely complicate matters. What did you do with the certificate?"

"I hid it in a book. Later, I went to the square for a drink and took it with me. While I was out, someone trashed my room."

Damien tapped a thoughtful finger on the table. "Jakome had a regular conference with his father on Tuesdays, the day of your visit. The doctor said Xavier died around two o'clock, which would have been an hour after his meeting with Jakome. When I got back to the castle after our lunch, the entire staff was assembled, but Jakome wasn't there. He came in a few minutes later, his clothes dusty and his manner distracted."

"Xavier must have told him he gave me the birth certificate, and he went to the hotel looking for it."

"I suppose so." He gave Lacey a speculative look. "Now that I think of it, Armand didn't clarify how he came into possession of the document. You couldn't have given it to him. You don't even know him. Do you?"

I don't have to lie, just skip over a few facts. "I didn't give it to him, no. I left the book in my backpack until I could figure out what to do with it." *Too implausible? Will he go for it?* Damien said nothing, so she went on. "A couple of days later I thought I'd...uh...go for a walk up the hill. I came across Ulisses Traficant in the woods on the west slope. He...he..."

"Traficant attacked you?" Damien slammed his fist on the table. Rupert took a step toward them but retreated when he saw Damien's expression. "The bastard—I knew he couldn't be trusted."

For once Damien's jealousy could be useful, since the story she'd concocted would otherwise be utterly unconvincing. And how sweet the revenge if one enemy got what was coming to him at the hands of the other. "You were so right, Damien." She simpered. "Thank God, some men happened along and gave me a lift back to town."

Damien frowned. "Don't you worry—I'll take care of him when I return."

"Oh, I hope so." Lacey fluttered her eyelashes at him.

He checked and gave her a hard look before going on. "So what happened to the book?"

She chirped airily, "I must have dropped my backpack in the scuffle. When I got back to town everything was in an uproar over Jakome's announcement, and then you sent me away and I...I guess it slipped my mind. Someone must have picked

up the pack, found the letter, and taken it to Armand."
Close enough.

Damien rubbed his chin. "Sounds improbable but not impossible. There are quite a few supporters of Armand around. Not enough to undermine Jakome's authority, of course," he added hastily.

He bought it. Yes! Rupert appeared and took her plate away, shaking his head with tender regret at the untouched rice and the picked over fish, but said nothing. "The question is, what happens next?"

"I don't know. I assumed Jakome was right, that the paper was a fake. He didn't bother to enlighten me. The situation's different now." He finished the wine. "Coffee? No? Why don't we get some fresh air?" He paid the bill, and they strolled down to the marina. Cabin cruisers bobbed next to sleek yachts in the slips, their shrouds and halyards whistling in the wind off the bay. The harbor lights streamed across the water, painting white stripes across the boats. They could hear the sound of laughter and the chink of glasses floating from open decks. She looked up at the sky. The half-moon reminded her of her last night in Paraiso. How she wished she could have said goodbye to Armand!

Damien took her hand. "I've been thinking. Lacey…" His voice dropped.

Oh no. Quick, quick. Change the subject. "You were saying things would be different now because of the birth certificate. What did you mean?"

He gave her hand a squeeze but let it go. "If the document checks out with the court-appointed experts, we'll regroup. I'm not worried—I'm sure I can come up with another way to discredit Armand and keep Jakome on the throne."

"But why?" Lacey was confused. Damien's loyalty to Jakome had seemed to be weakening. *Was I wrong?* "You have a job with Campbell now. What's it to you?"

He stared at her, shock etched in his face. "Are you kidding? And give up on all we've accomplished? All we plan to accomplish? I've got Campbell right where I want them—in our corner. From what I've heard of Armand, he's unlikely to consent to any of my—our—reforms. Jakome must remain the titular head of the duchy at all costs."

Still crazy after all these years. Lacey yawned. "Oh, will you look at the time. I must get home—I have to open the store early tomorrow. Thanks so much for dinner. Do you mind driving me home now?"

He said nothing, but she could sense his annoyance. Finally he said, "Sure, fine."

When the Cadillac pulled up to her house, he reached across her chest and opened the door. "I'll be here for a few more days. We still have other topics to discuss, Lacey."

Inside, Lacey let her breath out with a whoosh. She couldn't believe he'd given up without an argument. *Tomorrow won't be so easy.* Crispin came in. "Back so soon? How was your date?"

"Okay."

"So, tell me about him. What's he do for a living?"

"He's...um...a consultant."

"Consultant, huh? Is that why he's here in Sarasota?"

"You know something, I don't know. I forgot to ask." *When he sent me away from Paraiso, he said he'd come for me. Is that why he's here?*

"Must've been too busy flirting." Crispin winked.

"What? No! Look Crispin, Dam—I mean Danny—is…is not what he seems."

"What do you mean? Mother, you're not getting cold feet again!"

"I mean—" Might as well come clean. "He's not very honest. I don't like him very much, if you want to know the truth."

"I see. Well, I'll just have to find you someone else." He skipped out of reach. The telephone rang. He picked it up. "Yes? Lacey Delahaye?" He raised his eyebrows at her, and she vigorously shook her head. "I'm sorry. She's not available. May I take a message?" He wrote down a name. "I'll make sure she gets it." He hung up and handed the note to his mother. "It wasn't Danny, by the way."

She read the note and fell backwards onto the sofa. "That was Armand? Why didn't you tell me?"

"I'm sorry. I didn't know it mattered." He peered at her. "You haven't mentioned his name since you got back. I figured you were over him—you went out with Danny after all. Are you saying you still care for him?"

She brushed the question aside and reread the note. "There's no number here. How do I get hold of him?"

"He said he'd call again as soon as he had a chance, but that he doesn't have easy access to a telephone."

"Why not?"

"He's under house arrest."

"House arrest!" *Oh, why couldn't Crispin have given me the phone! How long will I have to wait to hear from him again? Damien—I'll have to grill Damien, even if it means making him think I'm still in love with him.*

Lacey went to bed but couldn't sleep. She went over and over the dinner conversation. Damien seemed to think he could get around the judge, defeat Armand, and reinstate Jakome. *Actually, without my story it might not be that hard to impugn the experts' conclusions.* A few bribes, strategically placed...Unless she were there to corroborate Armand's claim, they might just get away with it. The moon lit up her room, and she rose and went to the window. The bay was calm, glistening under the stars. Far out she saw a pair of dolphins leap in perfect unison. A loon called.

Forget Damien. I'm going to Paraiso.

Chapter Seventeen

Now when I was a little boy an' so me mother told me
Way haul away, we'll haul away Joe
That if I didn't kiss the girls me lips would grow all
moldy
Way haul away, we'll haul away Joe.
An' I sailed the sea for many a year not knowing what I
was missing
Way haul away, we'll haul away Joe.
Then I sets me sails afore the gales and started in
a'kissing.
~Traditional sea chanty
****

Crispin was not supportive of Lacey's sudden decision.

"Mother, this is ridiculous. You can't keep shuttling back and forth to Paraiso. The place is about as dysfunctional as the Simpsons. Why not let them sort out their affairs first, then go back for a holiday when everything's calm? Besides," he griped, "I just got here."

"Crispin, you have lots of friends here—you'll be fine." Lacey folded a slip and laid it in the suitcase. "It's not like I'm not already deeply involved in Paraiso's future. In fact, it may hinge on me. I'm the only one who can testify to the grand duke's last wish and prove the birth certificate is real. They'll have to believe me."

"Let's hope they do. You say Danny is really Damiano, Jakome's side kick? So his story of being an old friend was a lie?"

How to approach this? "No, it's true that I knew him many years ago. We…uh…went our separate ways."

"Before my father appeared on the scene, I presume."

"They…er…overlapped."

Crispin seemed to mull this over. "Why introduce himself as Danny Wynn then? I don't get it."

Hmm. "Danny…is his real name. He uses Damiano in Paraiso, I guess to blend in more and to lend an air of…er…gravitas." She closed the case and carried it to the kitchen. Grabbing juice, bread and jam, and a bowl of sliced kiwis from the refrigerator, she piled them on the table and began to make coffee.

Her son dropped two slices of bread in the toaster. "Let me get this straight. He just happened to be in Paraiso when you arrived?" He shook his head. "And his showing up in Florida had nothing to do with you? It was all merely a case of serendipity?"

"No, not at all. Well, the first part is true. We met by pure chance in Paraiso. But now he…he wants to renew our acquaintance. He claims he still carries a torch for me."

"Funny, you never mentioned him before." Crispin's lips twisted in a skeptical grimace. "I think I'd have known if there were another man in your life. Is there something you want to tell me, Mother?"

God no. "Not right now, okay?" Lacey didn't have the will to deliver another shock to her son's world.

He's going to find out about Damien eventually, but it can wait.

Crispin gave her a thoughtful look. "Okay, I'll back off." He slathered a piece of toast with mayhaw jelly and bit off a large chunk. "But if he was in Paraiso when you arrived on the island, how come he doesn't know about you and Prince Armand?"

"Because Traficant—"

"Your kidnapper?"

"Yes. Traficant hasn't told him, plus we thought I'd be more useful if we kept him in the dark."

"I see." Crispin took the plates to the sink. "Are you ready? We'd better get going."

"Give me a minute." Lacey found her purse and met her son in the garage.

They pulled out onto Gulf of Mexico Drive. Crispin drove in silence for a mile or so, then suddenly blurted, "Traficant works for Jakome too, doesn't he? Why wouldn't he tell him everything?"

"Ulisses is always looking for an angle—he has no real loyalty to anyone but himself. The night he caught me on my way to Anna Cay, he hinted that he'd struck a deal of some kind with Campbell. He must have his reasons not to advertise my relation to Prince Armand."

Crispin shook his head. "Like I said, that whole place is just warped. I don't like you going there."

"You can come with me."

"I just might. I'll ask Violet what she thinks."

She couldn't help it. "So you need to ask her consent?"

"Of course not—ah, here we are." He stopped at the departures entrance. "Let me get your bag. You call me when you get there, all right?"

Lacey kissed her son and headed into the airport.

****

As Lacey flew over the flat, peacock-blue water between Saint Andrews and Paraiso, it felt like she was coming home. Sure, she loved Longboat Key and her work there, but something more potent than any career or lifestyle drew her here. The wire connecting her to Armand tugged as the distance diminished. A man passed on his way to the restroom, and she caught a familiar scent. She closed her eyes the better to identify it. Cinnamon? And...ginger. Her eyes flew open. *I'm coming, Armand.*

She was surprised to see Inigo standing on the tarmac. "How did you know I'd be on the plane?"

"Your son called the Lady Maitea, and she told me to pick you up." He took her bag and strode along just ahead of Lacey. "They await you at Castle Aresti."

"Maitea and Edrigu are free? The bishop and the justice as well?"

"For the time being. Bishop Bunyan and Justice Winthrop went to their own houses. They all agreed it would be better to be in separate locations."

"And...Armand?"

Inigo gave her a sidelong glance. "He's in the grand duke's palace...with Prince Jakome."

Oh dear. "Is he a prisoner?"

"No, not exactly, although Prince Jakome has Mr. Traficant watching him around the clock to block him from directly communicating with the citizens. And now the prince has closed down the newspaper and scrambled the radio broadcasts. His public statements are the only source of information the people have."

"Paraiso is a small island. Surely he can't keep the

news of the birth certificate quiet."

"Oh no, everyone heard of Prince Armand's appearance in the court, but no one knows whether the document is legal or counterfeit. Prince Jakome has announced repeatedly that it is a forgery and suppressed the report of the court-appointed specialists. There is a lot of unrest, a lot of uncertainty." He flagged down a taxi.

"We're not going to the hotel?"

"First Secretary Edrigu feels you will be better protected in the castle."

Lacey wasn't so sure, but it seemed she had no choice. How she wished Armand were there! The ache only grew stronger as she drew nearer to him. She could almost feel his warm skin, his warm eyes on her, the touch of his lips…She sighed.

"Are you all right, Miss Lacey?"

"Yes. Um, Inigo. I don't suppose there's a way I could…could…"

"Meet with Prince Armand?" The boy cocked his head. "Already arranged. But first you must refresh yourself."

They climbed the winding cobblestone road up to Edrigu's castle, the blue and red flag of the first secretary flying proudly from the turret. Maitea stood at the gate. The girl hugged Lacey and ushered her inside where Edrigu waited. He kissed Lacey's forehead. "We are very glad to see you again. I've had your usual suite made ready. As soon as you are rested, come to my sitting room."

An hour later, as the sun set in glorious abandon, Lacey sat in the cozy living room in Edrigu's private quarters. Maitea handed her a cocktail. "Rum punch."

Lacey took a long, satisfying drink. "Thank you."

Edrigu leaned forward. "Now, tell us why you went away and why you have returned."

"You didn't receive my letter?"

"Letter? No."

So that's why he didn't reply. "I'd better explain." She told them about Damien's spiriting her out of the country and then about the grand duke's confession. "That's why I've come. To testify that Xavier gave me the papers and that they're authentic."

"That may not be easy." Edrigu pursed his lips. "Perhaps we should fill you in on recent events."

The two took turns relating what Lacey had missed in the last month, most of which she'd already heard from Damien. She told them of his intention to discredit Armand in any way possible and keep Jakome on the throne. "I should warn you. Traficant hinted to me that he has some kind of scheme of his own."

Edrigu steepled his fingers and sighed. "If only we Paraisans could be left to work out our difficulties by ourselves. These outsiders come in and stir up a hornet's nest, and we're left to pick up the pieces." He saw Lacey's face and caught himself. "I don't count you, of course, my dear. It's not your fault you were drawn into the maelstrom."

"Yes, if Armand hadn't washed up in my mangrove forest…" *I never would have found the love of my life.* Lacey fidgeted. Inigo said she would see Armand, but when? And how? She enjoyed Maitea's and Edrigu's company, but if she didn't find herself in Armand's arms soon she'd go stark raving mad.

"Dinner is served."

They filed into the dining room. Lacey peered into

every corner, hoping to see Armand. No one except the butler and a footman peered back. After dinner, Maitea suggested a stroll on the battlements. Lacey lagged behind in case Armand lay in wait for her. Nothing. They did two circuits and, as the moon rose, Maitea yawned. "It's been a long day. I'm sure you're tired. Come on, I'll walk you to your room."

No one waited for her there either. She even checked the shower just in case. At last, she undressed and lay down. She remembered this room and the bed and a beautiful night of lovemaking. Now she couldn't sleep. She went out on the balcony. The moon rode high, walking a carpet of stars. Their myriad needles of light bounced off something below. A terrace? No, a swimming pool. *Funny, I didn't notice it the last time I was here. A swim in the moonlight might relax me.* She slipped out of her nightgown, threw on a thin robe, and followed a set of rough, rock-hewn steps down.

At the bottom she found an oval pool, almost hidden by tall pink oleander and night-blooming jasmine. A waterfall tinkled at one end. She slipped into the water. It felt cool against her skin. She floated on her back, gazing up at the sky. Contentment filled her. *I can wait for Armand—there's all the time in the world. Anticipation is half the fun anyway.*

The whisper wafted across the ripples. "So you have come back to me." For a horrible second she thought Damien—or worse, Traficant—had found her. But then a wet head rose next to her and shook the glistening black locks out of a dear face.

"Armand!"

He swam a lap around her. "Who did you expect?"

Dazed, she touched his face. "I'd about given up

hope for tonight."

"I've been waiting here for you. Come to me."

If this were a scene suitable for children, the next few minutes would allude to sighs and chaste kisses. Or there would be a scene break with the words "romantic interlude" accompanied by a little light music.

But it's not.

Lacey rolled over in the water, placed a hand on Armand's head, and ducked him under. He came up spitting and laughing. "That's no way to treat a prince."

"That's the way I treat *my* princes. Where have you been, anyway?"

Armand didn't answer. He ducked under the water again. In the dark Lacey felt something gently touch her thigh, then pull it to the right. Bubbles rose up under her, tickling the lips of her vagina. She twisted, trying to cross her legs to get away from the sensation. A hand grabbed her other thigh and dragged it to the left. Lips replaced the bubbles, then a tongue speared her unprotected channel, darting in and out, prodding the nub of her clitoris. She took hold of Armand's shoulders and pulled his head closer. The orgasm kindled. Just as she slid over the edge, Armand's head came up. He gasped and sucked in a mouthful of air. "Armand, I was almost there! Why did you stop?"

He panted, "If you want more, you'll have to allow me to breathe now and then."

"All right—go ahead and rest a bit. Catch your breath." She dropped below the surface, circling around to Armand's rear. Reaching between his legs, she hefted his balls and rolled them in her hand. His fingers gently pried her hand away and pulled her between his thighs. His cock, hard as a shillelagh, bobbed before her. She caught it with her mouth and ran her tongue around it. Armand kicked his feet and rose to the surface, bringing Lacey with him. He held on to the coping with one hand to stabilize them and let Lacey finish her work. "Oh God, Lacey, that's it!" Warm, creamy fluid spurted out, dissipating in the water.

Armand swung her around so her back was to the pool wall and straddled her.

"Have you caught your breath yet?"

"Oh, yes." He held her waist and let the still rigid penis slide into her. The soft water cradled them as they moved in rhythm, making their own waves. In the dark Lacey could make out little except the saffron flashes in Armand's eyes. She kept her gaze locked on them while his thrusts lifted her almost out of the water. Like dolphins mating, they breached and plunged until the moment when man touched the innermost part of woman and fused. The wire connecting them across the miles, a wire that had been stretched almost to its limit, recoiled into its natural shape—a spring tightly coiled around them as they clung together.

Armand wrapped Lacey in his arms. "It's been so long," he whispered. He kissed the top of her head, her forehead, her nose. "I've imagined this moment—"

"Every day, every hour—"

"Every second."

His lips fastened on hers.

****

Lacey woke the next morning and stretched. She knew Armand had gone, so she relaxed, dwelling blissfully on the memory of the night before. Once they had taken care of their most pressing needs, they had sat under the waterfall, holding hands, while Armand recounted his version of the events.

"After Inigo brought me the documents, I came back to Port Huntington under cover of night, then the next day marched into the courtroom and presented them." He chuckled. "Not one of Jakome's best hours, I'm afraid." He shook his head. "I'm still puzzled as to how Inigo came by the papers. When I asked, he went all squiggly on me."

"I gave them to him."

"You? When? How?"

Lacey told him about Xavier and the monkey box. It was on the tip of her tongue to tell him about her aborted delivery attempt but realized she'd have to describe her encounter with Traficant. *It's not worth getting him riled up again.*

"Whew. So I have you to thank for my stroke of luck." For a few minutes, he demonstrated his gratitude in a most satisfactory manner.

When they came up for air, Lacey asked, "When are you going to tell the court about me?"

"You mean, that my father gave you the certificate? I don't see that it's relevant."

"What?"

He took Lacey's chin in his hand. "The document speaks for itself. There's no need to drag you into the conflict."

Lacey emphatically disagreed with his opinion, but she kept it to herself. *I must see the judge alone and tell him my story. Without my testimony, Armand is more vulnerable than he realizes.* She listened fondly as her lover went on to speak of his dreams for a resurgent Paraiso.

Contrary to Edrigu, he was positive that everything

would work out. His confidence gave her renewed vigor. *I'll forcefully plead his case before the judge. I'll blow the jury away with my unimpeachable evidence and winning self-assurance. Armand will take his rightful place and Jakome…well, I'm sure he'd be much happier back in his ivory tower where no one contradicts him.*

Maitea entered, behind her a maid with a tray. "Good morning, sleepyhead."

"Good morning! Oh, what a glorious day!"

Maitea sent the maid out and sat down on the bed. "*Hmm*, I surmise we had a busy night. Did you by any chance take a swim?"

"How did you—Oh. I guess everyone knows." It didn't really bother her. Everything seemed so wonderful. She felt quite magnanimous. She checked out the dishes on the tray. "This all looks delicious. Are those pancakes?"

"Banana fritters."

"Perfect. I'm starved." A crock filled with dark purple jam lay beside the fritters. She tasted it. "Wow—this is really different. What's it made from?"

Maitea took a small spoonful. "Jaboticaba berries. There's a tree in the courtyard. Cook makes up batches of it."

"I think I'll drop a dollop of it on my fritters." She finished her breakfast and took a sip of coffee. "By the way, how is your Gorko?"

Maitea examined her fingernails and mumbled, "I don't know."

"What do you mean?" Lacey suddenly remembered Damien's remark about the farmers. "I heard Jakome has consolidated the farmland into a commune or something?"

Maitea wailed, "It's been horrible, Lacey! They rounded up all the farmers, including Gorko, and made them live in one house on a tiny square of land on the ridge. Then they confiscated the individual plots and turned them into one huge plantation."

"The government took the planters' lands from them? Isn't that illegal?"

Maitea shook her head, her face a mask of misery. "Jakome declared the land necessary for public use and seized the farms under eminent domain. Even if the courts reverse his action, it will take years, and the damage will likely be irreversible."

"Who's doing the farming then?"

"He assigns designated sections to pairs of farmers. The produce goes directly to the grand duke's storehouses. Half of the crop is doled out to the population and the other half exported, but the treasury takes most of the profits and only returns a minuscule percentage to the farmers. Gorko was so distraught, he left Paraiso. I haven't seen or heard from him in two weeks."

"He didn't ask you to go?"

"No." Her lower lip trembled. "He came to see me before he left and he…and he said I was part of the problem, that my family had brought this on the island. He wanted to get as far away from me and Paraiso as he could. He asked for his ring back." She covered her face and burst into tears.

Lacey found a tissue and handed it to her. "I'm so sorry." It broke her heart to see the girl distraught. *Should I tell her that Gorko wouldn't have hesitated to turn her in?* No—that would probably only add insult to injury. She let her cry herself out. When the last tissue had been used and discarded, she took a more optimistic tack. "Are the changes permanent? Couldn't we just split up the fields again?"

Maitea sniffled. "Possibly, but that would only happen if Armand becomes the grand duke, and even then it will take a while. They…they cut down all the hedgerows!"

"Then they can build fences." Lacey refused to be affected by Maitea's despair. She rose and pulled on a dressing gown. "Look, I need to see the judge assigned to your case. Can you get me an appointment?"

"Of course." Maitea blew her nose and stood up. "We're so glad you're here, Lacey. It will give Armand the courage to stay the course. When you were gone…"

"How was he?" Lacey held her breath, hoping and not hoping he'd been as unhappy as she.

Maitea spoke eagerly. "We all expected him to break down, like he did the last time you left, but he didn't. He's a born leader, Lacey. He rallied us and led the defense in court. You should have seen his speech when he presented the birth certificate and told the story of his birth. Everyone was mesmerized." When Lacey's face fell, she added hastily, "No one could tell how much he missed you, how he longed for you. Think how much stronger he'll be with you to back him up. He loves you very much." The words seemed to depress her.

Lacey patted her hand. "Never mind, Maitea. If Gorko gave up so easily, he's not worth it. There are plenty of fish in the sea."

"Fish?"

"An American expression—mainly used in the

Midwest where there isn't any sea. Now, would you mind making that appointment?"

"Right away."

****

An old woman ushered Lacey into the judge's chambers. The sight of her reminded Lacey of Arrosa. *I wonder why she never came back.* She made a mental note to find out where she'd been those fateful days. The judge rose from his chair and shook her hand. "Obadiah Bastiaan Erramun Mather at your service."

"Mather?" In the bushel basket of names, she picked out one familiar one. *Maybe there are only a few surnames on the island.* "Are you by any chance related to Koldo, sergeant-at-arms to First Secretary Edrigu?"

"He is my son." He closed the door carefully and turned to face her. "Arrosa is my wife."

Aha. Things are looking up. "Then you know who I am."

"Yes, but not why you are here."

"First, is Arrosa all right? She never contacted me after the grand duke's death. In all the chaos, I worried she'd been arrested."

"Thank you for asking. She had a fall." A spasm of suspicion crossed his features. "It happened under rather unusual circumstances which I have asked the police to investigate. She is mostly recovered now. So…" He sat at his desk and indicated the chair opposite him. "What can I do for you?"

Lacey told him of Xavier's confession and his request that she give the birth certificate to Armand, of how she tried to get it to him, and of Traficant's intervention. "I know that Inigo managed to deliver the document to Armand, but I understand its validity is in question. I'd like to tell the court what happened."

"I see." The judge took a minute to cut the tip off a cigar and light it. He turned to the window and puffed a few times. "This is a remarkable story. I'm unclear on one point, however. Why didn't Prince Armand mention you in his statement?"

"He didn't know of my involvement then. And now he doesn't think my role as a go-between matters enough to drag me into the dispute."

"Ah, that is an assumption on which I would beg to differ." He stubbed out the cigar. "However, this must be done delicately. You are not a Paraisan citizen, and you have no diplomatic immunity, so the extent of your rights is unclear. Also, the prosecution will attempt to discredit you, especially if your close relationship with Armand is disclosed." He took another puff on the cigar. "This may take a little time. Why don't you return to Edrigu's castle while I determine the proper procedure?"

Lacey tried not to show her disappointment. He was right. She couldn't simply barge into the courtroom and announce that Armand was the rightful heir and expect everyone to believe her. She took her leave and walked down to the waterfront to collect her thoughts.

Inigo popped out of an alley. "I'm to watch over you. I—" Whatever he had to say was drowned in the sudden wailing of a siren. Lacey and the boy stepped out of the lane and watched as a scooter and then a black Mercedes roared through the square. The cobalt blue banner of the grand duchy fluttered on the hood. Just as it passed, the tinted window rolled down, revealing the unwelcome profile of Damien, locked in conversation with Prince Jakome. Lacey ducked, hoping they hadn't seen her, but the squeal of brakes and the wheezing of an engine unwillingly reined in told her otherwise. With a sinking heart, she raised her head.

"Why, Lacey Delahaye, whatever are you doing here in Paraiso?"

"I...uh—"

Damien interrupted. "When I called a couple of days ago, your son told me you had a family emergency and had to leave unexpectedly." The fury in Damien's eyes belied his light tone. "I didn't realize you had...relatives...in Paraiso. Lookee here, Jakome, your favorite American has come back. I wonder why." The prince's face appeared next to Damien's. His expression was, if anything, nastier than Damien's. "Why don't you pop in the car, and we'll take you up to the castle."

The cluster of market patrons who had closed in around the limousine during the exchange fell silent. Lacey felt like the snitch invited into the mobster's car for "a little ride." "Thank you, Sir Damiano, Prince Jakome. Unfortunately, I have an appointment I can't break." She skipped away before Jakome could order her to obey. After a minute, the Mercedes moved slowly up the hill to the castle. A slight sigh issued from the onlookers.

Inigo slithered into view. "I'd best take you home quickly." He took her hand and guided her through back alleys to a pony cart. "We'll take a short cut." The horse clumped along for a few minutes, then Inigo remarked, "So you spoke to my grandfather. Will he let you testify?"

"I don't know—he's considering his options. He is

on our side, isn't he?"

"My grandfather is a very upright man. He feels strongly that order should be maintained and traditions followed. Prince Jakome rightly expected him to be a conscientious arbiter, and he approached the case with an open mind—that is, until he learned that my bam-bam had been helping Armand. He began to suspect her accident was meant as a warning."

"Bam-bam?"

"My grandmother."

"Oh, yes." Lacey remembered Arrosa had used the Paraisan term. "You mean your grandmother's injury? He mentioned that."

"Yes, we all wondered how she came to fall, since my ibamai is known for her sure-footedness."

"When did the accident happen?"

"The night the grand duke died. She received a call that her cousin was ill and needed her. The cousin lives in Puebla Viejo, over the ridge. When my grandmother arrived, the cousin was perfectly fine and had no idea who had called or why. Puzzled, Bam-bam left, but on the way home, she tripped on a stone and fell down a rocky trail, breaking her leg. Luckily, my mother had gone in search of her and found her. Otherwise…" He left her fate unspoken.

The night Xavier died. *The same night someone ransacked my room.* Jakome? Did he want to make sure Arrosa was incapacitated? "Now I know why she didn't come when I signaled. I waited to hear from her for three days and finally decided to take the papers to Armand myself. Thank God Traficant didn't find them on me that night." She patted Inigo's shoulder. "If it weren't for your quick action, Armand would not have learned the truth about his birth. I never properly thanked you, Inigo."

Inigo turned the color of a ripe pomegranate. "I was...I was glad to be of assistance."

Lacey suddenly recalled the situation in which Inigo had found her. "You were very brave, Inigo. And very discreet." She patted his cheek. "And strong."

They arrived at the castle as twilight fell. Edrigu, Maitea, and Koldo waited in the study. Lacey told them what happened with the judge and of Damiano's return. "If Judge Mather refuses to let me tell my story in court, Armand could lose his appeal."

Edrigu put down his pipe. "And if Jakome learns you're to testify, he'll stop at nothing to silence you. I think you should stay here for the time being."

Lacey didn't quibble. She remembered with a shiver the twin looks of malice on the two men's faces. "We might as well wait until Judge Mather makes his decision."

A slight disturbance at the front door drew their attention. Koldo took Lacey's arm. "It could be that Jakome is taking preemptive action. Come with me— I'll hide you."

They were halfway across the bailey when Maitea called. "Wait! Come back!"

Lacey turned around to see a welcome sight. She ran forward, arms outstretched. "Crispin!"

Her son kissed her and touched Maitea's hand shyly. "I figured you could use the cavalry just about now."

Chapter Eighteen

Then three times round went our gallant ship,
And three times round went she.
Three times round went our gallant ship,
And she sank to the bottom of the sea.
~*~
Oh, the ocean waves do roll, they roll
And the stormy winds do blow.
But we poor sailors go skipping to the top,
While the landlubbers lie down below, below, below,
Oh, the landlubbers lie down below.
~ *"The Mermaid," a traditional sailing song*
****

A happy reunion ensued. Crispin heard all about recent events over dinner. Edrigu seated him next to Maitea, who chattered and burbled like a schoolgirl. Lacey watched them fondly. Maitea's color heightened, setting off her sparkling ebony eyes. After dinner, she offered to give Crispin a tour of the castle. No one pointed out that she'd guided him through it once before, and the young couple left, followed by amused looks.

Their growing affection reminded Lacey of how much she missed Armand—it was so hard to have him only a few miles away and yet beyond her reach. She said goodnight and trudged up to her room. *I probably won't see him again until the court hearing.* She wondered how he fared in the ducal castle—did he and Jakome speak? Was he locked in his room? She wandered out to her balcony.

"I thought you'd never come up to bed."

Lacey didn't jump but held her arms open as Armand emerged from the shadows. After a long, satisfying kiss, they settled on the bench looking out over the water. "Does Jakome know you're gone? I thought he assigned Traficant to guard you twenty-four-seven?"

Armand kissed her hair. "I have made a deal with the good Ulisses."

She jerked her head around. "Really? You know he's completely untrustworthy. He—" She stopped. Armand didn't know about her recent skirmish with Traficant, and it was best to leave it that way. He would only do something rash. "What kind of deal?"

"I think he's hedging his bets in case the judge rules in my favor. He allows me to move about freely during the night—which helps in communicating with the people. I just came from a meeting of farmers over in La Montaña. After Jakome razed the hedges, they came to me in a body declaring their support. I've got them gathering wood."

"To build fences?"

"Yes, how did you know?"

"What else would it be for?"

Armand tapped her nose. "You're very perceptive. Humans are territorial creatures—Jakome ignores this at his peril. We must have our own property to protect and improve, or we're miserable. I have most of the shopkeepers on my side as well. Now, if we can convince Campbell to reconsider, we'll be in a position to persuade Jakome to step down."

Campbell. What did Damien tell me about the mine? That's it. "Did you know that Damien's been in negotiations with Campbell to reopen the mine?"

"Yes, Pandanus told me. Gerald has been stringing him along, claiming to want to wait for the court's decision, but he has no intention of giving in to Damiano's demands."

Lacey thought of something. "Traficant is not the sort of man to let you roam freely without getting something more immediate and tangible in return. What does he want?"

"Well, aren't you the cynical thing? Yes, you're right. If we succeed in bringing back the mining operation, he wants a share of the profits—a direct cut of the net, not of the royalties."

"You can't give him that."

"No, but Pandanus can. Traficant says he'll throw his support behind me if I take his proposal to Campbell."

"Does he insist that Pandanus agree before he'll help you?"

"No. Just that I make the case for it."

There's something fishy here. Down below, a trawler chugged past the castle, its rigging glistening like a spider web in the moon's glow. Lacey wondered idly what it was doing out so late. "I think Ulisses has been planning to defect to our side for some time. Remember that purple file Jonathan Dooley gave me to give to you?"

"Yes. Traficant wanted it, didn't he? I wondered why."

"Me too. When I asked him, he said if you made it

public, Jakome would know who had collected the evidence for Pandanus. Who else could it be but Ulisses? Not only that, but when I tried to deliver the birth certificate to you he…he…" *Damn.*

Armand checked. "Wait a minute—you? What are you talking about? Inigo brought the papers to me. He didn't mention you were there. Why didn't you come to the island? *What happened, Lacey?*"

Various explanations fought for dominance in her brain. Anything but the truth. "Traficant…um… intercepted me before I could take the dinghy out to you. When he wasn't looking, I gave Inigo the envelope and sent him on."

"What was Traficant doing there?"

I can just skip the inflammatory bits. Lacey spoke quickly. "He had trailed you to the little beach and believed you were hiding on Santa Isabella. He was after the purple file and knew nothing about your father's documents. When his men appeared, he pretended to arrest me, and we all returned to Port Huntington. He deliberately misled them."

"He did, did he?" Armand rapped his fingers on the balustrade. "I suppose that gives credence to Traficant's promises. I don't mind working with him if it means we get the company back."

The trawler passed again, this time going north. *Maybe it's lost.*

Armand rose. "I have to be off." He gave a wry smile. "Curfew is midnight."

"So soon? Can't you stay a minute?" She tried to keep the frustration out of her voice. How she longed for a time when they didn't have so much business to talk over and could while away the hours whispering

313

sweet nothings.

He took her in his arms. "It won't be long now, my love." The kiss went on and on, reaching down into the roots of her soul. She opened herself to him—opened her mind, her heart, her body. She could almost feel her spirit move into his and meld. He tightened his grip. "I'll never leave you, Lacey. Never. You are mine."

"Yes."

****

She awoke to a hazy sky. The air tingled, and as she pulled the curtains open, lightning shot across the horizon. Rain pattered on the balcony. Something lay on the bench, and she ran out to pick it up. Armand's jacket. Back inside, she held it to her face and sniffed. No matter what troubles this day would bring, she would have the scent of his body to sustain her. She was dressing when the knock came. Maitea entered.

"Judge Mather called. He would like to see you in his chambers."

"When?"

"In an hour. Crispin and I will take you in my car—it's less conspicuous."

They drove along the coast road. The storm had moved on, and the sun sparkled on the blue water. Lacey, checking out the hillside to their right, saw nothing but row after row of straight, bamboo-like plants, marching like little soldiers down the slope. "What are those? And where are those beautiful citrus trees that used to line the verges?"

Maitea let out a sob. Crispin turned to Lacey in the back seat. "It's sugarcane. Maitea tells me Prince Jakome had all the orchards cut down to make room for his new export crop." He growled, "He obviously doesn't know that sugarcane, when grown as a monoculture, depletes the soil of most of its nutrients. His precious Paraiso will be a desert in a few generations."

Lacey doubted that it made any difference to Jakome.

When they reached the courthouse, the same old lady escorted Lacey inside. The judge shook her hand. "Good news, Ms. Delahaye." He winked. "I have decided to allow you to testify. It appears that, although the various parties have different ends in mind, most feel it would profit them to let you have your say."

What you hear is the sound of bus tires crunching over Prince Jakome's body. "When is the hearing?"

"Tomorrow at ten."

"I'll be there."

Lacey met Maitea and Crispin outside the courthouse. "It's a go. I have the impression that both Damiano and Traficant have jumped ship."

"You mean they've abandoned Prince Jakome?"

Lacey was distracted by a large crowd gathered on the waterfront. A man stood on a lobster trap shouting and waving his arms. *He looks awfully familiar. Now where have I seen him before?*

"Mom?"

"What? Oh, yes. Both men think they can make a separate deal with Campbell Metals. Damiano still espouses Jakome's policies—after all, they're his—but thinks the better approach is to milk the company dry. Traficant—true to form—just wants a slice of the profits."

Crispin steered around a truck. On its side a bearded pirate glared down at them next to the logo

"Satisfaction Spiced Rum—Henry Morgan's Favorite." "We should be able to use all their maneuverings to our advantage. Once Armand is the grand duke, it won't matter what games they've been playing."

Lacey hesitated. Should she tell them about Armand's deal with Traficant? *Everyone needs to be in the loop. There's only one secret I have to keep—Damien's relation to Crispin.* "Damiano will lose out, yes, but not Traficant."

"Why not? The guy's a crook."

"He's the reason Armand has been able to organize the opposition so effectively. Jakome and Damiano think he's tailing Armand, but—in exchange for Armand's interceding with Campbell on his behalf—he's giving him frcc passage in the evenings."

"Armand doesn't have to abide by any agreement made with a swindler like Traficant, does he?"

"Oh, Crispin, my sweet, you're so young. How would it look if he started his reign by betraying a trust?"

Maitea broke in. "Let's not forget that Armand has to win his petition first."

They pulled up in front of Castle Aresti behind a Bentley Lacey recognized. "Damn—that's Damiano. I don't think he's very happy with me."

"Because you left Florida so suddenly? You bet he isn't. He appeared just after I'd dropped you at the airport. I thought he was going to take my head off when I told him you'd gone. He's got a temper, doesn't he?"

"He didn't hit you, did he?" *I'll kill him with my bare hands.*

"No, no. In fact, once he cooled off, he took me to

dinner. We had a great time, Mom. It's like he...gets me, you know? He understands me. He had some great advice about...about..." He cast a quick glance at Maitea. "...how to handle Violet."

The girl in the front seat stiffened. "Violet?"

Lacey quickly opened the door. "I'll leave you two to discuss Violet. I'm going to have to face Damiano sometime."

She found her ex-husband in the study with Edrigu. Both men looked sullen, as though what little they had to say to each other would please neither. "Ah, Lacey, Sir Damiano has been asking for you."

"I was meeting with Judge Mather." She gave Damien a meaningful look. "My testimony is scheduled for tomorrow."

He didn't take the bait. "Lacey, I'm not here on business. Can we talk privately?"

Edrigu spoke. "With the lady's permission." Lacey bowed her head.

She led Damien to a small room filled with musical instruments. A beautiful grand piano graced one corner. She moved to it and ran her hand over the cold, smooth surface. Damien took her shoulder and turned her to face him. "Why did you run away, Lacey?"

"What are you talking about?"

"I thought we were reconnecting. And then all of a sudden you're gone, and I see you here in Paraiso set to tell the world your story. Why didn't you wait for me? I would have escorted you back."

He seemed genuinely hurt.

She decided to lie. "I got a call. From Maitea. She told me she'd heard Judge Mather was about to dismiss the case and asked me to come and help. She said to hurry." Really lame, Lacey.

"I see." He paused, then went on in a light tone, "Well, now that you're here we can have that date. Oh, by the way, I had a very agreeable visit with my son. I must say he turned out extremely well, thanks to you."

Lacey searched Damien's face for a hint of sarcasm, but found none. "Thanks, I guess."

He brought his face close and lowered his voice. "I'm serious, Lacey. I want to be in his life. I want to be back in your life. Won't you give me a chance?" He tapped the bulge in his pocket.

If he brings that ring out again, I'll…well, I don't know what I'll do. "I…I don't know, Damien. You have a lot of baggage."

"Can't you see your way past all that and forgive me?" His eyes pleaded.

No, I can't. "Look, I've got to go."

He stepped back. The light from the sconce behind him threw the shadow of a towering figure across the floor. "This isn't over, Lacey. At the very least, you have to let Crispin know who I am. It's only fair."

Her blood, currently at simmer, heated rapidly up to a boil. "Fair? You have a twisted definition of fair, Damien. Was it fair to opt out of our marriage? Was it fair to leave me almost destitute? Was it fair to abandon Crispin for twenty years? You had a chance to contribute, but you chose not to. Was that out of some grotesque interpretation of the golden rule? Did you want to support us but just didn't have the time? Or did you in fact simply not care that much?" Her chest heaved.

Damien hung his head. "I deserved that. What can I say? I'm a man. When we're not roped in and tamed,

318

we tend to forget and head out to undiscovered country. You didn't try all that hard, either. I—"

"That's enough!" Lacey marched to the door. "Don't blame me for your weakness. Get out, Damien."

Rage ignited in his face. He spit out, "You can't talk to me that way."

She lost it. "I can't? Who do you think you are? Here in Paraiso you may be the great Sir Damiano, liege to Prince Jakome, but to me you'll always be the pathetic drunk who slunk out of my house and disappeared twenty years ago. I owe you nothing."

Damien stood still, his face a mask. Finally, he brushed past her. "Like I said, Lacey, this isn't over."

She watched him out the door, tamping down the slight regret at her strong words. *I hope I haven't jeopardized Armand's position.* She couldn't bring herself to admit that Damien had in fact stepped up to the plate once, when he saved her from the riots. *Yes, he loves me. But he's still the same old cowardly rat who walked out on my son.*

****

Maitea and Crispin drove Lacey to the courthouse the next morning. They entered through a side door to find the hearing room packed. Edrigu, professing a slight cold, did not accompany them. Armand sat at the defense attorney's table. A muscle in his cheek twitched when she passed, but he deliberately kept his eyes glued on his companion. Damien sat next to the prosecutor, with Traficant in the pew behind them. Jakome wasn't there. Maitea and Crispin found a spot behind Armand, and Lacey took a seat near the back of the room.

When Judge Mather appeared, the prosecutor took

the floor. Recapitulating earlier proceedings, he pronounced all Armand's claims to be bogus, no matter what the court-appointed document analyst reported. He finished by adding, "Your Honor, I beg the court that we return to the original purpose of this trial, the charges of treason against the defendants."

The judge pounded his gavel. "I told you before, Leroy. I want to clear up this matter of the ducal birth order before we continue. If Prince Armand is in fact Lord Xavier's elder son, the charges will be moot." He turned to the defense table. "I understand the defense has a new witness, Edmund."

The man with Armand rose. "Yes, Your Honor. I'd like to call Ms. Lacey Delahaye to the stand."

Lacey walked slowly down the center aisle. She could feel a hundred pairs of eyes boring into her back. The judge smiled at her reassuringly. She took the oath and sat on the hard wooden chair.

The defense lawyer stepped to the center of the courtroom and faced her. "Ms. Delahaye, you are an American, correct? And you were visiting Paraiso when the events under discussion occurred?"

"Yes."

"According to your statement, you had made the acquaintance of Sir Damiano and expressed an interest in meeting Grand Duke Xavier."

"Yes."

"Tell us what happened."

Lacey related again her tête-à-tête with Xavier, how he'd confessed to the deception and given her the birth certificate.

"Did he tell you to take it to Prince Armand?" He gestured at Armand.

"Yes."

"And you did."

"I tried. I—"

"I object!" The prosecutor jumped up. "The witness had never met Prince Armand, so I'd like to ask—how could a tourist who'd never been in Paraiso before and had no idea what Prince Armand looked like think she could find him?"

The judge banged his gavel again. "Overruled, Leroy. Save your questions for the cross-examination." He turned to Lacey, "However, the Court would like to hear what made the grand duke believe you could deliver the papers."

Lacey opened her mouth, but the defense attorney interrupted. "That was going to be our next question, Your Honor." He tapped Lacey's hand. "Ms. Delahaye, the grand duke asked you, a foreigner, to seek out Prince Armand. By all accounts, you were not acquainted with the prince. Why did he make such a request of you and not one of his retainers?"

She looked at Armand. *It's time to stop lying. If I don't tell the truth now, Damien will never let me go, and Traficant will hold it over us.* "On the contrary, I know Prince Armand quite well. The grand duke had been made aware of that."

Murmurs swept through the audience. Traficant's brows went up, and Damien's eyes went from Armand to Lacey and back. The lawyer seemed as surprised as anyone. *Armand must not have told him, whether to protect me or...* A horrible thought occurred to her. *Oh no, now I'm no longer an impartial witness—I've compromised his case. The judge tried to warn me, didn't he? How could I have been so stupid!* The lawyer raised his voice. "Would you mind expanding on your statement?"

It's too late now. Wait—there may be a way out. Keeping her gaze locked on Traficant, she said slowly, "Prince Armand and I were kidnapped together and brought back here for ransom."

Judge Mather clucked his tongue. "The prince stated before this court that he had been abducted by pirates. He did not mention you, nor did he mention a ransom demand."

That must be part of Armand's deal with Traficant. Tough bananas. "Nevertheless, I was with him. When we arrived in Port Huntington, the kidnapper went into town to negotiate a deal. We were able to free ourselves and row to shore."

"And where is the kidnapper now?"

"He is here, Your Honor."

Edmund interrupted. "In Paraiso?" He glared at Armand.

It's now or never. "Yes. In fact, he's—" A commotion in the back of the courtroom drew everyone's attention. The bailiff made his way to the back. A burly man stood there waving his arms. *That's the man I saw on the waterfront yesterday. Wait…it's…it's Ulisses' partner. What the hell was his name?*

The man spoke with a thick Spanish accent. "Your Honor, I demand to be heard!"

Judge Mather gestured to the bailiff, who took the gate-crasher's arm and led him to the front. The judge regarded the man, his eyes stern. "I do not allow my courtroom to be disrupted in this way. Is there any reason why I shouldn't hold you in contempt?"

"No, sir. I mean, yes, sir. I come seeking justice, Your Honor."

"And your name?"

He opened his mouth wide, displaying a red cavern bereft of teeth. "I am Sandalio Cofresi."

Sandalio—that's right. The manatee smuggler. I wonder how he lost that last tooth?

"And what is this justice you seek?"

Cofresi, his shoulders hunched, his chin wobbling obsequiously, drawled, "Your Honor, I am but a poor fisherman from Aruba. I barely make enough to keep my family of twelve alive, and after the last hurricane, we've been desperate. The escolar are not running and the mahi mahi—"

"Yes, yes, get on with it, man."

Sandalio bobbed his head. His flinty, porcine eyes shifted from bailiff to judge. "Some months ago I agreed to do a small delivery job for a man—just to make a little extra money. For my poor sick wife and—" The judge rapped his gavel and he switched gears. "I left him with my partners in Aruba, but upon my return, I discovered all my money gone and my partners dead—murdered. I am here to demand compensation for the money he stole and punishment for the loss of my friends."

The audience seethed, fascinated with the drama playing out before it. Lacey, her mind a mass of conflicting thoughts, recalled in vivid color the cabin of a fishing boat and a man remarking, "I have decided not to share the proceeds with them." *So I was right—he did murder Belasco and the others.* The judge's astonished gaze went from Sandalio to Lacey and finally to Armand. When Lacey saw his glance fasten on Armand, she nearly choked. *He can't think Sandalio's talking about Armand. Can he?*

Traficant touched the prosecutor's shoulder and whispered in his ear. The latter sprang up. "Your Honor, this interruption is irrelevant to the proceedings. Can't the bailiff remove this man?" He glanced at Sandalio contemptuously. "He can have his day in court at another time. He may regret his outburst, since I'm informed that he is in fact a pirate."

"A pirate! No, sir. I'm only a poor fisherman." Sandalio shook his head regretfully. "Sometimes I may help out a friend or two when they need transportation, but that's all. Your Honor."

"I see." The judge seemed inclined to listen. "Can you tell the court why you chose to make your statement here?"

Sandalio brightened. "Your Honor, it has taken all this time to track this man down. I learned only this morning that he would be here today."

"And? Is he here?"

For answer, the pirate reeled and pointed a hairy finger at Traficant. "That is the murderer!"

Traficant responded with a blank stare. He leaned forward and whispered to the prosecutor again. Lacey watched Damien's face change as hope dawned that his rival might be eliminated. He pulled the prosecutor away from Traficant and spoke rapidly into his other ear. The poor attorney blinked twice and rose. "Your Honor, we request a recess."

"In a minute, Leroy. I want to hear Mr. Cofresi's accusations. Then I'll decide how to proceed. Ms. Delahaye, you are excused for the moment. Don't leave the courtroom. Henry, please swear in Mr. Cofresi."

Maitea made room for Lacey behind Armand.

Sandalio told his story, in which the smuggled manatees morphed into slightly less objectionable sea turtles, but otherwise stuck to the truth. He'd come back to his base on Aruba to find Tubal, Marko, and Belasco with their throats slit and no sign of Traficant. "Only the cook was spared."

"And you say Belasco told you he had two prisoners on board?"

"Yes."

"And they planned to hold them for ransom. Is that correct?"

"Yes."

"And do you know what happened to these prisoners?"

"Traficant took them when he stole Belasco's boat."

"And are they here in the courtroom?" Mather pointedly kept his eyes from Armand and Lacey.

Sandalio became suddenly uncomfortable. "I don't know, Your Honor."

"I see. So you never actually saw Belasco's captives?"

"N...no. But that's not why I'm here. I want—"

"Justice. Yes, I know. I think we shall deal with you later." He sat back. "Before we go any further, I'd like Ms. Delahaye to come forward again."

Sandalio stepped down, but when he tried to leave, the bailiff barred the door. Judge Mather raised his voice. "Henry, Mr. Cofresi will remain here. I may want to call him to the stand again."

Lacey sat and looked expectantly at the judge.

"Now, Ms. Delahaye, you're still under oath. Will

you testify to the truth of this man's allegations?" The judge pointed at Traficant. "That this man, Ulisses Traficant, kidnapped you and murdered three men?"

Traficant's eyes could have burned a hole in Lacey's chest. "Your Honor, I have no proof that he murdered the pirates, but he did capture me and Prince Armand and brought us here to Paraiso to demand ransom." *Should I mention that Damien refused to pay the ransom? Nah.* That tidbit might come in handy later.

Judge Mather nodded at the bailiff. "Henry, please take Mr. Traficant into custody and read him his rights." Ulisses didn't struggle, and as two policemen handcuffed him and led him away, Lacey observed her ex-husband's expression of astonished gratification mutate into one of calculation.

The judge resumed. "Let us return to the proceedings. Ms. Delahaye, we've established that you were previously acquainted with Prince Armand. Can you explain to the court why that shouldn't prejudice your testimony concerning the birth certificate?"

If it isn't one thing..."I...uh..."

At this point, the argument between Damien and the prosecutor became too loud to ignore. The judge banged his gavel. "Leroy, do you have something to share with the court?"

The prosecutor shot a furious look at Damien but rose. "Your Honor, the prosecution stipulates that the birth certificate is authentic."

"What? You're conceding the case?"

"Yes, Your Honor."

The judge pinched his lips together and beckoned the prosecutor to the bench. He said something under his breath, then called the defense lawyer. From her spot in the witness stand, Lacey could hear everything. Judge Mather folded his hands. "Leroy, let me be clear. If you make this stipulation, I will rule in Prince Armand's favor. He will be pronounced the new grand duke, and Prince Jakome must forfeit his claim."

"I understand."

"Edmund?"

The defense attorney seemed at a loss for words. Lacey wondered if he were torn between exulting at the speedy conclusion of the most sensitive case of his career and feeling vaguely robbed of victory. Mather waved both lawyers away and spoke loudly. "It is the judgment of this Court that the claim of Prince Armand to primogeniture and thus the title of grand duke is upheld. In light of this decision, all charges against the defendants are dropped. Witnesses are dismissed." He banged his gavel again.

The bailiff returned and shouted over the milling crowd at the judge. "Your Honor, what about Sandalio Cofresi?"

"Oh, yes. Arrest him too."

"On what charge?"

Mather flipped open a book on his desk, tipped his glasses down, and read aloud. "Under the Convention on International Trade in Endangered Species of Wild Fauna and Flora, he is charged with illegally harvesting a designated species, to wit, the green sea turtle." He disappeared behind the curtain.

Armand stood up and turned to the assembled people, who applauded lustily. "Long live Prince Armand! Long live the new grand duke!" Before he could stop them, two men hoisted him on their shoulders and carried him out to the market square. Cheers erupted outside.

Maitea and Crispin sat unmoving. Finally, Maitea said in a wondering voice, "It's over. We won." She touched Crispin's sleeve. "We won." Crispin drew her to him. Lacey left them kissing in the empty courtroom and made her way to the side door. She had just reached the car when a heavy hand landed on her wrist.

"Why didn't you tell me that Traficant kidnapped you along with the prince? For that matter, why did you lie about your acquaintance with Armand?"

"I…uh…" No excuse sprang to mind. *I forgot? I didn't think it was important? I didn't want to give you one more reason to persecute Armand?*

"No matter." Damien put his hand under her arm and pulled her away. "It got rid of Traficant. Now my way is clear."

"What do you mean? You just betrayed your mentor Jakome."

"Jakome my mentor? The other way around, my dear. He is—was—my protégé. I no longer need him. I already have a relationship with Gerald Pandanus. Whither goes Campbell go the fortunes of Paraiso."

"What about Prince Armand?"

He kissed her fingers. "That's where you come in. You two must have bonded while in captivity—"

You don't know the half of it, mister.

"—so I'm sure he'll listen to you when you persuade him to keep me on. Crispin can stay with us, and we'll all be one big happy family again."

"What on earth are you talking about?"

"When we get married, I want Crispin to live with us. I thought you'd like that."

Responses swirled in her head, some of which, if acted upon, would have had her facing a firing squad. "I need time to think, Damien." *Or, as the Wizard of Oz said, "Go away and come back tomorrow."*

"Sure, sure. Come on."

"Where are you taking me?"

"Back to Castle Zeruko."

She held back. "No! I mean, what about Jakome? He'll know what you did by now."

Damien halted. "Oh, God, you're right. I'd forgotten about him. All my plans falling into place, and there he is, marooned on that sinking ship." He pushed her away playfully. "You must be staying at the hotel—why don't you head on back there while I go soothe the savage beast?" He signaled to the chauffeur, jumped in the Bentley, and drove off.

Maitea and Crispin came around the corner. "There's no getting close to Armand. The entire population of Paraiso is celebrating in the square. Should we return to Edrigu's or go to the ducal palace?"

"Edrigu's. I need some time to take all this in."

No word came from Armand that afternoon, and the little band of friends had a quiet dinner. The public radio station broadcast the news of Traficant's arrest and the court's decision and announced that Prince Armand would make a formal proclamation the following day. Lacey poured herself a nightcap and went to bed. She said a prayer to the sickle moon, but its Cheshire cat grin gave her little comfort.

She slept deeply and peacefully. Late in the morning, she woke to a weak sun. Gray clouds passed in bubbles over the opaque sky, and thunder rumbled in the distance. She answered the knock to find a dreadfully pale Maitea. The young woman said nothing except, "Come down when you're ready."

Wondering what could have gone wrong this time, Lacey descended to the breakfast room. Edrigu and Crispin sat silently, staring at each other. "What is it? What's happened?"

Edrigu spoke, his gruff voice holding a hint of fear. "Damiano is dead."

"What! What happened?"

"Prince Jakome killed him."

Chapter Nineteen

O'er all those wide extended plains shines one eternal day,
There God the son forever reigns, and scatters night away.
No chilling winds or poisonous breath can reach that healthful shore,
Sickness and sorrow, pain and death, are felt and feared no more.

~*~

I am bound for the Promised Land
I am bound for the Promised Land
Oh who will come and go with me?
I am bound for the Promised Land
~Traditional hymn, Samuel Stennet, 1787

****

"Oh, my God." Lacey sat heavily on the remaining chair. Maitea pushed a cup of coffee toward her. She snuck a peek at Edrigu, vainly trying to remember if he knew of her relationship to Damien. She fervently hoped not, for then Crispin would be bound to find out. "Where is Jakome?"

"Disappeared. The royal sloop is gone, and they believe he is already far out to sea."

"How do they know he killed Dam...Damiano?"

"Are you sure you want to know?"

"Yes." Something clicked in her chest. "Yes."

331

"Damiano was stabbed several times—"

"Hundreds of times." Maitea turned slightly green.

"—but when Jakome left him, he was still alive. A footman found him crawling toward the hall. He moaned that when Jakome learned of the court's decision, he went berserk. He wrenched swords and knives from the walls and launched himself at Damiano."

Crispin spoke up. "He died before the ambulance arrived."

She should be sorry, but when she searched her heart, Lacey could only locate horror at the carnage…and relief. All their enemies had been eliminated in a single day. All, that is, except Jakome. How she wished she could be with Armand! "And Prince Armand?"

"He's at the ducal palace trying to sort it all out. I think we should stay out of his way until at least some of it is resolved."

They all agreed.

The day passed slowly. The rain kept them inside until after lunch. Crispin stayed glued to the radio and reported any new developments. Lacey bit her lip more than once to avoid disclosing Damien's relationship to the boy. *To find out now would be too cruel. And I couldn't even commiserate with Crispin's loss because I don't feel any grief.*

In the misty aftermath of the thunderstorm, she walked the battlements until her feet hurt, then took a long swim. Late in the afternoon, she knocked on Edrigu's study door. "What will you do, sir? Now that the grand duke is dead?"

He looked up from his book, his eyes tired.

"Whatever my lord Armand wishes, Miss Lacey. With any luck, I will be allowed to retire. He will need new blood to bring this island back to the paradise it was before Jakome began spinning his evil webs."

Lacey wondered where he'd find such supermen. "You have no children?"

He shook his head. "Only Maitea, my grand-niece. She came to me when her parents were killed. She and Lady Bacon…" At the mention of the older woman's name, contempt distorted his features. "…are my only living relatives."

Crispin burst in. "Armand has pardoned both Chief Justice Winthrop and Bishop Bunyan. Justice Winthrop has proclaimed Armand grand duke, pending formal installation. He has declared tomorrow a day of rejoicing."

"Has the date of the accession ceremony been announced?"

"Since preparations were already underway for Jakome's coronation, the bishop decided to hold the ceremony as planned, the day after tomorrow."

"Whew! Everything's happening so fast!" The others shot quizzical looks at Lacey. "Forgive me." She rose and went to the window, hoping to hide her sudden depression. The news reminded her that Armand belonged to his people now. He would have no time for her. He would have no room for her. An alarming thought struck her—would he follow through on his promise and marry Maitea? Before they could see the tears, she excused herself and ran to her room.

The wind had blown the clouds off to the east, and the western sky was awash in gold and cream and orange, like an enormous dreamsicle sea. She leaned on the parapet to watch the fishermen returning with their catch. They reminded her of the trawler she'd seen trolling back and forth. *That must have been Sandalio searching for Traficant.*

It all seemed like a faraway fantasy now, something she read in a book. *It's time to go home.* She went inside and began pulling dresses off the hangers. Busy with her sorting and folding, she didn't hear the door open.

"Don't pack yet, my dear. I think you'd better stay with Edrigu for a while. It wouldn't be proper for you to move in with me before the wedding."

"Armand!" The next few minutes were spent in pursuits other than conversation. When she was satisfied that she had hugged or squeezed every part of him she could reach without actually stripping him naked, Lacey laid her head on his chest.

Armand kissed her hair. "Now, do you want the wedding before or after my accession? If before, we'll have to go wake up Bishop Bunyan, but I'm sure he'd be willing to officiate in his pajamas."

"No, no. I want to savor it for a while."

Armand lifted Lacey's chin up. "Don't tell me you want some big elaborate event, do you? I don't think I can wait that long."

She smirked. "You can always scale the outer wall in the dead of night again."

"No can do. Now that I'm a big wig I have to preserve my reputation. Besides, Edrigu had that very handy trumpet vine cut down. He says he doesn't want me tempted to climb up and spirit you away."

Lacey looked up into his beloved face. "I see. So, no more trysts?"

He looked pained. "It will definitely be difficult. See, this is why I want to wake the bishop up now. We could skip all the—"

"But you're here now."

He stopped. "But—"

"I said, you're here now."

Understanding dawned and Armand's jet black eyes sparkled. "Why, yes I am. No rush to get home. Is there?"

"Who knows when you'll get a chance to come back?"

He slowly stretched out an arm and switched off the lamp.

****

The following days were a whirlwind of preparations, joyous semi-accidental meetings between the lovers, and endless paperwork. After so much hand-holding and longing gazes at the airport that Lacey almost missed her flight, she returned to Florida to close up her shop. She arranged to have the inventory and equipment shipped to Paraiso and, after much deliberation, decided to keep the house on Buccaneer Drive. When she called to tell him the news, Armand was quiet.

"Armand, are you there?"

Finally he said, "You decided not to sell the house after all?"

Is he worried I'm not ready to give up my old life? "I don't want to live there, of course, but the land has been in my family since...well, since the seventeenth century. Surely you understand about family ties." She waited anxiously.

After a minute, he spoke, his voice light. "I do

understand. In fact, perhaps we should spend our honeymoon on Longboat Key."

Lacey couldn't tell if he were making fun of her or not. A test? "Wonderful! You could hide in the mangroves, and I could find you and—"

"Wash me off?"

"Whatever you like. I could start with your toes and—"

Armand gave a delighted yelp. "Lacey, my dear, as long as you promise to come home soon, do whatever you want with the house."

She hung up and stared out at the bay. Oscar, her dolphin friend, had returned after the hurricane and raised his flipper in welcome. The cormorants roosting at the end of the pier turned in unison and stretched out their wings to the sun, like an avian chorus line. A pontoon boat chugged by. She sighed. It would be hard to leave this spot—not that she'd lived here long, but she remembered the thrill of starting a new life and a new business. *Isn't that what you're doing in Paraiso?* Only in Paraiso, she had just a little bit more. *The love of my life.*

She turned her back and took her suitcase out to wait for the taxi.

The next morning Maitea and Crispin met her at the Saint Andrews airport and drove her to the ferry for Paraiso.

"Where is Armand?"

Crispin spoke over his shoulder. "He's in a meeting with Gerald Pandanus. Since neither Damiano's nor Traficant's deals are valid any more, he wants to sign a new one with Campbell."

"Can't they go back to the old arrangement?"

"No. All the contracts were cancelled, so they have to be renegotiated. It's a tedious process, but Armand thinks Paraiso will be able to get a higher percentage of the royalties."

"If Damiano couldn't do it, what makes Armand think he can?"

Maitea said, "It turns out we have a...a...What's that expression, Crispin?"

Lacey's son pinched her cheek. "An ace in the hole. I keep forgetting that English is not your native language, hon."

Lacey leaned forward. "Hello? What is it?"

"It turns out that Campbell doesn't own the mineral rights to all of Paraiso."

Maitea broke in. "In the original contract, the Montegues retained two square miles."

"I forgot all about that!"

"What, Ma?"

"When Jonathan Dooley—the Campbell representative—came to my room that night with the file, he discovered that the Montegues still controlled some of the land. I think it had slipped everyone's mind. It's good to know they're honest at least."

"Well, now Campbell wants the subsurface rights to the acreage, and Armand is willing to sell. For a price."

Lacey had unpacked and settled on the balcony when Armand appeared. Following the mandatory interval for mutual physical gratification, he rolled over and reached for the telephone.

"Who are you calling?"

"Edrigu. I sent Koldo and his son to survey my property."

"You mean the two acres? Maitea told me about them."

"I haven't decided whether to keep the rights or sell them to Campbell. What do you think we should do?"

Lacey stretched. "We should keep them. Perhaps we can build a hideaway there." She tittered. "One a little more comfortable—and clean—than your den on Anna Cay."

Armand held up a finger and listened to the receiver. "Edrigu? Any report from Koldo?...He is?...No, no, I'm here. Tell them to meet me at Castle Zeruko in half an hour, will you? All right." He hung up.

Thirty minutes later Armand and Lacey stood in the once musty grand hall. It had been cleaned and aired and the dreary tapestries and ponderous Gothic furniture removed. Lacey admired the portrait of Xavier, which had been restored to its place over the fireplace. "It's so much fresher now. And brighter."

"Yes, I—"

A footman opened the door. "Your Highness, Sergeant-at-Arms Koldo Maarten Rackham Mather and his son Inigo Carolus Azarola Mather request an audience."

"Oh, for heaven's sake, George, let them in."

Inigo rushed in followed by his father. "Guess what!"

"Inigo!"

"Let him be, Koldo." Armand patted the boy's shoulder. "What is it?"

Inigo rocked on his heels, his face scarlet with excitement. "You'll never guess."

Two voices barked, "What?"

Koldo pushed his son aside. "As you commanded, Your Highness, I thoroughly examined the records of the two acres of land under question on the southwest side of the island. They have not been cultivated or used for any purpose since the seventeenth century. This morning we toured the property. It is overrun with vines, and there are many dead trees to be cleared, but it has great potential."

"Boy, oh, boy, does it!" interjected Inigo. "Can I tell them? Please, Father?"

Armand clapped his hands. "Will someone tell me?"

The sergeant-at-arms reluctantly gave way to his son. Inigo spread his feet and held his arms akimbo—

Just like Peter Pan.

—and crowed, "We found Henry Morgan's treasure!"

****

It seemed like forever, but it was only two weeks later that Lacey stood before a mirror admiring the long, ivory dress. The tailor had obligingly altered the duchess Amaia's wedding gown, and it fit perfectly. The princess lines and pinched waist hid her forty-year-old bumps admirably, and the mandarin collar and plunging neckline gave her an added inch of height. "It's beautiful."

"It is." Maitea let the lace train run through her fingers. "You will be the loveliest bride in the world." Crispin came in and threw an arm casually over Maitea's shoulders. She blushed. "Crispin!"

"What? Mother knows how we feel about each other. And your great uncle has already given his blessing." He picked up a bright red Surinam cherry from a bowl and popped it in his mouth.

Maitea's eyes crinkled with pleasure. "Yes, Uncle Edrigu says it's time Paraiso moved out of the dark ages. The old customs are outdated—"

"Some of the old customs, my dear." At the moment Lacey had no quarrel with primogeniture and ducal prerogatives.

"Yes, all right, some, but the rule that descendants of the original settlers may not marry later immigrants—"

Crispin interjected, "Or Floridians—"

Lacey cuffed him. "Or farmers…"

Maitea raised her voice. "That rule should be abolished."

"Oh, I don't know, Maitea. When it comes to farmers, a little discrimination is in order. There are good ones and bad ones." The trio fell silent, thinking of Gorka Jaso, who had recently been deported from Saint Andrews for trying to sell stolen bananas.

Crispin broke into their reverie. "Hey, guess what, Mom? Armand asked me if I would help train the farmers in some of the new sustainable agriculture techniques we developed at Arcadia. He wants to hire me as the new agronomy advisor!"

Lacey contemplated her son. Despite his twenty-three years, he had become so much more mature and self-assured in the last few months. She'd done the best she could in raising him, but spending time with a real man—in fact, several—had changed him. For one thing, he'd taken the news of his father's identity rather well, merely remarking, "Now I know why you didn't like him, Mom." *Youth are so resilient.* "At least he did the right thing in the end. He saved you from the riots."

Lacey had let that go. After all, if one overlooked Damien's motives, yes, he had indeed done the right thing. "Agronomy advisor! I'm so proud of you, honey." She kissed him.

"Mom!" Crispin dodged her lips. "Oh, by the way, Inigo told me that all citizens of Paraiso must have an income-producing job—even a Montegue."

"Since piracy is no longer an option," put in Maitea gravely.

Lacey giggled. "That's right, Edrigu told me about the custom. Armand's grandfather was a pawnbroker, and his father was…was"—she held her hand over her mouth—"an…an accountant."

Crispin's jaw dropped. "Really? How…er…"

"Dull? Prosaic?"

"Stupefying?"

Maitea looked from one to the other. "It's a perfectly acceptable and useful occupation. Unfortunately, as a youth, Armand was a bit of a…rebel, and refused to go into the family business."

Lacey realized Armand had never mentioned what he did—she'd assumed him to be the idle playboy, swooping up bikini-clad women for champagne-slurping sails on his yacht. But wait…hadn't he built an aqueduct in Ghana or Sierra Leone or some place? She touched Maitea's shoulder. "So what is his job?"

"He's an architect." She wrinkled her nose. "Now that's boring." She asked shyly, "And you, Lacey? What will you do?"

Lacey picked up a mango from the bowl, pressed it and sniffed the end. "What I've always done—make jelly."

Maitea nodded, satisfied. Crispin took her hand and went to the door. "I almost forgot to tell you. There's been another sighting of Prince Jakome's sloop."

Lacey's stomach tightened. "Where?"

"More than a hundred miles away—some place called Providencia. Not to worry—he knows if he comes back, he'll be hanged. "

Somehow, that didn't reassure Lacey. Jakome had indeed gone over the edge when he killed Damien. He was bound to try to regain his throne at some point, and until he was apprehended, Armand would not be safe. She'd even had a dream the night before that Jakome hid on the island, plotting his revenge.

"So, are you ready for Wednesday?"

Gulp. "Of course." The brave tone didn't fool anyone.

Maitea said, "The limousine will be at the door at two. It will take you up the island to the cathedral. They expect huge crowds along the route. People have come from Saint Andrews and many other islands. I heard a contingent of Puritan descendants has arrived from Massachusetts to pay their respects."

"Now that's just weird." Crispin ate another cherry.

"Let's hope we don't have a delegation of pirates." Lacey fluttered her fingers at them. "You two scram. I have things to do."

"Sheesh. Okay, I'm hungry. Do you suppose there's any more of that mombin jelly roll you taught Cook to make?"

Lacey watched them walk down the stairs, hand in hand. She had one more pilgrimage to make before the wedding two days' hence. She let the maid take off her dress and pulled on shorts and a T-shirt that said "Wild but Not Free—Lacey's Jams & Jellies." Slinging a backpack over her shoulder, she followed the path to Inigo's tiny secluded beach. When she reached it, she took a small package and a trowel out of the bag, dug a hole in the bank, and planted two beautyberry seedlings there. As she stood, admiring her work, she heard a twig break.

"Inigo?"

No one answered. "Armand?" She smiled fondly. "Now you know Edrigu needs you in Castle Zeruko. Get along with you."

Still no answer. She turned around. What she saw chilled her to the bone. A filthy creature, his once finely embroidered cloak in shreds, Jakome gawked at her. His eyes were red-rimmed, and he held a cane in one scrawny hand. He raised it over his head and shook it at her. "You!" he screamed. "You she-devil! You destroyed my life. You ruined my beautiful paradise."

"Prince Jakome, please."

"Please?" He blinked. In her terror, she could have sworn his eyes rolled up in his head. "Please what? Please kill you slowly? Or shall I rip you to shreds as I did the traitor Damiano? He loved you too. You turned everyone against me, even my father. I should have pushed you over the wall when I had the chance. You are a demon."

"No, no, Your Highness. I never meant to—"

"Ulisses told me. I know all about it. You brought Armand here to betray me. "

As he ranted, he advanced toward her. Lacey had her back to the water. On either side of her, Australian pines leaned at precarious angles over the eroded banks. A tangle of roots protruded through the mud. Jakome took another step. She edged away. *Can I make it? What if the roots break when I put my weight on them?* The sun broke out from behind a cloud and flashed off something in Jakome's other hand. Lacey took her eyes off his face for an instant. *Oh my God, he's got a knife.*

"Jakome, don't do this. Your brother loves you. He will pardon you, I'm sure."

The creature spat. "Don't be absurd. I murdered Damiano. Not even Armand is powerful enough to save me. Armand and his prissy ways—he never understood my greatness. I was always the more progressive one, the smarter one. That's why Father sent me to Princeton and Armand to that knuckle-dragging backwater Oxford." A tear coursed down his cheek, leaving a pink line in the grime. "Father loved me best—he wouldn't have let that little prick usurp my throne." He quieted, his eyes vague and troubled, then abruptly jerked as though he'd just remembered Lacey. "But you—you talked him into it. You forged that birth certificate. You tricked an old man into thinking Armand was his first-born son. How did you do it? Poison?"

Lacey was at a loss to answer. She forced herself to focus on her avenue of escape and inched toward the right bank, keeping her eyes on Jakome.

Apparently, Jakome didn't require a response. He began to fret. "And now Armand's going to take over and wreck Paraiso. Do you know, he rescinded all my lovely reforms? My beautiful revolution wiped out in its infancy…" He wiped his nose with the back of his hand. Just as Lacey thought he'd dissolve in tears, he looked straight at her, his yellow teeth bared. In a voice oozing venom, he cooed, "But if I'm going to die, I might as well take you with me." He held up the knife—a huge cleaver—and hurled it at her. She twisted her body to the side, and it whistled past her, barely missing her shoulder. Undeterred, Jakome hiked up his trouser leg and pulled a switchblade from a holster strapped to his calf. He pressed a button and a glistening six-inch blade flipped out. He crooked a dirty finger at her. "Come here, little one. Don't worry, I'll be quick."

Lacey backed away. Her left foot slipped on a clump of seaweed, and she went down. As she wallowed in the soft sand, Jakome waded toward her. He hovered above her, his knife held away from his body, slashing it as though imitating a scene from a horror movie. Suddenly he lunged. Lacey rolled away and leapt for the bank. She managed to get a toehold and scrambled up over the roots, but when she reached level ground, Jakome blocked her path. "Now I've got you. Go to hell, bride of Satan!" He raised the knife.

Bang. Jakome's eyes opened wide, and he fell forward onto her chest, slamming her to the ground. She gagged on the stink from his body, but her arms were pinned behind her and she could only wiggle helplessly. A shadow blocked the sun. Two hands snaked around the prince's thin shoulders and yanked him off. In his place Armand crouched, panting, his palms on his knees. "Now don't tell me I'm not supposed to see you before the wedding."

Koldo appeared, the Beretta in his hand still smoking. "Is he dead?"

Armand nudged his brother's body. "Yes. Come and take him away."

****

After that, the wedding went off without a hitch.

M. S. Spencer

Or almost.

Maitea, as maid of honor, positively scintillated with bliss. Crispin took his role as best man very seriously—even surprising Armand with a bachelor party, from which most participants emerged with eyes glazed and mouths shut. When Lacey asked Edrigu to give her away, a tear welled up in the old man's eye. "I would be honored."

The strains of Handel's *Water Music* filled the cathedral as Lacey and Edrigu came down the aisle. Armand stood at the altar in full dress uniform. Even though Lacey knew he'd borrowed it from Koldo, it nonetheless took her breath away. They floated through the customary prayers and homily, until finally Bishop Bunyan turned to Lacey and began, "Do you—" and stopped. He reread the paper twice before looking up, puzzled. "Is this your full name, Ms. Delahaye?"

Lacey kept her eyes fastened on the bishop, but she felt Armand go rigid at her side. "Yes."

The prelate shrugged. "All right. Do you, Charlotte Anne Dieu-le-Veut Bonny Read Delahaye, take Armand de Montegue to be your lawfully wedded husband?"

"I do."

Armand, his jaw hanging open, emitted an odd little animal cry, a cross between a hoot and a whinny. Lacey put out a hand and gently closed his mouth.

The bishop turned to the groom. "And do you, Armand Eneco Morgan Speirdyke Hastings Cromwell de Montegue"—he paused for breath—"take Charlotte Anne Dieu-le-Veut Bonny Read Delahaye to be your lawfully wedded wife?"

Armand could only nod.

The bishop closed his Bible. "I shall take that as an affirmative. I now pronounce you man and wife. You may kiss the bride."

****

Later that night, Armand opened one eye. "So, what do I call you now?"

"Besides Mrs. Montegue?"

He rolled over on his side. "You did tell me long ago that Lacey was a nickname. I never in my wildest dreams figured you for pirate's spawn."

"Pirate's spawn? How did you know?"

"The study of buccaneer history is required in Paraisan grammar school. So I know that Jacquotte Delahaye, Anne Bonny, Mary Read, Charlotte de Berry and Anne Dieu-le-Veut had disreputable but nonetheless glorious careers. Why didn't you confess when I asked you about it the night we first met?"

Lacey coughed. "It's not exactly something my family is proud of. We have about as long—and sordid—a connection to piracy as you do. I happen to be a direct descendent of Jacquotte Delahaye. She settled on Longboat Key after sweeping the Spanish Main."

"On the land near Buccaneer Drive?" Armand ran his fingers through her hair. "So that's how you came by your auburn locks."

"Yes." Lacey remarked to the ceiling, "In fact, she was rumored to have had dealings with Henry Morgan."

"Really? Did she relieve him of his treasure also?"

She swatted him. "She had her own treasure, thank you very much. Unfortunately, the Delahayes were somewhat profligate. The story goes that she lost it all to Henry in a card game."

"Apocryphal. Mark my words."

Lacey murmured, "My grandmother always insisted that Jacquotte had a fling with Morgan."

Armand threw up his hands in horror. "But that would mean we're related!"

"Maybe." She kissed him. "In fact, we could be second cousins."

"I see." He rubbed his chin thoughtfully. "So tradition is not defied, but wins the day after all?"

"Why not?" Lacey rose up in the bed and straddled her husband. "And what does tradition dictate for a wedding night?"

"I'll tell you what—let's wing it."

A word about the author…

Although M. S. Spencer has lived in Chicago, Boston, New York, France, Morocco, Turkey, Egypt, and England, the last thirty years have been spent mostly in Washington, D.C. as a librarian, Congressional staff assistant, speechwriter, editor, birdwatcher, kayaker, policy wonk, non-profit director, and parent. Once she escaped academia, she worked for the U.S. Senate, the U.S. Department of the Interior, in several library systems, both public and academic, and at the Torpedo Factory Art Center. She holds a BA from Vassar College, a Diploma in Arabic Studies from the American University in Cairo, and Masters in Anthropology and in Library Science from the University of Chicago. All of this tends to insinuate itself into her works.

Ms. Spencer has two fabulous grown children and an incredible granddaughter. She divides her time between the Gulf coast of Florida and a tiny village in Maine.

http://mssspencertalespinner.blogspot.com
https://www.facebook.com/msspencerromance
www.twitter.com/msspencerauthor

~*~

Other M. S. Spencer titles
available from The Wild Rose Press, Inc.:
*THE MASON'S MARK: LOVE AND DEATH
IN THE TOWER
THE PENHALLOW TRAIN INCIDENT
ARTFUL DODGING: THE TORPEDO FACTORY
MURDERS*

www.ingramcontent.com/pod-product-compliance
Lightning Source LLC
Chambersburg PA
CBHW071516260626
47170CB00002B/385